EVERYTHING

COUNTS.

REVISED EDITION

Steven Case

EVERYTHING

COUNTS.

A YEAR'S WORTH
OF DEVOTIONS ON
RADICAL LIVING

REVISED EDITION

 ZONDERVAN®

This edition is dedicated to my father, with admiration, respect and most of all love. Thanks Dad.

A WORD ABOUT
OSWALD CHAMBERS

started reading *My Utmost for His Highest* when I was in high school. Some days I thought, "This is great!" and other days I wondered what planet Oswald Chambers lived on. I pictured him as a stern old man sequestered somewhere writing profound thoughts about life and God. Years later, I was amazed to learn that he had died at the age of 43 and didn't "write" any of the books that bear his name.

Chambers was born in Aberdeen, Scotland, on July 24, 1874, the youngest son of a Baptist minister. He spent his boyhood years in Perth, then at the age of 15, he moved with his family to London. Shortly after, Oswald made his public profession of faith in Christ and became a member of a dynamic church. This marked a period of rapid spiritual growth, along with an intense struggle to find God's will and way for his life.

A gifted artist and musician, Chambers trained at London's Royal Academy of Art, sensing God's direction to be an ambassador for Christ in the world of the arts. While studying at the University of Edinburgh (1895–96), he decided, after an agonizing internal battle, to study for the ministry. He left the university and entered Dunoon College, near Glasgow, where he remained as a student, then a tutor, for nine years.

In 1906–07, he traveled around the world spending six months teaching at God's Bible School in Cincinnati, Ohio, then visiting the Tokyo Bible School in Japan. He married Gertrude Hobbs in 1910 and they had one daughter, Kathleen. During the last decade of his life, Chambers served in various ministries; he died in Cairo (where he was Y.M.C.A. chaplain to British Commonwealth soldiers in Egypt) on November 15, 1917, of complications following an emergency appendectomy.

During the seven years of their marriage, his wife had taken verbatim shorthand notes of nearly all of Oswald's lectures and sermons. After his death, she spent the rest of her life publishing her husband's spoken words. His best-known book, *My Utmost for His Highest*, has been continuously in print since being published in 1927. It has been translated into at least 13 languages and remains a best-selling book.

In a social setting, Oswald was the life of the party, but when he spoke about what it means to know and follow Jesus Christ, he was all business. Perhaps that's why people around the world still read his words every morning, more than 80 years after he died.

In this book, you'll encounter thoughts inspired by Chambers, and in the section titled **OZ Says**, you'll read the words of Oswald himself from *My Utmost*. Chambers won't let you off the hook, but he will challenge you to abandon yourself to Christ because he is completely trustworthy in every aspect of life.

—David McCasland

David is the author of the biography *Oswald Chambers: Abandoned to God* (Discovery House Publishers).

01.01

BEGIN AT THE BEGINNING

I eagerly expect and hope that I will in no way be ashamed, but will have sufficient courage so that now as always Christ will be exalted in my body, whether by life or by death.

[Philippians 1:20]

God. (That's it.) Just GOD. It starts there. It ends there. Got that? You have to understand that in order to get this next part. From this point . . . from this here and now. EVERYTHING COUNTS. Everything you do, everywhere you go . . . it all counts. It has to—God is at the beginning of it all. God is in all things. Therefore, with every person you meet, you have to treat them as if God placed them in your path for a reason. Everything that happens is part of God's plan. You must be willing to start and end with God's presence, or you are just reading words on a page. Once you have God's presence as a part of your innermost self . . . nobody can take that from you. You can give it away. You can share that oneness, but it cannot be taken from you. It's yours. It's God. Are you ready to begin?

—————————— OZ Says ——————————

An overweening consideration for ourselves is the thing that keeps us from that decision, though we put it that we are considering others. When we consider what it will cost others if we obey the call of Jesus, we tell God He does not know what our obedience will mean. Keep to the point; He does know. Shut out every other consideration and keep yourself before God for this one thing only—My Utmost for His Highest. I am determined to be absolutely and entirely for Him and for Him alone.

—————— Just Between You and God ——————

You have to be willing to give your whole self to this process. It takes time. It's a journey. Are you willing? Heart, mind, body, soul . . . are you willing? Okay. Say that to God . . . then listen.

God first. God last. God in all things. God in all ways. Can you handle that? Okay then, let's go.

01.02

RECALCULATING

Abraham . . . obeyed and went, even though he did not know where he was going.

[Hebrews 11:8]

Life is a journey. This is the ultimate road trip. We're going to ask you to do something scary now. Are you ready? Turn off the GPS. Put away any sort of directional gizmo. Fold the map any way you want and put it in the glove compartment. Better yet, pitch it out the window. Can you do that? From this point on, it's you and God. Can you surrender control? Can you follow the road without knowing where it's going? Yes, you can have a destination, but that's not exactly the same as knowing where the road is going. The coolest rest stops, the really fun tourist attractions, the best roadside snacks are not on the map. You drive. God will guide you. Listen. Just be in the moment. Roll down the window. Play your favorite tunes. Just be on the journey.

OZ Says

Each morning you wake it is to be a "going out," building in confidence on God . . . Have you been asking God what He is going to do? He will never tell you. God does not tell you what He is going to do; He reveals to you Who He is. Do you believe in a miracle-working God, and will you go out in surrender to Him until you are not surprised an atom at anything He does? Suppose God is the God you know Him to be when you are nearest to Him—what an impertinence worry is! Let the attitude of the life be a continual going out in dependence upon God, and your life will have an ineffable charm about it, which is a satisfaction to Jesus. You have to learn to go out of convictions, out of creeds, out of experiences, until so far as your faith is concerned, there is nothing between yourself and God.

Just Between You and God

When you close this book—say a prayer and give something to God. Simply hand over one thing that's been on your mind for a while. Give it to God, then stop stressing about it. He may not solve it for you right away. But it's God's now.

Put it into drive. Get ready. Imagine this distance in front of you. Road Tunes. Coffee. God. Snacks. Coffee. Ready? . . . Go.

01.03

SHINE OUT LOUD

Clouds and thick darkness surround him . . .

[Psalm 97:2]

These are more than just words. Jesus was more than just a really nice guy who told nice stories about nice things. There comes a point where the words become real, and then the very real sense of just who this man was settles into our minds. It's like a storm that's out there someplace and we are just beginning to hear the thunder or smell the wind. We come up with all sorts of ways to deal with our understanding of Jesus. We paint pictures and write songs. We create wonderful visuals of Jesus standing with his arm around our shoulder. Jesus as our friend is only the beginning. There's so much more. The sheer awesomeness is a light so bright it could knock us to the ground. (That actually happened to a few people in the Bible.)

OZ Says

The only possibility of understanding the teaching of Jesus is by the light of the Spirit of God on the inside. If we have never had the experience of taking our commonplace religious shoes off our commonplace religious feet, and getting rid of all the undue familiarity with which we approach God, it is questionable whether we have ever stood in His presence. The people who are flippant and familiar are those who have never yet been introduced to Jesus Christ. After the amazing delight and liberty of realizing what Jesus Christ does, comes the impenetrable darkness of realizing Who He is.

Just Between You and God

Can you go outside for this? Seriously. When you close the book, step outside. Feel the air on your skin. Open your arms. This is not a kneeling beside the bed prayer. This is throwing yourself open to God. This is letting the universe in. Can you pray like that?

This is deeper than you think. This is all far from over. You may be in over your head. Do you want to get wet?

01.04

COUNTDOWN

Peter asked, "Lord, why can't I follow you now? I will lay down my life for you."

[John 13:37]

Imagine your life as an airline pilot. You're sitting behind the controls reviewing your checklist. Every instrument is in order. Every gauge is working. Now you must sit and wait for clearance from the tower. It's completely normal to want to throw the throttle and take off down the runway, but God must give you the clearance. Wait. Listen to the comforting hum of the engines.

You're ready. God knows that. Listen for the signal. Timing is everything. Just because you're ready to take off doesn't mean you can. Just because the road is clear ahead of you doesn't mean it's safe. You promised you would trust him, remember? So relax for a minute. Ask God when to go. He will let you know when the time is right.

OZ Says

There are times when you cannot understand why you cannot do what you want to do. When God brings the blank space, see that you do not fill it in, but wait. The blank space may come in order to teach you what sanctification means, or it may come after sanctification to teach you what service means. Never run before God's guidance. If there is the slightest doubt, then He is not guiding. Whenever there is doubt—don't.

Just Between You and God

Patience. It's a hard thing for some people. You've been in training all this time and now you're ready . . . and God says wait. Wait? Why? Because God sees the whole picture. God sees the obstacles in your way. God is making sure that spot you're going to land on is empty and waiting for you. Right now, ask God for patience. It's all coming together on his side . . . he'll give you the signal when it's time.

Relax. God knows when. He'll tell you. Honest.

01.05

THE VIEW FROM UP HERE

**Simon Peter asked him, "Lord, where are you going?"
Jesus replied, "Where I am going, you cannot follow
now, but you will follow later."**

[John 13:36]

There is a brief moment, before you jump off the bungee platform, when
you are fully aware of your situation. Nothing you can do at that moment
will prepare you for what is about to happen. Entering into a friendship with
God is like this. All your preconceived notions are meaningless. You are
about to fall under the control of the Holy Spirit. Every cell of your being lights
up. Jesus said, "Follow me." He didn't say mostly, or nearly completely, he
just said, "Follow me." Up until now you have relied on your own beliefs, attitudes, talents, and ideas. Ditch them. Jesus wants your complete and total
devotion. Follow him.

———— OZ Says ————

No matter what changes God has wrought in you, never rely upon them; build
only on a Person, the Lord Jesus Christ, and on the Spirit He gives. All our vows
and resolutions end in denial because we have no power to carry them out.
When we have come to the end of ourselves, not in imagination but really, we
are able to receive the Holy Spirit. "Receive ye the Holy Ghost"—the idea is that
of invasion. There is only one lodestar in the life now, the Lord Jesus Christ.

———— Just Between You and God ————

You know that little thing you've been holding onto? Yeah, that one . . . stored
in the back of your mind. That bit of fear or doubt . . . or maybe it's guilt. It
can't exist inside this book. Just before you close the book to pray . . . place
it here. Closing the book will be a new beginning.

**Without Hesitation. Without complication. Follow.
Just follow.**

01.06

BUCKETS

From there he went on toward the hills east of Bethel and pitched his tent, with Bethel on the west and Ai on the east. There he built an altar to the LORD and called on the name of the LORD.

[Genesis 12:8]

For some people, there is an image that goes along with praying. They imagine themselves on their knees in a hot desert. Parched. Dying. And maybe *if . . .* just *maybe . . .* God is listening and will pull out his Godly eye-dropper and give you just one tiny drop of what he is. What if God had a bucket? What if God had a swimming pool filled with his love and he was about to hit you with a deluge that will knock you backwards? That is what God wants to give you, and all he asks for is a "thank you." How do you say "thank you" for something like that? Use what God gave you. Use the gifts. If you can paint . . . paint something for God. If you can sing . . . sing something for God. If you can make magic with numbers . . . there must be a kid out there who needs tutoring in math. God is pouring . . . are you ready to share?

--------------------- OZ Says ---------------------

Worship is giving God the best that He has given you. Be careful what you do with the best you have. Whenever you get a blessing from God, give it back to Him as a love gift. Take time to meditate before God and offer the blessing back to Him in a deliberate act of worship. If you hoard a thing for yourself, it will turn into spiritual dry rot, as the manna did when it was hoarded. God will never let you hold a spiritual thing for yourself; it has to be given back to Him that He may make it a blessing to others.

--------------- Just Between You and God ---------------

Consider a prayer of thanks. Thank God for your gifts. Thank him for those things that make you uniquely you—even those things that nobody else knows about you.

Take the blessing. Say thank you. Give it back. Repeat.

01.07

PERFECT FRIENDSHIP

Jesus answered: "Don't you know me, Philip, even after I have been among you such a long time? Anyone who has seen me has seen the Father. How can you say, 'Show us the Father'?"

[John 14:9]

Is there such a thing as friendship beyond friendship? Jesus' disciples traveled with him for years and most of the time they didn't understand him. They tried. Oh how they tried . . . but they could not get beyond the slap-him-on-the-back, sit-next-to-him-at-lunch, start a water-fight-in-the-stream Jesus. Jesus was more than that. Jesus was God. They didn't understand what Jesus was until he was nailed to a piece of wood. But that is when we meet Jesus. That's when it all begins.

─────────── OZ Says ───────────

When once we get intimate with Jesus we are never lonely, we never need sympathy, we can pour out all the time without being pathetic. The saint who is intimate with Jesus will never leave impressions of himself, but only the impression that Jesus is having unhindered way, because the last abyss of his nature has been satisfied by Jesus. The only impression left by such a life is that of the strong calm sanity that Our Lord gives to those who are intimate with Him.

─────────── Just Between You and God ───────────

Pray that others will see Jesus in you. That's a lot of responsibility. Jesus exists in the moments you offer yourself to others. Jesus is there when you put your hand on the shoulder of a friend who missed the basket . . . when you offer a look of encouragement before a test . . . when you point at their art hanging on the wall . . . when it would seem you have every right to go off on somebody and choose not to. Jesus is there. Ask God to show you these moments so that you can show Jesus to others.

Can you open yourself to a Jesus who is beyond physical? Can you let him in? Open yourself to that presence. Connect.

01.08

BAGGAGE

When they reached the place God had told him about, Abraham built an altar there and arranged the wood on it. He bound his son Isaac and laid him on the altar, on top of the wood.

[Genesis 22:9]

God has never asked you to give up the things that you love in order to prove your love for him. That's not how it works. God is not about sacrifice. God may ask you to give him all the things that keep you at a distance. The baggage you don't need . . . the fear . . . the guilt. You don't need these. God gets down on his knees like a parent and says, "Come to me." And we, in our so-called wisdom, say, "Just a minute" or "Be right there," and we drag this heavy suitcase filled with rocks across a gravel field. The luggage wheels break off and still we pull. "Just a minute, God. I'm on my way." As if the pulling and the suffering will get us there quicker. God says, "Leave it. I'm right here." You don't need to sacrifice. Jesus did that already. You can just run to God's arms.

OZ Says

God nowhere tells us to give up things for the sake of giving them up. He wants you to be a "living sacrifice," to let Him have all your powers that have been saved and sanctified through Jesus. This is the thing that is acceptable to God.

Just Between You and God

Okay, prayer time. Ask God to use you—all of you—all that you have and all that you will be. Ask him to give you the courage to let go of the things that keep you from being completely filled by his love. It's like lifting the stones from a pool of water. The water fills in the empty space. Ask God to fill you this way.

This is life. It's not about death and sacrifice. Get rid of what you don't need. Live.

01.09

WRECKING BALL

May God himself, the God of peace, sanctify you through and through. May your whole spirit, soul and body be kept blameless at the coming of our Lord Jesus Christ.

[1 Thessalonians 5:23]

God is bigger than your imagination. If you let your imagination run wild and think about all that God is, you won't even come close. Your connection with God is the same. Your spirit and all its capabilities are beyond your imagination. God wants to keep us clean by providing the faith and discipline needed to avoid the things that get in the way of our relationship with him. These things are like walls, keeping the spirit and God separate. If we consciously try to take these walls down—the unconscious will let our spirits soar.

OZ Says

Cleansing from sin is to the very heights and depths of our spirit if we will keep in the light as God is in the light, and the very Spirit that fed the life of Jesus Christ will feed the life of our spirits.

Just Between You and God

God knows you. You're not keeping anything from him. This allows you to pray with an open-ness. Tell God everything. Hold nothing back from him. The light outside the walls you've built is waiting to pour in. It's coming through the cracks. Pray for the strength to take down the walls that separate you from him.

Sometimes we must swing the wrecking ball from inside the house. Bring your walls down. God is waiting outside.

01.10

DOWNLOAD

. . . to open their eyes and turn them from darkness to light, and from the power of Satan to God, so that they may receive forgiveness of sins and a place among those who are sanctified by faith in me.

[Acts 26:18]

Deciding to follow God does not come with the special effects of a Hollywood blockbuster. It's not a matter of saying SHAZAM and the lightning bolt from the sky turns you into "Super Christian." The moment you decide to be a God-follower is usually a quiet one. It is not a decision taken lightly. It is not one anyone else can make for you. It's yours and it's between you and God. When you make the decision, it's not like special effects. Instead God puts something in your soul. Something unique. Something that's just for you. You begin to see the world differently. You begin to see God's presence in the world and in others. More importantly, the world begins to see God in you.

OZ Says

In sanctification the regenerated soul deliberately gives up his right to himself to Jesus Christ, and identifies himself entirely with God's interest in other men. "We are not here to tell God what to do with us, but to let Him use us as He chooses. Remember, God's main concern is that we are more interested in Him than in work for Him. Once you are rooted and grounded in Christ the greatest thing you can do is to be. Don't try and be useful; be yourself and God will use you to further His ends."

Just Between You and God

Part two of opening your heart to God is opening your life to him as well. Ask God to help you follow his call with your whole heart. Think of everything out there as being in darkness and once you say, "Amen," think of yourself as the light. God's light.

You are God's. That's a good thing. Not an easy thing, but a good thing. Darkness cannot stand up to the light. Not ever.

01.11

OVER SHARING

As the soldiers led him away, they seized Simon from Cyrene, who was on his way in from the country, and put the cross on him and made him carry it behind Jesus.

[Luke 23:26]

This changes everything. This journey you are on will change everything in your life and not just yours. Friends and family are affected too. You might lose friends. Your family might not understand. But you've signed up for this and God will live up to his end of the bargain. The place you end up may be far and away from where you are now. God will take care of those you live behind. They might have other journeys. They have other travels. You have to focus on this one. Trust God. This might be your first "road trip" but it's not his . . . not by a long shot.

─────── OZ Says ───────

If we obey God it will mean that other people's plans are upset, and they will gibe us with it—"You call this Christianity?" We can prevent the suffering; but if we are going to obey God, we must not prevent it, we must let the cost be paid . . . Beware of the inclination to dictate to God as to what you will allow to happen if you obey Him.

─────── Just Between You and God ───────

Pray a prayer of protection for those who can be hurt in some way by your decision to obey God. Pray for strength to stay on the path that God has set for you and avoid running off to solve everybody else's problems. God will take care of everything. That's not your job.

Everything has a cost. It's not always a cost to you. Trust God. He will take care of everything.

01.12

VOICEMAIL

He did not say anything to them without using a parable. But when he was alone with his own disciples, he explained everything.

[Mark 4:34]

We spend way too much time trying to figure ourselves out. How many times have you thought, "I just don't know who I am"? Well, guess what? You will never know exactly who you are. Not yet anyway. God is going to work through you. When you finally realize that you can't figure it all out—then God can use you. When God uses you, then you will start to know who you are.

—————— OZ Says ——————

Wherever there is any element of pride or of conceit, Jesus cannot expound a thing. He will take us through the disappointment of a wounded pride of intellect, through disappointment of heart. He will reveal inordinate affection—things over which we never thought He would have to get us alone.

—————— Just Between You and God ——————

Find a quiet place. Not a crowded bus or while you are driving. Turn off all the phones and devices. Make silence for this. Then sit and calm yourself. In this silence ask God who you are. Will you get a lightning bolt answer? Probably not. God will hear. God will make every attempt to bring you near to him. Then, in that quiet place, you can find your answer.

Get quiet. Open your heart. Let God show you who you are. Everything counts.

01.13

HELLO!! (HELLO . . . HELLO . . . HELLO . . . HELLO)

When he was alone, the Twelve and the others around him asked him about the parables.

[Mark 4:10]

How often do alone-with-God times happen only because we can't take it anymore? Everything is going wrong and we close ourselves off and say, "Why, God, why?" This is where God wants us. Know the reason? Because this is when he's sure we are listening. The rest of the time we are caught up in the details of our lives and the lives of others. It's only when we finally get to the end of ourselves that God says, "Okay, now let's talk."

--------------------- OZ Says ---------------------

If you are going on with God, the only thing that is clear to you, and the only thing God intends to be clear, is the way He deals with your own soul . . . There are whole tracts of stubbornness and ignorance to be revealed by the Holy Spirit in each one of us, and it can only be done when Jesus gets us alone.

--------------- Just Between You and God ---------------

The easy part about praying is that God has been waiting for you. Ready, and in a manner of friendship as with a cup of coffee in hand, he sits with his ears open, waiting to listen—longing for you. Don't wait for your life to go sour. He wants to hear the good things too.

God is listening. On the mountaintop and at rock bottom he's listening. Talk with him on the climb.

01.14

CLICK HERE IF YOU AGREE

"Whom shall I send? And who will go for us?" And I said, "Here am I. Send me!"

[Isaiah 6:8]

God says, "Who's going?" We say, "Send me." Notice there is no *if* or *only* or *maybe*. We don't say, "Send me, just give me a second to set up the DVR. I don't want to miss my favorite program." God doesn't say, "Well, it might be hard and difficult but I think you can make it work." God says, "Who's going?" We say, "Send me." It's a quick conversation that can make all the difference in our lives. God is not going to beg. This is God doing the inviting. What other choice is there? Send me.

—————————— OZ Says ——————————

"Many are called but few are chosen," that is, few prove themselves the chosen ones. The chosen ones are those who have come into a relationship with God through Jesus Christ whereby their disposition has been altered and their ears unstopped, and they hear the still small voice questioning all the time, "Who will go for us?" . . . If we let the Spirit of God bring us face to face with God, we too shall hear something akin to what Isaiah heard, the still small voice of God; and in perfect freedom will say, "Here am I; send me."

————— Just Between You and God —————

It's a short prayer. "Send me." Say it like you mean the words even if you are not sure. God knows your doubts and fears. Others have felt the same thing. God will give you what you need when the time comes. You just have to be ready to "go."

"I'll go." Say it loud. Then watch what happens next.

01.15

WAS

We were therefore buried with him . . . that . . . we too may live a new life.

[Romans 6:4]

Scripture is full of people becoming brand new. In many cases God (or his son) even changed their names. Sometimes there is no choice. Make a decision to start this journey and there is much you must leave behind along the way. Stuff you don't need. Stuff you cling to but only weighs you down. Leaving behind your past, your guilt, your pain, your prejudices . . . opens up new space inside you. God will fill that with something new.

──────────────── OZ Says ────────────────

If there has never been this crisis of death, sanctification is nothing more than a vision. There must be a "white funeral," a death that has only one resurrection—a resurrection into the life of Jesus Christ. Nothing can upset such a life; it is one with God for one purpose, to be a witness to Him.

──────────── Just Between You and God ────────────

Pray that God will show you just a piece of what lies ahead. This will make it easier to leave things behind. Don't be afraid to let these go. What God has in store is so much better, you can't even imagine.

Say a funeral prayer for the old you. The new you is here. Don't look back. Not even once.

01.16

UN-MUTE

Then I heard the voice of the Lord saying, "Whom shall I send?"

[Isaiah 6:8]

People who love to wander will talk about hearing the call of the open road. Sailors will tell you they hear the call of the sea. People like this are responding to a call that originates in something outside themselves. When we talk about the call of God, it is entirely different. If we hear the call of God, it is because God is in us. If we think about how this call will work with plans we already have, we may as well not listen at all. To listen to the call of God will change your life entirely.

OZ Says

When I am brought into relationship with God, I am in the condition Isaiah was in. Isaiah's soul was so attuned to God by the tremendous crisis he had gone through that he recorded the call of God to his amazed soul. The majority of us have no ear for anything but ourselves, we cannot hear a thing God says. To be brought into the zone of the call of God is to be profoundly altered.

Just Between You and God

Your call is a very personal thing. This calling is solely between you and your creator. As you pray, ask God for the ability to listen with your whole body. He can use more than your ears. Open all of yourself to hear his voice. You will know it when you hear it.

Everything you could possibly be is out there waiting. God is present. Listen. Listen. Listen.

01.17
GOING LIVE IN 3 . . . 2 . . . 1 . . .

But when God, who set me apart from my mother's womb and called me by his grace, was pleased to reveal his Son in me so that I might preach him among the Gentiles, my immediate response was not to consult any human being.

[Galatians 1:15–16]

Hearing the call of God does not mean you have to drop everything and become the next Mother Teresa. (Though some have heard that call and followed it.) Hearing that call and understanding who it is from means your life will show others you are following God. Live your life in extraordinary ways. You have heard the voice of God. It enters your soul and the two work together and create something wonderful.

OZ Says

Service is the natural part of my life. God gets me into a relationship with Himself whereby I understand His call, then I do things out of sheer love for Him on my own account. To serve God is the deliberate love-gift of a nature that has heard the call of God.

Just Between You and God

Ask God for guidance today. People think a "calling" is a job or a career. That's not necessarily the case. The "calling" is a life. Living a life worthy of the calling can lead you to some interesting career choices but they are not the same thing. Answering a "call" is like swallowing light. It shoots out of your hands and eyes and the tips of your fingers. The call is to light up a dark world.

Paints mix. New colors emerge. Take you. Add God. Be God's color. Be fully you.

01.18

CLICK HERE TO CONFIRM YOUR ORDER

Thomas said to him, "My Lord and my God!"

[John 20:28]

Remember not to get so caught up in serving God that you forget who you are serving. The important part of the phrase "servant of God" is not *servant*, it's *God*. Where God calls you to serve is not as important as the fact that God has called you. Regardless of where you are called to go, your heart must overflow with love for God, even if he calls you to some place nasty and unpleasant. Then it's not so easy to serve with a joyful heart. But if that's where you're called to serve, then you must jump in with both feet and make a God-splash that washes those nasty and unpleasant places.

OZ Says

How many of us are set upon Jesus Christ slaking our thirst when we ought to be satisfying Him? We should be pouring out now, spending to the last limit, not drawing on Him to satisfy us. "Ye shall be witnesses unto Me"—that means a life of unsullied, uncompromising and unbribed devotion to the Lord Jesus, a satisfaction to Him wherever He places us.

Just Between You and God

Don't get too hung up on your own needs and wants. God already knows what you like, what you're good at, what you're not so good at, what rings your chimes and floats your boat. Don't think about these things when you say, "I'm your servant, God." Trust God to have the best idea of what will make you a better person. God created the universe. God can handle your future.

Ask God to send you. Don't give him a list of suggestions or ideas. Ask to be sent. Then go.

01.19

NIGHT VISION APP

. . . and a thick and dreadful darkness came over him.

[Genesis 15:12]

God will show you the light, but he may also be the one to put his hand over your eyes. You get the vision. You get the inspiration. Eventually God will remove his hand and say, "Go!" That time of darkness when God has covered your face is a time to prepare. If you're pulling at the reins to get started, stop and think about why God has reigned you in. God's timing is perfect. He will make you ready for what you have to do. If you go running off before you're ready, you'll likely encounter a pitfall that could have been avoided, had you only waited until your blindfold was removed.

OZ Says

When God gives a vision and darkness follows, wait. God will make you in accordance with the vision He has given if you will wait His time. Never try and help God fulfill His word.

Just Between You and God

There is a joy in the anticipation. Like a child waiting to let loose on a birthday piñata. God may be holding you back for a reason. Your destination is not ready for you yet . . . or maybe you are the one not ready. God is sorting it out. Say thank you to God today for his judgment and be ready to run.

Be patient. Wait. Learn. Then run.

01.20

VIEW FROM THE CHEAP SEATS

Jesus replied, "Very truly I tell you, no one can see the kingdom of God unless they are born again."

[John 3:3]

Yes, you can get tired. Yes, sometimes the blanket is better than the cold kitchen. Sometimes you don't feel like discipling right now. The disciples felt that. Even Jesus needed to go off and be by himself some days. If a sense of staleness has been creeping into your life, it could be a sign that you've let something get between you and God. Jesus called his disciples to be one with him and one with God. There can be no room for anything in between. Examine your life. Ask God to help you remove the obstacles.

OZ Says

Keep all your life perennially open to Jesus Christ, don't pretend with Him. Are you drawing your life from any other source than God Himself? If you are depending upon anything but Him, you will never know when He is gone. Being born of the Spirit means much more than we generally take it to mean. It gives us a new vision and keeps us absolutely fresh for everything by the perennial supply of the life of God.

Just Between You and God

Ask God to remove all the petty little things that get in the way of being his servant. Jealousy. Anger. Selfishness. These are not things from the Holy Spirit. You don't need them. Pray and give these to God. He'll get rid of them so you can keep on serving.

Serve. Without questions or keeping lists. Just serve. Without keeping track of others. Serve.

01.21

BACK UP COMPLETED

Go and proclaim in the hearing of Jerusalem: "This is what the LORD says: 'I remember the devotion of your youth, how as a bride you loved me and followed me through the wilderness, through a land not sown.'"

[Jeremiah 2:2]

Take stock of yourself. Look back and think about what God sees when he looks back on your life. Have you lost that sense of "I'm yours, God"? Too often we think that once we've put in our time, God will lavish rewards on us and the hard work will be over. Guess what? It doesn't always work that way. Usually we forget God's promises when things get really bad. We get angry. "Didn't I do it right? Wasn't that what you told me to do?" If we base our continued love for God only on how he rewards us, then we are missing the mark.

―――――――――――― OZ Says ――――――――――――

Am I as spontaneously kind to God as I used to be, or am I only expecting God to be kind to me? Am I full of the little things that cheer His heart over me, or am I whimpering because things are going hardly with me? There is no joy in the soul that has forgotten what God prizes.

―――――――――― Just Between You and God ――――――――――

If you feel like you are wandering off the path, pray for a voice or a sign that will lead you back to where you are supposed to be. Thank God for all that he has already done, especially for what he asked his son to do. Then make a promise to continue the work regardless of what ends up in your shopping cart at the end of the trip.

Listen. Listen and then do what you're told. Most people forget that second part.

01.22

FROM THIS LOCATION

Turn to me and be saved, all you ends of the earth; for I am God, and there is no other.

[Isaiah 45:22]

For some reason we tend to think that God just wants to follow us around and give us his blessings. The Bible says, "Look to me." If we want these blessings, we have to go to God. Our focus must be on God. Notice the verse does not say, "You will be saved." It says, "Turn to me and be saved." If we are truly looking for a personal relationship with God, we need only turn our focus to God, not to what we wear or where we're going this weekend. Turn to God and be saved.

—————————— OZ Says ——————————

Rouse yourself up and look to God. Build your hope on Him. No matter if there are a hundred and one things that press, resolutely exclude them all and look to Him. "Look unto Me," and salvation is, the moment you look.

—————— Just Between You and God ——————

Pray alone in a quiet place with the lights dimmed. Try to blot out all physical and mental distractions. Put aside what you want from God. Put aside what you think God should be. Focus on who God is, and be in his presence.

Focus. Believe. Concentrate on him. Be saved.

01.23

UPGRADE WITH A VIEW

And we all, who with unveiled faces contemplate the Lord's glory, are being transformed into his image with ever-increasing glory, which comes from the Lord, who is the Spirit.

[2 Corinthians 3:18]

Ever see a reflection of light on the wall and try to figure out where it's coming from? Someone's watch? An earring? Ever sit with a small mirror in your hand and try to catch the light and send it somewhere else? This is what God calls us to do. We are mirrors. The love of Christ is the light. We catch that light and reflect it to others. That's why it's important to keep your mirror free of smudges. Let distractions come and go. Let criticism fall by the wayside, but never let anything get between you and the light of Jesus.

————————— OZ Says —————————

The golden rule for your life and mine is this concentrated keeping of the life open towards God. Let everything else — work, clothes, food, everything on earth — go by the board, saving that one thing. The rush of other things always tends to obscure this concentration on God. We have to maintain ourselves in the place of beholding, keeping the life absolutely spiritual all through.

————— Just Between You and God —————

Say a prayer that God will use you as the mirror. Pray for the skill to reflect his light to places that may be in continuous darkness. Pray that God will give you the strength to keep your glass clean and bright.

Wipe away life-smudges. Catch the light. Reflect.

01.24

WHEN CAN YOU START?

Now get up and stand on your feet. I have appeared to you to appoint you as a servant and as a witness of what you have seen and will see of me.

[Acts 26:16]

Anybody ever give you a good old fashioned dope slap? Saul was one of the lowest, most despised human beings ever. He dragged off people in chains and he enjoyed his work. Then Jesus came along, and through the power of the Holy Spirit, shoved Saul off the back of his horse. He literally knocked some sense into Saul and changed his name to Paul. Paul went on to do stuff like write the majority of the New Testament. Paul was a brand new person. Yes, you've decided to follow Jesus. Are you willing to leave the old you behind? You're not going to try and be someone you are not . . . you're going to be you . . . only new.

--- OZ Says ---

Paul was not given a message or a doctrine to proclaim, he was brought into a vivid, personal, overmastering relationship to Jesus Christ . . . There is nothing there apart from the personal relationship. Paul was devoted to a Person not to a cause. He was absolutely Jesus Christ's, he saw nothing else, he lived for nothing else.

--- Just Between You and God ---

Ask God to help you make him your priority. This is more than words in a book. Ask God to help you make the relationship real and vital. It's the most important friendship you have. Pray that God will strengthen the bonds that hold it together.

Listen. You get out of relationships what you put into them. What are you putting into the most important one of all?

01.25

BORDERS

But when God, who set me apart from my mother's womb and called me by his grace, was pleased . . .

[Galatians 1:15]

Okay, it's Summer. No, it's January but let's SAY it's August and you fill your glass with tea. It's hot outside. You're thirsty. So you fill that glass up to the brim. Now, how do you add ice, or a lemon wedge, or even a spoon to stir sugar? In our haste to fill our lives with meaning, we sometimes forget to leave room for God. God is what gives life flavor, makes it drinkable, even sweet. We don't know how God might make himself known but we must leave room so that God never gets crowded out.

—————— OZ Says ——————

That is the way to make room for Him. Expect Him to come, but do not expect Him only in a certain way. However much we may know God, the great lesson to learn is that at any minute He may break in. We are apt to overlook this element of surprise, yet God never works in any other way. All of a sudden God meets the life—"When it was the good pleasure of God . . ."

—————— Just Between You and God ——————

Invite God into your life when you pray. Make it an open invitation. Pray that your door will always be open for him and then clean out the stuff you don't need.

Clear a space. Open up. Invite. Receive.

01.26

STEP BACK AND LOOK AGAIN

If that is how God clothes the grass of the field, which is here today and tomorrow is thrown into the fire, will he not much more clothe you—you of little faith?

[Matthew 6:30]

The beauty of Jesus' message was in the simplicity. He was never complicated. He said, "Love God." "Love each other." "See the beauty in everything." Jesus wants us to step back and look at the flowers and enjoy the little things in life. If God will take care of these, won't he take care of us? We tend to think God is not living up to his promises when things in our lives go wrong. But things sometimes go wrong because of choices we make. God promises to take care of us in the midst of whatever is happening.

———————— OZ Says ————————

Consecration means the continual separating of myself to one particular thing. We cannot consecrate once and for all. Am I continually separating myself to consider God every day of my life?

———— Just Between You and God ————

Have you ever seen those viral videos where someone takes a single photograph of themselves every day for a few years and then runs them all together to show the changes? Day in and day out you might not see the change as it happens. God does not give you his blessings and then stop. It happens day in and day out. Today ask God to give you eyes that see the small moments.

Notice. See. Grant importance. Simplify.

01.27

FOR THE WIN

Therefore I tell you, do not worry about your life, what you will eat or drink; or about your body, what you will wear. Is not life more than food, and the body more than clothes?

[Matthew 6:25]

What do you mean I shouldn't eat and drink? If I don't wear the right clothes I won't get ahead or be popular. We tend to approach this teaching of Jesus as if he has no idea of what's going on in our lives. Not true. He knows what's going on in your life better than you do. Sure, you need to eat. But food does not need to be your number one priority; nor does fashion or how much money you have. Jesus does not want competition. He is number one over and above all else.

——————————— OZ Says ———————————

Whenever there is competition, be sure that you put your relationship to God first.

——————— Just Between You and God ———————

Make a priority list. Take a moment and actually write down the things that are important to you. Home? Family? Ice Cream? Good grades? Fill the paper if you want to. Now write the word *God* above the numbers. Yes, you can to squeeze it in. It's not that God doesn't want you to have the things on your list. He just doesn't want competition.

God is number one. That's it. No questions. God is number one. Always.

01.28

YOU HAVE (COULDA WOULDA SHOULDA) REACHED YOUR DESTINATION

We all fell to the ground, and I heard a voice saying to me in Aramaic, "Saul, Saul, why do you persecute me? It is hard for you to kick against the goads."

[Acts 26:14]

Okay cue the lasers! Full lighted dance floor! Big . . . and I mean BIG screens, floor to ceiling. Sound? We need trumpet blasts! Choirs of animatronic simulated angels praising God and singing. Ooooo. Holograms. Can we get holograms? Ready, three . . . two . . . cut to scruffy guy in the dirty white robe . . . "Hi. I'm Jesus and I want to tell you about my dad." Sometimes we get so busy trying to be holy we forget the holy one.

——————— OZ Says ———————

The Spirit of Jesus is conscious of one thing only—a perfect oneness with the Father, and He says, "Learn of Me, for I am meek and lowly in heart." All I do ought to be founded on a perfect oneness with Him, not on a self-willed determination to be godly. This will mean that I can be easily put upon, easily overreached, easily ignored; but if I submit to it for His sake, I prevent Jesus Christ from being persecuted.

——————— Just Between You and God ———————

Ask God to show you a mirror of yourself. When does your own selfishness get in the way of your message? Pray that God will help you get out of the way so his message can be clearly seen.

Remember why you started this. Get back on the path. Get past the obstacle—that is you.

01.29

HEY!

Then I asked, "Who are you, Lord?"
    "I am Jesus, whom you are persecuting," the Lord replied.

[Acts 26:15]

God often speaks to us in one of two ways. He will whisper in our ear, or smack us with a brick. Either way, we need to listen. It's when we lean on our own understanding that we get into trouble. When we serve God by doing what we think is right, or the way we want to serve, that's when God pulls the rug out from under us. Sometimes he needs to use drastic measures to get our attention. We can't say, "I think I'm doing what God wants me to do." With God there is no think. God makes his will known to us in ways he knows will be best for us.

—————————— OZ Says ——————————

God has to destroy our determined confidence in our own convictions. "I know this is what I should do"—and suddenly the voice of God speaks in a way that overwhelms us by revealing the depths of our ignorance. We have shown our ignorance of Him in the very way we determined to serve Him.

————— Just Between You and God —————

You should never ask God to speak up. You should never HAVE to ask God to speak up. Turn off the distractions, whatever they are in your life. It's not God's job to be understood. It's your job to listen. Pray today and then listen, not just with your ears but with your whole self . . . with all your senses. God is still speaking.

Listen for the whisper. Or wait for the brick. One way or the other, God will make himself known.

01.30

PRESS TO TALK

Samuel lay down until morning and then opened the doors of the house of the LORD. He was afraid to tell Eli the vision.

[1 Samuel 3:15]

First, understand that there is never a maybe with God. When God wants you to know something, you will know it. There will be no, "I wonder if that was God talking to me?" Prayer is not always about you *uploading* your soul into God's laptop. He wants to be heard as well. When God has something to say, he will say it, but only if he is sure you're listening. Jesus heard God speaking all the time. That is our goal as well.

--------- OZ Says ---------

Get into the habit of saying, "Speak, Lord"; and life will become a romance. Every time circumstances press, say, "Speak, Lord," make time to listen. Chastening is more than a means of discipline, it is meant to get me to the place of saying, "Speak, Lord."

--------- Just Between You and God ---------

Start with this prayer: "Talk to me, God . . . Amen." No frills. No music. No holy holy. Just say, "Talk to me, God . . . Amen." Pray this in the morning and the evening. Pray while driving and in school. This opens you. When he knows you are ready, he will speak.

Say, "Talk to me, God." Then listen. Really listen. The answer is just for you.

01.31

GRAB YOUR THINGS

. . . set apart for the gospel of God.

[Romans 1:1]

Here's your new word for today. Ready? *Redeemed*. Redeemed means that 100 percent is for God. Everything is now for his purposes. Our actions, talents, possessions, ideas, dedications, and time . . . that's all for God. Redeemed is about leaving behind those things which would get in the way of God. Nothing is for you anymore. Nothing is about you. It's about God. This is *not* restriction. Think of it as a retrieval or a recovery. Everything you are about was put in place by God anyway. Recognize it's now *for* God as well as *from* God. Whatever "it" is, examine it closely . . . whether thing or thought . . . ask yourself . . . can this bring me or someone else closer to the Creator? It is redeemed.

OZ Says

"Don't ask me to come into contact with the rugged reality of Redemption on behalf of the filth of human life as it is; what I want is anything God can do for me to make me more desirable in my own eyes." To talk in that way is a sign that the reality of the Gospel of God has not begun to touch me; there is no reckless abandon to God. God cannot deliver me while my interest is merely in my own character.

Just Between You and God

Make a list of things to pray for and then throw it away. That's not what you're here for. Pray that God will be the most important thing in your life. Pray that you will have the faith to walk into his outstretched arms without any baggage. Pray for the freedom to fully love God.

Be God's. Not religious. There is a difference. It will get better once you understand that.

02.01

TAB *A* FITS INTO SLOT *B*

For Christ did not send me to baptize, but to preach the gospel—not with wisdom and eloquence, lest the cross of Christ be emptied of its power.

[1 Corinthians 1:17]

There are many songs written about how the moon shines at night, but the moon does not shine. The moon in all its magic and power only reflects the light of the sun. So it is with us. We reflect the light of the Son. We can only be imperfect. We show the world the Creator the way one beggar shows another where the food is. Anything we ask that is for ourselves . . . our own glory . . . our own possession . . . is just getting in the way. The closer we get to understanding who God is (while accepting that we can never truly understand) all of the things we thought were important are not so important anymore.

—————————— OZ Says ——————————

The one passion of Paul's life was to proclaim the Gospel of God. He welcomed heartbreaks, disillusionments, tribulation, for one reason only, because these things kept him in unmoved devotion to the Gospel of God.

————— Just Between You and God —————

One of the dangers of being a Christian is thinking we are on par with Christ. Today, ask God to keep your head in the right place. You don't get to give the gifts—you can only show the one who does.

You don't have to stand in line to feel the rain. So it is with God. It's for everyone. Everywhere. Put away the umbrella.

02.02

HERE. WE. GO.

For when I preach the gospel, I cannot boast, since I am compelled to preach. Woe to me if I do not preach the gospel!

[1 Corinthians 9:16]

Once you start down this path with Christ, you will find there is no other way. You may see easier paths branching off from the one you are on. Or, you may see others having fun off to the side, but this is not for you. You chose this path when you chose to follow the way, which is Jesus. When Paul says, "Woe to me," he is referring to the fact that he would have blown it, if he hadn't used the gift of preaching that God had given to him. Now that you are on this journey, you will need to use your gifts. Art. Song. Poetry. Listening. What are your gifts?

―――――――― OZ Says ――――――――

Paul's words have to do with being made a servant of Jesus Christ, and our permission is never asked as to what we will do or where we will go. God makes us broken bread and poured-out wine to please Himself. To be "separated unto the gospel" means to hear the call of God; and when a man begins to overhear that call, then begins agony that is worthy of the name.

―――――――― Just Between You and God ――――――――

Some gifts from God shine or explode or resound. These are obvious ones. We see these in others and think God skipped us in the gift line. Those simply are not your gifts. Think about what it is you are doing when you feel the most alive. This is when you are closest to God. Today ask God to show you how to use your own gifts in the world he has given you to share.

How can you keep asking for more when your hands are full? Share.

02.03

WHO'S IN CHARGE AROUND HERE?

For it seems to me that God has put us apostles on display at the end of the procession, like those condemned to die in the arena. We have been made a spectacle to the whole universe, to angels as well as to human beings. We are fools for Christ, but you are so wise in Christ! We are weak, but you are strong! You are honored, we are dishonored! To this very hour we go hungry and thirsty, we are in rags, we are brutally treated, we are homeless. We work hard with our own hands. When we are cursed, we bless; when we are persecuted, we endure it; when we are slandered, we answer kindly. We have become the scum of the earth, the garbage of the world—right up to this moment.

[1 Corinthians 4:9–13]

Paul said anyone who follows Christ is a fool. You didn't get into this for the glory of it all. Sometimes it's going to be like being followed by dozens of paparazzi. They have cameras at the ready to post and tag you with horrible claims. They wait for you to screw up so they can point and say "SEE!" When you are mocked, respond with kindness. When you are hated, respond with love. When you are insulted, respond with compliments. When you are pushed down into the puddle, rise up, clean your face, and offer the rag to your tormentors. They're going to need it. They just don't know it yet.

—————————— OZ Says ——————————

The marvel of the Redemptive Reality of God is that the worst and the vilest can never get to the bottom of His love.

—————— Just Between You and God ——————

Pray for strength. You will need it. Patience. Kindness. Compassion. A sense of humor. You're going to need them all. Better start praying now.

When someone calls you "fool," take it as a compliment. Really. Yes, this is what you signed up for.

02.04

WHATEVER HAPPENED TO SOFTLY & TENDERLY?

For Christ's love compels us, because we are convinced that one died for all, and therefore all died.

[2 Corinthians 5:14]

Are you ready to do this totally? Everything? That's the goal here. Eventually you will want to get to the point where everything is for Jesus. Easy? Hardly. If you say everything is for him, then you better be prepared to go through what he went through. Exhaustion. Rejection. Persecution. Betrayal. Death. Yes, death—not of your body, but of your old life. You are going to be asked to leave it behind and get a new one. Are you ready for that? You can do it in his strength.

—————————— OZ Says ——————————

The one thing that held Paul, until there was nothing else on his horizon, was the love of God. "The love of Christ constraineth us"—when you hear that note in a man or woman, you can never mistake it. You know that the Spirit of God is getting unhindered way in that life . . . This abandon to the love of Christ is the one thing that bears fruit in the life, and it will always leave the impression of the holiness and of the power of God, never of our personal holiness.

—————— Just Between You and God ——————

This is one of those "big boss" levels. So much is in front of you but you have to get beyond this fight. Many quit. You can too. Put the book on the shelf and lie to the person who gave it to you . . . or you can keep going. It's like staring into the night. You know dawn is coming. It's going to start slow and then reveal the world. Are you willing to see it through?

Yes. As a matter of fact, it is hard—and it's going to get harder. But it's kind of like a hard rain. Change comes next.

02.05

TIPS

But even if I am being poured out like a drink offering on the sacrifice and service coming from your faith, I am glad and rejoice with all of you.

[Philippians 2:17]

The Bible is full of people who ask "Why God, why?" over and over. God almost always has the same answer. "Because I said so." There may not be banners with your name stretched across the door when you get back. That can't be even a small part of the reason you go. We go because God said, "Go." We do it because God said, "Do it." That's the reward. Recognized or unrecognized . . . we do it because God said so.

―――――――――――― OZ Says ――――――――――――

It is one thing to go on the lonely way with dignified heroism, but quite another thing if the line mapped out for you by God means being a doormat under other people's feet . . . Are you willing to spend and be spent; not seeking to be ministered unto, but to minister?

――――――― Just Between You and God ―――――――

Put aside your personal feelings and ask God today to "Send me." If you ask without the idea of "What's in it for me?" you might find the reply is different.

God will not always send you someplace pretty. You will not always get applause. You are a servant of God. Now, pray to be sent anyway.

02.06

SEVERED SERVANT

For I am already being poured out like a drink offering, and the time for my departure is near.

[2 Timothy 4:6]

You've heard the phrase, "Whatever doesn't kill me makes me stronger." It's true. We talk a lot about refining fires and that hard times are there to make us better people. But how many of us are willing to say, "Bring on the fire." No sensible person would willingly walk into the furnace. Even though we believe we will be stronger once it's over, we still avoid the pain if possible. We know that God will pick us up after we fall, but are we willing to make the jump when we know how badly it will hurt? We have to be able to say, "Bring on the fire. I'm ready." Once we win this inner battle, then our body just comes along for the ride.

OZ Says

Go through the crisis in will, then when it comes externally there will be no thought of the cost . . . After this way of fire, there is nothing that oppresses or depresses. When the crisis arises, you realize that things cannot touch you as they used to do.

Just Between You and God

Once you have stood up and said "Bring it," God will give you what you need when it has been "brung." It's the standing up in the first place that takes courage.

Take the step. Don't worry. God knows. Be brave.

02.07

BLAMING THE MIRROR

We had hoped that he was the one who was going to redeem Israel. And what is more, it is the third day since all this took place.

[Luke 24:21]

Who you are is who you choose to be. Who you are is not because your sister is prettier, your brother gets better grades, your mother smoked, or because your dad drank too much coffee. Who you are is who you choose to be. If your attitude is bad right now, it's not God's fault. Most likely, it's yours. We go through down-cycles in our lives and scream, "Why, God? Why are you doing this to me?" If we demand answers from God, we will get nothing. But if we truly seek God and live a life that honors him, he will give us the answers we're looking for.

OZ Says

Spiritual lust makes me demand an answer from God, instead of seeking God Who gives the answer . . . Whenever the insistence is on the point that God answers prayer, we are off the track. The meaning of prayer is that we get hold of God, not of the answer.

Just Between You and God

Stop shaking your fist at God and ask to see his face. Stop demanding answers and ask to feel his reassuring hand on your shoulder. The answers will come when you feel his presence, not when you demand his attention.

There's a reason God took the GPS from you.
Sometimes you have to choose a direction.

02.08

SQUIRREL!

May God himself, the God of peace, sanctify you through and through. May your whole spirit, soul and body be kept blameless at the coming of our Lord Jesus Christ. The one who calls you is faithful, and he will do it.

[1 Thessalonians 5:23–24]

Imagine every electronic gadget in the world in one big pile; every video game system, every laptop add-on, every smartphone, movies, music player—it's all there. Imagine it. Now off to the side we have the still small voice of God. The voice wants to talk to you. Can you hear it? Are you able? Can you concentrate enough so the noise doesn't distract you from what needs to be heard? This is what God wants of us. To become holy we must learn to shut out all the noise and learn to listen to God's voice.

––––––– OZ Says –––––––

Are we prepared to be caught up into the swing of this prayer of the apostle Paul's? Are we prepared to say—"Lord, make me as holy as You can make a sinner saved by grace?" Jesus has prayed that we might be one with Him as He is one with the Father. The one and only characteristic of the Holy Ghost in a man is a strong family likeness to Jesus Christ, and freedom from everything that is unlike Him.

––––––– Just Between You and God –––––––

This one is on you. God is not going to help you listen better. He is not going to speak up because you can't pay attention. All you can do is ask God to speak. Listening is entirely up to you.

That button right . . . there. Push it. Yes, it's the off button. What do you think you should do now? (Hint: It's called listening.)

02.09

STILL STANDING (BARELY)

Do you not know? Have you not heard? The LORD is the everlasting God, the Creator of the ends of the earth. He will not grow tired or weary, and his understanding no one can fathom.

[Isaiah 40:28]

Yes, you will get tired. If you start on this journey, if you follow the way, you will get tired. Some people don't understand this. They think if they follow Jesus he will constantly recharge their batteries and they will never feel fatigued. But most of us do grow weary. We set out to show Jesus to a hungry world, and we serve until we can't stand up. Those we are serving look to us for guidance and we just plain wear out. God is aware of this.

Think back to when you first said, "Send me, God," and evaluate where your energy came from then. When you return to God and say, "I'm really tired," not only will God give you strength, but he has been with you the whole time. It's really okay to admit you're tired. Just remember where your energy came from the first time.

———— OZ Says ————

Exhaustion means that the vital forces are worn right out. Spiritual exhaustion never comes through sin but only through service, and whether or not you are exhausted will depend upon where you get your supplies. Jesus said to Peter— "Feed My sheep," but He gave him nothing to feed them with. The process of being made broken bread and poured out wine means that you have to be the nourishment for other souls until they learn to feed on God.

———— Just Between You and God ————

God knows you're tired. No, he is not disappointed in you. Ask him for rest. Ask him for renewal. He gives these out freely in huge amounts. Whether it's spiritual caffeine or a holy pillow. He knows. Ask.

That whole loaves and fishes trick Jesus did? It's a metaphor for life. Are you giving away or shoving them in your backpack?

02.10

UN-LIMITED.

Lift your eyes and look to the heavens: Who created all these? He who brings out the starry host one by one and calls forth each of them by name. Because of his great power and mighty strength, not one of them is missing.

[Isaiah 40:26]

Everything you see in the Walt Disney Theme Parks started out on a table as an idea. There are professional imagineers whose only job is to think this stuff up. These people must be at the top of their creative game every day! However, these imagineers on their best day couldn't even begin to conceive all of who God is. When we think of God, we limit ourselves by what we already know. We think in terms of what our job is, what our concept of love is, what sounds and sights we associate with God's presence. Unlock your imagination. To think of God within the limits of our own existence puts limits on God. There is no such thing. Think about God and open your mind to every possibility. Think outside the bounds of color and noise and imagine the face of God.

OZ Says

In every wind that blows, in every night and day of the year, in every sign of the sky, in every blossoming and in every withering of the earth, there is a real coming of God to us if we will simply use our starved imagination to realize it.

Just Between You and God

Sight, smell, taste, hearing, touch . . . these are your senses. Think of them as limitations. God is more than this. Understand he's more and you are closer to him than you have ever been.

Beyond colors. Beyond sound. God exists there. And then some.

02.11

WHERE IT ALL STARTED

You will keep in perfect peace those whose minds are steadfast, because they trust in you.

[Isaiah 26:3]

Imagine. Imagine Walt Disney, Steve Jobs, Henry Ford, Vincent Van Gogh . . . all of them together around a table brainstorming. What they come up with would not be a blink of an eye to what God came up with. With a WORD, God spoke a universe into being. That spark that began the universe is still going on. Creator God is still creating. According to Scripture, that spark is in you. Right now. Sing, paint, compete, write, calculate, build . . . do all of these with that spark of God that lives, right now, in you. Imagine a God without limits, and it's easy to imagine a God that is with you . . . always.

OZ Says

Remember Whose you are and Whom you serve. Provoke yourself by recollection, and your affection for God will increase tenfold; your imagination will not be starved any longer, but will be quick and enthusiastic, and your hope will be inexpressibly bright.

Just Between You and God

Pray for a loosening of your mind. Don't put limits on your imagination. Let it continue forever, just like God.

Imagination. Ever try blowing up a balloon in a water bottle? Give those ideas room.

02.12

A LITTLE CHEESE WITH THAT WHINE?

... and said to Moses, "Speak to us yourself and we will listen. But do not have God speak to us or we will die."

[Exodus 20:19]

Imagine God . . . the Creator of all things. He's a one-man-band with cheerleader pom-poms tied to the end of his slide trombone. He's got a flashing neon sign on top of his Day-Glo hat. He's playing Lost and Found's "Lions" song. And we . . . we walk by like he's not there. We listen to God like a child listens to a parent. Not really paying attention. God is calling and we are too busy. It's like getting a text from your mother saying "Come home" and you finally head home after the fifth text . . . only to find she had made your favorite supper. Dishes now done. Supper's over. You lose. Listening for God works this way too.

—————— OZ Says ——————

We do not consciously disobey God, we simply do not heed Him. God has given us His commands; there they are, but we do not pay any attention to them, not because of willful disobedience but because we do not love and respect Him. "If ye love Me, ye will keep My commandments." When once we realize that we have been "disrespecting" God all the time, we are covered with shame and humiliation because we have not heeded Him.

—————— Just Between You and God ——————

Ask God for better ears, not the physical ones on the side of your head, but the ears in your heart and soul; the ones that are afraid of disappointing him. Don't ignore him. God will always love you. Pray for the ability to listen for his call.

Listen. Follow the sound. It's laughter. Don't be afraid.

02.13

OPEN EARS

The LORD came and stood there, calling as at the other times, "Samuel! Samuel!" Then Samuel said, "Speak, for your servant is listening."

[1 Samuel 3:10]

Sometimes a good friend doesn't have to say anything and you know exactly what they're thinking. Have you ever seen friends who are hurting and you think, "I should have listened better and been more attuned to what they were going through?" God wants to know us in this way. Our friendships develop because we listen to each other. Why can we not apply this same listening skill to God? We can hurt our relationships with our best friends simply by hearing, but not listening. We can do the same to our relationship with God. When he speaks, we need to do more than hear—we need to listen. By listening, we will begin to hear God, like a true friend, and do what he wants without having to be told over and over again.

—————— OZ Says ——————

What hinders me from hearing is that I am taken up with other things. It is not that I will not hear God, but I am not devoted in the right place. I am devoted to things, to service, to convictions, and God may say what He likes, but I do not hear Him.

—————— Just Between You and God ——————

Today, ask God for a better connection. Seek out that in-sync, don't-even-have-to-say-it kind of friendship. God is the one who has been waiting for you to find him. He's been teaching and advising and inviting all this time. Link up.

God is talking. Listen. God is. Are you still listening?

02.14

MUTE BUTTON

What I tell you in the dark, speak in the daylight; what is whispered in your ear, proclaim from the roofs.

[Matthew 10:27]

We all have those days that feel like we are experiencing life from down in a hole. As if everything we touch is going to fall apart in pieces on the floor just because we touched it. Especially plans. Those just break so easy. This is not the best time to talk with God. Days in the hole are the days God says, "Shut up for a second. It's my turn." These are the listening days. You could be in the hole just so God can get your attention. Listen. God needs to send someone a message and you're it. Listen. Listen. Are you listening yet?

────────── OZ Says ──────────

Are you in the dark just now in your circumstances, or in your life with God? Then remain quiet . . . Don't talk to other people about it; don't read books to find out the reason of the darkness, but listen and heed. If you talk to other people, you cannot hear what God is saying. When you are in the dark, listen, and God will give you a very precious message for someone else when you get into the light.

────────── Just Between You and God ──────────

Don't say a word. Don't ask God for ears or patience. Just sit quiet and stop talking long enough to hear what he's been trying to say to you.

Keep your mouth shut. It's God's turn. You're only here 'cause you didn't listen the first time.

02.15

NEVER ALONE

For none of us lives for ourselves alone, and none of us dies for ourselves alone.

[Romans 14:7]

You have gone from looking at the picture in the museum to being *in* the picture. You can no longer be an observer of life. You have to be a part of it. God needs someone to know something, and you are the messenger. You are an active part of the plan, not just a bystander. If you miss this . . . if you don't act like you are part of the plan, then everyone around you misses out. It's like playing a board game with your friends and you decide to put the dice in your pocket. Play the game. Play your part in God's plan.

─────────────── OZ Says ───────────────

How many of us are willing to spend every ounce of nervous energy, of mental, moral and spiritual energy we have for Jesus Christ? That is the meaning of a witness in God's sense of the word . . . My life as a worker is the way I say "thank you" to God for His unspeakable salvation.

─────────── Just Between You and God ───────────

Today, pray for perspective. Ask God to give you a glimpse of the big picture and ask him for a clear look at your little piece of it. Stop beating up on yourself for not being a "Super-Christian" and work hard at being a Christian.

It's a long time between exit ramps. There's nothing off road you need anyway. There's a reason they call Jesus "The Way."

02.16

LIGHT ME

Everything that is illuminated becomes a light. This is why it is said: "Wake up, sleeper, rise from the dead, and Christ will shine on you."

[Ephesians 5:13b–14]

Remember when you were a kid and joy was just a natural state of being? You thought you could do anything—a cape was all you needed to fly. As we grow older and mature, we stop finding joy in the little things. God says, "Wake up." God says, "Do the impossible." All those great ideas that we decided were impossible are not really impossible. God will give you spark and inspiration, but you have a job, too. You have to wake up and believe it's possible. Pull yourself out of that I'm-really-too-mature-for-this attitude and open yourself to the possibility that you can do the impossible thing God's calling you to do. Once you are in that frame of mind—God will bless you like you've never been blessed.

OZ Says

Our Lord said to the man with the withered hand—"Stretch forth thy hand," and as soon as the man did so, his hand was healed, but he had to take the initiative.

Just Between You and God

If you feel like you are churning out the same-old-same-old, perhaps it could be you are "inputting" the same-old-same-old. Ask God for new inputs today. Let the explosion of all that is God IN. You'll soon be letting it OUT.

Think different. Think new. Then the fun begins.

02.17

DOPE SLAP

Then he lay down under the bush and fell asleep. All at once an angel touched him and said, "Get up and eat."

[1 Kings 19:5]

Rocks are not capable of depression. It's not in their nature. Humans are. Depression happens. If we did not know depression, we could not know joy. When an angel came to the depressed Elijah, the angel didn't show him a big beautiful picture of a grand new heaven. The angel said, "Get up. Eat something." When we're depressed, it is often best to simply do something ordinary. God has always been in the ordinary things. We want to see him in a glorious vision, but we are more likely to see him in the simple sharing of a meal with a friend. We often see God in places we never thought he'd be. When we find him there, it's the first step on our way out of darkness.

―――――――― OZ Says ――――――――

If we do a thing in order to overcome depression, we deepen the depression; but if the Spirit of God makes us feel intuitively that we must do the thing, and we do it, the depression is gone. Immediately we arise and obey, we enter on a higher plane of life.

―――――――― Just Between You and God ――――――――

God is in all things, all places, all times, all people. God is quite literally everywhere. Yes, literally. Ask God to open your eyes to see him in the simplest places, the quiet places. He can lead you where you need to be.

Nobody lives in the puddle. Stay for as long as you want to . . . but why?

0 2.18

OUTLOOK

Rise! Let us go! Here comes my betrayer!

[Matthew 26:46]

When Jesus was experiencing his worst moment, he asked his friends to stay awake with him. Nothing else. Just stay awake. They let him down. Jesus was disappointed in them, and they knew it. We all feel that way sometimes. Just when someone needs something from us, we mess up and let them down. We are hard on ourselves. "I'm such a screw-up, I can't do anything right." But Jesus says, "Get up. Move on." What are you avoiding by being down in the dumps? There will always be another thing to move on to. Instead of sitting there and moaning about what a lousy person you must be, God says, "Get up. There's more."

─────────── OZ Says ───────────

Whenever we realize that we have not done that which we had a magnificent opportunity of doing, then we are apt to sink into despair; and Jesus Christ comes and says—"Sleep on now, that opportunity is lost forever, you cannot alter it, but arise and go to the next thing." Let the past sleep, but let it sleep on the bosom of Christ, and go out into the irresistible future with Him.

─────────── Just Between You and God ───────────

Sometimes when we pray, we put up our failures and imperfections like a deflector shield. Then they become a filter. We can't hear God's true voice. Put those aside and pray.

Really, it's not that bad. It'll buff right out. God has more on his to-do list. Quit whining.

02.19

CATCH

Arise, shine, for your light has come, and the glory of the LORD rises upon you.

[Isaiah 60:1]

Some jobs are just no fun—doing the dishes, emptying the trash, mopping up spills. These are mind-numbing jobs that often get assigned to the youngest child—you. So how do we make these jobs God-worthy? How do we remove the dullness and make them shine? Jesus took a lowly job (washing his disciples' feet) and turned it into something holy. When we do seemingly meaningless jobs with God in our heart, there is no way they can remain meaningless. God gives these jobs meaning. We can feel the Holy Spirit working through us, no matter what the job is. It doesn't have to be a grand-scale, stained-glass sort of job. When we allow God to work through us, something meaningless becomes meaningful.

OZ Says

Whenever God inspires, the initiative is a moral one. We must do the thing and not lie like a log. If we will arise and shine, drudgery becomes divinely transfigured . . . When the Lord does a thing through us, He always transfigures it.

Just Between You and God

Do *every*thing with your heart, mind, body, and soul—even those things you think are meaningless. God will help you turn those just-walking-around moments into an all-out dance-a-palooza.

Do the lowly jobs. Do them with God in your heart. They aren't lowly anymore.

02.20

AND YOU ARE WAITING FOR . . . ?

. . . but he comes so that the world may learn that I love the Father and do exactly what my Father has commanded me. "Come now; let us leave."

[John 14:31]

All your dreams, all your hopes, all your inspirations . . . let them come from God. They are his great gifts to you. But if you just sit around dreaming, hoping, and being inspired, how will things get done? You can sit and dream about painting a great masterpiece, but that doesn't create a painting. You can sit around dreaming about your girlfriend or boyfriend, but if you don't nurture your relationship, it will soon come to an end. That's what God expects of us in our relationship with him. God is God. God knows what he wants. If you merely sit and ponder on all that he wants, it sort of looks like you don't trust him. If you're supposed to do something—stop thinking about doing it and do it!

───────── OZ Says ─────────

When we are getting into contact with God in order to find out what He wants, dreaming is right; but when we are inclined to spend our time in dreaming over what we have been told to do, it is a bad thing and God's blessing is never on it. God's initiative is always in the nature of a stab against this kind of dreaming, the stab that bids us "neither sit nor stand but go" . . . Leave Him to be the source of all your dreams and joys and delights, and go out and obey what He has said.

───────── Just Between You and God ─────────

Ask God for a great big sparkling, singing, soaring pile of initiative. Ask for it in waves. Ask for it in piles shoved at you by angel-driven bulldozers. Now get up and go get it.

Dream all you want. Then do something about it. Otherwise you're just wasting your time—and God's.

02.21

WHAT?

"Leave her alone," said Jesus. "Why are you bothering her? She has done a beautiful thing to me."

[Mark 14:6]

If your love is sensible, stable, levelheaded, sane, rational, reasonable, logical, practical, realistic, or no-nonsense, then it isn't really love. Whether it is for another person or for God, love must function like one of those exploding dye-packs. It must be impractical, spontaneous, careless, unstructured, unplanned, over-the-top, indefinable, crazy, silly, and occasionally downright bizarre. God looks down to see if we are willing to come out of the shell we've created around ourselves and do something completely out there to show our love for him. If you think "Sorry, I don't do abandon," the world misses out on what you could have become.

———————————— OZ Says ————————————

Have I ever been carried away to do something for God not because it was my duty, nor because there was anything in it all beyond the fact that I love Him? . . . It is never a question of being of use, but of being of value to God Himself. When we are abandoned to God, He works through us all the time.

————————— Just Between You and God —————————

Do something that celebrates God. Don't ask him for anything today. Celebrate him in all things. Dance. Paint. Write. Sing. Do something—and make it for God alone.

Let go. Stop looking around to see who else is watching. Give over to the joy.

02.22

COME ON RISE UP.

Be still, and know that I am God; I will be exalted among the nations, I will be exalted in the earth.

[Psalm 46:10]

You see it in those great fantasy movies. The hero has dropped his sword; the villain has pushed it over the edge of a great cliff. The hero hangs on by his fingernails as the bad guy tries to stomp on his hands. Then from nowhere, the hero gets a sudden burst of determination, pulls himself up and keeps fighting. This is how we must live for Jesus. When we look around the world, it seems like all the things Jesus was about (love, peace, hope, kindness, justice, fairness, forgiveness) are hanging on by the tips of their fingers. We must be spiritually determined. When we stand in the face of all that would push us down, that is when, with God's power, we can pull ourselves up and keep going.

——————— OZ Says ———————

Tenacity is more than endurance, it is endurance combined with the absolute certainty that what we are looking for is going to transpire. Tenacity is more than hanging on, which may be but the weakness of being too afraid to fall off. Tenacity is the supreme effort of a man refusing to believe that his hero is going to be conquered.

——————— Just Between You and God ———————

New Word Alert: *intransigence*. Ask God for that today. That's like "the works" version of strength. With intransigence you get everything else you need with it—strength, determination, courage, and love.

The villain never wins. The hero will always rise. Usually the hero is just the guy tired of being handed the fuzzy end of the lollipop.

02.23

STICKY DISHES

. . . just as the Son of Man did not come to be served, but to serve, and to give his life as a ransom for many.

[Matthew 20:28]

Jesus of Nazareth was the Son of the Creator of the universe, and yet his behavior toward others was always characterized by humble service and love. Sometimes Christians will display their Christianity like a snooty waiter in a restaurant. "Look at me, I'm serving." "Yes, sir, coming right up." "Yes, ma'am, let me refill that for you." The fact is that Jesus calls us to be the busboy—the guy who cleans up after everyone. While the waiter is busy with other customers, the busboy slides in quietly and cleans off the table. Most of the time we don't even know he's there.

—————— OZ Says ——————

Paul's idea of service is the same as Our Lord's: "I am among you as He that serveth"; "ourselves your servants for Jesus' sake" . . . The mainspring of Paul's service is not love for men, but love for Jesus Christ. If we are devoted to the cause of humanity, we shall soon be crushed and broken-hearted, for we shall often meet with more ingratitude from men than we would from a dog; but if our motive is love to God, no ingratitude can hinder us from serving our fellow men.

—————— Just Between You and God ——————

When we're doing the lousy, nasty jobs, sometimes the only thing that gets us through the shift is the knowledge of quitting time. Eventually we will all be able to put the dish-tub down and walk with Jesus. Ask God to give you just a glimpse of that rest—that paradise we are all heading towards.

Sweat. Work. Feel like yours goes un-thanked? God knows.

02.24

IT'S ALL OUT THERE

So I will very gladly spend for you everything I have and expend myself as well.

[2 Corinthians 12:15a]

When we say we're going to give our lives to God, some people get a mental picture of tossing our lives away like a plastic Frisbee. Not even close. God is going to take our lives and spin them on his finger and start doing these impossible and graceful moves and turn what we flung away into an athletic kind of dance art. The art is not in the plastic disc. It's what God can do with what we gave him that amazes. Hold out your hand. God wants to give it back now. Your turn.

─────────── OZ Says ───────────

Paul became a sacramental personality; wherever he went, Jesus Christ helped Himself to his life. Many of us are after our own ends, and Jesus Christ cannot help Himself to our lives. If we are abandoned to Jesus, we have no ends of our own to serve. Paul said he knew how to be a "door-mat" without resenting it, because the mainspring of his life was devotion to Jesus.

─────────── Just Between You and God ───────────

Examine yourself for a moment and ask why you are on this path. Is it because you want to say, "Look, I'm a Christian," or is it because you can be a Christian whether anyone is looking or not?

Purposefully give your life. All of it. You're not tossing it over your shoulder. You're holding it out to Christ.

02.25

THAT'S EVERYTHING

If I love you more, will you love me less?

[2 Corinthians 12:15b]

There seems to be a bit of sideways thinking going on. As Christians, (by our very name Christians) people think we serve Jesus Christ, and we do. But Jesus himself said we are to serve him by serving others. Our real test is not in being preachers or teachers, but in being washers of each other's feet. Paul knew that his position as a servant of Christ would win him both friends and enemies, but this didn't matter to him. What mattered was his decision to completely and totally serve. The problems arise when we say, "I will serve completely and totally . . . as long as the pay is good, the weather is nice, it doesn't hurt, and the vacation package is negotiable." How "completely" and "totally" is that?

―――――――― OZ Says ――――――――

Paul delighted to spend himself out for God's interests in other people, and he did not care what it cost . . . Paul focuses Jesus Christ's idea of a New Testament saint in his life, viz., not one who proclaims the Gospel merely, but one who becomes broken bread and poured out wine in the hands of Jesus Christ for other lives.

―――――― Just Between You and God ――――――

Very often the close-ness we long for from God will come when we are up to our elbows in the sink at the shelter than it will on our knees in the sanctuary. Prayer is cleaner and less tiring. But which gets stuff done?

Are you willing to give it all up? I mean everything! That's what everything means.

02.26

RAISE YOUR HAND

"Sir," the woman said, "you have nothing to draw with and the well is deep."

[John 4:11]

Very often the ones who wave their arms and say, "Jesus is perfect and I am nothing," are those who think highly of themselves. They shout, "Look at me, everybody. See how humble I am?" But that's not being humble, is it? We say we look to Jesus for our answers, but do we really think he will help us? Will Jesus help me find a job for the summer? Will Jesus make my parents stay together? We want our Jesus to be like the one in the Children's Bible we had as kids. Handsome. Clean. Perfect. Eloquent. And eternally patient and giving. And if the Jesus we get is not the Jesus we want . . . who are we to get upset? This is Jesus we're talking about. We get to adjust *our* thinking.

―――――――――― OZ Says ――――――――――

It is all very well to say, "Trust in the Lord," but a man must live, and Jesus has nothing to draw with—nothing whereby to give us these things. Beware of the pious fraud in you which says—I have no misgivings about Jesus, only about myself. None of us ever had misgivings about ourselves; we know exactly what we cannot do, but we do have misgivings about Jesus. We are rather hurt at the idea that He can do what we cannot.

―――――――― Just Between You and God ――――――――

Go to God and lay out your frustrations and questions about him. Take your fears and doubts *about* the source directly *to* the source. He will understand.

When you say, "I trust" . . . trust. When you say, "I have faith" . . . have faith. If you have doubts, say, "I have doubts." But say all of this to the one who can do something about it.

02.27

IT'S DEEP TOO

Where can you get this living water?

[John 4:11]

When we say *Almighty*, do we really believe it? Most of our problems in Christianity come from the fact that we limit Jesus based on our own limitations. We say, "I love Jesus, but he can't pull me out of this one." Not so. If we believe it when we say, *All powerful*, *Son of God*, *Almighty*, then there is nothing Jesus cannot do. We have no problem thinking of Jesus as a comforter, healer, and nurturer, but the word "Almighty" causes us to pause because we have no concept of *Almighty*. No matter how deeply we hurt, Jesus can reach it. No matter how big our problems, Jesus is bigger.

———————— OZ Says ————————

Beware of the satisfaction of sinking back and saying—"It can't be done"; you know it can be done if you look to Jesus. The well of your incompleteness is deep, but make the effort and look away to Him.

———— Just Between You and God ————

What is the biggest word you know? Not the longest, but the word that means the "most big"? Is it *almighty*? *Omniscient*? *Supreme*? Choose a word like that and use it aloud when you pray, and understand this . . . it's absolutely true.

God does not play hide and seek. God plays hide and listen. You're hiding. Say it with me, God is . . .

02.28

AND???

"Now we can see that you know all things and that you
do not even need to have anyone ask you questions.
This makes us believe that you came from God."
"Do you now believe?" Jesus replied.

[John 16:30–31]

You've got your cool *Servant of God* t-shirt on, the one with the big "S" on the front. Now you're bounding forth doing God's good works. Look back. You're so far off the path, you can barely find your way back. One pitfall of signing on to be a servant is that we use the capital "S." We think this is *our* story, *our* plan, *our* idea. God began this long before you did. When we think the plan is ours, we usually create more problems and have to go clean it up before we can start again.

———————— OZ Says ————————

We need to rely on the resurrection life of Jesus much deeper down than we do, to get into the habit of steadily referring everything back to Him . . . We are not told to walk in the light of conscience or of a sense of duty, but to walk in the light as God is in the light. When we do anything from a sense of duty, we can back it up by argument; when we do anything in obedience to the Lord, there is no argument possible; that is why a saint can be easily ridiculed.

———— Just Between You and God ————

Ask God for a refresher course. We all wander off on our own, thinking we are working for God because we are of God. Talk with God about his plan, and he will straighten you out and put you back on the path again.

God's first words began a universe. The universe?
Still here. Still expanding. Maybe you should listen
to the plan that's working.

02.29

ALL THINGS . . .

"What do you want me to do for you?"
"Lord, I want to see," he replied.

[Luke 18:41]

Imagine all the water on earth in front of you in one gigantic ocean. You're standing on the beach with a teaspoon in your hand thinking, "If I start now, I may be able to empty this." The thought is incomprehensible; yet this is like our understanding of Jesus. We cannot begin to comprehend who Jesus is. We're forced to define him in terms we understand. That's the only way our minds can grasp it. To take in all that Jesus is would be unfathomable.

With this in mind, think about how you take your problems to him. Do you face difficult situations in terms of, "This is impossible"? Are you defining the abilities of the Son of God by the limits of your own abilities? If we hold back and say, "Here, Jesus, this is impossible," we are limiting him and are not operating by faith. Faith requires 100 percent belief. There will always be a shadow of doubt that says, "This is impossible." But nothing is impossible with Christ.

OZ Says

The most impossible thing to you is that you should be so identified with the Lord that there is nothing of the old life left. He will do it if you ask Him. But you have to come to the place where you believe Him to be Almighty. Faith is not in what Jesus says but in Himself; if we only look at what He says we shall never believe. When once we see Jesus, He does the impossible thing as naturally as breathing.

Just Between You and God

That problem you're hiding behind your back or that other one you can't even lift? God knows. He's got his hand out. Give it all to Him. He was waiting for you to ask.

Nothing is impossible. All things work out for those who love God and are in his will. Limit God and you limit what he can do for you.

03.01

NO EASY ANSWERS

Do you love me?

[John 21:17]

There are four words for love in the scriptures. *Agape. Eros. Storge. Phillos.* When Jesus asked "Do you love me?" He used the word *agape* (uncondi- tional). When Peter answered, he used the word *phillos* (brother). These are not the same. Peter had seen what happened to Jesus. Are any of us willing to make that leap? Are we able to run face first into the this-is-really-going- to-hurt kind of love? Ultimately it is Jesus who changes the question. He asks again using phillos. Peter finally says, "Yes Lord." Jesus will meet us where we are and lead us into the next question . . . the next answer. Yes Lord, I will love you . . . even if it hurts.

--------------------- OZ Says ---------------------

There is no possibility of being sentimental with the Lord's question; you can- not say nice things when the Lord speaks directly to you, the hurt is too terrific. It is such a hurt that it stings every other concern out of account. There never can be any mistake about the hurt of the Lord's word when it comes to His child; but the point of the hurt is the great point of revelation.

--------- Just Between You and God ---------

Tell God how much you love him. Tell him with your soul. The right answer comes with both joy and pain. Can you get through the pain to come into a joy that is beyond your imagination? Tell God that you love him, no matter how much it hurts, and you will find out how badly you need your faith.

The word "Yes" is the cornerstone to the cathedral. Blood. Sweat. Tears. Do you need me to repeat the question?

03.02

OKAY, I'LL SAY IT LOUDER

The third time he said to him, "Simon son of John, do you love me?"

Peter was hurt because Jesus asked him the third time, "Do you love me?" He said, "Lord, you know all things; you know that I love you."

[John 21:17]

Let's write I LOVE JESUS on a t-shirt and wear it to school. No, wait . . . let's put it in our phones so that every call will start out with I LOVE JESUS. No wait, let's write it on the blimp that flies over the stadium at the big game. If we could, we would re-arrange the stars to spell out I LOVE JESUS. Here's the problem. That's not the answer, at least not the one Jesus is looking for. The question comes in the quiet. The answer should be the same. No flashing lights. No production numbers. Do you love me? Yes. Can you be that direct? When the question comes in an unexpected moment . . . do you love me? We must answer with the same honesty and directness. Yes.

————— OZ Says —————

The patient directness and skill of Jesus Christ with Peter! Our Lord never asks questions until the right time. Rarely, but probably at least once, He will get us into a corner where He will hurt us with His undeviating questions, and we will realize that we do love Him far more deeply than any profession can ever show.

————— Just Between You and God —————

Clear your mind of all other things. Without a back-up list—without a working schedule—pray now and tell God how much you love him. This prayer is for nothing else.

Mean it.

03.03

NOT LUNCH . . . LAUNCH!

He said, "Lord, you know all things; you know that I love you."
Jesus said, "Feed my sheep."

[John 21:17]

Jesus' prayer was that the disciples would be one with him. Jesus was already one with God, so now he wanted that same connection for his disciples. He wants the same connection for us. Jesus doesn't always ask us to stand on top of a mountain and profess our faith. He also says, "Feed my sheep." "Do you love me? Good. Now take care of each other." We are the sheep. (Remember, "The Lord is my shepherd"?) Sheep can be disagreeable, nasty, smelly creatures—but no problem as long as they're left alone. However, trying to lead them is a whole new ballgame. Jesus said, "Feed my sheep, even if it's sometimes hard."

—————————— OZ Says ——————————

It is impossible to weary God's love, and it is impossible to weary that love in me if it springs from the one center. The love of God pays no attention to the distinctions made by natural individuality. If I love my Lord I have no business to be guided by natural temperament; I have to feed His sheep.

————— Just Between You and God —————

Let's say you are given a HOT new car. Are you going to say "Thanks" and never drive it? No. You will actually become the kind of person who would drive that kind of car. God says, "Here's love." What do you do next?

Sheep bite. Still want in on this whole "Do you love me? Feed my sheep" thing?

03.04

WHO, ME?

However, I consider my life worth nothing to me; my only aim is to finish the race and complete the task the Lord Jesus has given me—the task of testifying to the good news of God's grace.

[Acts 20:24]

Some people think, "Okay, now that I'm a Christian, I will live my life as a really, really good person. Okay, a really, really good person." In order for us to fully understand what God wants from us, we have to stop thinking of ourselves first. Paul tried not to consider himself at all. If you live without asking, "What's next, God?" you will undoubtedly live a life that has more free time, more money, and more success. But is that faith? We should ask, "How can I offer myself to God?" This is entirely different than going to God and saying, "Use me . . . but only if it works in my schedule."

––––––––––––– OZ Says –––––––––––––

But if once you receive a commission from Jesus Christ, the memory of what God wants will always come like a goad [sting]; you will no longer be able to work for Him on the common-sense basis . . . Never consider whether you are of use, but ever consider that you are not your own but His.

––––––––––––– Just Between You and God –––––––––––––

If you have a voice like an angel, are you still willing to serve if God says, "Shut up and feed the poor"? Give yourself to God and then go where you are sent.

You've got a lot of toys. Big deal. God gave them to you in the first place. He wants you. Not your stuff.

03.05

NO COPIES

However, I consider my life worth nothing to me; my only aim is to finish the race and complete the task the Lord Jesus has given me—the task of testifying to the good news of God's grace.

[Acts 20:24]

The magnificent writer Mark Twain once said "The two best days in a man's life are the day he was born and the day he finds out why." Real happiness does not come from doing something for God but from finding out what his purpose is for you. How? Good question. The more time you spend in God's presence, the closer you will get to that answer. If you can simply "be" with God, he will show you the way to yourself.

OZ Says

Think of the satisfaction it will be to hear Jesus say—"Well done, good and faithful servant"; to know that you have done what He sent you to do. We have all to find our niche in life, and spiritually we find it when we receive our ministry from the Lord. In order to do this we must have companied with Jesus; we must know Him as more than a personal Saviour.

Just Between You and God

Pray for God to be with you. Ask to feel his presence in all phases of your life. It is only in getting to know God that you can find out what he wants of you. Sometimes you may not learn the answer until years after you have finished high school. Sometimes you may find out as soon as you close this book.

Start now. Be with God. Closer. It's all just beginning.

03.06

TOMORROW AND TOMORROW

Rather, as servants of God we commend ourselves in every way: in great endurance; in troubles, hardships and distresses.

[2 Corinthians 6:4]

God is at work when we see that glorious sunrise (or sunset for you night people). All his handiwork on display, and we all stop in awe. Can you still be in awe on a day that is just a "day"? God is present in the boring moments. The gray moments. The moments of background-noise. Believe it or not, it takes more grace to step out of bed on the boring days than it does to stand on the mountain top. Anybody can find faith watching the aurora borealis. Can you find God when the days are like watching paint dry? This is where faith comes in.

──────────── OZ Says ────────────

The thing that tells in the long run for God and for men is the steady persevering work in the unseen, and the only way to keep the life uncrushed is to live looking to God. Ask God to keep the eyes of your spirit open to the Risen Christ, and it will be impossible for drudgery to damp you.

──────────── Just Between You and God ────────────

Thank God for moving even when you can't see him. Thank God for the inspiration even if you can't feel it. Thank God for the enormous amount of love he gives you even on days when you don't feel loved.

God is either cleaning up what you left behind, preparing the room for your arrival, or beside you singing along with the radio . . . or all three . . . at once.

03.07

NOW

No, in all these things we are more than conquerors through him who loved us.

[Romans 8:37]

Think about a surfer and a swimmer. The swimmer sees the oncoming wave and thinks, "Uh-oh!" The surfer sees the wave and thinks, "Cool!"—two different approaches to life. Verses in Romans talk about how nothing can separate God's children from the love of God. There are things that get in the way of your prayer life, relationship, soul dancing, and your devotion to God, but there is nothing that can separate you from God's love. It's this simple fact that turns us from swimmers into wave-riders. Surfers look at the oncoming wave and get excited over the possibilities. They skim over the tops of their troubles. Occasionally, a wipeout is possible. Okay, it's likely. But they crawl back up and do it again. There will always be another wave, but the mere fact that God is with them keeps them on top of the waves and occasionally sends them into the air. Are you a surfer or a swimmer?

OZ Says

The surf that distresses the ordinary swimmer produces in the surf-rider the super-joy of going clean through it. Apply that to our own circumstances, the severy things—tribulation, distress, persecution, produce in us the super-joy; they are not things to fight. We are more than conquerors through Him in all these things, not in spite of them, but in the midst of them. The saint never knows the joy of the Lord in spite of tribulation, but because of it . . . The experiences of life, terrible or monotonous, are impotent to touch the love of God, which is in Christ Jesus our Lord.

Just Between You and God

Sometimes you can just see problems coming, can't you? Ask God for his presence today. Ask for his reassuring hand on your shoulder. He's already there.

Ride. Soar. Crash. Rise. Ride.

03.08

LOST LUGGAGE (SAY IT LIKE IT'S A GOOD THING)

I have been crucified with Christ and I no longer live, but Christ lives in me. The life I now live in the body, I live by faith in the Son of God, who loved me and gave himself for me.

[Galatians 2:20]

If everything in your life, everything so far, could fit into one backpack, a time would come for you to open it and truthfully examine what's inside. Most of us wouldn't be shocked at the offenses and indulgences. We would be most surprised by how often our pride got in the way of following Christ. When we start down the way, that is, following Christ, we think we're required to toss out our bad behavior. Well, that's almost right, but we're required to toss out everything. The entire backpack needs to be chucked, and only then can we keep walking the path unhindered. There are things ahead of us we won't be able to get over if we're carrying any kind of stuff.

―――――― OZ Says ――――――

There is always a sharp painful disillusionment to go through before we do relinquish. When a man really sees himself as the Lord sees him, it is not the abominable sins of the flesh that shock him, but the awful nature of the pride of his own heart against Jesus Christ . . . If you are up against the question of relinquishing, go through the crisis, relinquish all, and God will make you fit for all that He requires of you.

―――――― Just Between You and God ――――――

Imagine you've paddled out into the ocean and dropped your backpack of guilt, shame, and grudges over the side. You watched it sink. It's gone. Don't search for it again. Once it's gone, believe that it's gone. Finding it again will serve no purpose. Trust God.

Check your bags. Chuck your bags. Get rid of the weight. You won't need it where you're going.

03.09

OPEN ROAD

"You do not want to leave too, do you?" Jesus asked the Twelve.

[John 6:67]

God has a plan. Undoubtedly there are times when the path God has for you will include ruts and holes. It will become so thick with branches and brambles that the sun won't shine through. There will be times when the muck will bog you down. He wouldn't have put you here if he weren't sure you could make it. But there may also be a path nearby that seems smoother and better lit. This will sometimes be the path God will allow you to travel. These are glorious parts of your way. This is when life will be like cruising down the road with the windows open and the perfect song on the radio. This too may sometimes be your path. Enjoy the smooth ride when God allows it and trust him when the path is rough.

—————————— OZ Says ——————————

If God gives a clear and emphatic realization to your soul of what He wants, do not try to keep yourself in that relationship by any particular method, but live a natural life of absolute dependence on Jesus Christ. Never try to live the life with God on any other line than God's line, and that line is absolute devotion to Him.

—————————— Just Between You and God ——————————

If you are beside life's highway changing a tire, ask God for strength. If you are cruising life's highway, windows open, good tunes, thank God for the blessing. It's all part of the same path and the connection with God must be maintained always.

Muck and mire. Loud tunes and mountain roads. Life is the path. Life is good.

03.10

THE MARCHING BAND REFUSED TO YIELD

Preach the word; be prepared in season and out of season; correct, rebuke and encourage—with great patience and careful instruction.

[2 Timothy 4:2]

This is more than leading the crowd in a cheer. "Gimme a J! Gimme an E! Gimme an S!" There's a difference between being a cheerleader for God and being a person of God. You can *have* a message and also *be* a message. The words that come out of you must be real. It's easy to spot a fake. You can't just say the words, you must also mean them. The crowd in the bleachers may be following the cheerleaders, but off to the side there will be a one-on-one where the message is being seen as well as being heard.

———————— OZ Says ————————

We are not saved to be "channels only," but to be sons and daughters of God. We are not turned into spiritual mediums, but into spiritual messengers; the message must be part of ourselves. The Son of God was His own message, His words were spirit and life; and as His disciples our lives must be the sacrament of our message. The natural heart will do any amount of serving, but it takes the heart broken by conviction of sin, and baptized by the Holy Ghost, and crumpled into the purpose of God before the life becomes the sacrament of its message.

———————— Just Between You and God ————————

If you like the crowds, ask God to show you the one in the bleachers who is not cheering. Seek out the ones who need to hear the message beyond the noise and commotion. If you're in the bleachers, look for the small crowd off to the side.

Hear the words. Preach the words. But mostly be the words.

03.11

IN SIGHT

So then, King Agrippa, I was not disobedient to the vision from heaven.

[Acts 26:19]

What happens to a helium balloon two days after the party? We'd love to keep the party going but sometimes we just feel . . . flat. We'll call that "spiritual leakage." Spiritual leakage comes when we try to maintain our God-lives separate from our real-world lives. They are not two different things. See the world with your God-eyes. Listen to the words of friends with your God-ears. Make God a part of your every-day-walking-around life and God will keep you filled. (Yes, you can make the 'hot-air' joke if you want to.)

——————————— OZ Says ———————————

Waiting for the vision that tarries is the test of our loyalty to God . . . Watch God's cyclones. The only way God sows His saints is by His whirlwind. Are you going to prove an empty pod? It will depend on whether or not you are actually living in the light of what you have seen. Let God fling you out, and do not go until He does. If you select your own spot, you will prove an empty pod. If God sows you, you will bring forth fruit.

————— Just Between You and God —————

Pray to be sent—not just sent, but flung. Try to live in the presence of God every moment of your life. When he is ready to fling you, you will be ready to be flung.

It's not where you are flung. It's the fling itself. Be ready.

03.12

GONE GONE

Peter spoke up, "We have left everything to follow you!"

[Mark 10:28]

When we say we are willing to give it all up for God, are we really willing to give it *all* up for God? We come to God with a list of wants. God, I need a job. God, I really want him to ask me out. Give me what I ask and I'll do what you want. This isn't prayer; it's bartering. Do I want the forgiveness and new life Jesus gives more than I want him? Am I interested only in what I can get? Some people give it all to God because they want to be put on a shelf in God's trophy room. "Look at me! I gave it all to God. See how wonderful I am." This isn't prayer. This is selfishness. If we're really willing to give ourselves to God, it should be because we want to be closer to God, and for no other reason. The fact that we get a new life, are made clean, or become God's chosen—is his blessing. We should want a closer relationship with God because we want to be close to God.

--------- OZ Says ---------

When we come up against the barriers of natural relationship, where is Jesus Christ? Most of us desert Him—"Yes, Lord, I did hear Thy call; but my mother is in the road, my wife, my self-interest, and I can go no further." "Then," Jesus says, "you cannot be my disciple."

--------- Just Between You and God ---------

Put away the wish list . . . this isn't the time for that. Put away your resume. God already knows. Today go to God with yourself. Just you. Open your heart and say, "I'm here." Now we can start.

Not for fame and glory. Not for new toys. Not to gain anything. Go to God for God.

03.13

ENOUGH

For God so loved the world that he gave his one and only Son, that whoever believes in him shall not perish but have eternal life.

[John 3:16]

When you start down the path that is the way, you can't be looking behind at what you gave up—or what might be coming up behind you—then you're not fully on the path. Giving yourself fully to God means looking only at what's ahead. Guilt and grief aren't things you can take with you; neither can you look at the consequences of the decision to follow Jesus. If you start thinking, "What will my friends say?" or "What am I giving up to do this?" then, again, you're not fully on the path. Being fully on the path is also known as abandonment. Without thoughts of the past or knowing the future, we step out of the boat—not into a black abyss or a storm, but into the full loving arms of Jesus.

--------- OZ Says ---------

Abandonment never produces the consciousness of its own effort, because the whole life is taken up with the One to Whom we abandon . . . and you will never know anything about it until you have realized that John 3:16 means that God gave Himself absolutely. In our abandonment we give ourselves over to God just as God gave Himself for us, without any calculation. The consequence of abandonment never enters into our outlook because our life is taken up with Him.

--------- Just Between You and God ---------

God isn't going to push you. God isn't going to give you a hint of what will happen if you make this step. Pray for courage. All you need is faith.

No, not presents . . . presence. Ask God for his presence. See, that works much better.

03.14

GIMMIES

Don't you know that when you offer yourselves to someone as obedient slaves, you are slaves of the one you obey—whether you are slaves to sin, which leads to death, or to obedience, which leads to righteousness?

[Romans 6:16]

What are the things that have control over us? What do we give in to every time it's offered? Alcohol? Cigarettes? It's easy to preach against the things our culture deems bad and evil, but what about the other things we know are bad for us? Caffeine? Sugar? Do we give in to these just as easily? What about our fears? Do we give in to these as well? Do we give in to long held prejudice about people we don't know? Do we give in to the screamers blogging about who to hate and when to hate them? If we give in to these fears and temptation all the while singing about how much we love God . . . then our faith is half-hearted. God must be "whole-heart" or the world loses out on what we could have done with just a little faith.

OZ Says

The first thing to do in examining the power that dominates me is to take hold of the unwelcome fact that I am responsible for being thus dominated. If I am a slave to myself, I am to blame because at a point away back I yielded to myself. Likewise, if I obey God I do so because I have yielded myself to Him.

Just Between You and God

Children cannot control their wants. They want everything. You're not a child. Today ask God for the maturity it takes to decide what is and what is not really important.

I want this." "I want that." Give it a rest. Want God.

03.15

BUDDY. CHRIST.

They were on their way up to Jerusalem, with Jesus leading the way, and the disciples were astonished, while those who followed were afraid. Again he took the Twelve aside and told them what was going to happen to him.

[Mark 10:32]

The way we believe in Jesus is in two parts. The first is the human side of Jesus. Since childhood you've seen pictures of the friendly man with children sitting on his lap. He is the baby born in a stable. He is the person who stands at the door and knocks. This image of Jesus is essential to our understanding of who God is. The second understanding is that this image is such a small part of who Jesus really is. Everything we've been taught about Jesus is like one snowflake in a blizzard—but there is so much more. Jesus was both completely God and completely human. How can you have two "completely's"?

Welcome to the debate scholars have argued about for centuries before you were born, and the argument that will go on after you're gone. At this point in the journey, you realize you'll never completely understand it all, but that's okay. You must have that image of Jesus in order to keep going.

―――――――――― OZ Says ――――――――――

At first I was confident that I understood Him, but now I am not so sure. I begin to realize there is a distance between Jesus Christ and me; I can no longer be familiar with Him. He is ahead of me and He never turns round; I have no idea where He is going, and the goal has become strangely far off.

――――――― Just Between You and God ―――――――

Today as you pray, think about the image you have of Jesus. Be as specific or as abstract as you want. Then say a prayer of thanks that he does not require you to know all of him in order to love him.

Jesus is bigger than you can imagine—beyond our sense of time, space, and reality. Understand completely that you will never completely understand.

03.16

CLICK TO RESTORE

For we must all appear before the judgment seat of Christ, so that each of us may receive what is due us for the things done while in the body, whether good or bad.

[2 Corinthians 5:10]

Ever meet someone who just seems to have a closed soul? They find fault with everything. They hurt others for no reason. They are quick to give and take offense. As Christians, we are all bathed in the light of Christ. His light shines on us and illumines our true selves. There will be some who, when they stand before Jesus, will show a cold stone where their heart should be. When John calls for us to be in the light (I John 1:7) he is not saying someday or eventually, he means in the here and now. Each day we must work to be in the light, loving God and living a life that pleases him. We must also love each other. If we can learn to do these things with our whole hearts, then we will never show Jesus a heart of stone.

OZ Says

If you learn to live in the white light of Christ here and now, judgment finally will cause you to delight in the work of God in you. Keep yourself steadily faced by the judgment seat of Christ; walk now in the light of the holiest you know.

Just Between You and God

Use this day . . . this moment right here right now . . . as your restore point. This day is what you'll come back to when you need help. Make this day the light that guides your future dark days. Tell God this day how much he means to you. Then rise. Move on.

Life is like night swimming. Take a rock or a bunch of glow sticks.

03.17

RIFF

So we make it our goal to please him, whether we are at home in the body or away from it.

[2 Corinthians 5:9]

Sometimes Christians like to keep score—the bigger the better. Let's see how many new churches we can start. Let's see how many people come forward at the altar call. Let's see how many kids show up for the youth event. We're ambitious about doing wonderful things for God, to get accepted by our society. We forget that we're in this to please God. God may not want you to build a church when he needs someone to give a blanket to a homeless person or visit a shut-in. Bigger is not necessarily better. What we think society expects of us as Christians and what Christ expects of us are not the same.

OZ Says

I have to learn to relate everything to the master ambition, and to maintain it without any cessation. My worth to God in public is what I am in private. Is my master ambition to please Him and be acceptable to Him, or is it something less, no matter how noble?

Just Between You and God

Let today be an ego-check. How much good can you get done in one day? How much good could you get done in one day if there was no chance of anyone knowing you ever did it? Are these two different answers? Think of God, not on what you do for him.

You're a musician. Are you playing to please the audience? Or are you playing to please the conductor?

03.18

SERVE

Since we have these promises, dear friends, let us purify ourselves from everything that contaminates body and spirit, perfecting holiness out of reverence for God.

[2 Corinthians 7:1]

If you were a cab driver and you knew Jesus was going to get in and ask for a ride, would you double check the map to make sure you knew the city backward and forward? If you were the chef in a restaurant and God was going to place an order, would you clean your stove and make sure all your ingredients were the best? Part of having God in our lives is that we need to clean up the place where he is going to live. God loves you for who you are. Yes, but if you love God for who he is, wouldn't you want to be at your best? Are there certain ways we act or talk or things we put in our bodies that keep us from being the crystal glass capable of holding the living water—Jesus?

––––––––––––––– OZ Says –––––––––––––––

Am I forming the mind of Christ, Who never spoke from His right to Himself, but maintained an inner watchfulness whereby He continually submitted His spirit to His Father? I have the responsibility of keeping my spirit in agreement with His Spirit . . . Is God getting His way with me, and are other people beginning to see God in my life more and more?

––––––––––– Just Between You and God –––––––––––

We all need power of the will. Pray that God gives you just a little more. Take care of yourself the way you would take care of a frame that will hold the painting created by God. You are a miracle. Think of yourself that way. God does.

You are a unique and amazing creation of a creator and creating God and you have the right to ignore anyone who tells you otherwise.

03.19

BLINDFOLD

By faith Abraham, when called to go to a place he would later receive as his inheritance, obeyed and went, even though he did not know where he was going.

[Hebrews 11:8]

Remember when you were a little kid and your mother took you some-place you'd never been before? Sometimes it was scary, but your mother would hold out her hand and you would walk together. That simple act of taking a hand and walking without knowing where you were going is pure faith. This is what God wants of us. If we put our entire trust, faith, and love in the one who is leading us, then where we're going isn't as important. Always having to know what's going to happen or where we're going gets in the way of faith.

OZ Says

Faith never knows where it is being led, but it loves and knows the One Who is leading. It is a life of faith, not of intellect and reason, but a life of knowing Who makes us "go." The root of faith is the knowledge of a Person, and one of the biggest snares is the idea that God is sure to lead us to success.

Just Between You and God

Today say a prayer to God and don't use the words *why, when, where, who,* or *what.* Pray and tell God only that you will follow.

Hold out your hand. Have faith. Follow.

03.20

LINK

Then the LORD said, "Shall I hide from Abraham what I am about to do?"

[Genesis 18:17]

Friendship with God goes beyond any friendship you've ever had. Imagine a friendship so close you never have to wonder if you're where you're supposed to be, doing the right thing, or growing the way you should. This is what Jesus wants for us—to be as intimately acquainted with God as he was. We mess up our friendship with God by putting ourselves first. When we see something we want and convince ourselves, that is what God wants, then it's for us and not him. Think of the last time you prayed. Did you pray to please God or did you pray selfishly? When we strengthen our friendship with God, he will make sure we have all that we need.

OZ Says

The point of asking is that you may get to know God better. "Delight thyself also in the Lord; and He shall give thee the desires of thine heart." Keep praying in order to get a perfect understanding of God Himself.

Just Between You and God

This is a three-word prayer. "God, I'm yours." Do not add "as long as" or "only if." Say it, and in your mind deem it as holy as any hymn or liturgy. Believe the words are sacred. When you truly believe the words, then you can think about adding more.

God wants a total access. An absolute network. Hold nothing back.

03.21

GOLD STAR

I have been crucified with Christ and I no longer live, but Christ lives in me. The life I now live in the body, I live by faith in the Son of God, who loved me and gave himself for me.

[Galatians 2:20]

Remember when we cut up a bed sheet and put it over you, then put a halo made of tinsel on your head and we called you an angel. There are no, or at least very few, Good Friday kids' pageants. Children aren't ready for that yet, but you are. You are ready for the crucifixion. If we truly believe that Jesus is such an intricate part of our lives, then we get crucified with him. You are no longer "playing" at Jesus. You are part of the real thing. That's a tremendous leap of faith. It's okay. God will catch you if you come up short.

OZ Says

When I come to such a moral decision and act upon it, then all that Christ wrought for me on the Cross is wrought in me. The free committal of myself to God gives the Holy Spirit the chance to impart to me the holiness of Jesus Christ.

Just Between You and God

Jesus and God are one. Jesus and you are one. You have a connection to God that no one can fully understand. Try anyway. When you pray today, ask God to make that connection clearer.

We are part of the connection. You are more than you think. Get the glitter.

03.22

SHINE ON

They asked each other, "Were not our hearts burning within us while he talked with us on the road and opened the Scriptures to us?"

[Luke 24:32]

Eventually we all have to come down off the mountain. Sometime you will have one of those wonderful experiences when you genuinely feel the Holy Spirit present in and around you. If you haven't had one of these, keep on this path and you will. Often these moments come on mission trips or retreats when we are away from our normal, everyday lives. We gather on a dock in the morning or around a fire in the evening, and suddenly we're so emotionally moved we can hardly speak. We don't want to leave the place, but that is exactly what God wants us to do: take that heart on fire and carry it into our normal, everyday life. This is hard. We have to learn to live every day with our hearts on fire and not go back to the ways of the world.

―――――――――― OZ Says ――――――――――

If the Spirit of God has stirred you, make as many things inevitable as possible, let the consequences be what they will. We cannot stay on the mount of trans-figuration, but we must obey the light we received there, we must act it out. When God gives a vision, transact business on that line, no matter what it costs.

―――――――― Just Between You and God ――――――――

Coming down off the mountain is scary. The mountain may be the first time we've ever truly felt whole and now we are asked to leave? Doesn't seem fair. That fire in your heart still exists no matter where you are. Today ask God to help you keep it burning. Use it to lead others or warm someone who is cold. It never truly goes out.

Heart's on fire. The light is in you. The world is dark. Hmmm. What do you think is next?

03.23

CAN'T GET NEXT TO YOU

You are still worldly. For since there is jealousy and quarreling among you, are you not worldly? Are you not acting like mere humans?

[1 Corinthians 3:3]

What, did you think you wouldn't have those feelings anymore? You decided to live as a God-servant . . . good for you? Did you think it would all be candy and unicorns? The world is full of people who struggle and many of them are good religious people. We are tempted to behave a certain way or believe a certain way that would certainly be easier and sometimes more fun. God is not asking you to be perfect. God is asking you to be you. God is not even telling you to fix your faults . . . he's asking to be let into your heart so he can do the fixing.

OZ Says

If the Spirit of God detects anything in you that is wrong, He does not ask you to put it right; He asks you to accept the light, and He will put it right. A child of the light confesses instantly and stands bared before God . . . When once the light breaks and the conviction of wrong comes, be a child of the light, and confess, and God will deal with what is wrong.

Just Between You and God

Some things are just that . . . between you and God. Take a quiet moment and bring everything to God. He will take them and replace them with something wonderful.

Confess. Unload. Refill. Live.

03.24

SCORE: YOU-0 GOD-LIKE A HUNDRED BAZILLION

He must become greater; I must become less.

[John 3:30]

Ready for the ego deflator? You are not God. You're all fired up and want-ing to share some of the amazing things that have happened to you since you started down this path, but there is an edge to you. You can only take this so far. Eventually you have to step back and let God take it from here. You can tell someone else about God but you cannot take the place of God, however satisfying that might be. Go right up to the edge of yourself and let God bring the person in. Remember, sometimes God has to break the pottery before he can reform it. It might hurt to watch someone else get their dish broken, but God made you whole and God will do the same for them. Just get out of his way.

OZ Says

If you become a necessity to a soul, you are out of God's order. As a worker, your great responsibility is to be a friend of the Bridegroom. When once you see a soul in sight of the claims of Jesus Christ, you know that your influence has been in the right direction, and instead of putting out a hand to prevent the throes, pray that they grow ten times stronger until there is no power on earth or in hell that can hold that soul away from Jesus Christ.

Just Between You and God

Say a prayer and ask God to remind you of who you are. You are his servant. Not his Son, not him. Pray that you won't take the idea of being the only Jesus some people will ever see too literally. Pray for your friends to find the way. Once they start down the right path, step out of the way and pray for their journey.

Bring a friend to God. Then move out of the way. God's done this before. Remember?

03.25

THERE WILL BE SNACKS

The bride belongs to the bridegroom. The friend who attends the bridegroom waits and listens for him, and is full of joy when he hears the bridegroom's voice. That joy is mine, and it is now complete.

[John 3:29]

Have you ever watched the way an airport works from the window near the gate? Imagine you have that cool job with the headset and the orange flashlights. That's you, got it? Now here comes a jet (we'll call that a soul). Your job it to guide that big boy into the hanger. (That's Jesus). You work for the same airline. Everybody has their special job. If you don't do yours and you try to be the pilot, you're going to cause a problem. It's the only job where you earn your wings by staying grounded.

———————————— OZ Says ————————————

Goodness and purity ought never to attract attention to themselves, they ought simply to be magnets to draw to Jesus Christ. If my holiness is not drawing towards Him, it is not holiness of the right order, but an influence that will awaken inordinate affection and lead souls away into side-eddies. A beautiful saint may be a hindrance if he does not present Jesus Christ but only what Christ has done for him. He will leave the impression—"What a fine character that man is!" That is not being a true friend of the Bridegroom; I am increasing all the time, He is not.

———————— Just Between You and God ————————

Pray today for your friends who aren't yet part of the passenger list. You've got the flight manifest—connect them with Jesus.

It's a party. The groom's waiting. Where's the bride?

03.26

DUSTPAN

Blessed are the pure in heart, for they will see God.
[Matthew 5:8]

Imagine you're the janitor in a magical church. This church is magic because the harder you work to clean and maintain the inside, the more beautiful the place becomes on the outside. Vacuum the carpets, and flowers grow outdoors. Dust the pews, and the broken stained-glass window becomes whole. You are like this magical church. In order to be an effective house of God, you sometimes have to clean out pew racks and sharpen the little golf pencils. It's not an easy job. Sometimes it's downright disgusting. But as you clean out the inside of your life, you will become beautiful, with Christ's love on the outside. Maintain the inside, and you will guard your outside from becoming tarnished.

OZ Says

The life with God may be right and the inner purity remain unsullied, and yet every now and again the bloom on the outside may be sullied. God does not shield us from this possibility, because in this way we realize the necessity of maintaining the vision by personal purity. If the spiritual bloom of our life with God is getting impaired in the tiniest degree, we must leave off everything and get it put right. Remember that vision depends on character—the pure in heart see God.

Just Between You and God

Ask God to get out that massive floor stripping device. Some of the dirt is pretty ground in. Some of the stains won't come up until you get under them. This part might hurt, but the end results will be amazing.

Get out the broom. Plug in the vacuum. Dust. Then watch the flowers grow outside.

03.27

THE VIEW FROM HERE

Come up here, and I will show you what must take place after this.

[Revelation 4:1]

Have you ever stood at the top of a tall building at night? Think about what the view is like from up there. You might see a light on the top of a taller building, but you never would have seen that higher light if you hadn't gone to the top of the first building. Life with God works this way. We try to live the kind of life that elevates us so we can see the view, and then he shows us a higher place where we can see even better. He shows us something new to work toward.

OZ Says

We have all been brought to see from a higher standpoint. Never let God give you one point of truth which you do not instantly live up to. Always work it out, keep in the light of it. Growth in grace is measured not by the fact that you have not gone back, but that you have an insight into where you are spiritually; you have heard God say "Come up higher," not to you personally, but to the insight of your character.

Just Between You and God

Today pray for strength and endurance. And as long as you are praying, ask for patience and discernment. You'll need them. Don't forget this is a journey and you are still on it. Say thank you to God for staying with you this far. There is more to go. God has never left anyone to travel alone.

Look up. See that light. That's the next stop. Climb. Reach.

03.28

HELLOOO? MCFLY? ANYBODY HOME?

**Then he said to his disciples, "Let us go back to Judea."
"But Rabbi," they said, "a short while ago the Jews
there tried to stone you, and yet you are going back?"**
[John 11:7-8]

The best part about getting lost is that you learn which way NOT to go. (Unless you found a really cool donut shop or ice cream place along the way.) God does not make mistakes when he gives you directions. Saying "Are you sure?" to God shows a lack of faith. God has been this way before. God created the "way." You're fussing about a turn that doesn't look right, and God has the whole map in his hand right down to the color of the sky when you reach the destination. Who has a better view?

——————— OZ Says ———————

To put my view of His honor in place of what He is plainly impelling me to do is never right, although it may arise from a real desire to prevent Him being put to open shame. I know when the proposition comes from God because of its quiet persistence: When I have to weigh the pros and cons, and doubt and debate come in, I am bringing in an element that is not of God, and I come to the conclusion that the suggestion was not a right one.

——————— Just Between You and God ———————

This may be difficult, but pray that God will let you see things from his side. This is difficult because you have to put away all your own opinions. Ask God for the vision and then ask for the energy to make it happen the way he showed it to you.

Follow. Don't question. Don't debate. Just follow. Do it.

03.29

TAPS YOU ON THE SHOULDER

You also must be ready, because the Son of Man will come at an hour when you do not expect him.

[Luke 12:40]

If you were driving a cab and Jesus got in the backseat, would that affect the way you drove? If Jesus were coming to your house for lunch, wouldn't that be the greatest grilled cheese sandwich you ever made? We don't know when Jesus is going to show up. More than likely, it won't be while we're being religious. It'll be when we're being ourselves. The trick is to make ourselves worthy of being surprised by Jesus—when he shows up at the door and asks if lunch is ready.

OZ Says

Jesus rarely comes where we expect Him; He appears where we least expect Him, and always in the most illogical connections. The only way a worker can keep true to God is by being ready for the Lord's surprise visits. It is not service that matters, but intense spiritual reality, expecting Jesus Christ at every turn.

Just Between You and God

Yes, you can say "tomorrow and tomorrow and tomorrow" over and over, but none of every single one of those tomorrows is up for grabs. What you do tomorrow is going to change tomorrow's tomorrow. Focus on one at a time. Ask God to give you a good tomorrow and worry about the others later.

Is he back yet? How 'bout now? How 'bout now? Still ready? How 'bout now?

03.30

BUFFET

He saw that there was no one, he was appalled that there was no one to intervene; so his own arm achieved salvation for him, and his own righteousness sustained him.

[Isaiah 59:16]

Too often we tend to visualize God as some sort of cosmic waiter. We go to church and give him our list (a new job, a hurtful relationship, healing for grandma's cancer); we place our order and wait. That's our idea of prayer. The fact is that prayer is finding out what God wants. We take God's order instead of giving him ours. That is what it means to pray and to worship. We must communicate with God with our entire beings. All that we are must come into play, or the whole place will go bankrupt.

―――――――― OZ Says ――――――――

Too often instead of worshipping God, we construct statements as to how prayer works. Are we worshipping or are we in dispute with God—"I don't see how You are going to do it." This is a sure sign that we are not worshipping. When we lose sight of God we become hard and dogmatic. We hurl our own petitions at God's throne and dictate to Him as to what we wish Him to do. We do not worship God, nor do we seek to form the mind of Christ.

―――――― Just Between You and God ――――――

Say a prayer today that has nothing to do with what you want from God—no bargaining. No I'll-do-this-if-you-do-that. Give yourself over to God and volunteer to be part of his plan. See how you can be his instrument to answer someone else's prayer. Rather than asking God about how to fit into this chaotic life, become part of the chaos, but be God's part of the chaos.

Prayer is conversation. Most of it is said without words. Use all of you. Move.

03.31

COME-'ERE

If you see any brother or sister commit a sin that does not lead to death, you should pray and God will give them life. I refer to those whose sin does not lead to death. There is a sin that leads to death. I am not saying that you should pray about that.

[1 John 5:16]

When some people hear the word *Christian*, they imagine a long-faced old man wearing a judge's robe and with a book under his arm. He points and scowls and tells people how they're messing up their lives. Actually, the biggest danger in being a Christian is giving others reason to have this image. When we become Christians, we don't get to jump in and fix people. That's not our job, especially since we usually need a lot of fixing ourselves. If we listen, God will let us know what to do. We will see others in trouble and in pain (sometimes of their own creation) and God will let us know the best course on how to help them. It's never finger-pointing.

OZ Says

One of the subtlest burdens God ever puts on us as saints is this burden of discernment concerning other souls. He reveals things so that we may take the burden of these souls before Him and form the mind of Christ about them, and as we intercede on His line, God says He will give us "life for them that sin not unto death." It is not that we bring God into touch with our minds, but that we rouse ourselves until God is able to convey His mind to us about the one for whom we intercede.

Just Between You and God

Get quiet. Think long and hard about a person you know who needs help. God will make something known to you. The answer may be to wait, or it may be to get involved. Be open to both answers and be ready to do what you are told.

There is only one God. He's already got the job. So don't apply. Listen. Just listen.

04.01

THE IN-BETWEENS

And he who searches our hearts knows the mind of the Spirit, because the Spirit intercedes for God's people in accordance with the will of God.

[Romans 8:27]

Ever feel like you're banging your head against a wall? Clubs, school, work, family, friends, sports—all of these just seem to be overwhelming at times. We make a list trying to prioritize, and God's place on the list just gets lower and lower. Do you ever stop and think that maybe, if God were higher on your list, the rest might not be quite so overwhelming? We are important to God, but how can God show us if we are not willing to make Him first on our list? If we take time to focus on God through worship and prayer for others, we open the door and allow the Holy Spirit to be a part of our lives, day in and day out.

--------- OZ Says ---------

Begin with the circumstances we are in—our homes, our business, our country, the present crisis as it touches us and others—are these things crushing us? Are they badgering us out of the presence of God and leaving us no time for worship? Then let us call a halt, and get into such living relationship with God that our relationship to others may be maintained on the line of intercession whereby God works His marvels.

--------- Just Between You and God ---------

God doesn't need you to give up your entire day. Use the drive in to school. Use ten minutes between school and homework. Set aside some time as belonging to God. Turn off your phone, open a journal or a sketchpad. Stare at the stars. God has a secret.

God does not get distracted. That would be you. Start again.

04.02

BATTING ORDER

Then Ananias went to the house and entered it. Placing his hands on Saul, he said, "Brother Saul, the Lord—Jesus, who appeared to you on the road as you were coming here—has sent me so that you may see again and be filled with the Holy Spirit."

[Acts 9:17]

Saul was a jerk. God had to literally knock the man off his horse in order to get him to listen. From that point on, Saul (whom God renamed Paul) did everything he could to make Jesus first in his life. It wasn't easy. Read his writings, and you will see that Paul really wanted to please God. Okay, everybody wants to please God, but Paul really, really wanted to please God. He was obsessed with it. That is how we should be. We should not just be after the really life, but the really, really life. People should look at us and see a person after God's own heart—not only through our preaching and the way we live, but also by what's in our hearts. The real heart. The true heart. The heart that shows God to the world.

OZ Says

The abiding characteristic of a spiritual man is the interpretation of the Lord Jesus Christ to himself, and the interpretation to others of the purposes of God. The one concentrated passion of the life is Jesus Christ. Whenever you meet this note in a man, you feel he is a man after God's own heart.

Just Between You and God

If these "Just Between You and God" moments are important to you . . . tell God. Let God know that you want to hear him, see him, understand him. Open yourself up to it and God will fill these moments and make them indispensable.

What's first? If it's not God, re-think and ask again.

04.03

'ROUND THE BEND

. . . and said, "If you, even you, had only known on this day what would bring you peace—but now it is hidden from your eyes."

[Luke 19:42]

Imagine walking along a train track and coming to a bridge. You can walk across the bridge to the other side, but what if a train comes while you're out there? You choose to cross and sure enough, you hear the blast of the whistle . . . you start to run.

Now, let's imagine this is your life. You're running along the track; there's no opportunity to jump or step to safety. However, over and over again God will open doors for you to take, but if you run past them you can't go back without running headlong into a train. You can wish, "I should have taken that door," but you can't go back. Memories are killers sometimes, but they serve to teach us a lesson. If you missed the last opportunity, it will open your eyes to see the next one.

OZ Says

The unfathomable sadness of the "might have been!" God never opens doors that have been closed. He opens other doors, but He reminds us that there are doors which we have shut, doors which need never have been shut, imaginations which need never have been sullied. Never be afraid when God brings back the past. Let memory have its way. It is a minister of God with its rebuke and chastisement and sorrow. God will turn the "might have been" into a wonderful culture for the future.

Just Between You and God

Memories can be like a stone in your shoe. Sometimes it hurts until you realize you don't need to carry it anymore.

Focus on God. Make the time. Look for his presence.

04.04

THE ALMOST

A time is coming and in fact has come when you will be scattered, each to your own home. You will leave me all alone. Yet I am not alone, for my Father is with me.

[John 16:32]

Have you ever driven on a road that only goes west? How about a roller coaster that only goes up? No? You've chosen to be on this journey into a better relationship with God. That means you get to experience the whole journey. You are going to fall. You are going to get lost. You are going to make mistakes and have to go back and fix them. Falling is part of the journey. It's not just moving from point A to point B. That's not a journey. That's a line.

Falling. Getting dirty. Messed up. It all happens when you're on this path. God sees the entire journey and knows what's ahead of you—even if you feel like you're sloshing through the muck. He sees the end of the path—where you will break through the trees and go running into his arms.

OZ Says

God is never in a hurry; if we wait, we shall see that God is pointing out that we have not been interested in Himself but only in His blessings. The sense of God's blessing is elemental. "Be of good cheer, I have overcome the world." Spiritual grit is what we need.

Just Between You and God

Sometimes you just have to keep going on faith. You're out of breath. You might need strength and rejuvenation. You just have to keep going. Tell God you are willing, even if it seems like he isn't listening.

Be patient. This is far from over. Keep walking.

04.05

LEVELING OFF

Then he said to them, "My soul is overwhelmed with sorrow to the point of death. Stay here and keep watch with me."

[Matthew 26:38]

No matter what you do, who you are, what you think you know . . . you can never know what it was like that night before the crucifixion. The Bible says that Jesus prayed so intensely that blood came from his pores. That sense of dread—that knowledge of what was going to be done to his body—was overwhelming. You and I cannot know. Ever. Jesus knew what was going to happen. If he had not stood up and said, "Let's do it," you would not be reading this book. Think about that. Whatever has brought you to this moment, your reading these words began with Jesus allowing himself to be arrested, tried, beaten, tortured, and murdered. Every member of the human race was affected by these actions.

OZ Says

The Cross of Christ is a triumph for the Son of Man. It was not only a sign that Our Lord had triumphed, but that He had triumphed to save the human race. Every human being can get through into the presence of God now because of what the Son of Man went through.

Just Between You and God

Don't even try to imagine it. You can't. Simply thank God. Say thank you. Mean the words when you say them, and then live your life like you mean them.

We cannot imagine the pain. We cannot imagine the agony. It was all done for one purpose. You.

04.06

BRIDGE

"He himself bore our sins" in his body on the cross, so that we might die to sins and live for righteousness; "by his wounds you have been healed."

[1 Peter 2:24]

Don't think of the cross itself as a symbol of suffering and death. The cross is a symbol of victory. The cross is a symbol of triumph. All that mankind could have been collides with all that mankind will be at the cross. Because of what Jesus did, we are free to create a world where "thy kingdom come" and "on earth as it is in heaven" are not just words recited in a prayer, but are incredibly real possibilities. Because of the cross, the good guys won. Life had been like a dark prison cell. Then someone gave the prisoner a hammer and allowed him to swing against the wall until it broke through and the light shone in. The cross occurred at that moment—when the wall broke open. We won't ever be in darkness again.

OZ Says

The Cross is not the cross of a man but the Cross of God, and the Cross of God can never be realized in human experience. The Cross is the exhibition of the nature of God, the gateway whereby any individual of the human race can enter into union with God. When we get to the Cross, we do not go through it; we abide in the life to which the Cross is the gateway.

Just Between You and God

Look for crosses today. They are everywhere. Power lines. Jet streams. The wires in your shopping cart. Seek them. We are surrounded. If you look for it, you will find it. If you seek Christ, you will find him the same way. Just look.

The cross does not equal death. The cross equals life. Yours.

04.07

CHASM

As they were coming down the mountain, Jesus gave them orders not to tell anyone what they had seen until the Son of Man had risen from the dead.

[Mark 9:9]

I don't get this."

"Why doesn't Jesus just come right out and say what he means?"

Imagine a jigsaw puzzle . . . one of those massive ones. A thousand pieces. You have the edge done. Certain sections are coming together by color. You still need one piece and you can finish up the corner. Nine hundred plus random pieces lay scattered in front of you. So you stare and stare and stare . . . then BANG. There it is. It's like reading a *Where's Waldo* book. It's easier the second time because you've trained your eyes to see the bigger picture. When we work on our relationship with Jesus, we understand more, little by little. The closer we get, the more understanding we receive. It's a continuing process.

—————————— OZ Says ——————————

Say nothing until the Son of Man is risen in you—until the life of the risen Christ so dominates you that you understand what the historic Christ taught. When you get to the right state on the inside, the word which Jesus has spoken is so plain that you are amazed you did not see it before. You could not understand it before, you were not in the place in disposition where it could be borne.

————— Just Between You and God —————

You can't ask God for understanding until you move closer to Jesus. Ask God to shrink the gap, and then you can ask for understanding. You'll discover that Jesus doesn't just *have* the answer—he *is* the answer.

Fake it 'til you make it.

04.08

EVIDENCE

Did not the Messiah have to suffer these things and then enter his glory?

[Luke 24:26]

If you hang a "Wet Paint" sign, most people will still touch to see if it's true. The human race can be obnoxious. God saw his children and was disappointed. He sent prophets and preachers over and over to tell them how to get close to him, and they still didn't listen. So God decided it was time for something drastic. He sent his Son. Jesus came and told them everything they needed to know and then was put to death, dying a death we deserve because of our sins against God. After three days in a grave, amazingly, Jesus conquered death and proved that everything he had said was true. All the things he said about God, all the things he said about loving each other— they were all true. Jesus had to go to the cross.

He died in the most horrible way possible so people would know beyond the shadow of a doubt that he was dead. Then he came back to call us to a new way of life unlike anything we had known before.

OZ Says

Our Lord's Cross is the gateway into His life: His Resurrection means that He has power now to convey His life to me . . . He rose to an absolutely new life, to a life He did not live before He was incarnate. He rose to a life that had never been before; and His resurrection means for us that we are raised to His risen life, not to our old life. One day we shall have a body like unto His glorious body, but we can know now the efficacy of His resurrection and walk in newness of life. "I would know Him in the power of His resurrection."

Just Between You and God

Jesus did what he did to prove then and now everything he said was true. Accept that. Accept that all those lessons are true and life just can't be the same.

Believe. Understand. Pray. Live.

04.09

ALREADY HERE

Afterward Jesus appeared in a different form to two of them while they were walking in the country.

[Mark 16:12]

The Bible tells us over and over again that Jesus laid it all out for the disciples, but they just didn't understand what he was talking about. Sometimes things can be right in front of us and we just don't see them. Then when we do, we wonder why it took us so long. Everyone wants to see Jesus. We look, hope, and pray for him—and all the time he's right in front of us saying, "I'm right here!" When we realize what Jesus has done for us, we start to see him. Until then, he remains invisible to us. Those who seek him just to say, "I saw Jesus" will miss him. Those who see what he has already done will get to experience the presence of Jesus.

OZ Says

The man blind from his birth did not know who Jesus was until He appeared and revealed Himself to him. Jesus appears to those for whom He has done something; but we cannot dictate when He will come. Suddenly at any turn He may come. "Now I see Him!"

Just Between You and God

Everything is connected to everything else. In ways we can't imagine, we are deeply connected to the creation. Today, thank the Creator for the connections you won't ever see. Believe they are there and say thank you.

You can't complain about stumbling around in the dark if you haven't tried the door. Open it. Let the light in.

04.10

LEFT BEHIND

For we know that our old self was crucified with him so that the body ruled by sin might be done away with, that we should no longer be slaves to sin.

[Romans 6:6]

A great many of Paul's letters are written to people who say, "I believe in Jesus" and then turn around and live exactly as they did before. Belief requires change or it isn't really belief. You get to leave your old life behind— the life that was filled with guilt and shame and pain. That's gone. It's on the cross. As Jesus came back brand new . . . so could we. Once we have a new life, it gets harder than ever not to think of the old one. It is when we tell God how much we love him and then deliberately turn away and follow the way we used to go that we get ourselves into trouble.

─────────── OZ Says ───────────

Have I entered into the glorious privilege of being crucified with Christ until all that is left is the life of Christ in my flesh and blood? "I am crucified with Christ; nevertheless I live; yet not I, but Christ liveth in me."

─────────── Just Between You and God ───────────

You have to mean it when you say it. You can't just say it like you mean it. You have to mean it. "God, I will follow you. God, I am your servant." Meaning it takes practice. Start now.

Hang the old life on a cross. Walk away. You don't need it anymore.

04.11

INTO MY LIFE

If we have been united with him in a death like his, we will certainly also be united with him in a resurrection like his.

[Romans 6:5]

To say, "God, here I am. Send me," is more than being a servant. Saying God is in charge is not giving our lives to God. To truly be a servant is letting God give us a life. He gives us our own life back. If we are willing to give it up and be crucified with Christ, then, like Christ, we will come back. God will give us a new being. Seeing the baby Jesus didn't make shepherding easier, but they were forever changed. Yes, it will be hard. Yes, it will be difficult. But it will never be the same.

OZ Says

The proof that I have been through crucifixion with Jesus is that I have a decided likeness to Him. The incoming of the Spirit of Jesus into me readjusts my personal life to God. The resurrection of Jesus has given Him authority to impart the life of God to me, and my experimental life must be constructed on the basis of His life. I can have the resurrection life of Jesus now, and it will show itself in holiness.

Just Between You and God

If there is an emptiness in you because you feel like you've given up something good in order to follow Jesus, then ask God to fill the empty space. You will receive an ocean's worth of love that will pour through your whole being. Ask God for it now and open yourself for the rush.

The dark becomes light. The night becomes day. The desert becomes an ocean. The space is filled.

04.12

STILL RUNNING DEEP

For we know that since Christ was raised from the dead, he cannot die again; death no longer has mastery over him. The death he died, he died to sin once for all; but the life he lives, he lives to God. In the same way, count yourselves dead to sin but alive to God in Christ Jesus.

[Romans 6:9–11]

It's easy for this all to seem confusing. Don't let people tell you they have it all figured out, because the process is a journey that doesn't end. There is a difference between getting a life from God and getting a life of God. God has already given you a life. What you do with it and how you use it is entirely up to you. Having the life of God begins when the Holy Spirit comes in to stay. The challenge is to make room for him. Our job is to look at our lives and say, "What am I willing to let go of?" "What is keeping me from a closer relationship with God?" We hang on to so many things we don't need, but as this journey continues, we must make room for the spirit of God in order to have that life of God.

––––––––– OZ Says –––––––––

The weakest saint can experience the power of the Deity of the Son of God if once he is willing to "let go." Any strand of our own energy will blur the life of Jesus. We have to keep letting go, and slowly and surely the great full life of God will invade us in every part, and men will take knowledge of us that we have been with Jesus.

––––––––– Just Between You and God –––––––––

Prayer is just that . . . between you and God . . . so what you say to him and what you give to him stays between the two of you. Dig something out of your soul that you have been carrying around for too long. Give it to him.

Stop fighting for the leftover crust . . . God has a whole pizza right behind you. No seriously, quite fighting . . . it's just crust.

04.13

FOR THE ASSIST

Cast your cares on the LORD and he will sustain you; he will never let the righteous be shaken.

[Psalm 55:22]

Imagine you are moving into a college dorm. Your best friend has given you a reclining chair, but the only way to get it up the stairs and into your room is if you ask the friend who gave it to you to help you carry it. Many of the weights we carry in life are of our own creation. We seem to look for ways to make living complicated, as if that's the reward. Being a servant of God means God will say, "Here. Carry this." God will never give you more than you can carry. When it's too much, God will help you. He will share the burden. He may even take the heavy end and walk backwards up the stairs, but it is a shared effort. No one does this alone.

OZ Says

If we undertake work for God and get out of touch with Him, the sense of responsibility will be overwhelmingly crushing; but if we roll back on God that which He has put upon us, He takes away the sense of responsibility by bringing in the realization of Himself.

Just Between You and God

We all have many burdens. Choose one. Be specific and ask for God's help in carrying it. He will lift one end and you can take the other. It's a partnership. God will not let you carry it alone if you ask for his help.

Lift with your knees. Ask for help. There's no reward for doing it by yourself.

04.14

SUPERMAN!

Take my yoke upon you and learn from me, for I am gentle and humble in heart, and you will find rest for your souls.

[Matthew 11:29]

God must have a great deal of patience. He wants to bring us into a closer relationship—and we start complaining. "I have to carry that? Come on, God, that's not fair." We need to step back and look at the big picture. God (the Creator of the universe, the Almighty, the everlasting, the beginning and the end) has asked us to share part of the load . . . to take one end of the recliner (borrowing from yesterday's illustration). God has asked us to do this so we can be in communion with him. We should be jumping for joy at this opportunity. We should be thanking him for the honor and for his faith in us, but we sometimes get things backward. God does not give us a weight to load us down. He gives us the weight to lift us up.

—————— OZ Says ——————

The fact that the peace and the light and the joy of God are there is proof that the burden is there too. The burden God places squeezes the grapes and out comes the wine; most of us see the wine only. No power on earth or in hell can conquer the Spirit of God in a human spirit; it is an inner unconquerableness.

—————— Just Between You and God ——————

If you think you can't help because you already have too much to carry . . . check what you are carrying. Do you really need it? The guilt? The anger? Do you need those? Put them aside. God is asking you to be in communion with him. Are you ready to receive?

Remember who it is that gave you the task. That shows his faith in you. You're your faith in him. Hold up your end.

04.15

REMOVE RESTORE RENEW

Although he did not remove the high places from Israel, Asa's heart was fully committed to the Lord all his life.

[2 Chronicles 15:17]

So there was this guy named Asa. He was given the task of cleaning out the kingdom, in a way. Everything that involved other gods was to be removed. There were even some changes needed in his immediate family. The entire kingdom needed a major renovation, both physically and spiritually. Imagine you need a new church building. A nice person in the community says, "Here. I have this old Peter Pepperoni Pizza Parlor. It's yours." You're going to need some renovation. (Although the giant talking pepperoni would be cool in the youth room.) The job is going to require a massive overhaul. The Bible refers to our bodies as temples. We must also care for our souls. Fixing. Cleaning. Repairing. Moving. Changing. God knows these tasks will take the rest of our lives. Don't let that stop you from continuing to grow. The joy of the Lord is your strength.

--------- OZ Says ---------

Beware of the thing of which you say—"Oh, that does not matter much." The fact that it does not matter much to you may mean that it matters a very great deal to God. Nothing is a light matter with a child of God. How much longer are some of us going to keep God trying to teach us one thing? He never loses patience.

--------- Just Between You and God ---------

Everybody has a to-do list when it comes to getting right with God. Ask God to help you make yours. Then he will be more than happy to help you get it done.

Overhaul. Create. Beautify. Uphold.

04.16

WAKE

"Believe in the light while you have the light, so that you may become children of light." When he had finished speaking, Jesus left and hid himself from them.

[John 12:36]

Oh those perfect days. You hit all the green lights. You find twenty bucks in an old coat pocket. The weather is perfect. Your homework is done and you are going to ace that test in English. As an added bonus, the prize that fell out of the box into your cereal is awesome. This is going to be a good day. Will tomorrow be like this? Probably not. Tomorrow may suck rocks. But this day . . . this day is good. Take this day and put it in your heart so you can remember it. You might have 63 bad days in a row but keep this one in mind. This one is the reminder that the pendulum swings both ways, that God gives us the good and the bad. Eventually, every day will be as good as this one.

──────── OZ Says ────────

Never allow a feeling which was stirred in you in the high hour to evaporate. Don't put your mental feet on the mantelpiece and say—"What a marvelous state of mind to be in!" Act immediately, do something, if only because you would rather not do it. If in a prayer meeting God has shown you something to do, don't say—"I'll do it;" do it! Take yourself by the scruff of the neck and shake off your incarnate laziness. Laziness is always seen in cravings for the high hour; we talk about working up to a time on the mount. We have to learn to live in the grey day according to what we saw on the mount.

──────── Just Between You and God ────────

We get good days and bad days. When we have a good day, it's like seeing the fall colors of the trees after living in the Mojave Desert for a year. Look around you now and appreciate what God has given to you. Say thanks.

Use the good days. Use them for God. And God will give you more. Watch.

04.17

CANNONBALL!

Then the disciple whom Jesus loved said to Peter, "It is the Lord!" As soon as Simon Peter heard him say, "It is the Lord," he wrapped his outer garment around him (for he had taken it off) and jumped into the water.

[John 21:7]

Some people approach a swimming pool by sticking their toes in to check the temperature of the water. They ease into the shallow end and walk, little by little, until they're waist high. Their arms are up in the air like they're afraid to get them wet. Others approach a pool by running full speed along the diving board, leaping into the air, yelling, "Cannnnnonballllllllllllllllll" as they splash with full force into the deep end. Jesus calls us to do a cannonball. Easing in and testing the waters shows a lack of faith. A life with Jesus requires a full-out leap. Total abandonment. He doesn't want us to stand on the side and say, "It looks cold," or "It's too deep." When we jump in with total abandon we can appreciate the deep love Jesus has for us when we come up for air.

---------------- OZ Says ----------------

Have you deliberately committed your will to Jesus Christ? It is a transaction of will, not of emotion . . . If you have heard Jesus Christ's voice on the billows, let your convictions go to the winds, let your consistency go to the winds, but maintain your relationship to Him.

---------------- Just Between You and God ----------------

Don't pray for courage to jump. Ask God to free you from everything keeping you from jumping. Are you afraid of looking silly? Are you afraid the water is cold? Is it too deep? To appreciate the splash, you must be free of what weighs you down.

Leap. Tuck. Splash. Go.

04.18

CALL

When the LORD saw that he had gone over to look, God called to him from within the bush, "Moses! Moses!"

And Moses said, "Here I am."

[Exodus 3:4]

We like to stand on the mountaintop, throw our arms out, and let the wind blow through our hair. We say, "I'm here, God!" We want to hear a booming voice like James Earl Jones' telling us what our glorious mission will be. Well . . . God doesn't call everyone like that. Sometimes God will whisper in your ear and say, "See her? She needs a compliment," or "He missed the free throw. Go put your hand on his shoulder." God may call us with the flashing neon sign, or he may use a little yellow sticky-note. The important thing is that we are ready. On the mountain in the wind or in the back of a school bus, we have to be ready to hear what God wants us to do, and then do it.

OZ Says

Readiness for God means that we are ready to do the tiniest little thing or the great big thing, it makes no difference. We have no choice in what we want to do, whatever God's program may be we are there, ready. When any duty presents itself we hear God's voice as Our Lord heard His Father's voice, and we are ready for it with all the alertness of our love for Him. Jesus Christ expects to do with us as His Father did with Him.

Just Between You and God

It's our egos that get us in trouble. We want the lightning and thunder. We want the burning bush. Ask God to help you keep your ego in check so when the still, small voice comes, you will hear it as clearly as you would a thunderstorm.

Be ready. Not get ready. If you have to get ready, you aren't ready to be ready.

04.19

IN PLACE

When the news reached Joab, who had conspired with Adonijah though not with Absalom, he fled to the tent of the LORD and took hold of the horns of the altar.

[1 Kings 2:28]

Imagine you're driving in a horrible storm. There's thunder and lightning. You've swerved around downed power lines. Branches have fallen from the trees, but you've steered clear. You're a new driver, maybe, but a good driver. Now the storm is passing. You can even turn off the windshield wipers. You reach over and grab your phone to check your texts and accidentally drive up over the curb and take out a mailbox. Life is sometimes like this. It's not always the storms of life that hurt us. We survive those. We're good at it. It's after the storm, when we take our eyes off the road for just a moment, that we get hurt. We've gained strength, wisdom, and experience along the way, but that means we must not forget—it's the small nail that will take out the tire.

_____ OZ Says _____

You have remained true to God under great and intense trials; now beware of the undercurrent. Do not be morbidly introspective, looking forward with dread, but keep alert; keep your memory bright before God.

_____ Just Between You and God _____

Ask God for the strength to keep going. Too often when we get through the crisis we think we can rest. This isn't always so. Surviving the avalanche will do you little good if you trip over a pebble in the path.

Open your eyes. Look forward, not behind you. You aren't done yet.

04.20

EXAMINE(D)

For no matter how many promises God has made, they are "Yes" in Christ. And so through him the "Amen" is spoken by us to the glory of God.

[2 Corinthians 1:20]

Too often we stand before God with a little paper cup saying, "Fill my cup, Lord." God fills our cup and then we start to look around and say, "Hey, he got more than I did. What's going on, God? How come that servant got more than I did?"

Don't forget that you are the one who went to God with, of all things, a paper cup. If you're going to God, take a bucket! Take a 30-gallon trash can. Grab some friends and take a swimming pool. God is there to give you what you need, but you have to be ready for what you might get. If you take a cup and then complain about how little you received—you weren't ready for more anyway.

OZ Says

Never forget that our capacity in spiritual matters is measured by the promises of God. Is God able to fulfill His promises? Our answer depends on whether we have received the Holy Spirit.

Just Between You and God

There is a process called "the examine." It means to take a good long, honest (yes honest) look at your own life. Are you ready for what God might give you? Have you made room in your life? Today, before you pray, check out your own life. Are you really ready?

God's love comes down like rain. You can open your mouth and catch the drops. Or you can open your life and catch a wave.

04.21

HANDS

Jesus answered: "Don't you know me, Philip, even after I have been among you such a long time? Anyone who has seen me has seen the Father. How can you say, 'Show us the Father'?"

[John 14:9]

So there's this guy . . . he's in his swim trunks and dives into a pool. Everyone sees him frantically searching the bottom of the pool. He comes up for air and he's down again. Over and over. Searching everywhere. After a long time, he finally climbs out of the pool dejected and sad. An old gentleman in a Hawaiian shirt walks up and says, "Son, what were you getting so worked up looking for?" The young guy says, "Water. I was looking for water." Didn't Jesus say, "I am with you always"? Jesus is right behind us, beside us, above us, below us; in fact, his spirit is within us. We miss him because we think we have to seek him. By thinking we must go and find Jesus, we're telling him we don't think he's with us. This is what Jesus meant by having the faith of a child. Tell a child and the child will believe. We make it hard for ourselves. We think it's a task, an assignment to find Jesus.

―――――――――――― OZ Says ――――――――――――

"Let not your heart be troubled"—then am I hurting Jesus by allowing my heart to be troubled? If I believe the character of Jesus, am I living up to my belief? Am I allowing anything to perturb my heart, any morbid questions to come in? I have to get to the implicit relationship that takes everything as it comes from Him. God never guides presently, but always now. Realize that the Lord is here now, and the emancipation is immediate.

――――――――― Just Between You and God ―――――――――

The walls that keep us from seeing the face of God were built by us. Ask God to help you take them down. The rules and regulations are in place only because we put them there.

Searching for God in your life is like swimming in the ocean and looking for water.

04.22

WASHED

And we all, who with unveiled faces contemplate the Lord's glory, are being transformed into his image with ever-increasing glory, which comes from the Lord, who is the Spirit.

[2 Corinthians 3:18]

It sounds like one of those bizarre extreme sport shows: RIVER FIGHTERS! Imagine standing in a dry river bed. They just blew the dam a mile away. The wave is coming. You can hear it. The guy next to you says, "Hold your ground!!" God stands on the back and says, "Or you could take this rope." You grab the rope and the guy next to you . . . well he's not there anymore. Strength comes from God, not from the stupid people who think they can stand up to a wave.

OZ Says

A servant of God must stand so much alone that he never knows he is alone. In the first phases of Christian life disheartenments come, people who used to be lights flicker out, and those who used to stand with us pass away. We have to get so used to it that we never know we are standing alone . . . We must build our faith, not on the fading light, but on the light that never fails.

Just Between You and God

Look to God. Go ahead and ask him for strength. Even the best of the best can get washed away in the raging water. Stand on your own. With God.

Plant your feet. The wave is coming. Take your eyes off God and you are gone.

04.23

SEXTON

For we are co-workers in God's service; you are God's field, God's building.

[1 Corinthians 3:9]

Let's build a church. We need stonecutters, carpenters, architects, artists, and ironworkers. Let's build a beautiful place where people from all over the world can come and see what we've done for God. In a word . . . wrong. The danger is in putting too much emphasis on the work, and not enough on God. The church we build should not take the place of God. God will build his church. God will put all the workers where they should be. Even the one who humbly cleans up behind others becomes a builder of the church. When God is first, nothing can stop the construction. But when the construction is first, we find ourselves far from God. Yes, this is another one of those our-lives-are-a-church analogies.

—————— OZ Says ——————

A worker without this solemn dominant note of concentration on God . . . becomes spent out and crushed. There is no freedom, no delight in life; nerves, mind and heart are so crushingly burdened that God's blessing cannot rest. But the other side is just as true—when once the concentration is on God, all the margins of life are free and under the dominance of God alone.

—————— Just Between You and God ——————

Love God, not what you do for him. Stop working for God for just a moment and take the time to pray and ask for nothing. Just tell God you love him.

It doesn't matter how tall the steeple is, how pretty the stained glass is. It doesn't matter how elegant the sanctuary is if all you're doing is blocking your view of God.

04.24

FAB

However, do not rejoice that the spirits submit to you, but rejoice that your names are written in heaven.

[Luke 10:20]

Once we become Christians, we realize that others are watching us. We start to think about what we should wear, what we should listen to, and what we should read. Sometimes we even allow other Christians to make us feel less than worthy if we don't dress, live, and worship as they do.

We become the person God wants us to be as we give our lives to God. This is what we show others, not the cardboard cutout of what a Christian "should" be, but a person who is in a personal growing relationship with God. Yours is different than mine. Mine is different than someone else's. God doesn't expect us all to be the same. He allows us to be disciples in our own way.

OZ Says

Unless the worker lives a life hidden with Christ in God, he is apt to become an irritating dictator instead of an indwelling disciple. Many of us are dictators, we dictate to people and to meetings. Jesus never dictates to us in that way.

Just Between You and God

If God wanted us to be the same, he would have made us that way. He would have given nothing but oatmeal, and Oreos would never have been invented. Today, thank God for the gift of your own uniqueness. Then live the unique life he gave you.

Be yourself. God likes you that way. God will use you that way. Nobody needs a clone.

04.25

A QUILT WITH YOUR NAME ON IT

Preach the word; be prepared in season and out of season; correct, rebuke and encourage—with great patience and careful instruction.

[2 Timothy 4:2]

Here's a shocker. Ready? You're not always going to feel like working for God. Big surprise! There are days when you'd rather roll over and stay in your nice, warm bed than go out and face another day. Nobody said this was going to be easy. It's those days when you'd rather be doing anything else that it's most important for you to get up and do it again. Those who say they give 110 percent to God 24/7 are kidding themselves. God knows better. Some days all we can give is sixty percent. It's amazing that God can take our sixty percent and use it for his glory. The real proof of a relationship with God is that I will do my best whether I feel like it or not.

--------- OZ Says ---------

When the Spirit of God gives you a time of inspiration and insight, you say—
"Now I will always be like this for God." No, you will not. God will take care you
are not. Those times are the gift of God entirely. You cannot give them to yourself when you choose If you make a god of your best moments, you will find
that God will fade out of your life and never come back until you do the duty
that lies nearest, and have learned not to make a fetish of your rare moments.

--------- Just Between You and God ---------

Is *purpose* in some sort of physical form. Does it look like rocks? Pillows? Does it come in Ben & Jerry's containers? Ask God for so much that you have to store the extra in the closet. You're going to need it some day. Store it up now.

Get up. Whether you feel like it or not. This is temporary. God is forever.

04.26

BURNING

Then God said, "Take your son, your only son, whom you love—Isaac—and go to the region of Moriah. Sacrifice him there as a burnt offering on a mountain I will show you."

[Genesis 22:2]

If we really wanted a traditional worship service, just like they did in the old days, we'd have a nice little pen behind the church where we'd keep the animals for our weekly sacrifice. (Wouldn't that tick off the custodian?) Fortunately, God had a better plan in mind. God put Abraham through a horrific ordeal to paint a picture that wouldn't be fully understood until thousands of years later. God already knew he would replace the ancient Jewish beliefs and traditions with a personal relationship—made possible through Christ Jesus. Today, closeness to God isn't about props and traditions, it's about understanding the gift of Jesus' love.

—————— OZ Says ——————

If you will remain true to God, God will lead you straight through every barrier into the inner chamber of the knowledge of Himself; but there is always this point of giving up convictions and traditional beliefs.

—————— Just Between You and God ——————

We teach children about God through the Jesus puzzles and the craft-time parables. As you get older, you don't need these. Imagine getting to the point where you don't need the tools at all . . . you can just "BE" in his presence. The day is coming.

Animal sacrifice is no longer needed. All the methods to get to God will someday be unnecessary. You have a ways to go. Keep praying.

04.27

RECEIVE

Should you then seek great things for yourself? Do not seek them. For I will bring disaster on all people, declares the LORD, but wherever you go I will let you escape with your life.

[Jeremiah 45:5]

Jesus said, "Ask and you will receive." Great. I want a new car. I want good grades. I want rest. I want peace of mind. I will enter into a closer relationship with God to get the things I want.

Back up, Sparky. Let's start over.

What are you asking for and why? Ask yourself these questions. Are you following God to get what you want, or to do what he wants? These two things may be incredibly different from each other. God knows what you need before you ask. As you get closer to him, he will give it to you as you need it. God's ultimate plan for you is complete joy and peace, but it may come to you in an unexpected way.

--------------------- OZ Says ---------------------

God always ignores the present perfection for the ultimate perfection. He is not concerned about making you blessed and happy just now; He is working out His ultimate perfection all the time—"that they may be one even as We are."

--------------------- Just Between You and God ---------------------

You can ask for *any*thing you want. But ask with the understanding that God will give you what you need when you need it. As you get closer to God, you might find that you really didn't need what you asked for in the first place.

God already knows. Be patient. You'll get what you need.

04.28

CATCH!

Should you then seek great things for yourself? Do not seek them. For I will bring disaster on all people, declares the LORD, but wherever you go I will let you escape with your life.

[Jeremiah 45:5]

There's the guy with the nice suit standing on top of the building emblazoned with his name on the side. Then there's the guy on the street corner singing "Stand By Me" with his battered guitar. Eventually the guy on the building will be sweeping the streets and the guy with the guitar is still singing. It's hard to keep singing, especially when we have to sing over the construction of the next big building project. But keep singing. Patience is hard. Keep singing. The mogul is smiling on top of the next building again. Keep singing. God is listening. It's his song.

─────────── OZ Says ───────────

Are you prepared to let God take you into union with Himself, and pay no more attention to what you call the great things? Are you prepared to abandon entirely and let go? The test of abandonment is in refusing to say—"Well, what about this?" . . . Abandon means to refuse yourself the luxury of asking any questions.

─────── Just Between You and God ───────

God will give you patience as you ask for it. This isn't the easiest part of the process to understand. Ask God for time and then see what happens.

The more you give up, the less you need. Puzzled? It's okay. Take your time. You'll get there.

04.29

$2 + 2 =$

Dear friends, now we are children of God, and what we will be has not yet been made known. But we know that when Christ appears, we shall be like him, for we shall see him as he is.

[1 John 3:2]

L ook at the math problem in the title of this page. It drives some people nuts not to have that last number in there. Math problems have solutions. Stories have conclusions. Symphonies have endings. Our lives are not always like that. Just beyond our view is uncertainty. Some fear it. Some guess at it. Some try to steer one way or the other, but ultimately God is the only one who knows what lies in that uncertainty. To totally believe in God is to totally understand there's nothing we can do to see that missing number. The trick is to approach this with trust. With God, that uncertainty should spark amazing anticipation. Not having the conclusion in advance can be a good thing. It's like getting on a roller coaster for the first time. The excitement is half the fun.

OZ Says

Certainty is the mark of the common-sense life: gracious uncertainty is the mark of the spiritual life. To be certain of God means that we are uncertain in all our ways, we do not know what a day may bring forth . . . The spiritual life is the life of a child. We are not uncertain of God, but uncertain of what He is going to do next. If we are only certain of our beliefs, we get dignified and severe and have the ban of finality about our views; but when we are rightly related to God, life is full of spontaneous, joyful uncertainty and expectancy.

Just Between You and God

Sometimes you don't get the answers. You just don't. Today thank God for the questions. If you have questions, at least you know the answers are out there somewhere. God has a journey ready for you to go and find the answer.

He's there. He's waiting. And he has got a surprise for you!

04.30

PAR-TAAAEE

Love is patient, love is kind. It does not envy, it does not boast, it is not proud. It does not dishonor others, it is not self-seeking, it is not easily angered, it keeps no record of wrongs. Love does not delight in evil but rejoices with the truth. It always protects, always trusts, always hopes, always perseveres. Love never fails. But where there are prophecies, they will cease; where there are tongues, they will be stilled; where there is knowledge, it will pass away. For we know in part and we prophesy in part . . .

[1 Corinthians 13:4–9]

Love is a surprise. You can't plan it. Love doesn't happen as a result of a formula or process. We don't even see it while it's happening. We have to look back and see, "Whoa, I think God was really there." If we try to make it happen, it won't. If we try to prove to God that we love him, we will fail. God will know we love him when, by the Holy Spirit, he shines through us and we give ourselves over to the surprise that is his very nature. That's when God shows up. It may be in the middle of a celebration or in a quiet moment in the dark, but it happens most when we stop trying to make it happen.

―――――――――― OZ Says ――――――――――

The characteristic of love is spontaneity. The springs of love are in God, not in us. It is absurd to look for the love of God in our hearts naturally; it is only there when it has been shed abroad in our hearts by the Holy Spirit.

――――――― Just Between You and God ―――――――

What if every now and then, just once in a while, the jack-in-the-box popped up something completely different. Wouldn't that change the way you wait for it?

God is waiting. Even when you're not ready, God will show up. Surprise!

05.01

HIDE AND SEEK

We live by faith, not by sight.

[2 Corinthians 5:7]

Yes, it's our own vanity that gets in the way. God makes us his servants and we want everyone to know it. We want to be held up, placed
on a mountain, have that heavenly light shine down on us while a choir of
angels sings a chorus of *Ahhhhhhs*. We don't get that. In fact, usually it's the
opposite. God usually doesn't send angels to work with humans. He sends
humans to work with humans. God tells us to go and serve, but we want
more. We want applause and special effects, but that isn't what we get. We
live by faith. That means we do what God asks because God asked us. We
do it knowing it's right because it was God who sent us to do it.

-------------------- OZ Says --------------------

*How many of us have laid ourselves by, as it were, and said—"I cannot do any
more until God appears to me." He never will, and without any inspiration,
without any sudden touch of God, we will have to get up. Then comes the
surprise—"Why, He was there all the time, and I never knew it!" Never live for
the rare moments, they are surprises. God will give us touches of inspiration
when He sees we are not in danger of being led away by them.*

--------- Just Between You and God ---------

That chair you're sitting in . . . do you believe it's going to be there in the next
second? Of course you do. What if you could apply that same sense of certainty to your life? It is possible. Start now. It will come to you.

**Sometimes there is no shining emerald city in the
distance. Sometimes you just go when God says,
"Go." It's about faith.**

05.02

CHILL

For the revelation awaits an appointed time; it speaks of the end and will not prove false. Though it linger, wait for it; it will certainly come and will not delay.

[Habakkuk 2:3]

Sometimes it takes your Internet 45 seconds to boot up instead of 15. Oh the horror. God give me patience! This is not the image you want for patience. Imagine your face carved into the side of a mountain by the sea while storm after storm and wave after wave pounds against you. Can you have that kind of patience? Can you take hit after hit and not think "Am I just being stupid?" Everyone doubts. Everyone questions. As we get closer to God, the storm and the waves mean nothing. This kind of patience will make us stronger. This is beyond patience. This is *resolve*.

—————— OZ Says ——————

A man with the vision of God is not devoted to a cause or to any particular issue; he is devoted to God Himself. You always know when the vision is of God because of the inspiration that comes with it; things come with largeness and tonic to the life because everything is energized by God.

——— Just Between You and God ———

It's okay to pray for patience, but sometimes God will use unpleasant circumstances to teach us. The more we endure, the stronger we become.

No matter what the world throws at you . . . don't throw back. God brought you through before. God will do it again.

05.03

CLICK THE HELP BUTTON

And pray in the Spirit on all occasions with all kinds of prayers and requests. With this in mind, be alert and always keep on praying for all the Lord's people.

[Ephesians 6:18]

When you pray for someone, God hears you. But you must remember that God works in everyone's life the same way he works in yours. He always knows what's best. When you see a friend's circumstances, you might feel sympathy and want to do something. But God has a plan, and guess what? You might not be part of his plan for that person. When we act on God's behalf in someone else's life, we have to be sure God asked us to do so. Otherwise, we're just getting in his way. Don't allow your own ego and emotions to make you think you know better than God.

―――――――――――― OZ Says ――――――――――――

The danger then is to begin to intercede in sympathy with those whom God was gradually lifting to a totally different sphere in answer to our prayers. Whenever we step back from identification with God's interest in others into sympathy with them, the vital connection with God has gone, we have put our sympathy, our consideration for them in the way, and this is a deliberate rebuke to God.

―――――― Just Between You and God ――――――

Pray for someone else today. Someone you know, a coworker, perhaps that woman behind you in line who looks like she's having a bad day. Ask God to intercede in their lives and then trust God will do it. He may even send you.

**There is only one job description that says, "God."
(Hint: it's not yours.) Pray and be patient.**

05.04

GOD IS GOD. I'M NOT.

Therefore, brothers and sisters, since we have confidence to enter the Most Holy Place by the blood of Jesus . . .

[Hebrews 10:19]

One of the most dangerous things we can say is, "I've prayed about this and I think that God agrees with me." We carry our own selfish desires to God and then pass them on to others because we think, "God said so." When we identify our own wants and communicate them as God's plan, we're building more than a wall between God and those we are trying to help. We're building a wall between God and ourselves. It may seem like the best idea to you, but that doesn't mean God agrees. God does not have to agree with you. We are there to do what God wants, not the other way around.

OZ Says

When we do not identify ourselves with God's interests in others, we get petulant with God; we are always ready with our own ideas, and intercession becomes the glorification of our own natural sympathies . . . Vicarious intercession means that we deliberately substitute God's interests in others for our natural sympathy with them.

Just Between You and God

If God wants to use you for something, he will let you know. If you think you can move your own agenda along by being God's servant, you've left God behind. Pray that God shows you the wisdom to know the difference.

Yeah, yeah, God has seen your wish list. Maybe it's not your turn. Did you think God doesn't know what you need?

05.05

BEYOND COMPREHENSION

For it is time for judgment to begin with God's household; and if it begins with us, what will the outcome be for those who do not obey the gospel of God?

[1 Peter 4:17]

There is no such thing as a God-expert. Think of who you know who seems to hold that title. In God's eyes, they are a rookie. God is so far beyond our comprehension that all we can do is understand we will never understand. Still there is the temptation to place ourselves like a lighthouse guiding in the lost ships at sea. That's not your job. Your job is to reach back across the river you just crossed and show someone else where the stepping stones are.

—————————— OZ Says ——————————

The Christian worker must never forget that salvation is God's thought, not man's . . . Never sympathize with a soul who finds it difficult to get to God, God is not to blame. It is not for us to find out the reason why it is difficult, but so to present the truth of God that the Spirit of God will show what is wrong. The great sterling test in preaching is that it brings everyone to judgment. The Spirit of God locates each one to himself.

————— Just Between You and God —————

Today, if you are praying for answers, thank God for questions. It's in the questions that we experience God's presence. In God's presence, rookies and experts are the same.

The creator of an expanding universe is also ever expanding. You can't know all of God. His decisions. His timing.

05.06

EDGE

It is for freedom that Christ has set us free. Stand firm, then, and do not let yourselves be burdened again by a yoke of slavery.

[Galatians 5:1]

Jesus said, "I am the way." We must follow the way. If Jesus says "Come this way" or "Do it this way" then we will follow and do. This life decision gives you great responsibility. You can't get so wrapped up in yourself that you feel you have the right to lay your guilt, pain, anger, and shame on someone else. That's not what Jesus did. You also can't hold yourself up as Jesus. Yes, you're following, but that doesn't make you the real thing. Can you simply follow? There is something about leading that is so very satisfying. Imagine you have a shirt that says, "Do not feed the ego." Wear it when you follow Jesus. Understand your role in this process. If God wants to use you to show others, he will do that. You don't need to do it for him.

—————————— OZ Says ——————————

Always keep your life measured by the standards of Jesus. Bow your neck to His yoke alone, and to no other yoke whatever; and be careful to see that you never bind a yoke on others that is not placed by Jesus Christ. It takes God a long time to get us out of the way of thinking that unless everyone sees as we do, they must be wrong.

————— Just Between You and God —————

Ask God for strength and humility. You will need the strength to carry what he wants you to carry. You will need the humility so you don't become proud when you succeed. Ask for both in equal amounts.

The Bible is like a map-app with all roads leading to Jesus. Your life works the same way.

05.07

BLUEPRINTS

Suppose one of you wants to build a tower. Won't you first sit down and estimate the cost to see if you have enough money to complete it?

[Luke 14:28]

Think of all that Jesus went through from his birth to his death. He grew up in a family that loved him; taught with wisdom and gently healed the sick; angered the government; was betrayed, tortured, and murdered. The world could point to the life of Christ and say that he was a failure. But what made his life meaningful was that everything he did, he did to please God.

Likewise, we must put God first if we want to succeed. God must be the one who approves our construction plans—then we can build. When we are finished, we can look back with the satisfaction of knowing we obeyed God.

OZ Says

Our Lord implies that the only men and women He will use in His building enterprises are those who love Him personally, passionately and devotedly beyond any of the closest ties on earth . . . These are days of tremendous enterprises, days when we are trying to work for God, and therein is the snare. Profoundly speaking, we can never work for God. Jesus takes us over for His enterprises, His building schemes entirely, and no soul has any right to claim where he shall be put.

Just Between You and God

Blueprints come in large rolls with dozens of pages. Lay them out on the table, hang them from the walls. Just don't start with the final drawing. Ask God to guide you through each phase and not get ahead of yourself.

Measure twice. Cut once. Be sure. God first = success.

05.08

AIM.

Since you have kept my command to endure patiently, I will also keep you from the hour of trial that is going to come on the whole world to test the inhabitants of the earth.

[Revelation 3:10]

Skilled archers will put an arrow in the bow and pull back. They won't release until they feel sure. There's so much more to this simple action than meets the eye. Certainty is essential to scoring the bull's-eye. Now imagine that you are the arrow and God is the archer. Don't ask questions. Don't doubt your place. God knows best. Don't lose patience while waiting for the release. Don't complain about the strain of being pulled back. God doesn't miss. Faith comes in the waiting. When the release comes, you can be sure you'll be heading in the direction God wants you.

—————— OZ Says ——————

God has ventured all in Jesus Christ to save us, now He wants us to venture our all in abandoned confidence in Him . . . The real meaning of eternal life is a life that can face anything it has to face without wavering. If we take this view, life becomes one great romance, a glorious opportunity for seeing marvelous things all the time. God is disciplining us to get us into this central place of power.

—————— Just Between You and God ——————

This is about faith. You've come this far and there is a temptation to say, "Ah ha! I've got this now." That's not how it works. Let God be in charge every step of the way. He sees what you can't. Ask for patience today.

Bungee jumping is a lot of faith in a rubber band. When you jump into your life, who's got the other end? (Hint: God.)

05.09

D'OH!

Where there is no revelation, people cast off restraint; but blessed is the one who heeds wisdom's instruction.

[Proverbs 29:18]

Occasionally we need a good smack to put us right. We need that "Oh, I get it" drummed into us so we can move on. We need the divine *D'oh!* We need understanding, not for ourselves, but for the rest of the world. We can do all sorts of wonderful things in God's name, but none of them counts for anything unless we know in advance what God is asking. All of this is based on an accurate view of who God is and what he can do. Unless we have a clear picture as we follow God, we're just wandering around looking holy—but not being holy.

OZ Says

When once we lose sight of God, we begin to be reckless, we cast off certain restraints, we cast off praying, we cast off the vision of God in little things, and begin to act on our own initiative. If we are eating what we have out of our own hand, doing things on our own initiative without expecting God to come in, we are on the downward path, we have lost the vision. Is our attitude today an attitude that springs from our vision of God? Are we expecting God to do greater things than He has ever done? Is there a freshness and vigor in our spiritual outlook?

Just Between You and God

You know that closet in your house that seems to be the home for everything that has no other place? What if that pile was in front of the front door. You'd de-clutter, right? Do that with your mind. Ask God to replace the clutter with vision. You'll be unstoppable.

Shut up long enough to listen. Stop looking long enough to see. Get the idea straight. Then do something about it.

05.10

LEVEL-UP

For this very reason, make every effort to add to your faith goodness; and to goodness, knowledge . . .

[2 Peter 1:5]

We're building a video game character. You get to choose what to add. Armor. Powers. Everything. Do you base your decisions on what looks good or what battles may come? If you've fought the dragon, you may not need the fireproof shield. Got it? Now, let's build you. What do you need to leave behind? What relationship should be fixed before you move on? Did you pack faith, goodness, knowledge, compassion? This is a lot more complicated than you think. There are requirements and then there are options and upgrades. Choose wisely. The more prepared you are, the better you will survive.

--------- OZ Says ---------

We cannot save ourselves nor sanctify ourselves, God does that; but God will not give us good habits, He will not give us character, He will not make us walk aright. We have to do all that ourselves; we have to work out the salvation God has worked in. "Add" means to get into the habit of doing things, and in the initial stages it is difficult. To take the initiative is to make a beginning, to instruct yourself in the way you have to go.

--------- Just Between You and God ---------

Knowledge and tools, that's what you need to ask for. Ask God where to find these things and then he'll show you the way. When you're prepared, then you can move forward.

Imagine there is only an "up" escalator. Why are you looking for the "down"?

05.11

UP

. . . and to godliness, mutual affection; and to mutual affection, love.

[2 Peter 1:7]

Peter's words are like a ladder. Each time we add to what we have, we get one rung higher to God. God loves us unconditionally. The very God who created the universe has decided that we are worthy of his love. In spite of our faults and the ways we hurt each other, God loves us with only one request—"love me and love each other." So we start up Peter's ladder, adding each new rung until we bump our heads against something. All too often that *something* is our inability to forgive, our anger at others, and our own selfishness. As long as these are in the way, we won't get any higher.

─────────── OZ Says ───────────

The knowledge that God has loved me to the uttermost . . . will send me forth into the world to love in the same way. God's love to me is inexhaustible, and I must love others from the bedrock of God's love to me. Growth in grace stops the moment I get huffed. I get huffed because I have a peculiar person to live with. Just think how disagreeable I have been to God! Am I prepared to be so identified with the Lord Jesus that His life and His sweetness are being poured out all the time? Neither natural love nor Divine love will remain unless it is cultivated.

─────────── Just Between You and God ───────────

As you climb, you're going to bump your head on some trapdoors. Let's call them "forgiveness." You have to push hard to move what's sitting on top. The object you need to move to forgive yourself may prove to be the heaviest. Ask God for strength. He's waiting to see you too.

Sawing the rungs off the ladder just makes the climb harder. Stop trying to ruin your own climb.

05.12

ALWAYS AWARE

For if you possess these qualities in increasing measure, they will keep you from being ineffective and unproductive in your knowledge of our Lord Jesus Christ.

[2 Peter 1:8]

For some people, the practice of going to church is more important than worshipping God. This happens. We get so busy being religious that we stop being with God. When we consciously practice being with God—using all we've learned—eventually we'll get to the place where it feels less and less like work. We can just be with God. The disciplines become second nature; in God's presence is where we belong. Obviously, this will come after lots of practice.

OZ Says

Your god may be your little Christian habit, the habit of prayer at stated times, or the habit of Bible reading. Watch how your Father will upset those times if you begin to worship your habit instead of what the habit symbolizes—I can't do that just now, I am praying; it is my hour with God. No, it is your hour with your habit . . . Love means that there is no habit visible, you have come to the place where the habit is lost, and by practice you do the thing unconsciously. If you are consciously holy, there are certain things you imagine you cannot do, certain relationships in which you are far from simple; that means there is something to be added.

Just Between You and God

Pray—about anything, it doesn't matter right now. Just pray. This is a step closer to God. Keep communicating with him and you will find yourself in his presence.

It takes years of practice to make it look effortless.

05.13

LIFE BY CHOICE

So I strive always to keep my conscience clear before God and man.

[Acts 24:16]

Think about everything you know about yourself. The pinnacle of who you are is your conscience. It's your conscience that points you to God. Everybody is like this. The challenge is to get the rest of you to live by your conscience. (And, hey, even this ability to choose was given to you by God). We must learn to listen with our conscience. If we open up our conscience the way we open our ears to our favorite music, God will let us know exactly what he wants from us. God will help us make decisions. He will point the way. If we close off our conscience, we'll have difficulty hearing God and obeying his directions.

──────────── OZ Says ────────────

The one thing that keeps the conscience sensitive to Him is the continual habit of being open to God on the inside. When there is any debate, quit. "Why shouldn't I do this?" You are on the wrong track. There is no debate possible when conscience speaks. At your peril, you allow one thing to obscure your inner communion with God. Drop it, whatever it is, and see that you keep your inner vision clear.

──────── Just Between You and God ────────

You know how sometimes you can stand with your feet in the ocean or on top of the mountain and just . . . listen? It's more than listening, isn't it? It's like your soul has ears. That's how you should listen for God.

God does not sound like Mufasa. God's voice speaks from within. You'll know it when you "hear it."

05.14

YES, THEM TOO

We always carry around in our body the death of Jesus, so that the life of Jesus may also be revealed in our body.

[2 Corinthians 4:10]

One of the toughest things about following Jesus is loving everyone, but that's what Jesus said we're to do. It's hard to imagine that we have to love those who go out of their way to make our lives miserable. It's not easy. Jesus didn't say it would be. But when you made the choice to follow this path, Jesus became more than a word or a part of history to you. Jesus became a very real part of who you are. Jesus loved even those who nailed him to the cross. (Talk about difficult to love.) But because Jesus is now a part of you—you can love those who hurt you. You can love those who don't love you. Once you start, you'll see how Jesus works inside of you.

─────── OZ Says ───────

The only thing that will enable me to enjoy the disagreeable is the keen enthusiasm of letting the life of the Son of God manifest itself in me. No matter how disagreeable a thing may be, say—"Lord, I am delighted to obey Thee in this matter," and instantly the Son of God will press to the front, and there will be manifested in my human life that which glorifies Jesus . . . The thing that ought to make the heart beat is a new way of manifesting the Son of God. It is one thing to choose the disagreeable, and another thing to go into the disagreeable by God's engineering. If God puts you there, He is amply sufficient.

─────── Just Between You and God ───────

This is not, not, not, not easy. If it was easy, everyone could do it. Ask God for perseverance because you won't get this right out of the gate. Start with, "No more hate. Hate impairs. Love wins. Hate breaks. Love heals." Seek the place where everybody wins. It's a good way to start.

Evvvvvvvvvv-reeeeeeeeeee-wonnnnne. Got it?

05.15

RUN

I pray that the eyes of your heart may be enlightened in order that you may know the hope to which he has called you, the riches of his glorious inheritance in his holy people.

[Ephesians 1:18]

Jesus said he was one with God. He also said he wanted us to be one with him. In doing so we can become one with God. Think about that—your purpose is to become one with the Creator of the universe. When you recognize this, life becomes a race. You're not racing against anyone else—it's just you. The hurdles you will face were placed there by God. Sometimes your back foot will catch and you'll go face down in the dust. Can you get back up? As you get farther down the road, you might notice the hurdles get higher. But you'll also notice how you can glide over them with ease. As you deepen your relationship with God, he becomes more a part of everything you do. Eventually you'll attempt to jump over a hurdle and find yourself flying.

OZ Says

May God not find the whine in us anymore, but may He find us full of spiritual pluck and athleticism, ready to face anything He brings. We have to exercise ourselves so that the Son of God may be manifested in our mortal flesh.

Just Between You and God

If life is a race, you don't need to ask for speed or endurance. You need to ask God to run beside you. If you get tired, God will encourage you. If you trip and fall, God will pick you up.

Trip. Fall. Stand. Run. Repeat.

05.16

THESE THINGS HAPPEN

Through these he has given us his very great and precious promises, so that through them you may participate in the divine nature, having escaped the corruption in the world caused by evil desires.

[2 Peter 1:4]

It's not God's fault if we are spiritually broke. When we get to the end of a day, exhausted or upset, and want to scream, "God, why are you doing this to me?" remember—God didn't cause your bad day. We may wonder how we can have a bad day when God is in us. On top of our frustrations is the pressure of being watched by those who don't believe. They're watching to see how a Christian will handle a lousy day. Once we recognize that God lives in us and we can draw on his resources, we'll no longer react the same to trials and hurdles in our lives. Rotten things will still happen, but our reactions will be different. Call out that God-part and the blessings will run to you and through you to others.

OZ Says

What does it matter if external circumstances are hard? Why should they not be! If we give way to self-pity and indulge in the luxury of misery, we banish God's riches from our own lives and hinder others from entering into His provision . . . When God is beginning to be satisfied with us He will impoverish everything in the nature of fictitious wealth, until we learn that all our fresh springs are in Him. If the majesty and grace and power of God are not being manifested in us . . . God holds us responsible. "God is able to make all grace abound;" then learn to lavish the grace of God on others.

Just Between You and God

God does not make bad stuff happen. Sometimes the bad stuff happens. God did not give you a bad day. Sometimes we have bad days. That's why God gave us each other. This line of thinking changes everything.

The God inside you has already seen, heard, and been through everything. Go there for advice, courage, and support. It really is all good.

05.17

TRANSFORMER

While he was blessing them, he left them and was taken up into heaven.

[Luke 24:51]

Think about this—after the Transfiguration (described in this passage) we can no longer fully identify with Christ. Up until then we could identify with his weariness, his joy, his thoughtfulness, his frustrations, and his temptation—we could identify with all these things. After the transfiguration, his focus became Calvary and we cannot really identify with what he went through at the Crucifixion, the Resurrection, and the Ascension. But it's here that we see hope for ourselves. Jesus, fully a man, was lifted straight to the throne of God. He shows us that it is possible for us to follow him. That is the greatest hope of all.

OZ Says

On the Mount of Ascension the Transfiguration is completed. If Jesus had gone to heaven from the Mount of Transfiguration, He would have gone alone; He would have been nothing more to us than a glorious Figure. But He turned His back on the glory, and came down from the mount to identify Himself with fallen humanity.

Just Between You and God

Until Jesus came we were just standing on the edge of a cliff. There was no hope. Everything was "over there." Then Jesus shows up and we have a bridge. Not a rope bridge but a giant steel girder bridge . . . called HOPE.

Jesus was the God/man. Nothing in the universe is harder to understand than that. Understand that you can't understand . . . then say thank you.

05.18

WHEN IT COMES TO CANARIES, YOU'RE WORTH A MILLION

Look at the birds of the air; they do not sow or reap or store away in barns, and yet your heavenly Father feeds them. Are you not much more valuable than they?

[Matthew 6:26]

Read that verse again and understand it is about more than birds. It's about the design of the universe. Rivers run by the trees, the trees provide food and protection. Everything . . . quite literally *every* thing works according to a plan. Now we get to choose to be a part of the plan or be an obstacle to it. We can follow the river to the ocean. We can feel the warmth of the sun on our faces or we can turn his sky into mud. God made the design and then put us into it. He gave us the choice to build the dam or go with the flow.

—————————— OZ Says ——————————

So often we mar God's designed influence through us by our self-conscious effort to be consistent and useful. Jesus says that there is only one way to develop spiritually, and that is by concentration on God. "Do not bother about being of use to others; believe in Me"—pay attention to the Source, and out of you will flow rivers of living water. We cannot get at the springs of our natural life by common sense, and Jesus is teaching that growth in spiritual life does not depend on our watching it, but on concentration on our Father in heaven. Our heavenly Father knows the circumstances we are in, and if we keep con-centrated on Him we will grow spiritually as the lilies.

————— Just Between You and God —————

Ask God to clear your mind and give you rest. You cannot see his perfect design if you yourself are the obstacle.

God cares for the birds, flowers, and trees. God cares for you too. The birds, flowers, and trees know how to receive it. How 'bout you?

05.19

TAKE IT EASY? (YEAH, THAT'S A QUESTION MARK.)

Who shall separate us from the love of Christ? Shall trouble or hardship or persecution or famine or nakedness or danger or sword?

[Romans 8:35]

When you started down this path, you didn't think God would keep you from problems and disappointments, did you? He won't. He never promised that he would. What God promises is that he will be with you all the time. When you face hunger, pain, loneliness, betrayal, and ignorance (and you will face all these just as you have before), God will be beside you. He was always beside you, but now you're aware of it. You can feel his hand on your shoulder, or you can feel his arms around you when you're scared. Open yourself up and let it happen. Nothing you do, nor what anyone else does, can separate you from God. Nothing.

—————— OZ Says ——————

God does not keep a man immune from trouble; He says—"I will be with him in trouble." It does not matter what actual troubles in the most extreme form get hold of a man's life, not one of them can separate him from his relationship to God. We are "more than conquerors in all these things." Paul is not talking of imaginary things, but of things that are desperately actual; and he says we are super-victors in the midst of them, not by our ingenuity, or by our courage, or by anything other than the fact that not one of them affects our relationship to God in Jesus Christ.

—————— Just Between You and God ——————

Look for: God above. God below. God beside. God east. God west. God here. God there. God within. God without. God . . . are you starting to get the idea?

God does not "show up." We do.

05.20
INVITED TO STAY
Stand firm, and you will win life.

[Luke 21:19]

God has a plan for you. You say, "God, I'm yours," and you think it's all going to happen at once. Remember, this is a process. It's a journey. It involves breaking you down and rebuilding you into a stronger person. It involves emptying you and refilling you with his presence. This takes time. The trick is not to bail when it gets tough. Lots of people make this mistake. They choose to follow God and then get sideswiped by life and say, "Well, this isn't what I expected," and then go back to their old lives. You know better. To make a really good piece of pottery, you sometimes have to smack the clay down on the wheel a few times, or it will never survive the fire.

―――――――― OZ Says ――――――――

We have to make an expression of the new life, to form the mind of Christ. "Acquire your soul with patience." Many of us prefer to stay at the threshold of the Christian life instead of going on to construct a soul in accordance with the new life God has put within. We fail because we are ignorant of the way we are made, we put things down to the devil instead of our own undisciplined natures. Think what we can be when we are roused!

―――――― Just Between You and God ――――――

God may use the storm to refine you. Lean into the wind. Clothes flapping all over the place. Rain pasting your hair to your head. Allow yourself to smile. You will make it through the storm. Sometimes it's not about the dawn. It's about relishing the night.

You know that moment on the dance floor just before the music starts? You might have to live there for a while . . . but the music is going to be really good.

05.21

WILD WONDER

But seek first his kingdom and his righteousness, and all these things will be given to you as well.

[Matthew 6:33]

We hear this and feel troubled because it's the exact opposite of how most of us live. We hear Jesus say this and we think, "What about food? I have to eat! I have to have clothes. Doesn't any of this stuff matter?"

People around you in your school or workplace have things backward. What they wear is the dominant concern of their lives. They measure themselves by what they wear. Others measure themselves by what they own, how they perform in sports, or what grades they get. These are the wrong measuring sticks. Jesus told us to concentrate on our relationship with God first. Get that in order and then work on the other things. Your sense of fashion, what car you drive, the starting position, reservations at a fancy restaurant where everybody goes . . . these have no real value or meaning in the great scheme of things if you are not rightly related to God.

OZ Says

Our Lord points out the utter unreasonableness from His standpoint of being so anxious over the means of living. Jesus is not saying that the man who takes thought for nothing is blessed—that man is a fool. Jesus taught that a disciple has to make his relationship to God the dominating concentration of his life, and to be carefully careless about everything else in comparison to that. Jesus is saying, "Don't make the ruling factor of your life what you shall eat and what you shall drink, but be concentrated absolutely on God."

Just Between You and God

Imagine your life in list form. All aspects of your life . . . in one big long list. Your stuff. Your beliefs. Your relationships. Your dreams—from your grand schemes to your minuscule moments. God is asking to be first. Keep it all. It's yours. Just put God first.

God first. (Yeah, that's it.)

05.22

CLOSE . . . CLOSER . . .

. . . that all of them may be one, Father, just as you are in me and I am in you. May they also be in us so that the world may believe that you have sent me.

[John 17:21]

Wouldn't you think that a prayer from Jesus would be the most important prayer God could answer? When Jesus prayed that his disciples would become one with God, he didn't just mean the group of guys sitting with him. He meant all of us. You started down this path to become a disciple, didn't you? So the most important thing you can do is to work toward that goal of being one with God. Your actions and reactions to life should reflect that. The troubles we go through will either make us better or bitter people. We get to choose—but which one will get us closer to the answer to Jesus' prayer?

OZ Says

The purpose of God is not to answer our prayers, but by our prayers we come to discern the mind of God, and this is revealed in John 17. There is one prayer God must answer, and that is the prayer of Jesus—"that they may be one, even as We are One." Are we as close to Jesus Christ as that?

Just Between You and God

Let's talk micro-movement. What would be the smallest possible movement you could make right now. What close-the-book-and-do-it-now movement can you make toward being one with God. Right now, now. Do that.

God answered our prayers. He gave us Christ. Don't you think it's about time we returned the favor?

05.23

SPECS

Therefore I tell you, do not worry about your life, what you will eat or drink; or about your body, what you will wear. Is not life more important than food, and the body more important than clothes?

[Matthew 6:25]

Is Jesus saying that it's okay to wear striped shirts and plaid pants together? No, Jesus would probably recognize bad fashion as much as the next person. When Jesus talks about not worrying about your food, and your drink, and your clothes, he's talking about the little things—those piddly little details that get in the way of living your life to the fullest. There is a bigger picture. Jesus still wants you to eat right and take care of yourself, but when the little things consume you, you lose sight of what's important. It's just like in Luke 10:40 when Martha was scurrying around the kitchen and Mary was sitting and listening to the message. Jesus essentially said, "Don't sweat the small stuff, Martha. Come have a seat."

OZ Says

The great word of Jesus to His disciples is abandon.

Just Between You and God

Think about the word *ever*. Ever-lasting. Ever-yone. Ever-ything. Ever-green. Ever-more. Ever-after. God is part of the *ever* not the *one* and not the *thing* and not the *more*.

It's not what you pray or how you pray . . . it's that you pray.

05.24

PLUMMETING

When I saw him, I fell at his feet as though dead. Then he placed his right hand on me and said: "Do not be afraid. I am the First and the Last."

[Revelation 1:17]

Sometimes life is unicorns and candy. Sometimes life is on your knees in a filthy parking lot trying to hide behind a rancid smelling dumpster to keep from getting drenched by a cold rain. Sometimes we must go all the way down. No hope. No peace. No rest. No joy. Sometimes it feels like we'd welcome death just so we could feel better. Yes, that happens. Then it turns around. The obvious question is why do we have to wait until we get that far down before God will step in and pick us up out of the puddle? Perhaps God gave us every possible opportunity to "correct the fall" before we got this low. We create our own situations. It is not God's fault. But God will always be there to pick us up.

—————————— OZ Says ——————————

Whenever His hand is laid upon you, it is ineffable peace and comfort, the sense that "underneath are the everlasting arms," full of sustaining and comfort and strength. When once His touch comes, nothing at all can cast you into fear again. In the midst of all His ascended glory the Lord Jesus comes to speak to an insignificant disciple, and to say—"Fear not." His tenderness is ineffably sweet. Do I know Him like that?

—————— Just Between You and God ——————

Say a prayer of thanks to God for his hand upon your life. Even if you haven't hit rock bottom yet, thank God that he will be there if you do.

Even at the bottom . . . God is here. Welcome, climb again. Need a boost?

05.25

BY CHOICE

Is not the whole land before you? Let's part company. If you go to the left, I'll go to the right; if you go to the right, I'll go to the left.

[Genesis 13:9]

Here's a hard one. It's easy to let God have control when things are really bad. When we're at our worst moments, we call on God and very often he'll pull our bacon from the fire. But what about when things are going really well? Here's the test: when things are going great, let God have control. Scary, isn't it? God may decide to send you back down to the bottom for a while—maybe to help someone else up; maybe 'cause you have something else to learn. But to give control to God and say, "I'm your servant," when all the good things in life are coming your way . . . that is faith.

—————— OZ Says ——————

God sometimes allows you to get into a place of testing where your own welfare would be the right and proper thing to consider if you were not living a life of faith; but if you are, you will joyfully waive your right and leave God to choose for you. This is the discipline by means of which the natural is transformed into the spiritual by obedience to the voice of God.

—————— Just Between You and God ——————

If you frequently find yourself shaking your fist at the sky shouting, "Why does this keep happening to me?", chances are it's because you didn't learn your lesson the last time it happened.

Good. Bad. God uses it all. For you.

05.26

THOUGHT-LESS.
THOUGHT-FULL.

Pray continually.

[1 Thessalonians 5:17]

Put your hand over your heart. Go ahead. Feel that? Have you thought at all today about whether or not your heart is beating? How about your blood? Flowing? How's your breathing? Did you wake up and say, "Start to breathe"? No, these things occur naturally. They don't have to be made to happen. This is how prayer should be. We think prayer happens when we hit our knees and fold our hands. We think prayer is what happens when we hold hands around the dinner table. Prayer happens all the time. Jesus taught us how to live. He is our connection to God. Therefore, by living the way Jesus taught us to, we are, in fact, praying without ceasing.

────────────── OZ Says ──────────────

Have we by the Spirit the unspeakable certainty that Jesus had about prayer, or do we think of the times when God does not seem to have answered prayer? "Every one that asketh receiveth." We say, "But . . . , but . . . ," God answers prayer in the best way, not sometimes, but every time, although the immediate manifestation of the answer in the domain in which we want it may not always follow.

────────── Just Between You and God ──────────

No, not "Living on a Prayer." You are a Living Prayer. Your life. Everything you are and do is a prayer. God listens. God knows. Open yourself up to God's presence in the smallest moments of your day. Every day is a day of prayer.

Every move you make. Every thought you think. Every word you say is prayer. What are you praying for?

05.27

STILL LIFE

I am going to send you what my Father has promised; but stay in the city until you have been clothed with power from on high.

[Luke 24:49]

Jesus' followers had to wait for something miraculous to happen and then they could go out and do wonderful things in his name. We don't have to wait. The miraculous has already happened. So we can go now. There are moments when we say we're feeling the movement of the Holy Spirit. That movement is a connection. That Holy Spirit is the same spirit that moved through the disciples in the upper room. But it's not connecting you to the past—or to the future, for that matter. The movement of the Holy Spirit connects you to now. God is not concerned with time. He is the beginning and the end. All things past and present are happening in the now to God. The Holy Spirit is your connection to God. Don't waste it when you feel it.

OZ Says

The Holy Spirit's influence and power were at work before Pentecost, but He was not here. Immediately Our Lord was glorified in Ascension, the Holy Spirit came into this world, and He has been here ever since. We have to receive the revelation that He is here. The reception of the Holy Spirit is the maintained attitude of a believer. When we receive the Holy Spirit, we receive quickening life from the ascended Lord.

Just Between You and God

The disciples thought it was over. It wasn't. Amazing things happen when you believe they happen. Pray that your life opens like a window in a stuffy room. Let the spirit in.

God is not the Internet. God is the eternal-net. Always open. Always accessible. No password. No code. Sign in.

05.28

A PLACE OF NO DISTANCE

In that day you will no longer ask me anything. Very truly I tell you, my Father will give you whatever you ask in my name.

[John 16:23]

Jesus talks about that day when there will be no need for questions. Jesus wants us to be one with him, and one with God. That is his most important goal for us. Right now we think of the distance between God and us as being endless, but it doesn't need to be. We can't close that space by just thinking about it or trying harder. That's not how it works. How we live affects the distance between God and us. We'll come to the place of no distance when we look at Jesus and trust him to duplicate his life in us. We'll have all that we need. We'll have the answers, or at least accept the questions.

—————— OZ Says ——————

Until the resurrection life of Jesus is manifested in you, you want to ask this and that; then after a while you find all questions gone, you do not seem to have any left to ask. You have come to the place of entire reliance on the resurrection life of Jesus which brings you into perfect contact with the purpose of God. Are you living that life now? If not, why shouldn't you?

—————— Just Between You and God ——————

When you pray today, let it come from your heart, not your head. Talk to God, and when you move on, keep that open-heart communication going. Think of prayer as a conversation with God. Chat with your friend.

With your mind you can build the bridge. With your soul you can move the mountain closer.

05.29

AND ON . . . AND ON . . . AND ON . . .

In that day you will ask in my name. I am not saying that I will ask the Father on your behalf. No, the Father himself loves you because you have loved me and have believed that I came from God.

[John 16:26–27]

When we reach that day, we will pray to God in Jesus' name. The idea is that we will become one with Jesus so that when we pray, it will be like God hearing from Jesus himself. So we ask again, "When is that day?" It's not out in your future. It's not something that's on God's eternal calendar. He doesn't own one, remember? That day for you may be different than that day for me. As we experience God's presence and find the place of no distance, we'll arrive at that day. We'll fulfill our journey and become one with Jesus.

OZ Says

Our Lord does not mean that life will be free from external perplexities, but that just as He knew the Father's heart and mind, so by the baptism of the Holy Ghost He can lift us into the heavenly places where He can reveal the counsels of God to us.

Just Between You and God

Believe that Jesus is with you. Ask to feel his hand on your shoulder. Through Jesus, God will hear you. The "place of no distance" (see 05.28) does not mean "place of no problems." Pray for the connection . . . pray to feel it; it's there already because of Jesus.

Think about all the possibilities involved in the word "limitless," then apply them all to God.

05.30

PLAY MESSAGES

Still another said, "I will follow you, Lord; but first let me go back and say goodbye to my family."

[Luke 9:61]

Yes, God, I will follow you—but what if my friends laugh at me; what if I get lost or lose all my money; what if following you hurts? We say we'll follow Jesus, but then we're asked to do something that goes against common sense and we step back and say, "You know, Jesus, I bet you wanted someone else." We're afraid of failure. We're afraid of dying.

Don't forget who has called you. Your challenges today might be huge—but Jesus wouldn't call you to do something if he knew you would fail. Where's your faith? Remember who it is that's calling you.

OZ Says

Jesus Christ demands that you risk everything you hold by common sense and leap into what He says, and immediately you do, you find that what He says fits on as solidly as common sense. At the bar of common sense Jesus Christ's statements may seem mad; but bring them to the bar of faith, and you begin to find with awestruck spirit that they are the words of God. Trust entirely in God, and when He brings you to the venture, see that you take it. We act like pagans in a crisis; only one out of a crowd is daring enough to bank his faith in the character of God.

Just Between You and God

That "right time right place" moment you've been waiting for to decide it's time? It's now. There are no more excuses. Jesus called Peter to step out of the boat. Yes, he sank after three steps but . . . THREE STEPS! How awesome would that be.

God is calling. God (yes, that's the one) is calling. Go.

05.31

ALPHA

Then he said, "Here I am, I have come to do your will." He sets aside the first to establish the second.

[Hebrews 10:9]

God is first because he was here before anything else. Anything you do, own, or become is because of God. Jesus never once questioned what God had in mind. He trusted God completely. So must we. The path we're on may be full of holes and pitfalls, but we'll make it because God said we would. To doubt is to lose trust in God. All that we are—all that we will be—is because of God. We must make ourselves worthy of the trust that God puts in us. His plan is for Christ to live in us. We must be trustworthy, so care for, nurture, and feed that relationship. God is completely aware of our situation. We must trust God.

OZ Says

A man's obedience is to what he sees to be a need; Our Lord's obedience was to the will of His Father. The cry today is—"We must get some work to do; the heathen are dying without God; we must go and tell them of Him." We have to see first of all that God's needs in us personally are being met . . . then He will open the way for us to realize His needs elsewhere.

Just Between You and God

GOD. Yes, just God. God is the reason . . . the beginning . . . the end . . . the "because" . . . and the "cause." Understand this. If you don't, it's okay to ask him for a better understanding. Be ready for the answer. It's pretty huge.

". . . and before that?" is a question only God can answer every time.

06.01

TRICK QUESTION

He asked me, "Son of man, can these bones live?" I said, "Sovereign Lord, you alone know."

[Ezekiel 37:3]

Those who tell you they have all the answers are either lying or selling something. There are many tough questions. Can a person who has walked away from God be brought back? Is this really what God wants? Why does bad stuff happen to good people? These are all great questions, but until we come face to face with the Creator and are able to ask him personally, any answers we get will be secondhand. Nobody knows the answers but God. Watch for those who say, "This is what God wants for you." How do they know? They try to define your enemies, choose your friends, and tell you what to do with your life—all in the name of God. They might be working for God, but they aren't necessarily working with him. There's a difference.

─────────── OZ Says ───────────

I despair of men in the degree in which I have never realized that God has done anything for me. Is my experience such a wonderful realization of God's power and might that I can never despair of anyone I see? Have I had any spiritual work done in me at all? . . . When God wants to show you what human nature is like apart from Himself, He has to show it to you in yourself. If the Spirit of God has given you a vision of what you are apart from the grace of God (and He only does it when His Spirit is at work), you know there is no criminal who is half so bad in actuality as you know yourself to be in possibility.

─────────── Just Between You and God ───────────

Go ahead. Ask the questions you've always wondered about. You may not get an answer right away. Worse, you may get an answer you don't want. But ask the questions of the Supreme Being, not from those who think they are.

Hard questions get either hard answers, or harder questions. Be careful who you ask.

06.02

BAND-AID

Who, then, are those who fear the LORD? He will instruct them in the ways they should choose.

[Psalm 25:12]

Remember when you were a little kid—you'd start to go somewhere you knew you weren't allowed, and you'd have the feeling your mom or dad was watching you? Remember when you fell off your bike and skinned your knee—you ran to your mom or dad for comfort? Still today, in a sense, your parents are always with you in your times of pain, even when they're not around. This is how our sense of God should be. He's watching us—keeping track of us—there for us when we're scared, hurt, depressed, or tired. We should never outgrow the sense that when things are at their worst, we can run into the arms of our loving Father, and he will hold us until we're ready to face the world again.

—————— OZ Says ——————

If we are haunted by God, nothing else can get in, no cares, no tribulation, no anxieties. We see now why Our Lord so emphasized the sin of worry. How can we dare be so utterly unbelieving when God is round about us? To be haunted by God is to have an effective barricade against all the onslaughts of the enemy.

—————— Just Between You and God ——————

Today say a thank-you prayer to the one who watches over you when you're headed for trouble—the one who bails you out when you get there—the one who makes sure nothing is going to hurt you and keeps you safe.

God stands on the wall. You're safe now. Rest.

06.03

PROMISES, PROMISES

The LORD confides in those who fear him; he makes his covenant known to them.

[Psalm 25:14]

Good friends listen to each other. Most likely you have a friend or two you can confide in. You can tell them all your secrets. They listen to you without judgment or trying to solve your problems; they just listen. True friends will also listen to your secret dreams—those things that make you giggling happy—those things you wish for, but can't share with anyone for fear of being laughed at. Have you ever listened to God's secret dreams for you? Usually we're too busy dumping our problems on him to listen to the dreams he has for us. We know the prayer—"Thy will be done on earth as it is in heaven"—but do we mean the words when we say them? God gets just as much joy out of the small everyday moments, where we hear his voice and appreciate his blessings, as when we do "giant" things to please him.

—————— OZ Says ——————

God guides us by our ordinary choices, and if we are going to choose what He does not want, He will check, and we must heed. Whenever there is doubt, stop at once. Never reason it out and say—"I wonder why I shouldn't?" God instructs us in what we choose, that is, He guides our common sense, and we no longer hinder His Spirit by continually saying—"Now, Lord, what is Thy will?"

—————— Just Between You and God ——————

Don't be quick with the AMEN today. Don't finish and move on until you've taken time to listen. God isn't a person you can just dump your soul-garbage on and then move along. It's a relationship—it's communication. What makes God happy?

Never approach prayer like you're taking a call at the table during a dinner date.

06.04

RIVER RUNS DEEP

Keep your lives free from the love of money and be content with what you have, because God has said, "Never will I leave you; never will I forsake you."

[Hebrews 13:5]

When you look at the ocean, do you see the wonder of God's creation, or do you see deep water that could easily drown you? Do you see the clouds that dot the sky or do you see the possible chance of rain? What good does being a pessimist or worrying do you? God says he will always be with you and will never leave you—so what good does it do to think about the possibility of . . . the very idea that we might . . . and you never know if . . . ? These thoughts keep you from God. He is trying to get through to you to say, "Hey, I'm right here. I'll hold your hand," while we say, "What if I trip and fall?" So where's your faith?

OZ Says

What line does my thought take? Does it turn to what God says or to what I fear? Am I learning to say not what God says, but to say something after I have heard what He says? "He hath said, I will never leave thee, nor forsake thee." So that we may boldly say, "The Lord is my helper, and I will not fear what man shall do unto me." "I will in no wise fail thee"—not for all my sin and selfishness and stubbornness and waywardness. Have I really let God say to me that He will never fail me? If I have listened to this say-so of God's, then let me listen again.

Just Between You and God

Look at the world like you are trying to read a book through a window. Those smudges and smears are not on the page. Look past them. Look at all that God created and see the beauty beneath it.

Worrying is as effective as using a toilet brush to change your cell phone battery. Worry says, "Sorry God, but I don't trust you." Yeah, don't do that.

06.05

TRUE

So we say with confidence, "The Lord is my helper; I will not be afraid. What can mere mortals do to me?"

[Hebrews 13:6]

Understand this. God says, "I'm here." If we start with this, then everything that could get in the way doesn't count for much. Whatever God wants us to do—we can do. Why? Because God says, "I'm here." That's it. End of story. The idea that we might fail shouldn't enter our minds. If we constantly seek communion with God and understand where he wants us and what he wants us to do, we shouldn't worry for a moment that we might fail. Why? Because God says, "I'm here." The dread and fear of losing is gone. We can walk into the lion's den with a smile. Why? Say it with me this time . . . because God says, "I'm here."

--- OZ Says ---

This does not mean that I will not be tempted to fear, but I will remember God's say-so. I will be full of courage, like a child "bucking himself up" to reach the standard his father wants. Faith in many a one falters when the apprehensions come, they forget the meaning of God's say-so, forget to take a deep breath spiritually. The only way to get the dread taken out of us is to listen to God's say-so.

--- Just Between You and God ---

You can't shake your fist at the sky and scream "What do you want from me?" God does not answer TO you. God might answer you if you ask . . . and if you are going to ask, be prepared to listen.

Stop, look, and listen . . . no, it's not a traffic thing. It's about prayer.

06.06

STASH

Therefore, my dear friends, as you have always obeyed—not only in my presence, but now much more in my absence—continue to work out your salvation with fear and trembling, for it is God who works in you to will and to act in order to fulfill his good purpose.

[Philippians 2:12–13]

One of the worst phrases to say is, "I don't think I can go on." It's not even a giving-up phrase. It's a phrase that recognizes there is more and yet we are choosing not to. There are events . . . Oh God . . . there are most assuredly events in your life when you stand in the midst of them and say, "I don't think I can go on" and then you do. God is in the "and then you do." God put that moment of strength, however small, in your soul. You've always had it. It's part of the human software. "And then you do" is strength and perseverance and love and sheer will. It is the response to every negative, progress-stopping thought. "And then you do."

─────────── OZ Says ───────────

You have to work out with concentration and care what God works in; not work your own salvation, but work it out, while you base resolutely in unshaken faith on the complete and perfect Redemption of the Lord. As you do this, you do not bring an opposed will to God's will. God's will is your will, and your natural choices are along the line of God's will, and the life is as natural as breathing. God is the source of your will; therefore you are able to work out His will.

─────────── Just Between You and God ───────────

It's already there, his inner strength. Even if you aren't up against something today, say thank you to God for the strength you will need sometime soon.

It's already there. You already have it. Stop asking God to give it to you. Bring it out. You can do anything.

06.07

NAMED. CLAIMED.

And I will do whatever you ask in my name, so that the Father may be glorified in the Son.

[John 14:13]

We can't spend our whole day on our knees or in our Bibles. That's not what God expects of us. When we decide to become followers, it doesn't mean we have to push everything else out of our lives. We can still go to movies, play sports, and dance at rock concerts. It's not the amount of time we spend doing God-things that makes us God-centered—it's whether or not God is at the center of all we do. Let the greatest influence in our everyday lives be God; making important decisions, making trivial decisions, not making decisions at all—just thinking about stuff. With God at our center we become who God wants us to be.

OZ Says

"Whatsoever ye shall ask in My name, that will I do." The disciple who abides in Jesus is the will of God, and his apparently free choices are God's foreordained decrees. Mysterious? Logically contradictory and absurd? Yes, but a glorious truth to a saint.

Just Between You and God

Don't listen to the voices that say "You're not doing enough for God!" Listen to the voice of God inside you that says, "That was fun. What do we do next?"

Maybe 10 percent is all I can give. But if God is 100 percent of that 10 percent, the math works out. God is first.

06.08

X, O, R1, XX, R1, DOWN ARROW

Now that you know these things, you will be blessed if you do them.

[John 13:17]

Remember Lara Croft in Tomb Raider? You controlled this virtual explorer with your game pad as she moved about various tunnels and tombs searching for treasure. At one point, in the second game, she had to jump backwards from one ledge to another. It wasn't that difficult. Three or four tries and you had it. Later in the game, the move got more difficult. This time Lara had to grab a wall on her jump, and if she missed she dropped into a pit of lava. Game over. Now if you hadn't mastered the earlier moves in the game, the tougher ones later on would have been impossible. Life is like this. God has a plan for you. He knows what you'll face farther down the road so he sets up something to prepare, refine, and make you ready for what you may face later on.

OZ Says

If you do not cut the moorings, God will have to break them by a storm and send you out. Launch all on God, go out on the great swelling tide of His purpose, and you will get your eyes open. If you believe in Jesus, you are not to spend all your time in the smooth waters just inside the harbor bar, full of delight, but always moored; you have to get out through the harbor bar into the great deeps of God and begin to know for yourself, begin to have spiritual discernment.

Just Between You and God

Thank God for your troubles. Yes, go ahead. It may be difficult, but do it anyway. Later down the line you will look back at this time and think "Oh, now I see why I had to do that."

God designed the video game. But the controller is in your hands. Got that? Save game. Start again.

06.09

BANANA WHO?

For everyone who asks receives; the one who seeks finds; and to the one who knocks, the door will be opened.

[Luke 11:10]

It's amazing how many of us go about our lives in pain. We think we deserve it. We think we can handle life on our own and continue to suffer day after day, refusing to ask for help. Jesus told us to ask, and we will receive. We receive from God because we are his children. A genuinely poor beggar on the street asks for help out of pure need. This is how we should approach God—out of need, not because we have a predetermined outcome in mind. We ask because we need something from God. It's not about selfish demands. That's not how it works. When we ask God to become a part of our lives, that is exactly what we get.

OZ Says

This does not mean you will not get if you do not ask, (cf. Matthew 5:45) but until you get to the point of asking you won't receive from God. To receive means you have come into the relationship of a child of God, and now you perceive with intelligent and moral appreciation and spiritual understanding that these things come from God.

Just Between You and God

Don't go to God with your Christmas list. Go to God with your emptiness and ask to experience his presence. Then see what you receive.

Ask. Receive. That about covers it.

06.10

AND IF THAT DOESN'T WORK . . .

So I say to you: Ask and it will be given to you; seek and you will find; knock and the door will be opened to you.

[Luke 11:9]

How exactly are we seeking? Are we seeking God because we've just royally messed up and driven our lives into the shredder? Do we seek God so we can be better people and show off to the world? Even if our intentions are good, God will not respond to these sorts of motives. God wants to hear us knock at the door so we can know him better—not for selfish reasons, but because this is what God wants of us. The gifts God has behind that door are better than anything you could get on this planet, but unless you are seeking and asking with correct motives, God can't give you his gifts.

OZ Says

Are you thirsty, or smugly indifferent—so satisfied with your experience that you want nothing more of God? Experience is a gateway, not an end. Beware of building your faith on experience, the metallic note will come in at once, the censorious note. You can never give another person that which you have found, but you can make him homesick for what you have.

Just Between You and God

People try to take selfies with their favorite celebrity. The Internet is full of these. Posting a picture of yourself with your favorite musician demeans all that their music has meant to you. Wearing God like He's a prize does the same thing. Show God with your actions not with your pictures.

Tattoo the cross on your arm or on your heart. One shows, the other "shows." Got it?

06.11

REST. STOP.

Come to me, all you who are weary and burdened, and I will give you rest.

[Matthew 11:28]

This verse has the answer to all of life's hard questions. Not questions like, "What toppings should we order on the pizza?" but the big ones you struggle with, like "Who am I? Where am I going? What should I do with my life and what is life all about anyway?" All of these can be answered by this one line from Jesus—"Come to me. Stop fussing. Stop straining. Come to me. I'm right here."

Jesus is there to give you rest—not to sing you a lullaby and hold your hand until you fall asleep. Not that kind of rest. He's talking about rest from the world; rest from the voices in your head; rest from the stress you inflict upon yourself day in and day out. That's the kind of rest that will get you out of bed and ready to face each day.

--- OZ Says ---

Jesus Christ makes Himself the touchstone. Watch how He used the word "come." At the most unexpected moments there is the whisper of the Lord— "Come unto Me," and you are drawn immediately. Personal contact with Jesus alters everything. Be stupid enough to come and commit yourself to what He says. The attitude of coming is that the will resolutely lets go of everything and deliberately commits all to Him.

--- Just Between You and God ---

Ask God for a whisper today. You'll find him when you move toward the sound of his voice. You can count on it. He'll be there.

Imagine playing the trust fall game with Jesus. Do you think he would ever let you hurt yourself? Trust him this way with everything.

06.12

RIGHT HERE. RIGHT NOW.

"Come," he replied, "and you will see." So they went and saw where he was staying, and they spent that day with him. It was about four in the afternoon.

[John 1:39]

Sometimes we get it all backwards. We think God wants us at the back of the line—to work without appreciation and put away all the things that make us who we are in order to be Christian. It's not like that. To say, "I'm not worthy" sounds like a self-esteem problem. Why aren't you worthy? Either because you don't want to be worthy or you don't think God knows what he's doing. Of course God knows what he's doing, and you're on this path in the first place because you chose to be here. So stop beating up on yourself and let God be God. He's going to do wonderful things with your life—just let yourself receive them.

OZ Says

Humility before men may be unconscious blasphemy before God. Why are you not a saint? If it is either that you do not want to be a saint, or that you do not believe God can make you one . . . Make no conditions, let Jesus be everything, and He will take you home with Him not only for a day, but forever.

Just Between You and God

Today get off your knees (literally and metaphorically). Stand up straight and, like the big bad servant of God that you are, talk with your creator.

In the history of creation, from its first moment until this one . . . God has never ever ever even one time said the word "oops." You are worth it.

06.13

AND NOW . . . HERE'S A THING

"Come, follow me," Jesus said, "and I will send you out to fish for people."

[Mark 1:17]

It's a very old secret. Are you sure you can handle it? Okay. When Jesus says, "Come to me," just do it. That's it. Go. Go now. Too often the Creator of the universe says, "Over here!" and we stand and look at him like he's going to send a car for us. When Jesus says, "Come," do it, but do it knowing that all you can take is yourself. We think we have to go and use our gifts for God. Well, the gifts weren't yours to begin with. What God wants is you. God will use you. God will put you where you need to be. He will give you what you need to get there and will tell you what to do once you're there. It's not something you can prepare for.

―――――――― OZ Says ――――――――

If you will give God your right to yourself, He will make a holy experiment out of you. God's experiments always succeed. The one mark of a saint is the moral originality which springs from abandonment to Jesus Christ. In the life of a saint there is this amazing wellspring of original life all the time . . . Never make a principle out of your experience; let God be as original with other people as He is with you.

―――――― Just Between You and God ――――――

That artist mind God gave you . . . while you plan your grand masterpiece, there's a kid with an 8 pack of crayons who needs some help (adjust that to your own particular gifts). When God says, "Here, take this," don't put it in your pocket for later.

Jesus is not playing hide and seek with you. He's right there. See?

06.14

REMAIN

Remain in me, as I also remain in you. No branch can bear fruit by itself; it must remain in the vine. Neither can you bear fruit unless you remain in me.

[John 15:4]

Let's talk about that word *abide*. It means "oneness." Jesus wants us to become one with him. Abide is not a goal . . . it is a state of being. That's like jumping in a pool and making a good solid effort to be wet. You really don't need to work at it, do you? Abiding works this way. It does take practice . . . and you can't stand on the edge of the pool and repeat "Abide with me" and not jump in. Jesus spent every moment living in oneness with his Father. There should be no difference between that wonderful mountaintop experience and the most average day of your life. Abiding in Jesus means experiencing each day to the fullest.

OZ Says

Think of the things that take you out of abiding in Christ—Yes, Lord, just a minute, I have got this to do; Yes, I will abide when once this is finished; when this week is over, it will be all right, I will abide then. Get a move on; begin to abide now. In the initial stages it is a continual effort until it becomes so much the law of life that you abide in Him unconsciously. Determine to abide in Jesus wherever you are placed.

Just Between You and God

Today ask God to be present in everything. Say a silent prayer as you change classes, take a test, or plan the weekend. Practice opening yourself up to his presence, and as you get better at it, you'll do it naturally.

If it's all God, it's all good.

06.15

BLEND

For this very reason, make every effort to add to your faith goodness; and to goodness, knowledge.

[2 Peter 1:5]

Peter wrote about life with simple lists that were easy to understand. He gave practical steps that could be easily understood. In this verse, he wrote about life as a recipe. No one is born naturally good, with strong character and good habits. We have to take the ingredients in this recipe and add them to our lives every day.

OZ Says

No man is born either naturally or supernaturally with character, he has to make character. Nor are we born with habits; we have to form habits on the basis of the new life God has put into us . . . It is the "adding" that is difficult. We say we do not expect God to carry us to heaven on flowery beds of ease, and yet we act as if we did! The tiniest detail in which I obey has all the omnipotent power of the grace of God behind it. If I do my duty, not for duty's sake, but because I believe God is engineering my circumstances, then at the very point of my obedience the whole superb grace of God is mine through the Atonement.

Just Between You and God

Talk to God today, not with a sense of urgency, but with a sense of certainty. Have no question in your mind that you are being heard. God hears when you scream from your knees on your worst day and when you sing from the mountain top. Just Pray.

It's like meatloaf. Add what you want. Mix well. Enjoy the sandwich.

06.16

MAKE ME. MOLD ME. HOLD ME. USE ME.

Greater love has no one than this: to lay down one's life for one's friends. I no longer call you servants, because a servant does not know his master's business. Instead, I have called you friends, for everything that I learned from my Father I have made known to you.

[John 15:13,15]

When Jesus talks about laying down your life, he isn't asking you to die. We think the ultimate sacrifice for God would be to die for his cause. When we begin to doubt whether or not we could die for God, we feel inadequate. Jesus didn't ask us to die. Instead, he asked us to lay down our lives. He asked us to give our lives to God. Our lives are to become God's modeling clay so that he can make and mold them into whatever he pleases. In some cases dying would be easier.

OZ Says

There was only one brilliant moment in the life of Jesus, and that was on the Mount of Transfiguration; then He emptied Himself the second time of His glory, and came down into the demon-possessed valley. For thirty-three years Jesus laid out His life to do the will of His Father, and, John says, "We ought to lay down our lives for the brethren." It is contrary to human nature to do it. If I am a friend of Jesus, I have deliberately and carefully to lay down my life for Him.

Just Between You and God

That confusing sensation? The potter's wheel is spinning. God's hands are . . . yeah GOD'S hands . . . molding and creating you. Yes, he may cut some pieces off, but nothing you need. Yes the whole project may collapse, but the potter starts again.

Imagine your life as art. God does.

06.17

NO "NO" VOTES

Do not judge, or you too will be judged.

[Matthew 7:1]

Not every fast-food worker is going to get your order right. Not every person you trust will keep your secrets. Sometimes teachers make mistakes. Sometimes parents screw up. What is the right way for you to judge the people who let you down? Surprise—there isn't. You don't get to judge anyone. That's not your job. God gets to judge them, not you. In the realm of God, nothing is accomplished by criticism. Only God can judge without hurting or wounding the one being criticized. It's even worse when people criticize in God's name. This pride gets in the way of our own relationship with God. God knows our faults and wants us to work on our own weaknesses, not point out other people's faults to them.

--- OZ Says ---

If I see the mote in your eye, it means I have a beam in my own. Every wrong thing that I see in you, God locates in me. Every time I judge, I condemn myself . . . Stop having a measuring rod for other people. There is always one fact more in every man's case about which we know nothing.

--- Just Between You and God ---

See that guy on the corner? The one with the suit and tie and waving a Bible while he calls people names and insults their integrity? See him? Yeah, you can ignore him. Better yet, ask God to give him some peace. Can't be fun to be that angry all the time.

Every single person you meet is fighting a battle you know nothing about. Save your judgments for something else.

06.18

WIND SURFING

"Come," he said. Then Peter got down out of the boat, walked on the water and came toward Jesus. But when he saw the wind, he was afraid and, beginning to sink, cried out, "Lord, save me!"

[Matthew 14:29–30]

Peter didn't care about the waves or the wind—not at first anyway. He saw Jesus. That was all he saw. Jesus said, "Come." Peter went. It wasn't until he started to pay attention to what was going on around him that he got into trouble. "Hey, there're waves. Hey, there's a storm. What am I doing out here?" And under he went. Sometimes we may feel like we have two lives—the one where we focus on Jesus and the one where we're walking alone. We shy away from focusing everything on Jesus because we're afraid of what our friends might think. We're afraid we'll miss out on something because we're too busy being Christian. It's when we take our eyes off Jesus that we create problems for ourselves. But Jesus is there. In spite of the storms and waves that bring us down, Jesus is there to lift us up, put us back in the boat, and let us try again.

―――――――――― OZ Says ――――――――――

If you debate for a second when God has spoken, it is all up. Never begin to say—"Well, I wonder if He did speak?" Be reckless immediately, fling it all out on Him. You do not know when His voice will come, but whenever the realization of God comes in the faintest way imaginable, recklessly abandon. It is only by abandon that you recognize Him. You will only realize His voice more clearly by recklessness.

―――――――― Just Between You and God ――――――――

When you listen and God says "Come on," he's got control over everything else. He's not leading you into a trap. Ask God to call you. Be ready when he does.

Jesus is waiting out in the worst storm of your life with open arms. Even if you sink, at least you took the step.

06.19

HERE MY SONG

Again Jesus said, "Simon son of John, do you love me?" He answered, "Yes, Lord, you know that I love you." Jesus said, "Take care of my sheep."

[John 21:16]

Jesus doesn't ask us to try to get people to think like us. The idea is not to convert people to our way of thinking. Jesus wants us to be disciples by caring for each other. We can't do that by pounding our beliefs into others. By being devoted to Jesus and feeding his sheep, we are living examples of him. That's the way to reach a waiting world. If we serve selfishly or because we've decided that's what we must do to get closer to God, then we'll get discouraged when the journey gets rough. If we are devoted to Jesus the service will be hard, but not at all hopeless.

OZ Says

Jesus Christ calls service what we are to Him, not what we do for Him. Discipleship is based on devotion to Jesus Christ, not on adherence to a belief or a creed . . . The secret of a disciple's life is devotion to Jesus Christ, and the characteristic of the life is its unobtrusiveness. It is like a corn of wheat, which falls into the ground and dies, but presently it will spring up and alter the whole landscape (John 12:24).

Just Between You and God

When Jesus said, "Feed my sheep," we seem to think of reasons not to do so. Sometimes we do so for the wrong reasons. (Ego or God-points.) What if we simply "fed the sheep" because the sheep are hungry. Kind of a WWJD thing there, yeah?

You can stop asking what would Jesus do. Just do what Jesus did. Because he was Jesus, that's why.

06.20

OH WAITER?

After Job had prayed for his friends, the LORD restored his fortunes and gave him twice as much as he had before.

[Job 42:10]

God is not like Santa Claus. We think if we work every day to make ourselves right with him we'll get a big present when we get to heaven. Truth is, we have already received the present. What God gave was the greatest gift anyone has ever received. Why spend so much time weeping and saying "Oh, I am not worthy of Christ's sacrifice." Well, obviously Jesus thought you were. Are you questioning his judgment? Stop fussing about worth and say "Thank you." Act like a person who has received this amazing grace gift and show THAT to the world.

OZ Says

If you are not getting the hundred-fold more, not getting insight into God's word, then start praying for your friends, enter into the ministry of the interior. "The Lord turned the captivity of Job when he prayed for his friends." The real business of your life as a saved soul is intercessory prayer.

Just Between You and God

Pray for the person who gave you this book. Pray for the people who think they must perform great miracles in order to get into the kingdom. Pray for those who have no idea what the kingdom is like. Pray for those closest to you who don't seem to understand why you spend so much time on your knees.

That guy who sits and laughs at you when you talk about God . . . yeah him. God loves him too. That's something you know that he doesn't.

06.21

PRICELESS

But you are a chosen people, a royal priesthood, a holy nation, God's special possession, that you may declare the praises of him who called you out of darkness into his wonderful light.

[1 Peter 2:9]

Okay, so you're not perfect. Big deal. Can you deal with that? Can you accept the idea that God loves you anyway? Can you accept it to the point where you stop praying for God to make you a better person and start asking God to help your friends and family? We operate under this mistaken idea that God won't listen to us until we are right with him. You're his child. You're in. Jesus took care of that. That's called grace. Now that you're in, perhaps you could spend less time praying for yourself and more time praying for your friends and family. There are lots of people out there who don't know about grace. Ask God to help them. Accept the fact that you're loved beyond measure and God won't abandon you. Now use your prayer time for someone else . . . anyone else . . . everyone else.

OZ Says

How long is it going to take God to free us from the morbid habit of thinking about ourselves? We must get sick unto death of ourselves, until there is no longer any surprise at anything God can tell us about ourselves . . . There is only one place where we are right, and that is in Christ Jesus. When we are there, then we have to pour out for all we are worth in this ministry of the interior.

Just Between You and God

You don't need to reach a certain prayer-level in order to be heard. Stop gaming ways to make yourself "better in God's eyes" so he'll hear you. He already hears you . . . already knows. So just pray for someone else.

Ever wonder how Grandma could hug all the grandkids at one time? It's a trick God taught her. Nobody gets left out. Ever.

06.22

FACE IT, DON'T FACEBOOK IT

For in the same way you judge others, you will be judged, and with the measure you use, it will be measured to you.

[Matthew 7:2]

For some reason we have a human need to feel superior. We stand with our arms folded and point out the frailties, inadequacies, and hypocrisies of others. What we need to understand is that, when we do this, we're creating the measuring stick by which we will be measured. We can spot these faults in others because we know what they look like—we've seen them in the mirror. Jesus said the way we judge others will be the way God will judge us. If you know people who say they're not scared by that idea, they're fooling themselves. When we pass judgment on others, it might make us feel good about ourselves. But beware—this is when God will humble you.

─────────── OZ Says ───────────

Jesus says—"Judge not, that ye be not judged"; if you do judge, it will be measured to you exactly as you have judged. Who of us would dare to stand before God and say—"My God, judge me as I have judged my fellow men"? We have judged our fellow men as sinners; if God should judge us like that we would be in hell. God judges us through the marvellous Atonement of Jesus Christ.

─────────── Just Between You and God ───────────

God wants you . . . the real you. Not the one you think you need to show the world. You see the guy talking to Jesus . . . the finger pointer. The one condemning all those around him while secretly hiding stuff in his heart. See him? We call that a Pharisee. Don't be that guy.

As soon as you start to feel superior to "those" people, look closely. Yeah, doesn't that one guy look like Jesus? Guess what?

06.23

ON PURPOSE

He was despised and rejected by mankind, a man of suffering, and familiar with pain. Like one from whom people hide their faces he was despised, and we held him in low esteem.

[Isaiah 53:3]

If we are made in the image of God, can we assume that God feels pain? Sadness? God gets frustrated sometimes? The book of Isaiah says God is acquainted with grief. So if God hurts . . . can we assume that we are the ones who hurt him? Frustrate him? Grieve him? Our problems are of our own creation. We know where we are supposed to go and yet we veer off the road and take the wrong exit every time. Nothing MADE us leave the path. We did it ourselves. For God it must be like watching your child learn to ride a bike. Scratches and scrapes are going to be part of the process but it doesn't make it hurt less . . . for anyone. But why would we think God will punish us if we can't get the hang of the peddles?

--------- OZ Says ---------

We take a rational view of life and say that a man by controlling his instincts, and by educating himself, can produce a life which will slowly evolve into the life of God. But as we go on, we find the presence of something that we have not taken into consideration . . . sin, and it upsets all our calculations. Sin has made the basis of things wild and not rational. We have to recognize that sin is a fact, not a defect; sin is red-handed mutiny against God. Either God or sin must die in my life. The New Testament brings us right down to this one issue. If sin rules in me, God's life in me will be killed; if God rules in me, sin in me will be killed. There is no possible ultimate but that.

--------- Just Between You and God ---------

Thank God for choice. He gave it to you. What you do with it is entirely up to you.

Want to know what sin is? To know God and turn away anyway. This is sin. Sin is by choice and the choice is entirely yours.

06.24

OVER HERE ON THE DARK SIDE

Every day I was with you in the temple courts, and you did not lay a hand on me. But this is your hour—when darkness reigns.

[Luke 22:53]

Cartoons and sitcoms like to show people with an angel on one shoulder and a devil on the other. It's a cheap illustration, but it's also incredibly true. Within each one of us is the capacity for good and evil. We deny it. We pretend it's not there. We say, "I'm a good person." We all think we are—but when we deny that devil on our shoulder, it's like pushing a beach ball under the water. When it comes up, it will be with a force you may not be ready for. When we accept that we have both good and evil within us, then we can go to God and say, "I am your servant." When we acknowledge what's inside of us, we can be the kind of servant God wants us to be.

––––––––– OZ Says –––––––––

If you refuse to agree with the fact that there is vice and self-seeking, something downright spiteful and wrong in human beings, instead of reconciling yourself to it, when it strikes your life, you will compromise with it and say it is of no use to battle against it . . . Always beware of an estimate of life which does not recognize the fact that there is sin.

––––––––– Just Between You and God –––––––––

God knows the part of you that no one else sees. You can tell the world it doesn't exist, but you won't convince God. Pray and ask God for the courage to be honest with yourself and the strength to deal with the truth.

Burying it doesn't make it go away. It just kills your garden.

06.25

KILN

"Now my soul is troubled, and what shall I say? 'Father, save me from this hour?' No, it was for this very reason I came to this hour. Father, glorify your name!" Then a voice came from heaven, "I have glorified it, and will glorify it again." The crowd that was there and heard it said it had thundered; others said an angel had spoken to him.

[John 12:27–29]

Ever watch a potter? Notice the way she clumps the clay and then slams it down on the wheel, again and again. A potter will also look for air bubbles. If she finds any she begins the process of slamming again, because the clay isn't ready to be molded. The air bubbles will cause the clay to explode when the kiln gets hot.

Such is life. We are like clay on a potter's wheel. We go through trials and tribulations. The hard times we go through are preparing us for something else. We're being made ready. When the fire gets hot, we'll survive because we've been through the slamming process. We will emerge from the fire as beautiful works of art.

———————————— OZ Says ————————————

You always know the man who has been through the fires of sorrow and received himself; you are certain you can go to him in trouble and find that he has ample leisure for you. If a man has not been through the fires of sorrow, he is apt to be contemptuous; he has no time for you. If you receive yourself in the fires of sorrow, God will make you nourishment for other people.

——————— Just Between You and God ———————

As hard as it may seem, you need to thank God for the pain and sorrow in your life. This shows faith. You must believe that God sees the whole picture even though you can only see what's happening right now.

Slam. Slam. Slam. It's all for the good. Really. Slam. Slam.

06.26

NO, YOU ARE NOT ON ANOTHER LINE

As God's co-workers we urge you not to receive God's grace in vain.

[2 Corinthians 6:1]

Too often we think of church buildings as some sort of direct funnel to God. Sanctuaries are wonderful places to pour out our hearts to God, but they're not the only places we can be heard. Sometimes we suffer through a rotten day and think, "I'll pray about this tonight before I go to sleep." What's wrong with praying now? Visualize grace as that whole cup-runneth-over-thing. God is pouring down his grace and your cup is there. God doesn't stop pouring, even when your cup is full. Imagine standing with a coffee mug at the base of Niagara Falls. That is what grace is like all the time. Don't wait for a specific moment to talk to God. Talk now. Pray now. Connect now. That grace is still flowing—why not use it?

OZ Says

The grace you had yesterday will not do for today. Grace is the overflowing favour of God; you can always reckon it is there to draw upon. In much patience, in afflictions, in necessities, in distresses—that is where the test for patience comes. Are you failing the grace of God there? Are you saying—Oh, well, I won't count this time? It is not a question of praying and asking God to help you; it is taking the grace of God now.

Just Between You and God

Pray now. That's it. Just pray now. You're still reading. Close the book. Pray now.

You didn't close the book. What did I just say? Put the book down and pray.

06.27

BAGGAGE

"Do not be afraid of them, for I am with you and will rescue you," declares the LORD.

[Jeremiah 1:8]

We're on a journey called life. Since none of us have done this before, we'll constantly be facing new things. Not all of them will be pleasant—but God has promised that he will get us through. He has said he'll be right next to us the whole time—not watching from far away—not waiting at the end of the path. When we start thinking about ourselves and focusing inward, we stop moving forward. We find a comfortable spot along the path, and we want to stay. Sometimes we stop to wallow in the misery of the moment. Neither of these is what God wants for us. Once you realize God's eternal presence, the things that block your way can be overcome.

OZ Says

Jesus says, in effect, Do not be bothered with whether you are being justly dealt with or not. To look for justice is a sign of deflection from devotion to Him. Never look for justice in this world, but never cease to give it. If we look for justice, we will begin to grouse and to indulge in the discontent of self-pity—Why should I be treated like this? If we are devoted to Jesus Christ we have nothing to do with what we meet, whether it is just or unjust. Jesus says—Go steadily on with what I have told you to do and I will guard your life.

Just Between You and God

Wherever you are on your journey right now . . . thank God for his companionship. If you're in a bad section of the trip, ask for just a glimpse of what is to come, to keep you going. If your walk now is easy, pause a moment to count the tears you have come through, and thank God that he brought you here.

Ever see anybody dance with a full suitcase?

06.28

GOTCHA

Not that I have already obtained all this, or have already arrived at my goal, but I press on to take hold of that for which Christ Jesus took hold of me.

[Philippians 3:12]

You're here because God wants you here. You followed the call. It's the people who stand up and say to the world, "Look at me. I'm special because I'm choosing to follow God," who will end up tripping along the path. God calls. We follow. Out of that great throng of people wandering this planet, God reached down and picked you out of the crowd. Not because you're better than anybody else, but because he has a purpose for you. You don't get to wear the flashing neon hat that says servant. You get to show a thirsty world where you found refreshing water.

OZ Says

What you are to preach is determined by God, not by your own natural inclinations. Keep your soul steadfastly related to God, and remember that you are called not to bear testimony only, but to preach the gospel. Every Christian must testify, but when it comes to the call to preach, there must be the agonizing grip of God's hand on you, your life is in the grip of God for that one thing.

Just Between You and God

A valet gets to drive some really amazing cars owned by some really amazing people who trust him/her with the keys. You are on the path God set out. He's given you the keys. Enjoy the ride, but remember who put you here.

That whole "you are the only Jesus" thing? Isn't that the scariest thought ever? Still true.

06.29

ROCK, PAPER . . . ?

And if your right hand causes you to stumble, cut it off and throw it away. It is better for you to lose one part of your body than for your whole body to go into hell.

[Matthew 5:30]

Remember that really cool Batman shirt you had as a kid? It was your favorite. You hated putting it in the wash and couldn't wait for it to come out of the dryer. What if you found it today? You couldn't even put it on. You aren't that person anymore. Physically, emotionally, spiritually. You can't go back. You are no longer the person you were when you started this journey. You are different. You can't go back. Most of the stuff you brought with you that you thought you might need? You can lose it now. Get rid of what you can. Be the new person you are becoming.

OZ Says

There never has been a saint yet who did not have to live a maimed life to start with. But it is better to enter into life maimed and lovely in God's sight than to be lovely in man's sight and lame in God's. In the beginning Jesus Christ by His Spirit has to check you from doing a great many things that may be perfectly right for everyone else but not right for you. See that you do not use your limitations to criticize someone else.

Just Between You and God

Ask God to help you go through your luggage. There are things you may be hanging onto that you don't even realize are holding you back. Examine them. Hold them up for God to see. He'll let you know when to toss them.

Look behind you. Is the path littered with your stuff the whole way back? If yes, you're on the right path. If not . . .

06.30

AND YOU'RE SITTING THERE WAITING FOR WHAT?

Settle matters quickly with your adversary who is taking you to court. Do it while you are still together on the way, or your adversary may hand you over to the judge, and the judge may hand you over to the officer, and you may be thrown into prison.

[Matthew 5:25]

Jesus tells us that we must settle disagreements quickly. He doesn't say, "Hold out until you get what you think you've got coming to you." He says, "Settle it." We want to say to God, "But he started it." "No, he did." "No, he did." What matters to God is how it ends. Finish it now. Settle up. Don't make me come down there. Look at the people you're arguing with and imagine what it would be like to eat, sleep, and live your life while giving them piggyback rides. Sounds silly, but do it. Imagine day in and day out, every waking and sleeping moment with someone clinging to your back. How long do you think you could last? This is what life will be like if you don't let it go. Without forgiveness you'll be carrying around that person until you can't stand up under the weight.

OZ Says

From our Lord's standpoint it does not matter whether I am defrauded or not; what does matter is that I do not defraud. Am I insisting on my rights, or am I paying what I owe from Jesus Christ's standpoint?

Just Between You and God

Ask God for some direct intervention here. Don't pray that your opposition will see the error of his ways and beg for your forgiveness. Ask God to take your blinders off and see what you need to do with the situation. Then do it.

Conflict builds walls. Arguments are like bricks. While you're mixing more cement, God is waiting for you to borrow his sledgehammer.

07.01

ROAD CONSTRUCTION

Truly I tell you, you will not get out until you have paid the last penny.

[Matthew 5:26]

A lot of this just doesn't make sense. Jesus' lessons about the kind of person we should be run contrary to the way the world thinks. The world says, "Step on the next person to get ahead." Jesus says, "Love your neighbor as yourself." Jesus' message doesn't seem to work in the real world: The meek don't inherit anything, the righteous get kicked in the teeth, and those who mourn are seen as weak.

We have to leave that sort of world-thinking behind. We must choose to move into God-thinking. We must attempt to heal broken relationships and be prepared to pay for our mistakes. God forgives, but life might still dish out some consequences. So . . . take a deep breath, and keep going. God will be beside us. These are some of the most difficult parts of the journey. We have to be willing to change if God is going to change us. We have to empty ourselves of the baggage we carry around so God can fill us again.

——————————— OZ Says ———————————

The moment you are willing that God should alter your disposition, His re-creating forces will begin to work. The moment you realize God's purpose, which is to get you rightly related to Himself and then to your fellow men, He will tax the last limit of the universe to help you take the right road. Decide it now—"Yes, Lord, I will write that letter to-night"; "I will be reconciled to that man now."

——————— Just Between You and God ———————

So the relationship is broken. Your apology or effort will mean nothing to them. That doesn't mean you don't make the move. Not every relationship is fixable. But you can take the broken part out of your system. You can remove it. Make space. Allow God to fill it in with love.

Road construction means to build roads . . . to fix roads. You can't get where you want to be until you do. What are you building?

07.02

LAAAAAAADIES AAAAAAND GENTLEMENNNNN

If anyone comes to me and does not hate father and mother, wife and children, brothers and sisters— yes, even their own life—such a person cannot be my disciple. And whoever does not carry their cross and follow me cannot be my disciple."

[Luke 14:26–27]

Let's not forget who is at the center of all this. Faith, belief, and spirituality can sometimes be like a three-ring circus. There is something going on no matter where you look. But sitting quietly watching the show with the rest of us is Jesus. Eventually we'll learn to ignore the chaos and the flashing colors that sometimes go along with belief. When we've tuned everything else out (even the sound of the band and laughter of the crowd) Jesus will turn to us and smile. It's as if some new ringleader has announced that you should direct your attention not to the center ring but to the seat next to you . . . to Jesus.

—————— OZ Says ——————

No man on earth has this passionate love to the Lord Jesus unless the Holy Ghost has imparted it to him. We may admire Him, we may respect Him and reverence Him, but we cannot love Him. The only Lover of the Lord Jesus is the Holy Ghost, and He shed abroad the very love of God in our hearts. Whenever the Holy Ghost sees a chance of glorifying Jesus, He will take your heart, your nerves, your whole personality, and simply make you blaze and glow with devotion to Jesus Christ.

—————— Just Between You and God ——————

Listen for God the way you listen when the doctor tests your hearing. Pay no attention to anything else. Focus on the words being said into your mind. Listen with all that you are. Listen this way . . . for Jesus.

Jesus is the star attraction. The rest of the world can be a circus. Don't forget the reason you bought the ticket.

07.03

HANDS DIRTY

"Woe to me!" I cried. "I am ruined! For I am a man of unclean lips, and I live among a people of unclean lips, and my eyes have seen the King, the LORD Almighty."

[Isaiah 6:5]

All of us have a deep secret that we don't talk about in polite company. Truthfully, we don't talk about it at all. But nothing is hidden from God. We may come into his presence and believe that we have buried things so deep he can't see them. (This is the same as a child hiding his dirty hands behind his back. Mom knows. Mom always knows.) Once we're in the presence of God—that is the time to bring it up. That is the time to place it before God. We can't live with guilt and fully love God. We must be willing to face our past mistakes, no matter how painful. However, we can do this with the full knowledge that nothing can ever separate us from the love of God.

OZ Says

There is never any vague sense of sin, but the concentration of sin in some personal particular. God begins by convicting us of the one thing fixed on in the mind that is prompted by His Spirit; if we will yield to His conviction on that point, He will lead us down to the great disposition of sin underneath. That is the way God always deals with us when we are consciously in His presence.

Just Between You and God

You don't need the fear. You don't need the pain or the guilt or the stress. Why would you want those inside you like gunk on your soul. God already knows about it. Tell it to God. Ask for help. There is nothing you can do to make him stop loving you. But you can make room for his love by giving up the gunk.

Did you think if you buried it that God wouldn't find it? He handed you the shovel. Dig it up. Give it to God. God knows what to do. He was just waiting for you to show it to him.

07.04

FRETS

**Refrain from anger and turn from wrath; do not fret—
it leads only to evil.**

[Psalm 37:8]

We've all heard it. "Don't sweat the small stuff." This verse in Psalms says, "Refrain from anger . . . do not fret." This is all well and good until we actually start living. Life is full of ups and downs. It's easy to not fret when life is good, but the moment things go wrong, we start fretting. We think God likes us in good times and ignores us in the bad. Your circumstances have nothing to do with your ability to fret not; this comes entirely from your relationship with God. Think of it this way . . .

You can stand in the river and punch the current because it isn't going the direction you want it to go, but you exhaust yourself, and the river doesn't seem to care. God has a plan. God has always had a plan. God knows what you are going through. Have a little faith. If you fuss and fret about the river, you might be missing the solution to the problem downstream.

OZ Says

. . . until we live, as so many are doing in tumult and anguish, is it possible then to rest in the Lord? If this "don't [fret]" does not work there, it will work nowhere. This "don't" must work in days of perplexity as well as in days of peace, or it never will work. And if it will not work in your particular case, it will not work in anyone else's case. Resting in the Lord does not depend on external circumstances at all, but on your relationship to God Himself.

Just Between You and God

Tell God you'll stop fretting. Even if it sounds hollow in your own ears, say it out loud so you can hear it. Tell God you trust him. Learn what you're supposed to learn and move on.

**God's plan is like a river. Swim upstream—it's tar.
Float downstream—it's water. Learn to go with the
flow.**

07.05

RECIPE

Commit your way to the LORD; trust in him and he will do this . . .

[Psalm 37:5]

E ver notice how we sometimes put together tremendous blueprints for our lives? We plan, schedule, calculate, and define all the possibilities of where we want to be at a given time, and what we want our lives to be like. Then suddenly the bottom falls out. Been there? When this happens we can usually look back and see that we didn't figure God into our plans. It's not that we have to check with God as some sort of spiritual boss-man, but we need to actually include God in our plans. It's easy to do on Sunday, but the rest of the week we tend to put God aside. Imagine living each day, looking ahead to the rest of our lives, knowing that God will be part of every day. Some of us are different people on Sunday. God wants us to be the same person every day of the week—to come as we are.

─────────── OZ Says ───────────

God seems to have a delightful way of upsetting the things we have calculated on without taking Him into account. We get into circumstances which were not chosen by God, and suddenly we find we have been calculating without God; He has not entered in as a living factor. The one thing that keeps us from the possibility of worrying is bringing God in as the greatest factor in all our calculations.

─────── Just Between You and God ───────

Today look at the blueprint. Dream big. Where do you want to be and what do you want to be doing ten years from now? Twenty years? Now take that blueprint to God and say, "Where do you want to fit in?"

Baking with God . . . cookies! Baking without God . . . hockey pucks. Yeah, it's pretty much that easy.

07.06

FINGER PAINT

The burning sand will become a pool, the thirsty ground bubbling springs. In the haunts where jackals once lay, grass and reeds and papyrus will grow.

[Isaiah 35:7]

It's inspiring to see the special "eye" of artists as they stare at a blank canvas. Where we see white, the artist sees the landscape, profile, shape, and color . . . the finished painting in the "mind's eye." God has that same eye when he looks at us and sees our potential. The artist's canvas must be prepared—woven, primed, stretched, and tacked. So it is with us. We're not ready on our own to become a masterpiece. God may allow us to go through pain and hard times in preparation. This hurts. But in the end we'll become all that the Artist envisions us to be.

―――――――――― OZ Says ――――――――――

In the light of the glory of the vision we go forth to do things, but the vision is not real in us yet; and God has to take us into the valley, and put us through fires and floods to batter us into shape, until we get to the place where He can trust us with the veritable reality. Ever since we had the vision God has been at work, getting us into the shape of the ideal, and over and over again we escape from His hand and try to batter ourselves into our own shape.

―――――――― Just Between You and God ――――――――

Perhaps you feel like you are still encased in rock . . . an unfinished statue. You just want to be free. Be patient. If the artist hasn't finished with you yet there is a reason. See yourself with the eyes of the artist . . . there is so much more to come.

You are the canvas. Trust God. Believe in God. And you will be the art.

07.07

HARDER TIMES

Enter through the narrow gate. For wide is the gate and broad is the road that leads to destruction, and many enter through it. But small is the gate and narrow the road that leads to life, and only a few find it.

[Matthew 7:13–14]

If following Jesus Christ was easy, everybody would do it. It's harder to live your life as a believer than as a non-believer. But there's a difference between believers and non-believers. Believers don't shy away from something because it's hard. That's not who we are. Yes, the life we've chosen is hard. But it's this belief that makes us the kind of people we are. When a crisis comes, believers stand up to the storm while non-believers hide. It's when we stand up to the storm that we discover something amazing about our own new nature. We discover that God has put amazing power inside us. We're strong. We're brave. Living this life takes a tremendous amount of discipline, faith, and courage. If you didn't have that—you wouldn't be here, would you?

OZ Says

If we are going to live as disciples of Jesus, we have to remember that all noble things are difficult. The Christian life is gloriously difficult, but the difficulty of it does not make us faint and cave in, it rouses us up to overcome. Do we so appreciate the marvellous salvation of Jesus Christ that we are our utmost for His highest?

Just Between You and God

Stand up when you pray today. Strike your best "bring-it" pose. Ask the world, "Is that all you've got?" Pray loud if it helps. This is between you and God. If God is there, nothing . . . not one thing . . . can stand in your way.

Did you think this was going to be easy? But God is here. If he weren't, you wouldn't be either.

07.08

WE ARE DECIDED

But if serving the Lord seems undesirable to you, then choose for yourselves this day whom you will serve, whether the gods your ancestors served beyond the Euphrates, or the gods of the Amorites, in whose land you are living. But as for me and my household, we will serve the Lord.

[Joshua 24:15]

Remember, this was your decision. You made the choice to walk this path. You can't just float along waiting for God to do something. You've chosen to live as Jesus said to live. This is between you and God—what the rest of the world thinks doesn't matter. Even though your friends may have your best interest at heart, they don't figure into this decision. Jesus said, "Come," and you said, "Yes." That's it. Nothing else matters in this process. There's not a list of pros and cons and deep calculations. This is a determined, definite, resolute, single-minded, unwavering decision. It does not happen to you. You happen.

--------- OZ Says ---------

The Lord has been putting before us all some big propositions, and the best thing to do is to remember what you did when you were touched by God before—the time when you were saved, or first saw Jesus, or realized some truth. It was easy then to yield allegiance to God; recall those moments now as the Spirit of God brings before you some new proposition.

--------- Just Between You and God ---------

Quiet yourself. Be alone for this prayer. Re-state your decision. Say it to yourself as much as you say it to God. Promise to listen. Promise to learn. Promise to act. Say, "I am your servant." Say it again.

You can't choose a direction and then stay put. Move.

07.09

READY?

Joshua said to the people, "You are not able to serve the LORD. He is a holy God; he is a jealous God. He will not forgive your rebellion and your sins."

[Joshua 24:19]

If we could all be perfect servants of God, this would be so much easier—but we aren't perfect. We tell God to use us and we still have that tiny part inside of us that says, "But what about . . ." or "Maybe I'm not really . . ." We can't help but feel this way. We can, however, position ourselves to be used. We can be prepared to be put in the right place at the right time. When we feel we aren't worthy, that's when we're most worthy. Those with the most to lose will be the last to follow the call. Those of us who think we have nothing to offer are the ones who will be filled, when grace pours in like a flood.

OZ Says

Have you the slightest reliance on anything other than God? Is there a remnant of reliance left on any natural virtue, any set of circumstances? Are you relying on yourself in any particular in this new proposition that God has put before you? That is what the probing means. It is quite true to say—"I cannot live a holy life," but you can decide to let Jesus Christ make you holy.

Just Between You and God

Take your empty self to God. The broken self. The screw-up self. Take yourself to God with no promises and no expectations. God wants you when you are this way. This way he knows you're listening. This way he knows the message gets through.

Go to God with your empty bucket. Not to ask but to offer. Hold up your bucket of zilch. God sends a flood.

07.10

INSPIRED

And let us consider how we may spur one another on toward love and good deeds, not giving up meeting together, as some are in the habit of doing, but encouraging one another—and all the more as you see the Day approaching.

[Hebrews 10:24–25]

Ah, that wonderful vision . . . swinging back and forth in a hammock. We listen to the sound of the surf as we peruse the Scriptures and experience that one-on-one conversation with God. Ahhhhh.

Guess what? That's not what this is about and you aren't the only one on this path. As you walk, you will walk with others. You will run up against instances of injustice, hatred, and unfairness. You are part of God's people. As a part, you must be willing to receive a spiritual kick in the pants. You must be willing to provide one as well. We need to inspire each other along the path to do what God's called us to do.

——————————— OZ Says ———————————

It is a most disturbing thing to be smitten in the ribs by some provoker of God, by someone who is full of spiritual activity. Active work and spiritual activity are not the same thing. Active work may be the counterfeit of spiritual activity. The danger of spiritual sluggishness is that we do not wish to be stirred up, all we want to hear about is spiritual retirement. Jesus Christ never encourages the idea of retirement—"Go tell My brethren . . ."

——————— Just Between You and God ———————

If you stand by the side of the road and repeat "God send me" over and over with all your heart but you never move, you can't really say God's not living up to his end of the deal, can you? Part of "I'll go where you send me!" is that whole "going" thing.

It's easier to find God in the clang and clatter of a busy kitchen than in the back of your eyelids. Do something! God is.

07.11

"LIKE" JESUS

I want to know Christ—yes, to know the power of his resurrection and participation in his sufferings, becoming like him in his death . . .

[Philippians 3:10]

Perhaps the question "What would Jesus do?" is a bit misleading. A better statement is, "Be what Jesus would be." Our most important goal is not to right the wrongs of the world. Our goal is to be like Jesus—who calmed storms and washed his disciples' feet. If we're to be what Jesus would be, then the world will see Jesus through us. Jesus wanted us to be one with him. By being like him we are making him known to the world. We're to be like Jesus in all we say and do. When believers live like him, then we truly can say that Jesus is in the world.

––––––––––– OZ Says –––––––––––

The initiative of the saint is not towards self-realization, but towards knowing Jesus Christ. The spiritual saint never believes circumstances to be haphazard, or thinks of his life as secular and sacred; he sees everything he is dumped down in as the means of securing the knowledge of Jesus Christ. There is a reckless abandonment about him. The Holy Spirit is determined that we shall realize Jesus Christ in every domain of life, and He will bring us back to the same point again and again until we do.

––––––––––– Just Between You and God –––––––––––

What would Jesus be? In your life—where you are now—what would Jesus be? Ask God. Then be that.

You are what Jesus would be if he was still here and he was you.

07.12

HERE WE ARE

. . . until we all reach unity in the faith and in the knowledge of the Son of God and become mature, attaining to the whole measure of the fullness of Christ.

[Ephesians 4:13]

A famous comedian who used to smash watermelons with a sledge hammer once said, "Church is the weekly reminder there's something worse than school." Instead of thinking about church as that two hours they rip out of your weekend . . . let's think of church as a verb. Church is to make something sacred. Church occurs daily outside of the building in the place where we live the rest of our lives. Church is sharing God's love with the world. Everyone. Everywhere. Time to go to "church."

──────── OZ Says ────────

The rehabilitation of the human race on Jesus Christ's plan means the realization of Jesus Christ in corporate life as well as in individual life. Jesus Christ sent apostles and teachers for this purpose—that the corporate Personality might be realized. We are not here to develop a spiritual life of our own, or to enjoy spiritual retirement; we are here so to realize Jesus Christ that the Body of Christ may be built up.

──────── Just Between You and God ────────

Pray with someone else today. Call a friend. Grab a family member and pray together. Ask that the link bonding the two of you will be strengthened and ask God how to make it larger.

God is group work.

07.13

ON VIBRATE

In the year that King Uzziah died, I saw the Lord, high and exalted, seated on a throne; and the train of his robe filled the temple.

[Isaiah 6:1]

God has a funny way of getting our attention. Not funny-ha ha, but funny-strange. We may not always be prepared for it. If God wants to be the most important part of your life, he may come up with ways to make that happen in your life. Good experiences and bad experiences bring us closer to God. The one who wants to be admired may find himself at the bottom of the heap. The one who is in love with the sound of her own voice may wonder why it seems like everyone is interrupting her. God may make changes in your life so that you pay attention to the plan he has for you. Chances are it's better than the one you had for yourself.

OZ Says

My vision of God depends upon the state of my character. Character determines revelation. Before I can say "I saw also the Lord," there must be something corresponding to God in my character. Until I am born again and begin to see the Kingdom of God, I see along the line of my prejudices only; I need the surgical operation of external events and an internal purification.

Just Between You and God

Putting God first in your life won't keep bad things from happening to you. God will use the good and the bad to work together so he'll become number one in your life.

What color ribbon do you give for "before first"?
That one is God's.

07.14

UN-EXPECTATIONS

But I tell you, do not resist an evil person. If anyone slaps you on the right cheek, turn to them the other cheek also.

[Matthew 5:39]

Do what is unexpected. When Jesus taught, he often took ideas that had been accepted for generations and turned them around. The meek shall be powerful. The last shall be first. The leader shall be the servant. Over and over we're faced with situations in which the world expects us to react one way and our faith calls us to act another. Therefore we can dance on the tables when life seems to dump garbage on our plate. We are handed an opportunity to live the lesson. Hard? Sure. But imagine the excitement of doing everything Jesus' way—do the unexpected!

OZ Says

You cannot imitate the disposition of Jesus; it is either there or it is not. To the saint personal insult becomes the occasion of revealing the incredible sweetness of the Lord Jesus. The teaching of the Sermon on the Mount is not—Do your duty, but—Do what is not your duty. It is not your duty to go the second mile, to turn the other cheek, but Jesus says if we are His disciples we shall always do these things. There will be no spirit of—"Oh, well, I cannot do any more, I have been so misrepresented and misunderstood." Every time I insist upon my rights, I hurt the Son of God; whereas I can prevent Jesus from being hurt if I take the blow myself.

Just Between You and God

This one is so very difficult to pull off. When your life is like the computer crash that eats your term paper the night before it's due . . . celebrate. Fist pump the air and say, "YESSSS!" God had something else entirely in mind for your life at the moment. You get to find out what it is.

Last is first. Weak is strong. Questions are answers. Tragedy is comedy. God is good.

07.15

POTTER'S WHEEL

I am obligated both to Greeks and non-Greeks, both to the wise and the foolish.

[Romans 1:14]

Everything good comes from God. Everything that we like about ourselves is a result of God's work. Paul considered himself to be forever in debt to Jesus because it was Jesus who made him who he was. Can we consider anything different?

How do you respond to the Creator of the universe who made you all that you are? The answer is by being there for God. Being the example. Being his servant. Showing the love that you've been shown so that anyone who looks at you, hears you, or thinks of you, will think about the love of Jesus.

OZ Says

I am not to be a superior person amongst men, but a bondslave of the Lord Jesus. "Ye are not your own." Paul sold himself to Jesus Christ. He says—I am a debtor to everyone on the face of the earth because of the Gospel of Jesus; I am free to be an absolute slave only. That is the characteristic of the life when once this point of spiritual honour is realized. Quit praying about yourself and be spent for others as the bondslave of Jesus. That is the meaning of being made broken bread and poured-out wine in reality.

Just Between You and God

Say thank you for the gifts you've been given by giving them back to the One who gave them to you. Whatever your gifts, find a way today to use them specifically for his purpose.

The best way to say thank you to God for the gifts is by becoming one.

07.16

XXXL

If you, then, though you are evil, know how to give good gifts to your children, how much more will your Father in heaven give good gifts to those who ask him!

[Matthew 7:11]

God is in charge and he loves you. There—that's pretty much all you need today. In fact, that's pretty much all you need in life. Understand and accept that one idea, and everything else will fall into place. Don't know where your life is going? That's okay. God is in charge and he loves you. Life going into the shredder lately? Don't worry. God is in charge and he loves you. Need something? Seeking something? Lose something? A friend is sick? A friend is in trouble? God is in charge and he loves you.

OZ Says

There are times, says Jesus, when God cannot lift the darkness from you, but trust Him. God will appear like an unkind friend, but He is not; He will appear like an unnatural Father, but He is not; He will appear like an unjust judge, but He is not. Keep the notion of the mind of God behind all things strong and growing. Nothing happens in any particular unless God's will is behind it; therefore you can rest in perfect confidence in Him.

Just Between You and God

Answer this out loud. No matter where you sit reading this. Do you believe in God? (Remember to say it aloud.) You: "Yes." There. Now you can begin again.

Life can be like spending a day in a t-shirt that's two sizes too small. God is your fuzzy jammies.

07.17

SCRABBLE

And so it was with me, brothers and sisters. When I came to you, I did not come with eloquence or human wisdom as I proclaimed to you the testimony about God. For I resolved to know nothing while I was with you except Jesus Christ and him crucified. I came to you in weakness with great fear and trembling. My message and my preaching were not with wise and persuasive words, but with a demonstration of the Spirit's power, so that your faith might not rest on human wisdom, but on God's power.

[1 Corinthians 2:1–5]

Paul wasn't a great speaker, but the message he delivered was powerful. We have to understand, it's the words that bring us closer to God, not the one who's preaching them. If we're preaching and we want our words to bring people closer to God, we've missed the ball. Likewise, if we listen to the words merely because we like the preacher, we aren't getting any closer to God either. If the Word speaks for itself, we better not interrupt.

OZ Says

The creative power of the Redemption comes through the preaching of the Gospel, but never because of the personality of the preacher. The real fasting of the preacher is not from food, but rather from eloquence, from impressiveness and exquisite diction, from everything that might hinder the Gospel of God being presented. The preacher is there as the representative of God—"as though God did beseech you by us." He is there to present the Gospel of God.

Just Between You and God

Intelligence is about learning your lessons. Wisdom is understanding that your lessons can come from anywhere. God is going to teach you. Never discount the teacher.

The Bible is a story that you are part of. Read it aloud. Live it aloud.

07.18

RECEIVING

"Who are you, Lord?" Saul asked. "I am Jesus, whom you are persecuting," he replied. "Now get up and go into the city, and you will be told what you must do."

[Acts 9:5–6]

Human beings are interesting creatures. We have a desire to explain everything. We're uncomfortable with things we can't understand. Jesus asks us to just do it—so to speak. Don't ask questions. Don't try to reason it out. It's God, the ultimate authority who is asking us to go—so just go. We make our lists of do's and don'ts and put them in our little rulebook and label it religion. But God does not come to us because we're being religious. God may come to us without an explanation and say, "Go," and we must go. If we say, "No, thanks, not today, too busy," God won't push us. But someplace down the road we're going to look back and say, "I guess I should have . . ."

--------- OZ Says ---------

When I stand face to face with Jesus Christ and say—I will not, He will never insist; but I am backing away from the re-creating power of His Redemption. It is a matter of indifference to God's grace how abominable I am if I come to the light; but woe be to me if I refuse the light . . .

--------- Just Between You and God ---------

Take the OPEN 24 HOURS sign flashing in the diner window and imagine it on your soul. God is going to send you someplace. You can't put up the CLOSED sign. You'll miss out on some amazing opportunities.

You are the text. God is going to push SEND to a random number. What are you going to say?

07.19

HAND UP

You call me "Teacher" and "Lord," and rightly so, for that is what I am.

[John 13:13]

The belief that Jesus was the Son of God and through him all things are possible . . . is *entirely* your choice. Once we *decide* to believe that Jesus is the son of God and through him all things are possible . . . we see the world in a way that makes us appreciate that the decision was up to us. If Jesus had made it a requirement, the relationship would be different. He gave us the choice. Jesus lets us come to the conclusion on our own. That is the secret of a relationship with him. He was there all along and was waiting for us to show up. All those times when we couldn't quite make the leap, Jesus was still there waiting to catch us. This way we appreciate so much more when he does.

OZ Says

If our Lord insisted upon obedience He would become a taskmaster, and He would cease to have any authority. He never insists on obedience, but when we do see Him we obey Him instantly. He is easily Lord, and we live in adoration of Him from morning till night. The revelation of my growth in grace is the way in which I look upon obedience. We have to rescue the word "obedience" from the mire.

Just Between You and God

Thank God for the ability to choose whether to believe in him or not. Even if you aren't sure you believe, thank him anyway. If you believe with certainty, thank God for that.

Choosing God is like looking back after you already arrived. It's only hard until you decide.

07.20

THE WHOLE TIME

. . . but those who hope in the LORD will renew their strength. They will soar on wings like eagles; they will run and not grow weary, they will walk and not be faint.

[Isaiah 40:31]

We go for the rush. We go for the thrills out of a desire to push ourselves to extremes. But no bungee jump, no skateboard trick, no leap out of a plane can produce the adrenaline rush we get when we finally experience the presence of God in the fullest sense. God is in a league of his own. The rush of God will affect us mentally, emotionally, spiritually, and in ways we can't even imagine. Then when it happens we'll see something we didn't realize— God was with us through it all.

OZ Says

The reality of God's presence is not dependent on any place, but only dependent upon the determination to set the Lord always before us. Our problems come when we refuse to bank on the reality of His presence. The experience the Psalmist speaks of—"Therefore will we not fear, though . . ." will be ours when once we are based on Reality, not the consciousness of God's presence but the reality of it—Why, He has been here all the time!

Just Between You and God

We put up walls. We think we've got it covered. We think we can handle the stress. We think things will get better if we just put up with a little more or push a little harder. In the meantime, God's wave is getting higher. When you open the door and let him in, it's like nothing you've ever experienced. The rush is waiting.

. . . 6 . . . 5 . . . 4 . . . You have no idea what "extreme" means yet. But you're about to . . . 3 . . . 2 . . . 1 . . .

07.21

DIRECTIONS FROM HERE

Blessed are the poor in spirit, for theirs is the kingdom of heaven.

[Matthew 5:3]

There is a point in the journey with Jesus where we make the leap from man to God. All the books, Sunday school take-home papers, the hymns, the pageants . . . that's all a pre-game. There is another level to understanding. It comes when we understand and completely accept that we will never fully understand. It's too big. It's more than our minds can grasp. It is THEN we can truly understand the blessing. It is then we can truly be ready for what happens next.

OZ Says

Beware of placing Our Lord as a Teacher first. If Jesus Christ is a Teacher only, then all He can do is to tantalize me by erecting a standard I cannot attain. What is the use of presenting me with an ideal I cannot possibly come near? I am happier without knowing it. What is the good of telling me to be what I never can be—to be pure in heart, to do more than my duty, to be perfectly devoted to God? I must know Jesus Christ as Saviour before His teaching has any meaning for me other than that of an ideal which leads to despair. But when I am born again of the Spirit of God, I know that Jesus Christ did not come to teach only: He came to make me what He teaches I should be.

Just Between You and God

Ask God to increase your understanding—even just a little. When you finally come to the understanding that all you can offer God is yourself—that is when he will use you.

It's like asking for the directions without plugging in the destination. Somehow God tells you anyway.

07.22

MAKING SACRED—PART 1

It is God's will that you should be sanctified . . .

[1 Thessalonians 4:3]

This journey is about life and death, but today's thoughts are about death. Does God want you to go belly up in the tank so you can meet him face to face? That would defeat the purpose of being his servant, wouldn't it? God wants your old life to die so that your new life can live. In your old life you've let a lot of things be more important than him. That's what has to go. Your life is still there. You can still live it. But the things that you used to put above God are now gone. What's left is the new you, the one who really wants to please God.

OZ Says

God has to deal with us on the death side as well as on the life side. Many of us spend so much time in the place of death that we get sepulchral. There is always a battle royal before sanctification, always something that tugs with resentment against the demands of Jesus Christ. Immediately the Spirit of God begins to show us what sanctification means, the struggle begins. "If any man come to Me and hate not . . . his own life, he cannot be My disciple."

Just Between You and God

Today, ask God "What is sacred?" God may let you in on what is possible. He may show you a mirror. Once you see what is possible, all that "was" is irrelevant. Everything you were becomes like stone. Are you going to drag it behind you or let it go so you can run?

The perfect road tunes don't matter if you're towing a parked bulldozer.

07.23

MAKING SACRED—PART 2

It is because of him that you are in Christ Jesus, who has become for us wisdom from God—that is, our righteousness, holiness and redemption.

[1 Corinthians 1:30]

We're not role-playing Jesus. That's not the idea. If we want to become truly holy, we don't walk around like actors playing a part. We become sacred when we're willing to say to God, "Okay, I'm ready." Then something happens. All the best parts of Jesus—his love, faith, compassion, kindness, justice, patience, and godliness—all of these become part of us. We're not merely imitating Jesus, we're allowing him to become part of our very being. Once these things become part of us, we can slowly begin to live the life that is worthy of being one with the Son—who is one with the Creator of the universe.

———— OZ Says ————

The one marvellous secret of a holy life lies not in imitating Jesus, but in letting the perfections of Jesus manifest themselves in my mortal flesh. Sanctification is "Christ in you." It is His wonderful life that is imparted by faith as a sovereign gift of God's grace. Am I willing for God to make sanctification as real in me as it is in His word?

———— Just Between You and God ————

Imagine a hole in the window screen. Jesus can weave himself into that hole. Painstakingly slow. Incredibly precise. Jesus can be a part of your life. Now you can open the windows and let the air in. Jesus is part of you.

You remember the "love chapter" in Corinthians? Remember God is love? Now read it again.

07.24
ATTITUDE DETERMINES ALTITUDE

For I tell you that unless your righteousness surpasses that of the Pharisees and the teachers of the law, you will certainly not enter the kingdom of heaven.

[Matthew 5:20]

The Pharisees were a group of religious leaders who spent more time trying to look holy than be holy. If you're giving someone a birthday gift purely because you have to—keep it. Why bother if the sentiment isn't there? Our actions for God work the same way. More important than doing right is being right. A child can break a favorite vase and go to the parent to ask forgiveness. The parent won't hate the child, but will see the child's love and sincerity. Eventually we will all stand before the Almighty Father, who will look at us and see the Christ-like qualities of his own Son. We will be welcomed in.

OZ Says

The purity which God demands is impossible unless I can be remade within, and that is what Jesus has undertaken to do by His Redemption. No man can make himself pure by obeying laws. Jesus Christ does not give us rules and regulations; His teachings are truths that can only be interpreted by the disposition He puts in. The great marvel of Jesus Christ's salvation is that He alters heredity. He does not alter human nature; He alters its mainspring.

Just Between You and God

There is much to learn. Today when you talk with God, ask him to show you the areas you need to work at. You've already asked Jesus in, now ask God what out of the Jesus-supply you need to draw on most right now.

Don't just try and give the right answers . . . try and "be" right. It matters.

07.25

SPIRITUAL GRENADE

Blessed are the poor in spirit, for theirs is the kingdom of heaven.

[Matthew 5:3]

Look up the rest of the Beatitudes (Matt. 5:3–10). They are such familiar little sayings—you've heard them a hundred times. But there's more there than meets the eye. As with many of Jesus' lessons, the full impact hits us later. The lessons explode. Can we really apply what Jesus is saying when we're in the thick of things—when it hurts and goes against all that we've learned about our world? Can we really do this? This is not fluff. This is the full-out assignment for a saint.

─────────── OZ Says ───────────

The teaching of Jesus is out of all proportion to our natural way of looking at things and it comes with astonishing discomfort to begin with. We have slowly to form our walk and conversation on the line of the precepts of Jesus Christ as the Holy Spirit applies them to our circumstances. The Sermon on the Mount is not a set of rules and regulations: it is a statement of the life we will live when the Holy Spirit is getting His way with us.

─────────── Just Between You and God ───────────

This is a two-part prayer today. Ask God to help you remember these lessons when you're in the thick of the situation . . . then ask him for the strength to actually pull it off.

Live your life like a rainbow-colored exploding dye-pack.

07.26

LAUNDRY

But the things that come out of a person's mouth come from the heart, and these defile them. For out of the heart come evil thoughts—murder, adultery, sexual immorality, theft, false testimony, slander. These are what defile a person; but eating with unwashed hands does not defile them.

[Matthew 15:18–20]

If we (and that's a "we" as in everybody) look deep inside ourselves, we'll find things that make us uncomfortable. There are things about us that we don't like to stand up and talk about in front of others. We think if we ignore them they'll go away. We think if we slander someone out of our own warped sense of righteous judgment, it doesn't count as slander. These awful things are inside us all—but they don't exist alone. Deep inside we will also find what is good, pure, and right. By asking Jesus to help and by allowing God to come into our hearts, the good inside of us will win over the bad.

―――――――― OZ Says ――――――――

We begin by trusting our ignorance and calling it innocence, by trusting our innocence and calling it purity; and when we hear these rugged statements of Our Lord's, we shrink and say—but I never felt any of those awful things in my heart. We resent what Jesus Christ reveals. Either Jesus Christ is the supreme Authority on the human heart, or He is not worth paying any attention to.

―――――― Just Between You and God ――――――

Invite God in today. Don't be afraid for him to see what's inside. You're human. But when God is a living, breathing part of your existence, you can be the person God wants you to be.

Good. Bad. God. Human. Mix well. Pour.

07.27

CERTAINTY

Anyone who chooses to do the will of God will find out whether my teaching comes from God or whether I speak on my own.

[John 7:17]

Science and faith are unusual things. Science will tell you the size of the universe as best it can. As we grow, so does our ability to explain our place in the universe. I'll say that again. This time read it not in a science mind but in a God-mind. Ready? As we grow, so does our ability to explain our place in the universe. Got it? To study the universe with the science-mind, you must use a telescope. To study the universe with a God-mind, you must use the Word of God. Biblical truth won't help if you don't get off your chair and do something with what you've learned. Until you begin to live the life that God intended for you, you won't increase your understanding of the universe around you and why you are here.

—————————— OZ Says ——————————

No man ever receives a word from God without instantly being put to the test over it. We disobey and then wonder why we don't go on spiritually. "If when you come to the altar," said Jesus, "there you remember your brother hath ought against you . . . don't say another word to Me, but first go and put that thing right." The teaching of Jesus hits us where we live. We cannot stand as humbugs before Him for one second. He educates us down to the scruple. The Spirit of God unearths the spirit of self-vindication; He makes us sensitive to things we never thought of before.

—————————— Just Between You and God ——————————

Stare at the stars all you want. Imagine other planets and say, "God send me!" But be ready. God may send you next door to the neighbor who simply needs help with her windows. With God there is no zero.

God can keep answering the question "What was before that?" God can also answer "What happens next?"

07.28

RECALCULATING

Immediately Jesus made his disciples get into the boat and go on ahead of him . . .

[Mark 6:45]

Okay, so now I'm loving God. I'm working every day to follow the lessons of Jesus, and if I keep doing this, God will allow me to be successful. Right? Buzzzzzzzz. I'm sorry, that's not correct, but thanks for playing our game.

We have this mistaken notion that our following will lead us somewhere. To God, the fact that we're following is the success. That is the end result. God may not lead you to wealth or to what the world considers success. In fact, it may wind up being the exact opposite. Jesus walked on the water. He didn't want to catch a ride in the boat. He was not near the shore. He was just out there in the middle of the wind and the rain. This is where this following may lead you—into the storm. But you will not be there alone. You will be walking into the wide open arms of Jesus.

OZ Says

God's training is for now, not presently. His purpose is for this minute, not for something in the future. We have nothing to do with the afterwards of obedience; we get wrong when we think of the afterwards. What men call training and preparation, God calls the end.

Just Between You and God

Don't be the kid in God's backseat saying, "Are we there yet? Are we there yet? Are we there yet?" There is a whole world out the window. Pay attention to the journey. You'll miss something if you're too hung up on the destination.

Jesus didn't say, "I am the destination." He said, "I am the way." Jesus is the journey itself.

07.29

LOOK, UP IN THE SKY!

"Look, he is coming with the clouds," and "every eye will see him, even those who pierced him"; and all peoples on earth "will mourn because of him." So shall it be! Amen.

[Revelation 1:7]

Remember when you were a kid and someone told you that thunder was just the angels bowling? How about this one? The clouds are just the dust on God's shoes. Throughout the Bible, clouds are associated with the presence of God, the white clouds that drift on a summer day and the dark clouds that tell us there's a storm ahead.

God doesn't come to us in a full glaring light that spells out everything in obvious terms. God may come to us in the clouds or the light peeking out from behind. He lets us know he's there and at the same time asks for our faith. We need to think of ourselves as children sitting on a grassy hill and making pictures from the shape of the clouds. The faith is simple. The imagination is supreme. The relationship with God—simple.

OZ Says

What a revelation it is to know that sorrow and bereavement and suffering are the clouds that come along with God! God cannot come near without clouds, He does not come in clear shining. It is not true to say that God wants to teach us something in our trials: through every cloud He brings, He wants us to unlearn something. His purpose in the cloud is to simplify our belief until our relationship to Him is exactly that of a child—God and my own soul . . .

Just Between You and God

Stare at some clouds today or at least remember a time when you did. Thank God for his continual presence when you're aware of it . . . and when you're not.

"Sky"—it's a much bigger word than you imagine. Now think of the word "Encompass." Combine them.

07.30

HERE AND NOW

But Jesus would not entrust himself to them, for he knew all people. He did not need any testimony about mankind, for he knew what was in each person.

[John 2:24–25]

Many of us live with illusions. We think things are one way, and when we learn otherwise, it's like having the rug pulled out from under us. Jesus saw human beings for who they are—flawed and imperfect. Too many followers of Jesus think that following makes them Jesus, so they have the right to point out the flaws and imperfections of others. These people are missing the point.

Jesus saw our flaws and imperfections and loved us anyway. He didn't judge. He didn't accuse. He knew everything that could possibly be wrong with the human race and still was willing to be nailed to a tree so we would eventually get the idea. Awakening from our illusions may be unsettling, but it shouldn't make us cynical. It should open our eyes to what Jesus was trying to teach us and how amazing it is that he did what he did.

─────────── OZ Says ───────────

Disillusionment means that there are no more false judgments in life. To be undeceived by disillusionment may leave us cynical and unkindly severe in our judgment of others, but the disillusionment, which comes from God, brings us to the place where we see men and women as they really are, and yet there is no cynicism, we have no stinging, bitter things to say.

─────── Just Between You and God ───────

Being a follower of Christ does not mean we only see the rainbows after the storm. It means we see the storm's destruction, pain in its wake, the suffering in the rebuilding. We see all that and love God anyway.

Open your eyes. See. Don't turn away. This is what it's all about.

07.31

SHINE

Let perseverance finish its work so that you may be mature and complete, not lacking anything.

[James 1:4]

Ever watch a parent walking with a child in a mall? Distractions like toys in windows and ice cream shops make little kids go scrambling off on their own. The parent then brings the child back and says, "Stay beside me." God often shows us the way, but we get distracted and go scrambling off on our own. God brings us back and says, "Stay beside me." Eventually, like children, we get the idea. Once God is sure we're going to stay with him, he can move onto the next lesson. "Look both ways." "Don't touch." "Listen." One by one we learn. God doesn't run out of patience. He sees what the finished product will be.

————————— OZ Says —————————

Not only must our relationship to God be right, but the external expression of that relationship must be right. Ultimately God will let nothing escape, every detail is under His scrutiny. In numberless ways God will bring us back to the same point over and over again. He never tires of bringing us to the one point until we learn the lesson, because He is producing the finished product.

————— Just Between You and God —————

The only thing you get to say to God today is . . . "I'm listening." If you start to add more, shut up. You can't say "I'm listening" and then interrupt. Listen with your mind, body, and soul, and God will let you know.

Think of all those instructions you received when you were just starting to learn to read. Now apply them to your understanding of God. You'll get there.

08.01

IMPATIENCE

After Jesus had finished instructing his twelve disciples, he went on from there to teach and preach in the towns of Galilee.

[Matthew 11:1]

God tells you when to go. God tells you where to go, but he may not tell you what to do when you get there. Part of serving God is waiting for him. Ever play checkers? Have you ever tried to set up that one big move where you can jump your piece from one side of the board to the other? God works this way. All things must be in place, and then he begins to move. If you've said, "I'm your servant, God," then he'll place you where you need to be. The big move may come right away, or you may have to be patient. This does not mean you sit with your hands folded and twiddle your thumbs. If something is coming, you have to make yourself ready. Even if you don't know what it is, you have to be ready when the time comes.

——————————— OZ Says ———————————

Are we playing the spiritual amateur providence in other lives? Are we so noisy in our instruction of others that God cannot get anywhere near them? We have to keep our mouths shut and our spirits alert. God wants to instruct us in regard to His Son, He wants to turn our times of prayer into mounts of transfiguration, and we will not let Him. When we are certain of the way God is going to work, He will never work in that way any more.

——————— Just Between You and God ———————

Pay attention. You must be ready. God decides when you have a teachable moment in front of you. God will show it to you. You must wait for this moment like you wait for the red light to turn green. Do not check your phone or play with the radio. God's "Go" is coming.

Who? What? When? Where? Why? And how? Never thought of them as prayers, did you?

08.02

COME AGAIN NO MORE

I have told you these things, so that in me you may have peace. In this world you will have trouble. But take heart! I have overcome the world.

[John 16:33]

People have the wrong idea about Christianity. They think it means that God will solve all their problems. That's the wrong way to look at it. Being a Christian doesn't mean that God will rescue you from your troubles—it means that God will rescue you in your troubles. Isn't that the same thing? No. You can't appreciate amazing blessings if you have no troubles. You can't appreciate light unless you're in a dark place. When everything that can go wrong, does, God will be there beside you. He will give you hope, strength, patience, and love. Will he reach down and pick you up out of the muck and mire? Not always, but he did promise to be in the muck and mire with you and guide you until you are once again on solid footing.

OZ Says

If you are a child of God, there certainly will be troubles to meet, but Jesus says do not be surprised when they come. "In the world ye shall have tribulation: but be of good cheer, I have overcome the world, there is nothing for you to fear."

Just Between You and God

Don't ask God for things. Don't ask God for intervention. Don't ask God for a song in your heart. Today just ask God for his presence. Ask for him to simply be there. You can do this on your own. It helps to have a hand on your shoulder.

Sometimes you don't need an answer or a solution or a suggestion . . . you just need someone to listen. God is here.

08.03

COMING SOON

Jesus took the Twelve aside and told them, "We are going up to Jerusalem, and everything that is written by the prophets about the Son of Man will be fulfilled."

[Luke 18:31]

Jesus knew that by going to Jerusalem he was heading for the conclusion of his time here on earth. God has a plan for each and every one of us. Our goal must not be to become what we want, but to become what God wants us to be. These could be the same, but often they're not. We may start down one path without any thought as to "Is this where I am supposed to go?" We will face life-changing choices until we're finally heading in the direction that God wants. The frustrating part is that once we start on the path, the goal doesn't necessarily become clearer. We don't always get to see the flashing light in the distance that lets us know we're close. We just need to walk. God will let us know the *wheres*, *whens*, and *whys* when we need to know. In the meantime, we just get to keep the faith and keep walking.

OZ Says

The great thing to remember is that we go up to Jerusalem to fulfill God's purpose, not our own. Naturally, our ambitions are our own; in the Christian life we have no aim of our own. There is so much said today about our decisions for Christ, our determination to be Christians, our decisions for this and that, but in the New Testament it is the aspect of God's compelling that is brought out. "Ye have not chosen Me, but I have chosen you." We are not taken up into conscious agreement with God's purpose; we are taken up into God's purpose without any consciousness at all.

Just Between You and God

Don't ask God for directions. Don't ask for a vision of your future. Ask him, "Right here. Right now. Is this where you want me?"

The lessons come from the journey, not the arrival. If you are still on the journey, you still have lessons to learn.

08.04

TRAVEL LIGHT

Jesus took the Twelve aside and told them, "We are going up to Jerusalem, and everything that is written by the prophets about the Son of Man will be fulfilled."

[Luke 18:31]

As you walk along, you may want to leave some things by the side of the road—pride, for instance. Those who walk along with their noses in the air thinking, "Look at me. I'm walking with God," will more than likely stumble and find themselves biting the dust. You might think you have amazing abilities that you can use for God along the way. That's good, but you don't need them. All you need on this path is you. Just you. Nothing else. Anything else you need on the way God will give you because he's always there. If you think, "I'm nothing. I have nothing to offer," then you're in the best position because that is how God wants you to walk with him. Anything else would mean you have your own ideas and they would just get in the way.

OZ Says

The bravery of God in trusting us! You say—"But He has been unwise to choose me, because there is nothing in me; I am not of any value." That is why He chose you. As long as you think there is something in you, He cannot choose you because you have ends of your own to serve; but if you have let Him bring you to the end of your self-sufficiency then He can choose you to go with Him to Jerusalem, and that will mean the fulfillment of purposes which He does not discuss with you.

Just Between You and God

You don't need an agenda. You need a traveling companion. Ask God to ride shot-gun. God knows the best road tunes. God knows how to work the GPS. God will even pick the pickles off your burger. You are on this journey for the long haul. There's nothing that says you have to travel alone. Pray for company.

The road is long but not lonely . . . scary but not debilitating . . . dangerous but not unpassable. By the way, Jesus likes to sing from the passenger seat.

08.05

OBJECTS IN THE MIRROR

The disciples did not understand any of this. Its meaning was hidden from them, and they did not know what he was talking about.

[Luke 18:34]

By every standard of today, Jesus' ministry was a failure. He chose the worst possible people to follow him. One of his best friends betrayed him. His own town turned against him. He was beaten and killed, and his ministry was scattered to the winds. But by God's standards, it was the greatest triumph. When we're on the path and wondering what's in store for us, we wonder based on the standards we already know. We don't know what God has in mind. We don't know God's measuring stick. Once we are in communion with God, we will stop asking.

――――――― OZ Says ―――――――

There comes the baffling call of God in our lives also. The call of God can never be stated explicitly; it is implicit. The call of God is like the call of the sea; no one hears it but the one who has the nature of the sea in him. It cannot be stated definitely what the call of God is to, because His call is to be in comradeship with Himself for His own purposes, and the test is to believe that God knows what He is after. The things that happen do not happen by chance, they happen entirely in the decree of God. God is working out His purposes.

――――――― Just Between You and God ―――――――

You may be standing looking at the mountain ahead of you, but if you turn around you'll see the wreckage of everything that tried to stop you from getting to this point. You're here. The mountain is large. God got you this far. Pray and ask for his continued presence.

Can you turn off the GPS and keep driving? Just enjoy the road.

08.06

ANYBODY LISTENING?

In that day you will ask in my name. I am not saying that I will ask the Father on your behalf.

[John 16:26]

Why pray? If God knows us, has a plan, and knows our problems before we tell him, then what is the point of praying? Isn't it a waste of time?

The point of prayer is not to get an answer from God. If you're only praying to get answers, then you're praying for all the wrong reasons. Prayers that seem unanswered open the door for you to get angry and frustrated because the answer doesn't come when you want it, in the way you want. The point of prayer is to communicate with God. Jesus said he wanted us to be one with the Father. How can you do that if you don't talk to God or listen to him? Prayer is communication, not a monologue. Does it seem like you're talking to yourself? Then perhaps you should listen to what you're saying.

--------- OZ Says ---------

We are too much given to thinking of the Cross as something we have to get through; we get through it only in order to get into it. The Cross stands for one thing only for us—a complete and entire and absolute identification with the Lord Jesus Christ, and there is nothing in which this identification is realized more than in prayer.

--------- Just Between You and God ---------

Let's put it into practice. Pray—but don't put expectations on the time or tone of an answer. God is listening. Just talk. You talk to friends. You talk to strangers every day. Just talk to God.

God answers all prayers. Sometimes the answer is no. Deal with it.

08.07

SANCTUARY

"Why were you searching for me?" he asked. "Didn't you know I had to be in my Father's house?"

[Luke 2:49]

When do you talk with the Father? Do you wait until things go wrong and then ask God to bail you out? Things aren't what you want them to be today, so do you pray and ask God to turn them around?

Sometimes we may legitimately need the help of God, and we hit our knees in desperation and ask for help. There's nothing wrong with that, but do we also say, "Thanks," when we get what we asked for? Do we compliment God on the wonderful day, as well as complain about the bad ones? We should forever be aware of the presence of our heavenly Father in our lives.

OZ Says

Narrow it down to your individual circumstances—are you so identified with the Lord's life that you are simply a child of God, continually talking to Him and realizing that all things come from His hands? Is the Eternal Child in you living in the Father's house? Are the graces of His ministering life working out through you in your home, in your business, in your domestic circle? Have you been wondering why you are going through the things you are? It is not that you have to go through them; it is because of the relation into which the Son of God has come in His Father's providence in your particular sainthood. Let Him have His way, keep in perfect union with Him.

Just Between You and God

Pray constantly today. Pray in the drive-thru line. Pray on the school bus. Pray as you open your locker. Pray as you wait for your video game to load. Let today be about quantity. God has been waiting to hear. Try saying "Hey Dad" instead of "Oh heavenly Father." Listen with the same attitude.

You know that little vertical-line icon at the top or bottom of your computer screen? The one that says you're connected? Be that.

08.08

DECEN-DANCE

The angel answered, "The Holy Spirit will come on you, and the power of the Most High will overshadow you. So the holy one to be born will be called the Son of God."

[Luke 1:35]

The angel of God came to a normal, everyday young lady and said, "Surprise! It's you." The Creator of the universe arrived on this earth in human form owing, in large part, to the obedience of a normal, everyday girl. We're not that different from Mary. Jesus exists on this planet today . . . in us. We are the bodily representation of him. If we're here, then he's here. We know that when Jesus was here on earth he was in constant contact with his Father. So, if Jesus is here . . . now . . . in us . . . living in us by his spirit, we need to be in contact with God, just like Jesus was. All those things Jesus did when he was here on earth, he can still do through us. Because of this: Jesus is still around.

OZ Says

Is the Son of God praying in me or am I dictating to Him? Is He ministering in me as He did in the days of His flesh? Is the Son of God in me going through His passion for His own purposes? The more one knows of the inner life of God's ripest saints, the more one sees what God's purpose is—"filling up that which is behind of the affliction of Christ." There is always something to be done in the sense of "filling up."

Just Between You and God

Mary accepted the responsibility of bringing Jesus into the world. She was a little surprised and probably more than a little shocked, but we know she said, "I am the Lord's servant" without hesitation. So should we. Use these words when you pray today. Ask what you can do for God, not the other way around.

Jesus said he'd be here always. He was right. Look in the mirror.

08.09

CONNECTIONS

So they took away the stone. Then Jesus looked up and said, "Father, I thank you that you have heard me."

[John 11:41]

Follow along. Stay with me. Here we go . . . Jesus and God are one. Jesus said so. He told his disciples. Jesus also wants to be one with us. So Jesus and I are one. Jesus is in me; therefore God is in me also. You are there too. You and Jesus, you and God, God and you—all one. Got that? Now, God is a three in one—Father, Son, and Holy Spirit. The Holy Spirit is God's presence here on earth. He moves like wind. (Sometimes like a storm.) Jesus and God and the Holy Spirit are one. You are one with them. It's all about connections. Now, if you've asked Jesus to be a part of you, you are part of this connection. If we're willing to make that connection with God, Jesus, and the Holy Spirit, we have to live our lives as part of that connection. We live our every-day-walking-around lives with God in us. What a privilege!

OZ Says

Is the Son of God getting His chance in me? Is the direct simplicity of the life of God's Son being worked out exactly as it was worked out in His historic life? When I come in contact with the occurrences of life as an ordinary human being, is the prayer of God's Eternal Son to His Father being prayed in me? "In that day ye shall ask in My name . . ." What day? The day when the Holy Ghost has come to me and made me effectually one with my Lord.

Just Between You and God

Notice the wi-fi icon grows upward and outward. The farther we are away from the source, the more distance we cover. This is why we need others. Let there be no place that we cannot make someone else feel connected. Pray to God today for coverage.

Life is wireless. The possibilities are endless.

08.10

EXPECT DELAYS

So then, those who suffer according to God's will should commit themselves to their faithful Creator and continue to do good.

[1 Peter 4:19]

Some people take the hard path for all the wrong reasons. If God tells you to take the hard path, then by all means take the hard path. If God says, let's take the easy road . . . do not say, "No my father let me suffer for thee. I will walk the hardest path!" Suffering needlessly does not impress God. Obedience impresses God. Suffering needlessly is usually about wanting people to see you suffer for God, in which case it becomes about you . . . not God. Go where God sends you. If you suffer on purpose, you're wasting your time . . . and God's.

—————————— OZ Says ——————————

To choose to suffer means that there is something wrong; to choose God's will even if it means suffering is a very different thing. No healthy saint ever chooses suffering; he chooses God's will, as Jesus did, whether it means suffering or not. No saint dare interfere with the discipline of suffering in another saint.

—————— Just Between You and God ——————

Pray this: "I'll go where you send me." Then listen. If God doesn't want you to walk through hard times, why would you put yourself there? If God does want you to walk through hard times (for reasons he'll explain later), then why would you do anything else?

Take the hard road. But only if God says, "Take the hard road."

08.11

GONE GONE GONE

Elisha saw this and cried out, "My father! My father! The chariots and horsemen of Israel!" And Elisha saw him no more. Then he took hold of his garment and tore it in two.

[2 Kings 2:12]

One of the wonderful things about following the way of Jesus is that we're rarely alone. God provides us with mentors, teachers, and friends to walk beside us. They encourage and lift us up when we fall down. They are gifts from God. However, eventually we hit the point when we must travel alone. As much as we want to take a friend with us when life gets scary, there are certain times when we must face life on our own. We take what we've learned. We take his love. We take the knowledge that God is with us. And we venture off by ourselves. Sometimes the path splits and we must choose one. Sometimes we are called to make our own path, but God is always with us.

―――――――― OZ Says ――――――――

It is not wrong to depend upon Elijah as long as God gives him to you, but remember the time will come when he will have to go; when he stands no more to you as your guide and leader, because God does not intend he should. You say—"I cannot go on without Elijah." God says you must.

―――― Just Between You and God ――――

When you come to the great chasm and the bridge is barely wide enough for one person to cross at a time, this does not mean you leave God behind at the edge. It doesn't mean God must be waiting for you at the end. God is beside you always. Everywhere. Every moment. You aren't alone even if you feel like you are.

Ask for the light. Ask for the song. Ask for the reminder in the scary moments: Go by yourself but go with God.

08.12

PANIC

He replied, "You of little faith, why are you so afraid?" Then he got up and rebuked the winds and the waves, and it was completely calm.

[Matthew 8:26]

People who haven't chosen to follow God usually pray only when their circumstances get really bad. They seldom give God a second thought until the bottom falls out of their lives and then they hit their knees. You're different. You've made a choice to follow God. For you to revert to panic prayers is like saying, "Yeah, I believe you're a kind and loving God with my best interests at heart, but do you see what I'm going through here?" As a believer, you have confidence in God that unbelievers don't have. It's this confidence that will carry you to the breaking point and beyond. Others hit that point and fall apart. You won't. You have faith. Others may start looking to you when they lose their footing because you're always on solid ground.

OZ Says

"O ye of little faith!" What a pang must have shot through the disciples— "Missed it again!" And what a pang will go through us when we suddenly realize that we might have produced downright joy in the heart of Jesus by remaining absolutely confident in Him, no matter what was ahead.

Just Between You and God

Pray this: "God I'm yours." Say it with as much confidence as you can muster. When walking into a storm . . . "God I'm yours." When you feel like you've been beaten down . . . "God I'm yours." When you reach the summit of your climb . . . "God I'm yours." It's an all-purpose prayer. Pray it like you mean it.

Say what you mean. Mean what you say. One thing leads to another.

08.13

A BETTER LIGHT

Do not quench the Spirit.

[1 Thessalonians 5:19]

Ever hang out with a group of friends and notice there's always one person who doesn't want to do anything? "Hey, why don't we . . ." "Yeah, let's do that." "Sure, that'd be great," and then one voice says, "Nah, we better not. We'll get in trouble. That's boring. I don't feel like it."

The spirit of God is around you all the time. He's like a flame that doesn't burn, who leaps, jumps, and surrounds you, and if you turn yourself off to his presence, it's just like that friend who kills the spirit of every idea. Feeling the presence of God is not a one-time thing. It didn't happen to you once a long time ago. It's happening all the time. If you don't feel it, then perhaps the problem isn't that the Holy Spirit hasn't come by in a while, perhaps it's that you haven't been around to answer the door.

————————— OZ Says —————————

If you get out of the light you become a sentimental Christian and live on memories, your testimony has a hard, metallic note. Beware of trying to patch up a present refusal to walk in the light by recalling past experiences when you did walk in the light. Whenever the Spirit checks, call a halt and get the thing right, or you will go on grieving Him without knowing it.

————— Just Between You and God —————

Closing your eyes, sticking your fingers in your hears and screaming "lalala-lalalalalalalala!" is not the best way to go through life. It's amazing how many people do this when it comes to the Holy Spirit. The Spirit is there like it or not. You can't not be in the presence. Connect and be part of something bigger than yourself.

There is more to the "presence" than being present. Actions speak louder.

08.14

TARGET

And have you completely forgotten this word of encouragement that addresses you as a father addresses his son? It says, "My son, do not make light of the Lord's discipline, and do not lose heart when he rebukes you."

[Hebrews 12:5]

Don't think being on this journey is going to make you perfect. We make mistakes. We do really stupid things. Sometimes God has to reach down and whack us to get our attention. It hurts. If God sends a smack, don't get upset about it. Don't say, "Oh, God hates me. I must be a wretch not worthy of living. Oh why, oh why, oh why?" Give it a rest. If God wants you to change your current behavior, he'll let you know. So learn, change, and keep moving. We're big enough to take a few lumps if we deserve them. That's part of the journey.

─────────── OZ Says ───────────

Never quench the Spirit, and do not despise Him when He says to you—"Don't be blind on this point any more; you are not where you thought you were. Up to the present I have not been able to reveal it to you, but I reveal it now." When the Lord chastens you like that, let Him have His way. Let Him relate you rightly to God.

─────────── Just Between You and God ───────────

Sometimes you have to lose your footing and fall back down to the bottom to learn where to put your feet. Today, thank God for the pain caused by the correction. It serves as the reminder and the teacher. Just think how banged up you'd be if you fell from higher up?

The mistakes you made are in the past. Piled by the side of the road. Why are you setting up a memorial to them? Move on.

08.15

REFRESHED

You should not be surprised at my saying, "You must be born again."

[John 3:7]

A sking Jesus to be a part of your everyday life is like being offered a drink of water while crossing the desert. It would be unbelievable to think you would just keep walking and sweating and never drink. When Jesus talks about being born again he's saying, "Helloooo . . . right here, have a sip." But we choose to keep right on walking. We must make the conscious choice to drink, be refreshed, and to stop wandering around hot and sweaty. Seems like that'd be an easy choice, doesn't it? You'd be surprised, *my friend*, you'd be surprised.

OZ Says

The answer to the question "How can a man be born when he is old?" is— When he is old enough to die—to die right out to his "rag rights," to his virtues, to his religion, to everything, and to receive into himself the life which never was there before. The new life manifests itself in conscious repentance and unconscious holiness.

Just Between You and God

Once someone offers you the "drink" and you choose not to take it, the onus is on you. No more complaining about the heat. You had a choice and you didn't drink. The good part is that you can still ask and it will still be there.

You know how sometimes you just have to hold the can to your forehead before drinking? God is like that.

08.16

HEY! _____ (YOUR NAME HERE)

The gatekeeper opens the gate for him, and the sheep listen to his voice. He calls his own sheep by name and leads them out.

[John 10:3]

A mother was once shopping for groceries with her son. She pushed the cart while he followed behind texting to his friends with his phone. She made a left turn into the cereal aisle and he kept walking. She decided to let him go. She spotted him a few minutes later following another woman, with a similar coat, through the store. She called his name just before he tried to put a jar of peanut butter in the other woman's cart.

He put the phone in his pocket and pushed his mother's cart through the rest of the store. Sometimes we follow like lost sheep because following is what we do. It is when God calls us by name that we are snapped to attention. (Hopefully before we do something stupid.) When God calls our name, the only response is to put the phone away and be a part of the world around us.

—————————— OZ Says ——————————

Have I a personal history with Jesus Christ? The one sign of discipleship is intimate connection with Him, a knowledge of Jesus Christ which nothing can shake.

—————— Just Between You and God ——————

Thank God today for his persistence. He really loves you—that's why he keeps calling. The plan he has is bigger than your doubts. First thank. Then listen.

Now Hear This!! (You're supposed to stop there and listen. Kind of what it means.)

08.17

HEARD

When Jesus heard this, he said to him, "You still lack one thing. Sell everything you have and give to the poor, and you will have treasure in heaven. Then come, follow me."

[Luke 18:22]

One of the sobering things about walking this path is that we often understand more than we're willing to admit. We hear Jesus' words and understand what's expected of us and yet—because it's hard—we choose not to obey. We say, "I don't understand. I'm still studying it," when the truth is we understand perfectly well. We're choosing not to act because it will hurt, it may alienate our friends, or it could cause disruption in our family. God knows perfectly well what's on our minds. He also knows that sooner or later we'll choose to obey. When that moment comes is entirely up to us. God won't push. He says, "Here's the lesson. Take it or leave it." Which do you do?

--------------------- OZ Says ---------------------

Have I ever heard Jesus say a hard word? Has He said something personally to me to which I have deliberately listened? . . . Our Lord knows perfectly that when once His word is heard, it will bear fruit sooner or later. The terrible thing is that some of us prevent it bearing fruit in actual life. I wonder what we will say when we do make up our minds to be devoted to Him on that particular point? One thing is certain, He will never cast anything up at us.

--------------------- Just Between You and God ---------------------

Nobody likes a whiner. God doesn't need you to tell him some of his lessons are hard. He knows. Instead of praying for God to take this heavy burden from our shoulders, ask for patience, persistence, or whatever it is you think you need to learn the lesson God is trying to teach you at the moment.

Here's the lesson. Learn it now. Learn it later. Your choice. (Personally, I'd say the sooner the better.)

08.18

BLANK

When he heard this, he became very sad, because he was very wealthy.

Luke 18:23

Do you think your pile of stuff impresses God? You can have the complete collection of . . . well . . . just about anything, and it isn't going to get you a spot at God's table. Likewise, you can bring nothing to the table except your intelligence, and that's not going to get you very far either. God doesn't want your things. God doesn't want your mind. God wants you—nothing more, nothing less. God wants you to come to him with a blank canvas. Don't come to God with expectations of what you will receive, or with a preconceived notion of what you can do for God. Notice in the Bible story that Jesus didn't chase after the man. He won't chase after you either, but he will be there when you finally get it and come back to him like a clean canvas and say, "Use me, I'm yours."

---------------- OZ Says ----------------

I can be so rich in poverty, so rich in the consciousness that I am nobody, that I shall never be a disciple of Jesus; and I can be so rich in the consciousness that I am somebody that I shall never be a disciple. Am I willing to be destitute of the sense that I am destitute? This is where discouragement comes in. Discouragement is disenchanted self-love, and self-love may be love of my devotion to Jesus.

---------------- Just Between You and God ----------------

You may be a great artist (builder, writer, coach, analyst) but if you go to God with your own plan for how wonderful your life could be, you're going to be disappointed. God already knows what he wants for you. It's better to let him tell you than stuff his suggestion box.

Anything God wants . . . God can have. He is God, after all. Everything except you. That part is a choice.

08.19

KNOWN

Come to me, all you who are weary and burdened.

[Matthew 11:28]

Picture yourself driving in a sleet storm. The rain freezes almost as instantly as it hits your windshield. The roads are treacherous and you can't keep going. Up ahead is a flashing neon sign: *Open All Night.* You pull in. A kind waitress gives you hot coffee and conversation. A favorite song comes on the jukebox. As you look out the window, you see that the sign is now flashing *Jesus* in bright neon letters. You're safe. All of this . . . the atmosphere, the combination of securities is what it's like to live in the heart of Christ. We have to be willing to be a part of Jesus with all our senses. We have to be willing to be part of Christ morally, spiritually, intellectually, emotionally, and whole-heartedly. Anything that we hold back and keep for ourselves is wasted.

OZ Says

Never allow the dividing up of your life in Christ to remain without facing it. Beware of leakage, of the dividing up of your life by the influence of friends or of circumstances; beware of anything that is going to split up your oneness with Him and make you see yourself separately. Nothing is so important as to keep right spiritually. The great solution is the simple one—"Come unto Me."

Just Between You and God

Jesus is like a big plate of hot fluffy blueberry pancakes (insert your own favorite diner food if it helps.) The moment the plate hits the table, you know all is right with the world . . . even if it's just for that moment. It's allllllll good. Jesus wants you to feel that way *every* moment.

"Got your back" is an understatement. Jesus starts from the inside out. He's got it all.

08.20

WHOLE

. . . I will give you rest.

[Matthew 11:28]

There comes a point on this journey when we no longer ask questions about the existence of God. We don't ask if God answers prayers. We know that. We don't ask if Jesus was real. We know that too. But do we know it with our hearts? When we pray, there should be no question in our minds about whether or not our prayers will be answered. We may not get the answer we want, but we know there'll be an answer. We stop looking for evidence and proof about God because we know he exists. There's solidity in arriving at this place. It's the point where the concrete hardens and there are no more questions about the reality of God. The questions of where, what, why, and how are natural and may continue, but the basic idea of yes or no about God is gone.

OZ Says

The complete life is the life of a child. When I am consciously conscious, there is something wrong. It is the sick man who knows what health is. The child of God is not conscious of the will of God because he is the will of God. When there has been the slightest deviation from the will of God, we begin to ask— What is Thy will? A child of God never prays to be conscious that God answers prayer, he is so restfully certain that God always does answer prayer.

Just Between You and God

Be convinced. Nothing can separate you from God. When you pray, have no doubt that you are heard. NO doubt. NONE. If you don't get what you want, it doesn't mean you were ignored. It means God knows better.

Water is wet. Air is necessary. Try and pray with the same certainty.

08.21

BACKSTAGE

Blessed are the poor in spirit, for theirs is the kingdom of heaven.

[Matthew 5:3]

For every movie star who steps up to accept an award, there are many others who deserve to stand there also—the make-up girl, the lighting guy, the grip, the gaffer, the producer, the director, and the screenplay writer—to name a few. All of these helped put the star on the stage. Our world is full of these others. While the world gives standing ovations to those in the spotlight, Jesus said the ones who will receive special blessings from God are those who'll never take a bow, never get a private dressing room, and never see their faces on the front page. The back stagers are the truly blessed. Think about the people who have influenced you the most. Most likely they're the ones who never realized the impact they've had on our lives—teachers, parents, ministers, tutors, friends—these are the blessed.

OZ Says

At the basis of Jesus Christ's Kingdom is the unaffected loveliness of the commonplace. The thing I am blessed in is my poverty. If I know I have no strength of will, no nobility of disposition, then Jesus says—Blessed are you, because it is through this poverty that I enter His Kingdom. I cannot enter His Kingdom as a good man or woman, I can only enter it as a pauper. The true character of the loveliness that tells for God is always unconscious.

Just Between You and God

Thank God for the stagehands. Those people never get credit or sometimes even a second look, but every one of them played a part in getting you there. Think of the obvious ones, then the not-so-obvious, then the completely missed. Ask God to bless them all and say thank you.

You can be in the play but you are not "of" the play. Say your lines and then hang out with the cast backstage.

08.22

IN BETWEENS

I baptize you with water for repentance. But after me comes one who is more powerful than I, whose sandals I am not worthy to carry. He will baptize you with the Holy Spirit and fire.

[Matthew 3:11]

There are pages in the back of this book with blankness on them. In a manner of speaking, it's in life's blank spots where we will meet Jesus. This book and books like it are full of thoughts and ideas to make you think, but it's in the blank places, the blank moments, where Jesus comes. Our lives can be made up of one good or one bad action after another, but when we're willing to break down and say, "You know what? I'm lost," Jesus will come. In the places where we have no expectations, in the places where we have no attitudes, in those blank places—we will meet Jesus.

—————————— OZ Says ——————————

I indeed am at an end, I cannot do a thing: but He begins just there—He does the things no one else can ever do. Am I prepared for His coming? Jesus cannot come as long as there is anything in the way either of goodness or badness. When He comes am I prepared for Him to drag into the light every wrong thing I have done? It is just there that He comes. Wherever I know I am unclean, He will put His feet; wherever I think I am clean, He will withdraw them.

————— Just Between You and God —————

Be a blank page for God. Even if there's a slight part of you that wants to say, "It's not my fault," or "This isn't really a bad thing to do," you're not yet blank. Pray and give God everything you are carrying.

Walk on new snow. Be the first to break the surface of the peanut butter. This is the life you give to God.

08.23

BETWEEN YOU AND GOD

But when you pray, go into your room, close the door and pray to your Father, who is unseen. Then your Father, who sees what is done in secret, will reward you.

[Matthew 6:6]

Maybe you have a special place where you like to pray—a quiet room, a sanctuary, a tree, a rooftop. These are all good places to pray. Prayer is a conversation between you and the Almighty. There should be no distractions. A prayer closet is a good thing, whatever form it takes. A prayer closet must also be mental. We must learn to shut out the distractions of this crazy world. We must concentrate on our prayer and focus on what we're saying. Eventually we can become so focused that our prayer closet can be found on a crowded bus, in a classroom, or in a stadium full of cheering fans.

─────────── OZ Says ───────────

Jesus didn't say—Dream about thy Father in secret—but pray to thy Father in secret. Prayer is an effort of the will. After we have entered our secret place and have shut the door, the most difficult thing to do is to pray; we cannot get our minds into working order, and the first thing that conflicts is wandering thoughts. The great battle in private prayer is the overcoming of mental wool-gathering. We have to discipline our minds and concentrate on willful prayer.

─────────── Just Between You and God ───────────

Even with your hands in the dishwater, you can be a thousand miles away. Alone. Soaring in the stars. Taking in the wonder of the universe while you scrub dried cereal off a bowl. Pray today in the crowded place. Just don't let your mind be crowded.

Pray. Just pray. Now.

08.24

ALLOW TO RISE

Which of you, if his son asks for bread, will give him a stone?

[Matthew 7:9]

Imagine a bakery where the breads, cookies, and pastries are so delicious they can't be measured on a chart. There aren't enough stars to properly rate the work of this baker. Now imagine that all of these sweet treats are free and it's at the baker's discretion to give them to you, or not. The baker knows your life. Are you right in your relationships? Are your other accounts settled? Are you on the path or are you still being distracted and chasing after things off to the side? Jesus said that it's God's pleasure to give you what you want—but he didn't say God had to give it to you on demand.

—————— OZ Says ——————

We mistake defiance for devotion; arguing with God for abandonment. We will not look at the index. Have I been asking God to give me money for something I want when there is something I have not paid for? Have I been asking God for liberty while I am withholding it from someone who belongs to me? I have not forgiven someone his trespasses; I have not been kind to him; I have not been living as God's child among my relatives and friends.

—————— Just Between You and God ——————

Before you pray, think of a broken place in your life—an unkind word you said, a mean text, a bad grade. Make an effort—even a small one—to fix that broken place and *then* say a prayer. God will wait right here.

How well do you wait in a restaurant? Impatient? Angry? Annoyed? What if the food tasted the same way you waited for it? How's that sandwich?

08.25

GIVING. UP.

I no longer call you servants, because a servant does not know his master's business. Instead, I have called you friends, for everything that I learned from my Father I have made known to you.

[John 15:15]

Have you ever met someone who quit smoking? Have you ever known someone who dieted and lost some weight? There's a smile inside them that says, "I did it." Sometimes those who make sacrifices to become better people may lose friends and family in the process. But there's a certain satisfaction or pleasure that comes in making sacrifices to become a better person. This is how God wants us to come to him. We may have to give up certain things. There may be parts of our lives that God doesn't want us to bring along. We willingly sacrifice for the joy of obedience, not for another reason or reward. We give things up because God has asked us to do so. It's our pleasure to do as we're told.

-------------------- OZ Says --------------------

Our Lord is our example in the life of self-sacrifice—"I delight to do Thy will, O my God." He went on with His sacrifice with exuberant joy. Have I ever yielded in absolute submission to Jesus Christ? If Jesus Christ is not the lodestar, there is no benefit in the sacrifice; but when the sacrifice is made with the eyes on Him, slowly and surely the molding influence begins to tell.

-------------- Just Between You and God --------------

Imagine a picture of yourself dancing like no one is watching. It is a joyous dance in the stars. No burdens. No pain. Just pure joy. Now imagine a list of all the things you tend to put before God in your life. Look at that list. Is any of it worth it if you lose the dance to keep it?

The delivery truck is coming. It sounds like it's loaded. Have you made room? Better get busy! If it doesn't fit, they ship it back.

08.26

BLISS

Peace I leave with you; my peace I give you. I do not give to you as the world gives. Do not let your hearts be troubled and do not be afraid.

[John 14:27]

You've probably heard the saying "Ignorance is bliss," or maybe "Those who are happy are too stupid to know what to worry about." Some of the happiest, least stressed people are those who have no clue about what's going on in the world. That's not the kind of peace Jesus is talking about. Choosing this path of following Jesus can throw our lives into chaos instead of peace. This walk is full of pitfalls and challenges, not smooth paths and nice weather. The peace that Christ talks about comes from being in the right place at the right time. It comes from the complete and total confidence in God that everything is going to be all right.

—————————— OZ Says ——————————

Are you looking unto Jesus now, in the immediate matter that is pressing, and receiving from Him peace? If so, He will be a gracious benediction of peace in and through you. But if you try to worry it out, you obliterate Him and deserve all you get. We get disturbed because we have not been considering Him. When one confers with Jesus Christ the perplexity goes, because He has no perplexity, and our only concern is to abide in Him. Lay it all out before Him, and in the face of difficulty, bereavement and sorrow, hear Him say, "Let not your heart be troubled."

————— Just Between You and God —————

Being "at peace" does not mean your problems went away. Of course they are still there. Being at peace means you simply face them without letting them control you. Jesus will be there with you. There's a reason they call him Prince of Peace.

Shhhhhhhhhhhhhhhh . . .

08.27

REALITY TV IS ANYTHING BUT REALITY

Then Jesus told them, "You are going to have the light just a little while longer. Walk while you have the light, before darkness overtakes you. Whoever walks in the dark does not know where they are going."

[John 12:35]

Nnone of this is for show. This book isn't meant to look nice on your shelf. The cross hanging around your neck or from your ear means nothing if you wear it only for decoration. You have a responsibility if you've gotten this far. All this—everything we've talked about so far, everything in the Bible, every spiritual truth you've arrived at on your own—all of this is real and must be acted upon. True spirituality isn't about looking good on the outside. It takes effort every step of the way.

––––––––––––––––– OZ Says –––––––––––––––––

Beware of not acting upon what you see in your moments on the mount with God. If you do not obey the light, it will turn into darkness. "If therefore the light that is in thee be darkness, how great is that darkness!" The second you waive the question of sanctification or any other thing upon which God gave you light, you begin to get dry rot in your spiritual life. Continually bring the truth out into actuality; work it out in every domain, or the very light you have will prove a curse.

––––––––––– Just Between You and God –––––––––––

Would you spend years learning watch repair and then go to work driving bulldozers? Probably not. You know how it works. It's time to use what you learned.

Now you're learning. Put it into practice. Don't just believe. Do.

08.28

MEANING. WHAT?

One day Jesus was praying in a certain place. When he finished, one of his disciples said to him, "Lord, teach us to pray, just as John taught his disciples."

[Luke 11:1]

Now and then you may be asked, "What's the point of praying? Prayer doesn't change things." There are some things prayer will never change. A blue coffee mug will always be blue no matter how hard you pray for it to become yellow. Sometimes the purpose of prayer is to change me. I pray. God changes me and then I can change things. Painting a coffee mug is of little consequence. But I can pray for the homeless, or I can pray for strength and resources—and then I can go out and give the homeless blankets and food. Prayer is my communication with God. It's how God knows I'm here and how I know God is there. Prayer is my connection.

—————— OZ Says ——————

Be yourself before God and present your problems, the things you know you have come to your wit's end over. As long as you are self-sufficient, you do not need to ask God for anything.

—————— Just Between You and God ——————

Turn off the part of your mind that confines you. Surrender to the infinite possibilities. Let your mind go where it will and find something way "out there" to pray about. Let your imagination take you and then bring something back.

Why do you pray? To change the world? Or for the strength to change it? Pray.

08.29

MAKE IT SO

Then Jesus said, "Did I not tell you that if you believe, you will see the glory of God?"

[John 11:40]

If you go looking for a debate, you'll find one. If you go looking for reasons to say, "Following God is a waste of time," you'll find them, too. The world of faith and the world of common sense are two different things, and trying to bring them together into one big ball of putty is impossible. Faith doesn't require common sense. This doesn't mean we need to hide from the world— just the opposite. In order to make a vase shiny and capable of holding water, it must be put through the fire. It's in testing that our faith grows stronger. Don't be afraid to put your breakable vase out there where others can throw things at it. Even if they get a lucky shot and shatter it, God will be there to pick up the pieces and mold them back together into something even stronger.

OZ Says

Faith must be tested, because it can be turned into a personal possession only through conflict. What is your faith up against just now? The test will either prove that your faith is right, or it will kill it. "Blessed is he whosoever shall not be offended in Me." The final thing is confidence in Jesus. Believe steadfastly on Him and all you come up against will develop your faith. There is continual testing in the life of faith, and the last great test is death. May God keep us in fighting trim! Faith is unutterable trust in God, trust which never dreams that He will not stand by us.

Just Between You and God

Faith is the certainty that God hears you. Common sense says you're talking to the ceiling fan. Go with faith . . . common sense has an off switch.

You are heard. Never doubt that. Most of the time you are heard before you even open your mouth.

08.30

I. ME. MINE. I. AM. YOURS.

I have given you authority to trample on snakes and scorpions and to overcome all the power of the enemy; nothing will harm you. However, do not rejoice that the spirits submit to you, but rejoice that your names are written in heaven.

[Luke 10:19–20]

There are some people who, if given the chance, would walk around wearing a giant hat with the word *Christian* in flashing letters. They don't mind getting dirty or sweating it out building houses for the homeless as long as they have a new set of batteries to keep their hat flashing. God pours down a waterfall of blessing and allows it to come through us. It's not that we're doing the work that counts, it's that God's work is being done. The flashing light on top of our hat is not the real light. God is the real light. When we stand in the light of God, we have worth.

——————— OZ Says ———————

The tendency today is to put the emphasis on service. Beware of the people who make usefulness their ground of appeal. If you make usefulness the test, then Jesus Christ was the greatest failure that ever lived. The lodestar of the saint is God Himself, not estimated usefulness. It is the work that God does through us that counts, not what we do for Him. All that Our Lord heeds in a man's life is the relationship of worth to His Father. Jesus is bringing many sons to glory.

——————— Just Between You and God ———————

Take off your hat. Ask God to be a part of your everyday, every-breath life—so each moment can be for him and what he does, and not for you and what you do.

Imagine you have the greatest singing voice anyone ever had, ever, ever, ever. Would you still sing if you were alone? This is life in God.

08.31

LAUGHING AT CLOUDS

I have told you this so that my joy may be in you and that your joy may be complete.

[John 15:11]

Our happiness is like squirting a friend with a squirt gun. The joy that Jesus wants us to have would be like throwing a water balloon the size of Cleveland. We'd get washed away in it. The things that get in the way of our relationship with God are the same things that get in the way of the joy we could be experiencing. Think about your circumstances, your stuff, and about your place in the scheme of things and you'll merely be putting up umbrellas that will keep the water from getting you completely wet in joy.

--- OZ Says ---

The joy of Jesus was the absolute self-surrender and self-sacrifice of Himself to His father, the joy of doing that which the Father sent Him to do . . . Be rightly related to God, find your joy there, and out of you will flow rivers of living water. Stop being self-conscious, stop being a sanctified prig, and live the life hid with Christ. The life that is rightly related to God is as natural as breathing wherever it goes. The lives that have been of most blessing to you are those who were unconscious of it.

--- Just Between You and God ---

Ever wonder why the people on the inside scowling at those who are playing in the rain outside are ones scowling? The people in the rain are laughing. The most puzzling part is . . . it's all a choice. Pray for the scowlers. They need help too.

Two important words . . . "with abandon." A child in the rain, a dancer with new music, a chef in an empty kitchen. You and God. Get it?

09.01

HOLY, HOLY, HOLY

. . . for it is written: "Be holy, because I am holy."

[1 Peter 1:16]

All of life . . . all the things that make up your life . . . all the bits and pieces . . . all the big chunks . . . everything . . . has one purpose. Do you want to know what it is? Are you ready? All of life is for the purpose of making us more like God. That's why we're here. That's the meaning of it all—to be more like him. God sent prophets and preachers to tell us. God sent his Son to tell us. God tells us every day. Our main purpose here on earth is to be one with God. Things that don't work toward that goal are in the way. Some are easy to get rid of. Some take a bit longer. Eventually we must reach the point where we have nothing blocking our way and we can walk unencumbered into God's outstretched arms. Until then—keep working at it.

————————— OZ Says —————————

God has one destined end for mankind, viz., holiness. His one aim is the production of saints. God is not an eternal blessing-machine for men; He did not come to save men out of pity: He came to save men because He had created them to be holy. The Atonement means that God can put me back into perfect union with Himself, without a shadow between, through the Death of Jesus Christ.

————————— Just Between You and God —————————

The end of the journey is God—a complete and total sense of "oneness" with the creator of the universe. That's the light you see in the distance. Today ask God to light the immediate path in front of you—just enough so you don't stumble. Pray for light.

Be one with God, the reason for everything. Be one with God. Everything for that reason.

09.02

SACRED LOSS

Whoever believes in me, as the Scripture has said, rivers of living water will flow from within them.

[John 7:38]

Imagine the earth as one big ice cream stand and God has given us the sweetest, creamiest, most delicious ice cream that has ever been created. (Probably something with big chunks of chocolate and peanut butter, but that's just me.) So here we are. We have the ice cream. The question is, do we eat it ourselves or do we begin making amazing milkshakes, sundaes, and cones to share with everyone? You might think, "I should save it in case I run out," or "If I give just a little bit and mix it with plain vanilla, it will last longer." God calls us to use what we have been given and to be extravagant with it. Give it to everyone. Don't measure. Don't keep track. Just give it away. There may not even be enough left for an ice cream cone when you're done, but that's the sacred loss. You've given your all for God and that isn't a loss in God's eyes.

OZ Says

When Mary of Bethany broke the box of precious ointment and poured it on Jesus' head, it was an act for which no one else saw any occasion; the disciples said it was a waste. But Jesus commended Mary for her extravagant act of devotion, and said that wherever His gospel was preached "this also that she hath done shall be spoken of for a memorial of her." Our Lord is carried beyond Himself with joy when He sees any of us doing what Mary did, not being set on this or that economy, but being abandoned to Him. God spilt the life of His Son that the world might be saved; are we prepared to spill out our lives for Him?

Just Between You and God

This is harder for some people. You have three. You don't want to give away one because then you'd only have two. Perfectly sensible to some people. But since when was Jesus sensible? Ask God for trust and then start sharing.

Yeah, it's going to hurt sometimes. That's how you know it's real.

09.03

SPLOOSH

So the three mighty warriors broke through the Philistine lines, drew water from the well near the gate of Bethlehem and carried it back to David. But he refused to drink it; instead, he poured it out before the LORD.

[2 Samuel 23:16]

Think of it this way. It's a hot August day. Your father has just handed you a water balloon filled with cool clear water. You can easily break it open and refresh yourself, or you can take it to a friend's house, hide in a tree, and when they walk beneath you—let it go. We have the same choice with God's love. If you keep it to yourself, you're the only one who experiences it. If you share (or use) it on someone else, you'll immediately change two lives—yours and theirs. And when they do the same for someone else, the kingdom of God grows.

——————— OZ Says ———————

What has been like water from the well of Bethlehem to you recently—love, friendship, spiritual blessing? Then at the peril of your soul, you take it to satisfy yourself. If you do, you cannot pour it out before the Lord. You can never sanctify to God that with which you long to satisfy yourself. If you satisfy yourself with a blessing from God, it will corrupt you; you must sacrifice it, pour it out, do with it what common sense says is an absurd waste.

——————— Just Between You and God ———————

Take stock of all your blessings today. Look around and then look within. There are so many. When it comes down to it, you have been blessed beyond words. Now choose one of those countless blessings and share with someone.

Wait for it. Waaaaaaaait for it. Sploooooosh.

09.04

BELONGING

I have revealed you to those whom you gave me out of the world. They were yours; you gave them to me and they have obeyed your word.

[John 17:6]

This one is hard to understand. Ready? There's a difference between a follower and a disciple of God. Some don't like to hear that. Some use it to their advantage. But there is in fact a difference. A disciple says, "I am your servant, God, send me." A follower tries to add on statements like "As long as it doesn't hurt," or "As long as it's convenient." To say, "I am your servant" without any conditions is to be a disciple. To be willing to go when and where God says is being a disciple. This is hard. It might hurt. It might take most of your life. It might take your life. To be a follower is not a bad thing—in fact it's wonderful. But are you ready to be a disciple? Are you ready to go when God says, "Go"—unconditionally?

———— OZ Says ————

The missionary is one in whom the Holy Ghost has wrought this realization— "Ye are not your own." To say, "I am not my own" is to have reached a great point in spiritual nobility. The true nature of the life in the actual whirl is the deliberate giving up of myself to another in sovereign preference, and that other is Jesus Christ. The Holy Spirit expounds the nature of Jesus to me in order to make me one with my Lord, not that I might go off as a showroom exhibit. Our Lord never sent any of the disciples out on the ground of what He had done for them. It was not until after the Resurrection, when the disciples had perceived by the power of the Holy Spirit Whom He was, that Jesus said "Go."

———— Just Between You and God ————

Being a disciple means exactly two things. "Been there" and "Done that." Have you? Then you can be a disciple. Not many other qualifications involved.

The follow up to "Speak Lord your servant is listening" is actually doing what you're told.

09.05

ALL ALONG THE WATCHTOWER

Then he returned to his disciples and found them sleeping. "Couldn't you men keep watch with me for one hour?" he asked Peter.

[Matthew 26:40]

In the early stages of our journey, we watch for Jesus. We're always looking, always waiting. "Jesus will be here soon . . . look busy." As we go on, we get to the point where Jesus says, "Watch *with* me," not *for* me. This is different. When our journey began, we were like the child who holds the tools while dad fixes the car. We watch. We learn, even if we're not aware of what we're learning. The disciples could not watch with Jesus. In their doubt and exhaustion, they fell asleep. Yet later when they were given the Holy Spirit, they took the message of Jesus into the world. We must eventually move onto the "watching with" stage of our relationship with Christ. Even if we feel ineffective, something very big is coming.

OZ Says

We do not watch with Him through the revelation of the Bible; in the circumstances of our lives. Our Lord is trying to introduce us to identification with Himself in a particular Gethsemane, and we will not go; we say—"No, Lord, I cannot see the meaning of this, it is bitter." How can we possibly watch with Someone Who is inscrutable? How are we going to understand Jesus sufficiently to watch with Him in His Gethsemane, when we do not know even what His suffering is for? We do not know how to watch with Him; we are only used to the idea of Jesus watching with us.

Just Between You and God

Imagine your soul as a bookshelf or an external hard drive if you prefer. You have volumes about fear and stress and pain. You really don't need these. God is tech support. He'll help you delete these to make room for what's coming. (Hint: It's love.)

It's the difference between Candy Land and chess. No more chance. No more spinners. Every move requires you to look deeper.

09.06

RIVERS

Whoever believes in me, as Scripture has said, rivers of living water will flow from within him.

[John 7:38]

When animals come down to a river to drink, they have no concept of where the water is coming from or where it's going. God is the source of living water. When our lives become this water, we can roll down the mountain and touch the lives of many. We may weaken and become a mere trickle, or we can grow and become mighty, washing away anything that gets in our way. Rivers don't care about obstacles. They go around, through—rolling, never stopping. God uses our lives to touch others. They, in turn, touch more lives. We'll never know how many lives we've touched.

——————— OZ Says ———————

A river touches places of which its source knows nothing, and Jesus says if we have received of His fullness, however small the visible measure of our lives, out of us will flow the rivers that will bless to the uttermost parts of the earth. We have nothing to do with the outflow—"This is the work of God that ye believe . . ." God rarely allows a soul to see how great a blessing he is.

——————— Just Between You and God ———————

Don't get wrapped up in who and where. Ask God to keep you moving in and around. Ask for the strength to keep going when you're weary. Ask for the patience to reach everywhere you need to go.

Fishing. Wading. Cooling. Surviving the rapids. All this changes when we understand we are the river. God is the source.

09.07

DRINK THIS

... but whoever drinks the water I give them will never thirst. Indeed, the water I give them will become in them a spring of water welling up to eternal life.

[John 4:14]

Okay, you've got the whole we-are-the-river concept right? Now what is God? What is Jesus? God is the source of the water—ever since the moment of creation when he dug out the channels with his thumb. God is the source. If God is the source, then Jesus is the fountain. A spectacular glorious fountain full of light and sound and mist and . . . rivers. It is tempting to want to be the fountain. Too late. That job is taken. We are the river that expands and rages and feeds and guides. Often the people who come to the river have never seen the fountain. They aren't aware of the source. They know only the river's life-giving water. The world is thirsty.

—————— OZ Says ——————

Keep at the Source, guard well your belief in Jesus Christ and your relationship to Him, and there will be a steady flow for other lives, no dryness and no deadness. Is it not too extravagant to say that out of an individual believer rivers are going to flow? "I do not see the rivers," you say. Never look at yourself from the standpoint of—Who am I? In the history of God's work you will nearly always find that it has started from the obscure, the unknown, the ignored, but the steadfastly true to Jesus Christ.

—————— Just Between You and God ——————

Never feel unworthy to be the river. God wouldn't have chosen you if he didn't think you would be able to keep going. Pray that when you feel weary, God will send rain, or an underground source of pure water, or an overflowing fountain to fill you again.

Moses prayed for water in the desert. God sent a fountain (like Niagara Falls in reverse.) This is how we view answered prayers. Oh, yeah, sometimes the answer God sends is *you*.

09.08

DO IT YOURSELF

We demolish arguments and every pretension that sets itself up against the knowledge of God . . .

[2 Corinthians 10:5]

God is the source of the water. Jesus is the fountain. We are the river. Now what happens when the path is blocked? What happens when we are confronted with obstacles?

We have the power of God. What can get in our way? There will always be obstacles. Sin. Unforgiveness. Racism. Ignorance. Apathy. These will get in our way, but with the help of God, nothing can stop us. We're not deterred. We may face these problems, but they don't stop us. They may hold us back for a moment, but it's only temporary. Our strength gathers. Our ideals grow. We'll eventually push through anything that stands in our way. Obstacles created by man cannot hold back God. There is no compromise here. Some things must be washed away.

——————————— OZ Says ———————————

The conflict is along the line of turning our natural life into a spiritual life, and this is never done easily, nor does God intend it to be done easily. It is done only by a series of moral choices. God does not make us holy in the sense of character . . .

——————— Just Between You and God ———————

Today ask God for power and perseverance. Not power as in control, but power as in force. You'll need power when the river runs up against seemingly unmovable obstacles. You'll need perseverance to keep pushing. There is no compromise here.

River meets boulder. River goes over, around, or through.

09.09

DO IT YOURSELF AGAIN

. . . we take captive every thought to make it obedient to Christ.

[2 Corinthians 10:5]

Okay, last river analogy. We're on God's time, not our own. Every drop of water that falls on a stone shapes it, just a little. The transformation is so small it can't be detected, but generations from now will see a different stone. God sometimes puts obstacles in our way to mold, shape, and create new paths that we won't ever see changed. Some things are changed in ways so small that we may never see the results. God may want us to slowly wear away a stone. But we want to create the crash of a dam as we splinter it with the waves. This causes a spectacular sight, but it's gone in an instant and can cause damage. We need patience—God's timing.

OZ Says

We are apt to forget that a man is not only committed to Jesus Christ for salvation; he is committed to Jesus Christ's view of God, of the world, of sin and of the devil, and this will mean that he must recognize the responsibility of being transformed by the renewing of his mind.

Just Between You and God

Ask God for some big-picture thinking. Yes, the deer drinks from the river, but downstream the river rages and rips away trees. Sometimes we are there simply to help the deer. Other times we change the whole landscape. Ask God which he wants from you at this moment.

"Go with the flow" is probably one of the deepest lessons you can learn. Understand.

09.10

THIS LOOKS LIKE A JOB FOR . . .

"How do you know me?" Nathanael asked. Jesus answered, "I saw you while you were still under the fig tree before Philip called you."

[John 1:48]

Sometimes big events in your life tend to blindside you when you least expect them. These experiences will often reveal your true character. They will not, however, put anything new in you. In fact, you may not survive the event if you aren't ready for it. If you were on a plane and the pilot had a heart attack, you wouldn't take the controls if you'd never read a flight manual. This is the same thing. We must be ready. We must be prepared. If you call on God only when you need something, how well can you expect to do? A relationship with God must be molded, formed, and practiced every day. Nathaniel was spending time just sitting under the fig tree. When God calls us, are we goofing off or are we prepared for what's around the corner?

—————— OZ Says ——————

The private relationship of worshipping God is the great essential of fitness. The time comes when there is no more "fig-tree" life possible, when it is out into the open, out into the glare and into the work, and you will find yourself of no value there if you have not been worshipping as occasion serves you in your home. Worship aright in your private relationships, then when God sets you free you will be ready, because in the unseen life which no one saw but God you have become perfectly fit, and when the strain comes you can be relied upon by God.

—————— Just Between You and God ——————

Spend time in prayer. Spend time in the Bible. Spend time in meditation. Learn all you can. When the crisis comes, you'll rise. You'll survive. You'll become stronger.

What if "that's an oven" was the only cooking lesson you ever received. You've got to learn this. The banquet is near.

09.11

DISHES

Now that I, your Lord and Teacher, have washed your feet, you also should wash one another's feet.

[John 13:14]

When we make a promise to be a servant of God, we sometimes get a mental picture of ourselves standing on top of a mountain with a raised sword, lightning crashing, and a multitude of angels flying behind us. Realistically, we're more likely to go with a group to plant trees or build a church in a far-off country, but does being a servant mean a mission trip? Jesus took a towel and washed his disciples' feet—right where he was. There is work that needs to be done all around you. You don't necessarily need to go out there to do his work. His work is waiting for you right where you are.

OZ Says

Ministering as opportunity surrounds us does not mean selecting our surroundings, it means being very selectly God's in any haphazard surroundings which He engineers for us. The characteristics we manifest in our immediate surroundings are indications of what we will be like in other surroundings. The things that Jesus did were of the most menial and commonplace order, and this is an indication that it takes all God's power in me to do the most commonplace things in His way.

Just Between You and God

God has a list too. God's list says if someone is hungry, feed them. If someone is cold, give them a blanket. If someone is lonely, visit them. There's nothing on that list about standing on the mountain top. Sometimes servants get their hands dirty.

Yes, you can dance to God's music under stars . . . but there's a sink full of dishes in the homeless shelter.

09.12

UNDERSTANDING

"You don't know what you are asking," Jesus said to them. "Can you drink the cup I am going to drink?" "We can," they answered.

[Matthew 20:22]

It's okay if you don't get it. It's okay if you are struggling to find an answer. It's okay, because when you feel this way, it means you recognize that the outcome of all your mental wrestling is important. Don't stress over confusion. The answer to being confused, puzzled, baffled, perplexed, or mystified is not to complain about being confused, puzzled, baffled, perplexed, or mystified, or to wish you weren't feeling this way. This is a matter of faith. God will sometimes lead you into a place where you'll have no idea what's going on. When this happens, have faith that God will explain everything down the line, but for now . . . just for now . . . you have to move on faith.

OZ Says

There are times in spiritual life when there is confusion, and it is no way out to say that there ought not to be confusion. It is not a question of right and wrong, but a question of God taking you by a way which in the meantime you do not understand, and it is only by going through the confusion that you will get at what God wants.

Just Between You and God

Pray this prayer: "God, I don't understand why I'm going through this right now, but I believe that you will tell me when it's time for me to know. Until then, I will have faith." Say it again like you mean it.

All things eventually.

09.13

SWEET SURRENDER

I have brought you glory on earth by finishing the work you gave me to do.

[John 17:4]

Sometimes we have to give up. That's not to say we give up being a Christian or give up following the Carpenter. Sometimes we have to give up and say, "Jesus, I can't do this by myself." Sometimes we have to give up ourselves and say, "I'm not God. Only God is God. I'm God's servant." Sometimes we have to surrender ourselves to God. We surrender our lives because God has asked us to do so. Many have done it before us, and many will do it after we're long gone. Giving up like this is never easy, but once we do it with our whole hearts, we'll be in constant communion with the Creator of the universe.

---------------------------- OZ Says ----------------------------

Surrender is not the surrender of the external life, but of the will; when that is done, all is done. There are very few crises in life; the great crisis is the surrender of the will. God never crushes a man's will into surrender; He never beseeches him, He waits until the man yields up his will to Him. That battle never needs to be re-fought.

---------------------------- Just Between You and God ----------------------------

You've built your life like that game with the little wooden blocks. Sometimes it's very precarious, but you've put a lot of time into it. Today, choose one block—just one aspect of your life—and give it to God. It will actually make your tower stronger.

Surrender. Give in. Give up. You'll get it back.

09.14

CLARITY

But I am afraid that just as Eve was deceived by the serpent's cunning, your minds may somehow be led astray from your sincere and pure devotion to Christ.

[2 Corinthians 11:3]

Sometimes we find ourselves spiritually befuddled. We can't understand why we are where we are. We don't know why God would ask us to do things that don't make sense. We feel like our spiritual life is being lived on a child's merry-go-round. It's in these times that God will use our imagination to give us inspiration. You may feel like God is putting pressure on you. You may see images again and again in your dreams. You may find yourself thinking about the same things over and over. God may be leading you out of your confusion and you don't even know it. The only thing to do is to follow God. God will lead you out of your befuddlement if you only listen and follow.

OZ Says

Spiritual muddle is only made plain by obedience. Immediately we obey, we discern. This is humiliating; because when we are muddled we know the reason is in the temper of our mind. When the natural power of vision is devoted to the Holy Spirit, it becomes the power of perceiving God's will and the whole life is kept in simplicity.

Just Between You and God

We say we want to hear God's voice and see God's face, but how often does it get lost in the white noise of our everyday lives. Today ask God not to speak louder, but to help you shut off the rest of the world's noise so you can hear him clearly.

Stop, look, listen . . . it's not about traffic. Add the word "follow," and it becomes about growth.

09.15

SPIRITUAL SPELL-CHECK

. . . we have renounced secret and shameful ways; we do not use deception, nor do we distort the word of God. On the contrary, by setting forth the truth plainly we commend ourselves to everyone's conscience in the sight of God.

[2 Corinthians 4:2]

Sometimes a self-test is necessary—a serious inward look at ourselves. When you started on this journey, you promised God that lying, cheating, envy, distrust, coldness, cruelty, and self-indulgence would be a thing of the past. Are they still a part of you? Yes, they're a part of every human being, but you don't need to live by them. Take a look at your everyday life. Do these still play a part in all you do? Do you try to get what you want by using these things that don't please God? The path ahead has pitfalls and challenges. If you're still living 24/7 for yourself, you may be tempted to turn back when the going gets tough. Stay on the path. With God's help, honesty, truthfulness, trust, kindness, compassion, and patience will keep you there.

OZ Says

Others are doing things which to you would be walking in craftiness, but it may not be so with them: God has given you another standpoint. Never blunt the sense of your Utmost for His Highest. For you to do a certain thing would mean the incoming of craftiness for an end other than the highest, and the blunting of the motive God has given you. Many have gone back because they are afraid of looking at things from God's standpoint. The great crisis comes spiritually when a man has to emerge a bit farther on than the creed he has accepted.

Just Between You and God

Ask God for clarity. A good honest, true picture of your life as it is right here, right now. Remember all those things you promised God you'd work on? How's that going? Ask God for help with those too.

Mirrors can't lie. It's not in their nature. What if a mirror showed you within? What would you see . . . honestly?

09.16

NON-PUBLIC BROADCASTING

But when you pray, go into your room, close the door and pray to your Father, who is unseen. Then your Father, who sees what is done in secret, will reward you.

[Matthew 6:6]

Texting is not conversation. Gentlemen do not ask for a date via text. Never start or end a relationship via texting. Conversation is done in person. We must make the time if we want the relationship to get stronger. Prayer is not a monologue, it is conversation. You can't go to God like it's a text. God wants you fully engaged. (BONUS: You can talk to God while you drive.) This journey requires quiet time. It requires that you shut out the distractions and talk with the Creator. Ever have a friend so close they could finish your sentences for you? God is so close he could finish your life for you. Our goal is to connect with God.

—————— OZ Says ——————

The main idea in the region of religion is—Your eyes upon God, not on men. Do not have as your motive the desire to be known as a praying man. Get an inner chamber in which to pray where no one knows you are praying, shut the door and talk to God in secret. Have no other motive than to know your Father in heaven. It is impossible to conduct your life as a disciple without definite times of secret prayer.

—————— Just Between You and God ——————

Read the heading just above again. That's the idea. Your life is just between you and God. Talk with God today. Tell him everything about your life—your concerns, your fears, your delights, and your dreams.

Sometimes it's about the candle . . . not the spotlight.

09.17

WANT SOME OF THAT?

No temptation has overtaken you except what is common to mankind. And God is faithful; he will not let you be tempted beyond what you can bear. But when you are tempted, he will also provide a way out so that you can endure it.

[1 Corinthians 10:13]

Being tempted is not a sin. Temptation does not rip us from the path of good and send us down the wet, muddy slide of evil. Temptation can give us a look inside ourselves as to what is missing. We're human beings and in being so we're going to experience temptation. Temptation presents us with shortcuts. If our ultimate goal is that deep satisfaction we'll get when we're one with God, temptation suggests a shortcut that we think will get us there sooner. God wants that oneness as much as we do, but he knows better how to get us there. He knows there are temptations (both good and bad) and he will not take them from us. He will offer us a reassuring hand on our shoulder, however, when we're deep in the middle of them.

--------- OZ Says ---------

The word "temptation" has come down in the world; we are apt to use it wrongly. Temptation is not sin, it is the thing we are bound to meet if we are men. Not to be tempted would be to be beneath contempt. Many of us, however, suffer from temptations from which we have no business to suffer, simply because we have refused to let God lift us to a higher plane where we would face temptations of another order.

--------- Just Between You and God ---------

God is your best resource in any situation. Good or bad. Harmful or helpful. Anytime you feel the pull from the path, ask God. He's been at this a very long time. You aren't dealing with anything he hasn't seen before. Just ask.

You know that big giant gooey sticky cinnamon roll you just bought at the airport? That was your cab fare. Maybe you can enjoy it while you're walking to the hotel.

09.18

HOLY ATTRACTION

For we do not have a high priest who is unable to empathize with our weaknesses, but we have one who has been tempted in every way, just as we are— yet he did not sin.

[Hebrews 4:15]

If our ultimate goal is to become one with God, and we do this by striving to become one with Jesus, what does that say about the temptations we face?

The temptations Jesus faced were not that dissimilar to ours. It was all about identity. Who are you at your very core? Are you chasing what you want or what you need? Are you putting God first in all things? What forces out there are making you doubt that you are an amazing creation of a creator God? Jesus answered the voice of temptation by putting God first. As we continue to travel this path with Jesus riding shot-gun, it will get easier not to pull off for donuts and coffee every other exit.

—————— OZ Says ——————

Temptation means the test by an alien power of the possessions held by a personality. This makes the temptation of Our Lord explainable. After Jesus in His baptism had accepted the vocation of bearing away the sin of the world, He was immediately put by God's Spirit into the testing machine of the devil, but He did not tire, He went through the temptation "without sin," and He retained the possessions of His personality intact.

—————— Just Between You and God ——————

Today spend some time recognizing the place of God in your life. See if there are places where you put your own ideas and will in front of his. Did you find any? Pray about them.

So . . . you made a really good PB&J sandwich. God is the creator of the universe. Hmmm. Who do you think is in charge?

09.19

UNFRIEND

You are those who have stood by me in my trials.

[Luke 22:28]

Jesus had a way of thinning out the crowds when things got a little chaotic. "Hey, if you follow me, your friends and family will hate you and you could die. Ready? Come on." The challenges we face when we follow Jesus can help us get closer to him. One of these challenges might involve giving up friendships that mean a lot to us. Are we really prepared to let important parts of our lives go? We may be asked to do that.

─────────── OZ Says ───────────

We have the idea that we ought to shield ourselves from some of the things God brings round us. Never! God engineers circumstances and whatever they may be like we have to see that we face them while abiding continually with Him in His temptations. They are His temptations, not temptations to us, but temptations to the life of the Son of God in us. The honour of Jesus Christ is at stake in your bodily life. Are you remaining loyal to the Son of God in the things which beset His life in you?

─────────── Just Between You and God ───────────

If you truly look at the situation, you may find you really can indeed take more. Despite the exhaustion and the pain, you will be amazed at how often "I can't take this anymore!" can turn into "Bring it, Sparky" when you turn to God for help.

Are you sure? Really sure? Okay, then. Let's move on.

09.20

NOBODY

Be perfect, therefore, as your heavenly Father is perfect.

[Matthew 5:48]

The perfection achieved by Jesus meant that he was fulfilling God's purpose. As we attempt to reach perfection, we're going to make a lot of mistakes along the way. We'll meet all kinds of people on our path—some nice, some not so nice. We'll be in all kinds of places on our journey—some safe, some not so safe. But in our attempts to reach the God-sort of perfection, we'll receive from God what we need to exist in all situations with all sorts of people.

──────────── OZ Says ────────────

The secret of a Christian is that the supernatural is made natural in him by the grace of God, and the experience of this works out in the practical details of life, not in times of communion with God. When we come in contact with things that create a buzz, we find to our amazement that we have power to keep wonderfully poised in the center of it all.

──────── Just Between You and God ────────

God is a part of you. God connects with you through grace. It's that grace of God that will get you through the times when things are at their worst. Ask for a warming of the God that is inside you. You'll need it.

**Nobody is perfect. Not by our standards, anyway.
You can be one with God. That would be perfect.**

09.21
BABY, I WAS BORN THIS WAY

And now the LORD says—he who formed me in the womb to be his servant to bring Jacob back to him and gather Israel to himself, for I am honored in the eyes of the LORD and my God has been my strength . . .

[Isaiah 49:5]

This should be a video game character. Picture a former assassin, now a monk. He looks like an oak tree in a robe. Bad guys are rampaging the town and Brother Bad rolls up his sleeve and we see a cross tattoo. Above it reads "SERVANT" and beneath "BORN FOR THIS." This is how we must face the journey. We were born for this long before our parents even met. The world can be a dark and scary place. When we step up and say, "I am a servant of God," the world becomes our home. God's children become family. Are you ready to roll up your sleeves and begin?

--------- OZ Says ---------

The purpose for which the missionary is created is that he may be God's servant, one in whom God is glorified. When once we realize that through the salvation of Jesus Christ we are made perfectly fit for God, we shall understand why Jesus Christ is so ruthless in His demands. He demands absolute rectitude from His servants, because He has put into them the very nature of God. Beware lest you forget God's purpose for your life.

--------- Just Between You and God ---------

Say a prayer for the entire planet. When you are a servant, God will take the concerns of the world and shove them into a single heart. Your heart better be massive. Then again, if it wasn't already, you wouldn't have made it this far.

(Cue the Music.) Ba ba ba ba baaaaaa. We have been created for this purpose. We are the servants of God.

09.22

MASTER

You call me "Teacher" and "Lord," and rightly so, for that is what I am.

[John 13:13]

To have a master is not the same thing as to be mastered. To have a master is to have someone who knows you better than you know yourself, someone who is closer than a friend, someone who can look into the depths of your soul and give you what you need. Your master is not someone who will gleefully taunt you and tell you what to do and chuckle at your inability, but is one who will send you into harm's way and then gladly die for you so you can perform the task. If we stand up and shout to the world, "Nobody will tell me what to do. I am my own master," we have already lost. It's all about humble obedience.

OZ Says

Our Lord never enforces obedience; He does not take means to make me do what He wants. At certain times I wish God would master me and make me do the thing, but He will not; in other moods I wish He would leave me alone, but He does not . . . He wants us in the relationship in which He is easily Master without our conscious knowledge of it, all we know is that we are His to obey.

Just Between You and God

Say it again. "I am a servant of God." Say it knowing there is suffering coming. Say it knowing that God is real. Say it knowing you will come up against walls in your path. Servants go around. Servants go over. Servants go through. They do not stop.

Rise up out of the wreckage. Nothing can keep me down. Yeah, I'm right here! Bring it! (Repeat as necessary.)

09.23

IT'S A SHORT LIST

Jesus took the Twelve aside and told them, "We are going up to Jerusalem, and everything that is written by the prophets about the Son of Man will be fulfilled."

[Luke 18:31]

You've probably had to make a list of your life goals in school. Ask adults about it and they'll tell you how their lists have changed over the years.

Ask missionaries (regardless of age—12 or 112) and they'll tell you they had one goal—God. God first. God last. God in all things. Not to go out and feed the hungry, shelter the homeless, make busy with conversion activity, but God first. With God as the goal, the homeless get a roof, the hungry get fed, the cold get warmed, the lonely get a friend, and the wanderer finds a way. Salvation comes.

--------- OZ Says ---------

In Our Lord's life Jerusalem was the place where He reached the climax of His Father's will upon the Cross, and unless we go with Jesus there we will have no companionship with Him. Nothing ever discouraged Our Lord on His way to Jerusalem. He never hurried through certain villages where He was persecuted, or lingered in others where He was blessed. Neither gratitude nor ingratitude turned Our Lord one hair's breadth away from His purpose to go up to Jerusalem.

--------- Just Between You and God ---------

You are on this journey. Ask God for what you need to pack in order to keep going—patience, strength, courage, compassion, kindness, justice, humor, loyalty, perseverance, faith, and love. Ask for all of them. It's okay. God has them all.

Missionary life goal list: ready?
1. God.
End of list.

09.24

"GO" IS A BIG WORD

Therefore, if you are offering your gift at the altar and there remember that your brother or sister has something against you, leave your gift there in front of the altar.

[Matthew 5:23–24]

Are you ready for this? Are you sure? The idea of being the hero for God is appealing in many ways. We say, "I can do that." But a careful examination of our baggage may show that we're bringing along things that are of no use on this trip and will only weigh us down. When you take a quiet moment with God before setting out, certain things may pop up in your mind. Perhaps God is bringing these to mind as a way of saying, "Are you sure about this?" There are certain things in all of us that people wouldn't be ready to hear if we said them out loud. There are things buried deep in your baggage that you don't need. Before you leave on the I-Am-Your-Servant Tour, give these to God. You don't need them. He's been waiting for you to hand them over.

OZ Says

Never discard a conviction. If it is important enough for the Spirit of God to have brought it to your mind, it is that thing He is detecting. You were looking for a great thing to give up. God is telling you of some tiny thing; but at the back of it there lies the central citadel of obstinacy: I will not give up my right to myself—the thing God intends you to give up if ever you are going to be a disciple of Jesus Christ.

Just Between You and God

See that heading? Between you and God. What you take to God stays between you and God. God is not a snitch. That's not how he works, but remember you can't hide anything from God. Look deep within yourself, take those things you don't want the world to see, and give them to God.

Ever notice how much of "God" is made up of "go"? (No, this is not a spelling lesson.)

09.25

IMPOSSIBLE

If anyone forces you to go one mile, go with them two miles.

[Matthew 5:41]

Here's a puzzle . . . the work God is going to ask you to do is not possible without him. Think about that. God will ask you to do the impossible. It's work that no human can do, but it's work that God and a human can do together. And if God and you do it together, it's not impossible. (You can go back and read that part again if you want.) The power that is given to us (the inspiration and perspiration, call it) is given to us by God for the purpose of doing the work he has asked us to do. We can't create it. We can't manufacture it on our own. The only place to get the power to do what God has asked us to do is from God.

OZ Says

The summing up of Our Lord's teaching is that the relationship which He demands is an impossible one unless He has done a supernatural work in us. Jesus Christ demands that there be not the slightest trace of resentment even suppressed in the heart of a disciple when he meets with tyranny and injustice. No enthusiasm will ever stand the strain that Jesus Christ will put upon His worker, only one thing will, and that is a personal relationship to Himself which has gone through the mill of His spring cleaning until there is only one purpose left—I am here for God to send me where He will. Every other thing may get fogged, but this relationship to Jesus Christ must never be.

Just Between You and God

Impossible looks like "I'm possible." That's what it really comes down to. It's not about the task, it's about the faith God has in you. With God all things are possible. So are you.

You: "I can't." God: "Yes, you can." You: "How do you know?" God: "I said so." You: "Good enough for me."

09.26

READY? SET? UH . . . UM . . .

First go and be reconciled to them; then come and offer your gift.

[Matthew 5:24]

You may be fired up and ready to go. You may have the walkin' shoes you need and a bag over your shoulder. Your walking staff is in your hand and you're waiting for God to say, "Now!" But there's something you need to fix. Everybody has something to fix—the unsaid apology, the unspoken gratitude, the buried anger, or the lost chance. These are things that must be fixed before you can leave. You don't just walk out the door before a vacation; you make arrangements to have things taken care of. This is your life we're talking about. Fix what needs fixing—then come back to the starting line.

OZ Says

The process is clearly marked. First, the heroic spirit of self-sacrifice, then the sudden checking by the sensitiveness of the Holy Spirit, and the stoppage at the point of conviction, then the way of obedience to the word of God, constructing an unblameable attitude of mind and temper to the one with whom you have been in the wrong; then the glad, simple, unhindered offering of your gift to God.

Just Between You and God

God is a details guy. You think you can gloss over some of the preparations, but you can't. You must be completely ready. Not "I'll-work-on-that-as-I-go" ready. Fix what you need to fix. God is a details guy, yes. But he's patient. He'll wait. Go fix.

You know that last weight you hid in your suitcase. Yeah, that one. You can't hide it. You're going to have to leave it.

09.27

THE BUT . . .

As they were walking along the road, a man said to him, "I will follow you wherever you go."

[Luke 9:57]

It's a wonder sometimes that God bothers with us at all. We stand up and say, "I'll follow," and then we get a good look at the to-do list and say, "Yes, God . . . but." We come up with our list of reasons why we can't do what's expected of us. Even when we say, "Anything! Anything, God, you just name it and I'll do it," it's often followed by, "Uhhhh . . . okay, anything but that." Jesus didn't play the nice guy when he dealt with these people in the verses that follow the one above. Jesus' answers to our hesitations are often what we need to hear, not what we want to hear. But if we didn't hear the words that hurt sometimes, we wouldn't be strong enough to keep up, let alone finish the journey with him.

--------- OZ Says ---------

The words of the Lord hurt and offend until there is nothing left to hurt or offend. Jesus Christ has no tenderness whatever toward anything that is ultimately going to ruin a man in the service of God. Our Lord's answers are based not on caprice, but on a knowledge of what is in man. If the Spirit of God brings to your mind a word of the Lord that hurts you, you may be sure that there is something He wants to hurt to death.

--------- Just Between You and God ---------

God doesn't sugar coat anything. He'll never beat around the bush. (He might burn it, but that's to get your attention.) Don't ask for God's honest evaluation if you think it's going to come with ice cream. You signed up for this. Stand up and take it.

Ask. Listen. Ouch. Learn. Go.

09.28

YOUR NAME IS NOT *GAP*

Jesus looked at him and loved him. "One thing you lack," he said. "Go, sell everything you have and give to the poor, and you will have treasure in heaven. Then come, follow me."

[Mark 10:21]

We often define ourselves by what we have. Do we have the right name written on our back pocket? Do we have the right things on our feet? When the man asked Jesus, "What must I do?" he was out to save his own soul. He was out to be a big shot on the Jesus Team. That's not what Jesus is asking. Jesus wants us to define ourselves not by what we own, but by what is inside of us. He wants us to follow him—to be empty and free inside so he can fill us with his love and compassion. If that is going to happen, we have to make room in our lives.

―――――――――― OZ Says ――――――――――

"Sell whatsoever thou hast . . ." I must reduce myself until I am a mere conscious man, I must fundamentally renounce possessions of all kinds, not to save my soul (only one thing saves a man—absolute reliance upon Jesus Christ)—but in order to follow Jesus. "Come, and follow Me." And the road is the way He went.

――――――― Just Between You and God ―――――――

If you signed on to this so you could get a free pair of "chucks" (or "trainers") with Jesus on the side giving the thumbs up . . . you're in it for the wrong reason. None of this is about fashion or recognition or self-glorification. It's all about God. Jesus will give you the thumbs-up even without the shoes.

For God. Not for you. That's the order. Deal with it.

09.29

IT'S FOR YOU

For when I preach the gospel, I cannot boast, since I am compelled to preach. Woe to me if I do not preach the gospel!

[1 Corinthians 9:16]

If people tell you with great authority, "This is what a call is" and "This is how it comes" and "This is what it sounds like"—then it's truly doubtful they have ever received a call of their own. We're the church. We believe in the call of God. It may come like a loud, unexpected "Hey! You!" It may come as a gradual realization when we stop and look back at all the God-intervening-moments in our life and we say, "Wow, God has brought me all this way for a reason!"

When God calls guys or girls, there is nothing that is going to stand in the way. Everything that happens does so that God's plan will be realized. You may take the long way around, but you'll come back to the point where God wants you to be.

OZ Says

If you have been obliterating the great supernatural call of God in your life, take a review of your circumstances and see where God has not been first, but your ideas of service, or your temperamental abilities. Paul said—"Woe is unto me, if I preach not the gospel!" He had realized the call of God, and there was no competitor for his strength.

Just Between You and God

Look back over your life. Look at the greatest, most life-changing moments. (Make a list, if that makes you feel better.) God was wholly (and holy) present at each of those times. The reasons might not be clear now, but they'll become clear. Thank God for his presence in your greatest and worst moments.

The roller coaster is not going to change course randomly someday. You got on. Now hang on.

09.30

CHISEL

Now I rejoice in what I am suffering for you, and I fill up in my flesh what is still lacking in regard to Christ's afflictions, for the sake of his body, which is the church.

[Colossians 1:24]

We are the uncarved block. God is the sculptor. Okay, we've got that. God will use his divine hands to carve us into great works of art. We're even willing to put up with the pain of the carving knife and the chisel, because they're God's and we love him and we know he has a plan. But what if God uses someone else's hands? What if those who give you the hardest time are put there by God to hack away at you—to help you become a great piece of art? Can you love them? Can you still love the process? Usually we start griping. Until we can love those who sculpt us, whether it's God or our biggest detractors, we'll never be the art God wants us to be.

OZ Says

If ever we are going to be made into wine, we will have to be crushed; you cannot drink grapes. Grapes become wine only when they have been squeezed. I wonder what kind of finger and thumb God has been using to squeeze you, and you have been like a marble and escaped? You are not ripe yet, and if God had squeezed you, the wine would have been remarkably bitter. To be a sacramental personality means that the elements of the natural life are presenced by God as they are broken providentially in His service. We have to be adjusted into God before we can be broken bread in His hands. Keep right with God and let Him do what He likes, and you will find that He is producing the kind of bread and wine that will benefit His other children.

Just Between You and God

We've said it before. You are an amazing and unique creation of a creator and creating God. You are the masterpiece. Now trust the artist.

There is one who sees the art beneath the stone. The sculptor knows what you need and what you don't. Painful? Yes, of course . . . but worth it.

10.01

COMING DOWN AGAIN

After six days Jesus took Peter, James and John with him and led them up a high mountain, where they were all alone. There he was transfigured before them.

[Mark 9:2]

Most of us have been on top of the mountain. We're not talking about a physical mountain, but a feeling deep inside that seems to say, "I'm in the presence of something bigger than myself." It may happen at a concert of some sort, or perhaps on the last night of a mission trip or weekend retreat. There are candles and music and someone's arm is around your shoulder. Suddenly you feel overcome with a presence. The bummer is that you have to go home. You have to come down off the mountain. As much as you'd like to stay there and have that feeling forever, you have to come down. God doesn't intend for us to live on the mountaintop always. There are times when we will live in the valley. God gives us those mountaintop moments so we can survive the days in the valley and show others the path up the mountain.

––––––––––––– OZ Says –––––––––––––

We are apt to think that everything that happens is to be turned into useful teaching, it is to be turned into something better than teaching, viz., into character. The mount is not meant to teach us anything, it is meant to make us something. There is a great snare in asking—What is the use of it? In spiritual matters we can never calculate on that line. The moments on the mountaintops are rare moments, and they are meant for something in God's purpose.

––––––––––– Just Between You and God –––––––––––

If you're in need of a mountaintop moment, or if you're still remembering how it felt and don't want the feeling to end, ask God for a crystal-clear reminder of your experience—a song, a fragrance, the stars, whatever. Meditate on your reminder and thank God for your experience.

The mountaintop was not meant for living. It's a temporary place. Life occurs in the valley. You've been to the top. Now, lead an expedition.

10.02

THE VALLEY SO LOW

It has often thrown him into fire or water to kill him. But if you can do anything, take pity on us and help us.

[Mark 9:22]

There are times when we have to live in the valley. Unfortunately, it seems like the higher our mountaintop experience, the lower we come down. The fact that we have been on top of the mountain makes the bottom of the valley that much harder. In the valley, life can be drab, cold, and humiliating to someone who professes belief and then must endure the barbs of those who haven't experienced the mountaintop. The valley is also the place we're most likely to get discouraged and lose faith. We want that mountaintop so badly, but we must remember there are things God wants to teach us that we need to learn in the valley. We must sometimes live in the valley, but we don't *have* to live in the valley. Get it?

―――――――――― OZ Says ――――――――――

It is in the sphere of humiliation that we find our true worth to God, that is where our faithfulness is revealed. Most of us can do things if we are always at the heroic pitch because of the natural selfishness of our hearts, but God wants us at the drab commonplace pitch, where we live in the valley according to our personal relationship to Him. Peter thought it would be a fine thing for them to remain on the mount, but Jesus Christ took the disciples down from the mount into the valley, the place where the meaning of the vision is explained.

―――――― Just Between You and God ――――――

Everyone "comes down" after being on the mountain. Jesus did. "How low can you go?" is a question best left unanswered. God knows. God knows exactly what you are feeling. You can go to him and ask for strength, perseverance, faith. Whatever. Ask for a double portion.

Dark in the valley. Light on the mountain. You can't live up there. Life is down here. Keep the light.

10.03
BE GIVEN

He replied, "This kind can come out only by prayer."

[Mark 9:29]

Doing the work of Jesus without knowing him is like thinking you can perform a miracle because you have a picture of Jesus on your t-shirt. Prayer and concentration on Jesus will give you his presence. When others laugh, point, and snicker at you for your faith (valley-living), the presence of Christ will get you through. But it doesn't just happen. It must be made to happen. Focus on him. Remove the obstacles (physical, mental, emotional, and spiritual) that stand between you and Jesus. Coming down off the mountain into the harsh reality is like that disorienting feeling you get when walking out of the bright sunshine into a dark theater. We can't live on the mountaintop, but the mountaintop feeling is still available in the valley.

─────────── OZ Says ───────────

We must be able to mount up with wings as eagles; but we must also know how to come down. The power of the saint lies in the coming down and the living down. "I can do all things through Christ which strengtheneth me," said Paul, and the things he referred to were mostly humiliating things. It is in our power to refuse to be humiliated and to say—"No, thank you, I much prefer to be on the mountain top with God." Can I face things as they actually are in the light of the reality of Jesus Christ, or do things as they are efface altogether my faith in Him, and put me into a panic?

─────────── Just Between You and God ───────────

Think about Jesus today. Think of all you ever learned about Jesus in Sunday school, books, movies, and music. Here's a word: *dwell*. Dwell on Jesus. Fill your mind with your favorite images of him. Imagine him here. Now. Talk with him. Tell him everything.

Jesus needs a haircut. Jesus with dirt between his toes. Jesus with BO. Jesus with bad breath. Jesus with that smile. Jesus is real.

10.04
WILL I AM NOW

To the church of God in Corinth, to those sanctified in Christ Jesus and called to be his holy people, together with all those everywhere who call on the name of our Lord Jesus Christ—their Lord and ours.

[1 Corinthians 1:2]

Follow this one. It gets tricky. There's a reason why you are where you are spiritually right now. You have a vision of the *you* that you will be someday, but you're not that *you* now. You're a different you. The you that you are now can't live as the you that you will become, because you're not ready for that you. God knows that other you—the one you'll be someday; the one you'll be when you achieve the vision. You have a long way to go to get to that you. God will use the ordinary things in your life to make you into you. For now, your assignment is to keep the faith and not turn back, so that you can become you.

OZ Says

There are times when we do know what God's purpose is; whether we will let the vision be turned into actual character depends upon us, not upon God. If we prefer to loll on the mount and live in the memory of the vision, we will be of no use actually in the ordinary stuff of which human life is made up. We have to learn to live in reliance on what we saw in the vision, not in ecstasies and conscious contemplation of God, but to live in actualities in the light of the vision until we get to the veritable reality. Every bit of our training is in that direction. Learn to thank God for making known His demands.

Just Between You and God

The five-year-old version of you would probably pray for puppies and candy. That version would not do well in this journey. This journey you have undertaken is about "becoming." You are in process. You are growing. This time . . . this right-here-right-now is completely necessary. Understand that and you'll see the possibilities.

Ingredients become cookies. The ingredients are not the cookies. It takes a lot of work. Are you ready to become?

10.05

AN INFINITELY MORE PROFOUND REVELATION

Therefore, just as sin entered the world through one man, and death through sin, and in this way death came to all people, because all sinned . . .

[Romans 5:12]

Let's talk about sin. All of us sin, whether we want to admit it or not. Sin is profound separation from God. This separation can express itself as a beautiful looking self-righteousness, or as an ugly immoral existence. Both represent separation from God. Both make a person feel like, "I am my own god."

Sin is a part of us all. When we make the conscious choice not to live as one who has experienced the grace of God, we are in sin.

―――――――――――― OZ Says ――――――――――――

The disposition of sin is not immorality and wrong-doing, but the disposition of self-realization—I am my own god. This disposition may work out in decorous morality or in indecorous immorality, but it has the one basis, my claim to my right to myself. When Our Lord faced men with all the forces of evil in them, and men who were clean living and moral and upright, He did not pay any attention to the moral degradation of the one or to the moral attainment of the other; He looked at something we do not see, viz., the disposition . . . The condemnation is not that I am born with a heredity of sin, but if when I realize Jesus Christ came to deliver me from it, I refuse to let Him do so, from that moment I begin to get the seal of damnation.

―――――――― Just Between You and God ――――――――

Pray against those things that can separate you from God. They might be of your own creation or not, but they exist.

Sin equals separation. Not bad behavior. Not immoral thoughts. Separation. And that's a choice . . . and it is yours.

10.06

NEW CREATION

But when God, who set me apart from my mother's womb and called me by his grace, was pleased to reveal his Son in me so that I might preach him among the Gentiles, my immediate response was not to consult any human being.

[Galatians 1:15–16]

Remember that old song about foot bones connected to ankle bones and ankle bones connected to shin bones? The song comes from a scripture passage where God knits together a valley of bones. He stretches skin over them. He sends blood coursing through veins. He asks Ezekiel, "Are these bones alive?" Answer: No, they are not. They are not new until God breathes the breath of life into them. We often spend much time feeling like dry bones. We desperately want to be NEW. We make every effort on our own but it is not until God breathes a spirit into us that we are truly new. We can't become new until we see that we need to become new. This takes honesty and a deep introspection and we often have to get pretty low before we are willing to even look.

―――――――――― OZ Says ――――――――――

The moral miracle of Redemption is that God can put into me a new disposition whereby I can live a totally new life. When I reach the frontier of need and know my limitations, Jesus says—"Blessed are you." But I have to get there. God cannot put into me, a responsible moral being, the disposition that was in Jesus Christ unless I am conscious I need it.

―――――――― Just Between You and God ――――――――

Are you aware? Look inside and see the things you could do without. Ask God to pour his Holy Spirit into you and fill the empty spaces. You are the highest creation of the Creator of the universe. You are a new creation.

Life lesson: If you can bring yourself to throw away that old cup . . . God will give you a bucket. Which do you want when it rains blessings?

10.07

COME TOGETHER

God made him who had no sin to be sin for us, so that in him we might become the righteousness of God.

[2 Corinthians 5:21]

There are those who believe God sends his angels down like angelic paparazzi. Taking secret videos and pictures of our every move. Oh there's a sin. (click) There's another one. (click) Ohhhh there's a BIG one. (click) God does not keep a record of wrongs. (It says so in Corinthians.) It's not about keeping score. Sin is separation and it is of our own creation. We choose to live a life separate from God. God tried prophets and people killed the prophets. So God sent his Son. Watched his own Son die and then brought him back . . . so that people would know what he said was all true. We are part of God. God is part of us. Jesus said so. If there is separation between us and God, it is solely by our own creation—that is sin. If we can choose to be separate from God. It must be so much easier to be *in* God.

─────────── OZ Says ───────────

Sin is . . . not wrong doing, it is wrong, deliberate and emphatic independence of God . . . Jesus Christ rehabilitated the human race; He put it back to where God designed it to be, and anyone can enter into union with God on the ground of what Our Lord has done on the Cross.

─────────── Just Between You and God ───────────

Have you ever said thank you to Jesus? Sounds like the right thing to do, doesn't it? Do it today. The Son of God will hear. All that you have and all that you will be is because he allowed himself to be nailed to that chunk of wood. Doesn't that deserve appreciation?

We were lost. We are found. Thank you, Jesus.

EVERYTHING COUNTS

10.08

ONLY ONE

Come to me, all you who are weary and burdened, and I will give you rest.

[Matthew 11:28]

Three words—"Come to me." Notice that it's only three words. There is no *if* or *only* or *when*. Jesus said, "Come to me." That means you can go to him with anything. Better than that, you should go to him with everything. We think we need to reserve going to Jesus for when we've hit bottom. Jesus didn't say that. Every possible thing can be brought to Jesus—the smallest concern, the grandest gratitude—everything. And there's not a mile-long list of instructions, rules, or ceremonies. Jesus just gave one simple invitation, "Come."

OZ Says

How often have you come to God with your requests and gone away with the feeling—Oh, well, I have done it this time! And yet you go away with nothing, whilst all the time God has stood with outstretched hands not only to take you, but for you to take Him. Think of the invincible, unconquerable, unwearying patience of Jesus—"Come unto Me."

Just Between You and God

Here's one you've heard before. "I'll deal with this on my own." We think God is out saving the world and doesn't have time for us. God is farther than the moon and as close as your skin. Nothing should be held back if you truly want to move forward.

When Jesus calls you to him, it's to lighten the load, not to increase it. Why would Jesus give you more to carry?

10.09

SOLELY

. . . but rather offer yourselves to God, as those who have been brought from death to life; and offer every part of yourself to him as an instrument of righteousness.

[Romans 6:13]

We can't right the wrongs of this world. We can't make good what is bad. We can't make holy what is unholy. We can't fix what is unfixable—all of these can only be done by God. Once we grasp the idea of what Jesus did for us, we have a responsibility to recognize that it will affect everything we do. Do we take this Godly knowledge into our everyday lives? Do we make our decisions based on this? This is what is meant by obedience. Watch out for people who think they have the corner on what God wants and have his one time approval for everything they do. Obedience is something that must happen again and again. It's not a one-time thing.

─────────── OZ Says ───────────

If I construct my faith on my experience, I produce that most unscriptural type, an isolated life, my eyes fixed on my own whiteness. Beware of the piety that has no pre-supposition in the Atonement of the Lord. It is of no use for anything but a sequestered life; it is useless to God and a nuisance to man. Measure every type of experience by our Lord Himself. We cannot do anything pleasing to God unless we deliberately build on the pre-supposition of the Atonement.

─────────── Just Between You and God ───────────

What's on your plate today? What decisions wait for you at your job, school, relationship? Too many decisions can be like juggling eggs. Eventually you're going to have a problem. Go to God now. Small decisions can have big consequences.

Can't decide? Ask God. Already decided? Ask God anyway.

10.10

THE DOORS

At that time Jesus said, "I praise you, Father, Lord of heaven and earth, because you have hidden these things from the wise and learned, and revealed them to little children."

[Matthew 11:25]

Think of your spiritual life as a series of doors in a long hallway. They're all closed and locked and there's nothing you can do on your own to open them. If you can get to the last one, you'll receive a spiritual understanding. You can try to pick the locks on the doors. You can push, shove, and pull. You can read books on how to get through the doors. You can hurl yourself against them. But you'll never be able to open the doors on your own power. When you say, "I will live as God wants me to live," and then actually do it, the doors will open. God opens them. God throws them open and invites you in.

─────────── OZ Says ───────────

Obey God in the thing He shows you, and instantly the next thing is opened up. One reads tomes on the work of the Holy Spirit, when five minutes of drastic obedience would make things as clear as a sunbeam. "I suppose I shall understand these things someday!" You can understand them now. It is not study that does it, but obedience. The tiniest fragment of obedience, and heaven opens and the profoundest truths of God are yours straight away. God will never reveal what you know already. Beware of becoming "wise and prudent."

─────────── Just Between You and God ───────────

You've said it before. "I am your servant, God." Promise it again now. Show that you can pull it off without question or complaint, and God will open the door for you.

Can't pick the lock. Can't bust it open. God is waiting to open it from the other side. Give him the password—(your name here).

10.11

REMEDY

So when he heard that Lazarus was sick, he stayed where he was two more days.

[John 11:6]

We have a tendency to hit our knees, say our prayers, and then expect a glorious light show. We want pyrotechnics and special effects. We want the full choir of angels to come down and say, "Your prayer is answered." But often when we pray we get silence. Silence is sometimes God's answer. Silence means God trusts you to accept this as his answer. Silence is sometimes temporary. God may want to bless you beyond measure, but you might have to wait. Things happen in his time, not ours. So to be met with silence is to be trusted. You may be told, "What I have planned for you is unbelievable, so just wait for now." The secret here is to have faith that God has heard you, so you don't go back again and again, frustrated and angry in the false belief that God doesn't listen. You can't put limits on God. There is nothing God can't do in his time. So take the silence as a sign that God trusts you. How's that for a compliment?

OZ Says

A wonderful thing about God's silence is that the contagion of His stillness gets into you and you become perfectly confident — "I know God has heard me." His silence is the proof that He has. As long as you have the idea that God will bless you in answer to prayer, He will do it, but He will never give you the grace of silence. If Jesus Christ is bringing you into the understanding that prayer is for the glorifying of His Father, He will give you the first sign of His intimacy — silence.

Just Between You and God

Follow the example today. Find a place and sit in silence. Sit in the silence of God. Listen, but don't expect. Look, but don't plan on a vision—just be in God's silence.

Shhh. Listen. Hear that? That's a good thing.

10.12

PACE YOURSELF

Enoch walked faithfully with God; then he was no more, because God took him away.

[Genesis 5:24]

It's not the great and wonderful moments of our spiritual lives that show the world who we are—it's the ordinary moments. How well do we experience the God-connection on the same-old-same-old days? Getting into the stride of God is difficult because God is always changing directions, slowing down, speeding up, and often unpredictably. We must pay attention during the big moments as well as the little ones. Once we get into the same stride as God, things begin to happen. Things we never thought we could have done in a million years suddenly are do-able.

—————————— OZ Says ——————————

God's Spirit alters the atmosphere of our way of looking at things, and things begin to be possible which never were possible before. Getting into the stride of God means nothing less than union with Himself. It takes a long time to get there, but keep at it. Don't give in because the pain is bad just now, get on with it, and before long you will find you have a new vision and a new purpose.

————— Just Between You and God —————

Having an ordinary day? Focus your attention on God. This isn't a mountaintop—this is regular life. Apply your mountaintop thinking to this ordinary moment and you'll find yourself keeping up with the Creator of the universe.

Run. Catch up. Keep going. God will give you a second wind.

10.13

BALLOONS

One day, after Moses had grown up, he went out to where his own people were and watched them at their hard labor. He saw an Egyptian beating a Hebrew, one of his own people.

[Exodus 2:11]

Have you ever given any serious thought to a balloon? It's a simple design—no complicated parts. The simplicity of it is what makes it cool. Is there anyone who can't appreciate the simple joy of playing with a balloon? We are like balloons. God breathes into us. Just a little. Just enough to begin to stretch us out and move our boundaries. Then the air goes out. We feel discouraged. After a while God breathes into us again—more this time, and we become larger and fuller with the presence of God. Then we deflate. God will breathe into us again and again, eventually filling us to our fullest so we can become a source of joy to those around us.

OZ Says

We may have the vision of God and a very clear understanding of what God wants, and we start to do the thing, then comes something equivalent to the forty years in the wilderness, as if God had ignored the whole thing, and when we are thoroughly discouraged God comes back and revives the call, and we get the quaver in and say—"Oh, who am I!" We have to learn the first great stride of God—"I am THAT I am hath sent thee". We fix on the individual aspect of things; we have the vision—"This is what God wants me to do;" but we have not got into God's stride. If you are going through a time of discouragement, there is a big personal enlargement ahead.

Just Between You and God

Feeling discouraged—like a flat, lifeless balloon? It's temporary. God will breathe into you, and the lightness that seems to be lacking will become commonplace. Pray to be filled. Allow the joy to happen.

All things in time. All things in order. All things happen. Breathe in. Breathe out. Repeat.

10.14

CAUSE

Therefore go and make disciples of all nations, baptizing them in the name of the Father and of the Son and of the Holy Spirit, and teaching them to obey everything I have commanded you. And surely I am with you always, to the very end of the age.

[Matthew 28:19–20]

We go because Jesus said to go—not because we think we're needed, but because we've been told to go by the Son of God. *Go* doesn't necessarily mean get up, leave, and fly to the ends of the earth. *Go* means to live. Be a disciple. Live as a disciple. Where we go is not up to us. That's up to God. When we say, "I am your servant," God will send us where he wants us to be. Our job is to go (to live) as we have been instructed to do by his Son. Jesus says, "I am in you and you are in me." That is how we keep going.

--------------------- OZ Says ---------------------

"Go ye therefore . . ." Go simply means live. Acts 1:8 is the description of how to go. Jesus did not say—Go into Jerusalem and Judea and Samaria, but, "Ye shall be witnesses unto Me" in all these places. He undertakes to establish the goings. "If ye abide in Me, and My words abide in you . . ."—that is the way to keep going in our personal lives. Where we are placed is a matter of indifference; God engineers the goings.

--------------------- Just Between You and God ---------------------

All that you are waiting to become is out there. Real life. Real faith. Real love. Real relationship with God. It's there. God is waiting. You have to go get it. Waiting for it to come to you is wasted time. Live the journey.

Go. Live. Same thing.

10.15

ALLITERATION

He is the atoning sacrifice for our sins, and not only for ours but also for the sins of the whole world.

[1 John 2:2]

Think about the concept of "timeless." Being outside the boundaries of time. God said he was both beginning and end. The lessons of Jesus are outside of time itself. Before the world began and after it all ends, Jesus' words will still exist and still be true. Love God. Love others—four words that are beyond time and understanding and yet guide us in every moment of our existence. God is speaking. Are we listening?

─────────── OZ Says ───────────

The key to the missionary message is the propitiation of Christ Jesus. Take any phase of Christ's work—the healing phase, the saving and sanctifying phase; there is nothing limitless about those. "The Lamb of God which taketh away the sin of the world!"—that is limitless. The missionary message is the limitless significance of Jesus Christ as the propitiation for our sins, and a missionary is one who is soaked in that revelation.

─────────── Just Between You and God ───────────

Immerse yourself in the words of Christ today. Read a Bible. If you don't have access to one right now, meditate on the words that you know by heart. Back off their meaning and just think about the idea of how long they have endured and how long they will endure. This alone is proof that something beyond us is going on.

Christ above. Christ below. Christ beside. Christ yesterday. Christ today. Christ tomorrow. Christ in the ever-present now.

10.16

APPLY WITHIN

Ask the Lord of the harvest, therefore, to send out workers into his harvest field.

[Matthew 9:38]

If you're ever part of a mission trip—if 15 to 30 of your friends pile into a plane or bus to go and do your annual youth mission trip—remember the most important thing is not that you do the work. The most important thing is to get closer to God. That is the purpose. The work will get done, but it's important to use the time to grow closer to God. Every day should begin and end with prayer. Your friends at home will also be praying for you every day. Prayer is the key. No one is so important that God can't do his work without them. If you're a missionary, then you're a missionary for God, and God will put you where you need to be. That's where you really can become a disciple of Jesus.

OZ Says

We are taken up with active work while people all round are ripe to harvest, and we do not reap one of them, but waste our Lord's time in over-energized activities. Suppose the crisis comes in your father's life, in your brother's life, are you there as a labourer to reap the harvest for Jesus Christ? "Oh, but I have a special work to do!" No Christian has a special work to do. A Christian is called to be Jesus Christ's own, one who is not above his Master, one who does not dictate to Jesus Christ what he intends to do. Our Lord calls to no special work: He calls to Himself. "Pray ye therefore the Lord of the harvest," and He will engineer circumstances and thrust you out.

Just Between You and God

Say a prayer today for someone who heard the word "Go" and took it very seriously. There are people all over this planet who "went" when God said "go." These people need strength, patience, courage, and love. Say a prayer for one of them.

Prayer. Not work. Work will happen. Prayer becomes.

10.17

RECOGNIZE

Very truly I tell you, whoever believes in me will do the works I have been doing, and they will do even greater things than these, because I am going to the Father.

[John 14:12]

When we pray for a miracle, we may not realize that prayer itself is a miracle. When we pray in the name of Jesus, we're connecting with God. That is a miracle in its truest form. By praying, we're acknowledging that Jesus is a part of us. Jesus himself said that we would be able to do even more than he did here on earth because we're able to connect with God, just as he did. How's that for a miracle? We must understand that God is in charge. God designed this game. We may hold the control pad, but God designed the game. If we think we're not any good to God—and maybe someday we'll be of use, but not now—we're wrong. God will use us wherever he needs to. The key to finding out where is prayer.

OZ Says

Prayer is the battle; it is a matter of indifference where you are. Whichever way God engineers circumstances, the duty is to pray. Never allow the thought—"I am of no use where I am;" because you certainly can be of no use where you are not. Wherever God has dumped you down in circumstances pray . . . He says pray.

Just Between You and God

"Go ye into all the world." May start with your backyard . . . the kid in school who eats by himself every day, the kind word to a bus driver, the adding of your voice to a choir. Ask God to send, but know that he might just tell you to stay put.

Pray. Here. Now. Be used.

10.18

ROUSE

It was for the sake of the Name that they went out, receiving no help from the pagans.

[3 John 1:7]

Jesus said to love God with our whole selves. We do this by recognizing God's presence in all things (not just our favorite things, the happy things, the pleasant things, the easy things, or the religious things). Sometimes this makes people uncomfortable. Sometimes being like Jesus really upsets some of the most religious people. God will use everyone. The ordinary and the celebrity. Those who have been educated and those who have been "schooled." The only requirement for a missionary is a strong assurance of God's presence in their lives. Sometimes being a missionary is just about one beggar showing another where to find bread.

OZ Says

The key to missionary devotion means being attached to nothing and no one saving Our Lord Himself, not being detached from things externally. Our Lord was amazingly in and out among ordinary things; His detachment was on the inside towards God. External detachment is often an indication of a secret vital attachment to the things we keep away from externally. The loyalty of a missionary is to keep his soul concentratedly open to the nature of the Lord Jesus Christ. The men and women Our Lord sends out on His enterprises are the ordinary human stuff, plus dominating devotion to Himself wrought by the Holy Ghost.

Just Between You and God

The more you live in the presence of God, the more you will see it. If you ask to see it—you won't. If you do what God asks of you—you will become so aware of his presence you won't know how you missed it.

You don't need a list (to-do or wish). You don't need an agenda. That's a work thing. When you go to God . . . let it be because of God.

10.19

THE PARK IS NOW CLOSED

Jesus said, "My kingdom is not of this world. If it were, my servants would fight to prevent my arrest by the Jewish leaders. But now my kingdom is from another place."

[John 18:36]

Ever go driving on a summer day and suddenly the perfect driving song comes on the radio? The music is playing. The wind feels good on your face and your arm as your elbow is out the window. Got the picture? Now imagine living in this place—where everything seems to be perfect. This is what the kingdom of God is like. The kingdom of God is not a place you can visit. The kingdom of God happens inside of you. It's not even a place you can think of going to. You can't get there. To get there suggests that the kingdom is someplace else—somewhere in the future. The kingdom is here and now and inside you. To be at the right place and time in your heart, mind, and soul—that's the kingdom.

—————————— OZ Says ——————————

You have no idea of where God is going to engineer your circumstances, no knowledge of what strain is going to be put on you either at home or abroad, and if you waste your time in over-active energies instead of getting into soak on the great fundamental truths of God's Redemption, you will snap when the strain comes; but if this time of soaking before God is being spent in getting rooted and grounded in God on the unpractical line, you will remain true to Him what ever happens.

————— Just Between You and God —————

The whole "in-God's-presence" thing is not a destination. Don't listen to the people who tell you "someday" or "eventually" or "if you work harder." Put away all those reasons you think you can't get in the kingdom and realize you already are.

No rides. No tickets. But you'll never want to leave.

MASON JARS

It is God's will that you should be sanctified.

[1 Thessalonians 4:3]

Imagine a clear glass mason jar. You know the kind. Like Grandma's jelly jars. This jar label says, "LIFE." Now we fill that jar with stones, but there's still room. We can put pebbles or gravel in to fill in those extra spaces. There's still space. Let's add sand. Now every bit of our LIFE is packed full. God comes along and says, "I have this living water. Do you want a drink?" We must be willing to clean out every bit of the jar before we drink. Otherwise we might taste the grit or get a bit of sand in our teeth. The jar must be cleaned out and scrubbed before we are ready to take a drink of what God has to offer.

OZ Says

Receive Jesus Christ to be made sanctification to you in implicit faith, and the great marvel of the Atonement of Jesus will be made real in you. All that Jesus made possible is made mine by the free loving gift of God on the ground of what He performed . . . Sanctification makes me one with Jesus Christ, and in Him one with God, and it is done only through the superb Atonement of Christ. Never put the effect as the cause. The effect in me is obedience and service and prayer, and is the outcome of speechless thanks and adoration for the marvellous sanctification wrought out in me because of the Atonement.

Just Between You and God

Ask God for the water. Pray to be filled. If you still have some stones and sand, you'll see the places that still need a little work.

It is the in-betweens that keep us from the God-life. God seeps in like water into stone. There is still room for water in a jar of sand.

10.21

GAINS

But you, dear friends, by building yourselves up in your most holy faith and praying in the Holy Spirit . . .

[Jude 1:20]

Would you believe that it's easier to walk on water than it is to walk in The Way, that is Jesus? Living day in and day out as a servant of God and a follower of Jesus is the hardest thing you'll ever do. Some people think they don't need God's grace to get them through the hard times. Our human design is to be at our best when things are at their worst. But God never intended us to live life on our own. When we live each day as a servant and a follower, we experience God's grace.

—————————— OZ Says ——————————

We do not need the grace of God to stand crises, human nature and pride are sufficient, we can face the strain magnificently; but it does require the supernatural grace of God to live twenty-four hours in every day as a saint, to go through drudgery as a disciple, to live an ordinary, unobserved, ignored existence as a disciple of Jesus. It is inbred in us that we have to do exceptional things for God; but we have not. We have to be exceptional in the ordinary things, to be holy in mean streets, among mean people, and this is not learned in five minutes.

————— Just Between You and God —————

If you're in the middle of an absolutely ordinary day, thank God for it and promise to keep trying to follow the path he has laid out for you.

It's a beautiful daaaaaaaaaaaaaaaaaaaaaaaay. Don't let it get away.

10.22

VOCALIZE

The Spirit himself testifies with our spirit that we are God's children.

[Romans 8:16]

This is the God parade. Celebrate! We've got giant balloons of the disciples. We've got bands and dancers, and we stand on the float tossing out pieces of candy to anyone who wants to reach out. Now, whenever we have a desire to push our agenda and not God's love . . . we come to a detour. The whole parade must now go around. We push our ideas, our rules, our reasons . . . the detours become road blocks. We must turn an entire parade around in the street. People at the end of the route miss out. People nearby lose interest and start to go home. We are left in the middle of the street trying to do a 360 in a parade float because we lost sight of the reason for the celebration.

OZ Says

The Spirit of God witnesses to the Redemption of Our Lord, He does not witness to anything else; He cannot witness to our reason. The simplicity that comes from our natural common-sense decisions is apt to be mistaken for the witness of the Spirit, but the Spirit witnesses only to His own nature, and to the work of Redemption, never to our reason. If we try to make Him witness to our reason, it is no wonder we are in darkness and perplexity. Fling it all overboard, trust in Him, and He will give the witness.

Just Between You and God

God is in you. We've known that. So God telling you about God is like God talking to himself in some ways. The trick is to let the God part of you out of the strong metal box you've sort of put him in, so you can hear him with your soul.

You can listen or you can hear. Yes, there is a difference. God is speaking . . . are you listening?

10.23

ERASED

Therefore, if anyone is in Christ, the new creation has come: The old has gone, the new is here!

[2 Corinthians 5:17]

Ever eat at a diner or restaurant where they write the daily specials on a board outside? Even if it's wiped off every day, there's still a trace of the old specials. Even if it's scrubbed off, there will always be a trace of the old marker . . . even if it's on a molecular level. God does not wipe away. God does not clean. God creates a brand new board—fresh and unused. All that you were is gone. All that stuff you worried about no longer counts. When you make this decision, you're a new creation.

―――――――――― OZ Says ――――――――――

When we are born again, the Holy Spirit begins to work His new creation in us, and there will come a time when there is not a bit of the old order left; the old solemnity goes, the old attitude to things goes, and "all things are of God." How are we going to get the life that has no lust, no self-interest, no sensitiveness to pokes, the love that is not provoked, that thinketh no evil, that is always kind? The only way is by allowing not a bit of the old life to be left; but only simple perfect trust in God, such trust that we no longer want God's blessings, but only want Himself. Have we come to the place where God can withdraw His blessings and it does not affect our trust in Him? When once we see God at work, we will never bother our heads about things that happen, because we are actually trusting in our Father in Heaven Whom the world cannot see.

―――――――― Just Between You and God ――――――――

Stop worrying about that stuff. Stop thinking that God won't take you because of something you did or something you didn't do. You're a clean slate. You're at the starting line. Say a prayer to the God of second chances and start again.

Start here. Do not pass Go. Do not collect two hundred dollars. This is a brand-new game.

10.24

UNENDING

But thanks be to God, who always leads us as captives in Christ's triumphal procession and uses us to spread the aroma of the knowledge of him everywhere.

[2 Corinthians 2:14]

When we're at the highest point we can go, God is still higher. We may work day in and day out to get a little higher up the mountain, but there will always be more climbing to do. But that's okay because with God, the climb is what's important. With each of God's victories in our lives we move higher and higher, but God will always be higher than we can go. At the same time, God will be there next to us as we climb. If we slip and slide back down, God will catch us. If we have to stop and rest, God will warm us, and give us strength. Understand that the climb is the thing—not the summit.

OZ Says

. . . we are here to exhibit one thing—the absolute captivity of our lives to Jesus Christ . . . Paul says—I am in the train of a conqueror, and it does not matter what the difficulties are, I am always led in triumph. Is this idea being worked out practically in us? Paul's secret joy was that God took him, a red-handed rebel against Jesus Christ, and made him a captive, and now that is all he is here for. Paul's joy was to be a captive of the Lord; he had no other interest in heaven or in earth.

Just Between You and God

If you need rest, pray for rest. If you need your vision renewed, pray for that. If you need strength, courage, and affirmation, pray for these, but understand that the climb keeps going.

Can you walk and think at the same time? Do you let your mind wander while you are shaving? Then you can make God possible in all things.

10.25

IN NOT *OF*

To the weak I became weak, to win the weak. I have become all things to all people so that by all possible means I might save some.

[1 Corinthians 9:22]

Picture a master class in Shakespeare's plays—a gathering of great actors, directors, scholars, and writers—all there because they love the Bard and are eager to hear new ideas and learn new things about his work. You're sitting at the back trying not to look conspicuous. Someone from the outside slips you a note. "Professor is sick. You teach."

This is what it can feel like when we share God with others. We feel unqualified. The apostle Paul went through this all the time. Paul said this is what it's like to be a servant. We can't know all of God, yet we are asked to describe him—to teach others about him. This is where we must trust that God will use us, somehow. In some way God will get through us and into the lives of others. We can't plan for it. We simply must allow God to use us for his purposes.

OZ Says

A Christian worker has to learn how to be God's noble man or woman amid a crowd of ignoble things. Never make this plea—If only I were somewhere else! All God's men are ordinary men made extraordinary by the matter He has given them. Unless we have the right matter in our minds intellectually and in our hearts affectionately, we will be hustled out of usefulness to God. We are not workers for God by choice. Many people deliberately choose to be workers, but they have no matter in them of God's almighty grace, no matter of His mighty word.

Just Between You and God

You're not the one out of place. You're with God and God is never out of place. Ask God to strengthen your connection to him, and you'll be able to go anywhere.

Maybe the reason you don't fit in is because God wants you for a different puzzle. New box. Better picture.

10.26

AIM

Again Jesus said, "Peace be with you! As the Father has sent me, I am sending you."

[John 20:21]

We hear the word "missionary" and many of us picture a guy wearing an explorer's hat, hacking his way through the jungle with a machete in one hand and a Bible in the other. He finds the remote village and somehow manages to bring the entire tribe to Jesus. The truth is that a missionary is any person who is sent by Jesus as God sent him. The missionary doesn't know what lies ahead. God knows what lies ahead, and the missionary trusts that God will be there. You can plan a great trip to work in a homeless shelter, but if you're going primarily to show people how holy *you* are—that's not mission. The purpose of mission is to show the world God. Those you are serving should see God alive in you.

OZ Says

In the New Testament the inspiration is put behind us, the Lord Jesus. The ideal is to be true to Him, to carry out His enterprises. Personal attachment to the Lord Jesus and His point of view is the one thing that must not be overlooked. In missionary enterprise the great danger is that God's call is effaced by the needs of the people until human sympathy absolutely overwhelms the meaning of being sent by Jesus. The needs are so enormous, the conditions so perplexing, that every power of mind falters and fails. We forget that the one great reason underneath all missionary enterprise is not first the elevation of the people, nor the education of the people, nor their needs; but first and foremost the command of Jesus Christ—"Go ye therefore, and teach all nations."

Just Between You and God

"Here I am Lord. Send me." These are dangerous, scary, challenging, wonderful, rewarding, and amazing words. If you are going to say them, you better mean them.

God: "Go." You: "Okay." (That's pretty much it right there.)

10.27

HOW DO I GO?

There's an old song that gets sung at Christmas time—"Children go where I send thee. How shall I send thee?"

Perhaps a better question for us is "God, how do I go?" Part of the answer comes by looking into ourselves. If we're willing to go and make disciples as Jesus told us, don't we have to be disciples ourselves? Are we doing this so others will come to know Jesus, or are we doing this so we can be Jesus to others? Are our reasons selfish or unselfish? Do we want the world to come around to our point of view, or to see God's view? Before we take the first step in a mission for God, before we can invite others to walk with us, we have to be sure we're on the right path ourselves.

OZ Says

The one great challenge is—Do I know my Risen Lord? Do I know the power of His indwelling Spirit? Am I wise enough in God's sight, and foolish enough according to the world, to bank on what Jesus Christ has said, or am I abandoning the great supernatural position, which is the only call for a missionary, viz., boundless confidence in Christ Jesus? If I take up any other method I depart altogether from the methods laid down by Our Lord—"All power is given unto Me . . . therefore go ye."

Just Between You and God

Take some time today and think about what God wants. Compare this to your own ideas and then toss yours out. God wants us to go into the world—some will not leave their church, others will go to the ends of the earth. Are you ready?

You know how some people write their destination on the back window? "Cleveland bound" or "Spring Break Rules." What if it said, "God"? It'd be an interesting trip.

10.28

B-CAUSE & A-FFECT

For if, while we were God's enemies, we were reconciled to him through the death of his Son, how much more, having been reconciled, shall we be saved through his life!

[Romans 5:10]

Everything we do, everything that exists—this book, your favorite song, the church, the weather—everything is because of God. We know God by our connection to Jesus. We know Jesus because of God. There aren't enough underlines to emphasize the importance of this fact. God is everything. To hold ourselves up as Christians, or to think that because we're Christians we can make the world right, is putting the effect above the cause. All the good we can do, all the people we can reach . . . everything is because of God.

--------- OZ Says ---------

. . . men and women can be changed into new creatures, not by their repentance or their belief, but by the marvellous work of God in Christ Jesus which is prior to all experience. The impregnable safety of justification and sanctification is God Himself. We have not to work out these things ourselves; they have been worked out by the Atonement. The supernatural becomes natural by the miracle of God; there is the realization of what Jesus Christ has already done—"It is finished."

--------- Just Between You and God ---------

There's not a single thing you can think of that doesn't exist because of God. Even concrete and abstract things all exist in the universe because of God. God created the universe they exist in. Pray out loud to God, and thank him for being there before there was anything else.

God knows how it all started because he was there. That would make him the authority on the . . . well, everything.

10.29

CHASM MEET BRIDGE

God made him who had no sin to be sin for us, so that in him we might become the righteousness of God.

[2 Corinthians 5:21]

There's no need for us to feel separated from God. We create amazing problems for ourselves when we purposely turn away from God and separate ourselves from his love. Jesus died on the cross so we would never have to feel separated from God again. God sent Jesus here for that reason. He didn't want to be separated from us either. God took the first step by sending his Son to close the gap. Now any separation that exists is because of our choice. Separation from God is never necessary.

--------------------- OZ Says ---------------------

That Christ died for me, therefore I go scot free, is never taught in the New Testament. What is taught in the New Testament is that "He died for all" (not—He died my death), and that by identification with His death I can be freed from sin, and have imparted to me His very righteousness. The substitution taught in the New Testament is twofold: "He hath made Him to be sin for us, who knew no sin; that we might be made the righteousness of God in Him." It is not Christ for me unless I am determined to have Christ formed in me.

--------------------- Just Between You and God ---------------------

You're on this journey for one reason—because Jesus died, and then came back, to prove that everything he said was the absolute truth. Today pick up a Bible and study the words of the Son of God.

Let's amend the title of this one. See it? Let's change it to Chasm Meet Ramp. That's more like it.

10.30

FAITH BUILDS BRIDGES

And without faith it is impossible to please God, because anyone who comes to him must believe that he exists and that he rewards those who earnestly seek him.

[Hebrews 11:6]

Imagine a bridge that spans halfway across a vast chasm. From the other side another bridge reaches out. Right there in the middle is an empty space. These two bridges don't meet. The gap is too big to jump across. That gap—that space—is called faith. Nothing impossible can happen without faith. When every rational, common-sense notion says, "You can't; there's no way," we must make the last step using faith, and then we can walk into the impossible. God lives in that space. All that God is exists in that place between what the world says is possible and impossible. With faith we can cross the bridge and do everything the world says we can't do.

OZ Says

Common sense is not faith, and faith is not common sense; they stand in the relation of the natural and the spiritual; of impulse and inspiration. Nothing Jesus Christ ever said is common sense, it is revelation sense, and it reaches the shores where common sense fails. Faith must be tried before the reality of faith is actual. "We know that all things work together for good," then no matter what happens, the alchemy of God's providence transfigures the ideal faith into actual reality. Faith always works on the personal line, the whole purpose of God being to see that the ideal faith is made real in His children.

Just Between You and God

In 1978 Christopher Reeve starred as Superman. A train was headed toward certain death and Superman lay down in the gap of the broken track and allowed the train to run over him. You're the engineer. Guess where God is?

That moment where possible ends, impossible begins. God is there. Have faith. All things are possible with God.

10.31

STRUCTURE

He replied, "Because you have so little faith. Truly
I tell you, if you have faith as small as a mustard
seed, you can say to this mountain, 'Move from here
to there' and it will move. Nothing will be impossible
for you."

[Matthew 17:20]

Life falls apart sometimes. The wrong Jenga block gets pushed and pulled and it all comes down. Life falls apart sometimes. You climb out of the rubble and stand on top of the remnants of your life. You want to scream "Why GOD why?" It wells up from deep within you. At this moment, can you turn your face to the storm and say, "I am your servant!" This is faith. A life of faith hurts sometimes. Faith gets tested. We face the trials and tribulations knowing (having faith that) a life of faith can also bring us indescribable joy. Have faith.

OZ Says

Faith by its very nature must be tried, and the real trial of faith is not that we find it difficult to trust God, but that God's character has to be cleared in our own minds. Faith in its actual working out has to go through spells of unsyllabled isolation. Never confound the trial of faith with the ordinary discipline of life, much that we call the trial of faith is the inevitable result of being alive. Faith in the Bible is faith in God against everything that contradicts Him—I will remain true to God's character whatever He may do. "Though He slay me, yet will I trust Him"— this is the most sublime utterance of faith in the whole of the Bible.

Just Between You and God

God can give you faith, so ask for it. You may be tested when you least expect it. You're going to need all you can get. Asking is not weakness; it's strength.

I gotta have faith, faith, faith . . . I gotta have faith,
faith, faith . . . (pause) Bay-Beee.

11.01

HOME WRECKER

Do you not know that your bodies are temples of the Holy Spirit, who is in you, whom you have received from God? You are not your own.

[1 Corinthians 6:19]

Have you ever known someone with a lot of scars? Someone who has had open heart surgery or some other major operation? What about emotional scars? Do you know someone who has been put through the wringer? There is something special about these people. They seem less interested in the trivial . . . as if the pain that caused the scar has brought them to a new way of thinking. Now imagine a life like this only spiritual. This is what often happens when you say "yes" to God. "Yes Lord, I will be your servant" comes with pain but scars heal. God will bring you into a relationship with himself that is unlike anything you have ever experienced. It will be worth the pain.

OZ Says

The first thing God does with us is to get us based on rugged Reality until we do not care what becomes of us individually as long as He gets His way for the purpose of His Redemption. Why shouldn't we go through heartbreaks? Through those doorways God is opening up ways of fellowship with His Son. Most of us fall and collapse at the first grip of pain; we sit down on the threshold of God's purpose and die away of self-pity, and all so-called Christian sympathy will aid us to our death bed. But God will not. He comes with the grip of the pierced hand of His Son, and says—"Enter into fellowship with Me; arise and shine."

Just Between You and God

Are you ready to say it and mean it? "I am a servant of God." It comes with more than you think. It requires more faith than most people possess. But if God didn't think you could handle it, you wouldn't be hearing that voice deep in your gut that says, "This is the way to go."

At this point in the journey the world is open to you. Everything is possible except one thing. Stopping. Rest? Yes. Stop? Nope.

11.02

I, ME, MINE, I, ME, MINE, I AM

If you love me, keep my commands.

[John 14:15]

ere's the beautiful and crazy part about this whole servant thing. God doesn't make you do it. He doesn't require it. He doesn't force it. He sets up the process, and then we choose whether to follow. It's beautiful because we're given the choice. God, the Father almighty, Creator of the universe, is giving us the choice of whether or not to follow the path. It's crazy because we decide to actually do it! No sane people would put themselves through this. God lays out the rules and says, "It's up to you." When we choose the path of being a servant it will lead into a deep, incredible relationship with God that we would never be able to experience if we instead choose to say, "Maybe later," or "I'm not worthy to walk this path," or "I'll let someone else."

—————— OZ Says ——————

The Lord does not give me rules, He makes His standard very clear, and if my relationship to Him is that of love, I will do what He says without any hesitation. If I hesitate, it is because I love some one else in competition with Him, viz., myself. Jesus Christ will not help me to obey Him, I must obey Him; and when I do obey Him, I fulfill my spiritual destiny . . . If I obey Jesus Christ, the Redemption of God will rush through me to other lives, because behind the deed of obedience is the Reality of Almighty God.

—————— Just Between You and God ——————

Stand up and say this aloud. "I am a servant of the living God." Repeat it a few times. Sometimes it helps to hear it. Put your finger in the book and say it again. One more time. Good. Yes, God heard you. Yes, he's pleased.

A straight line is the shortest distance between two points, but it is absolutely not the most interesting.

11.03

PUSH/PULL

I have been crucified with Christ and I no longer live, but Christ lives in me. The life I now live in the body, I live by faith in the Son of God, who loved me and gave himself for me.

[Galatians 2:20]

Who are you living for? Are you living for yourself or are you living for God? Think of a door. Beyond that door is a life with Jesus that will involve both pitfalls and blessings. Behind you is the life you've lived up until now. God can bring you up to this door 365 days a year, but he won't push you through it. You have to step through. This is not a door into another Twilight Zone(ish) dimension. It's basically a doorframe in the middle of the path. Step through, and you may not feel all that different. You'll be the same person you are now, but the purpose for your life will have changed. Stepping through the door doesn't change you—it does, however, change everything you're heading toward from this point on.

OZ Says

It means breaking the husk of my individual independence of God, and the emancipating of my personality into oneness with Himself, not for my own ideas, but for absolute loyalty to Jesus. There is no possibility of dispute when once I am there. Very few of us know anything about loyalty to Christ—"For My Sake." It is that which makes the iron saint.

Just Between You and God

Someone can't point to the sunrise and explain the rotation of the earth. They explain the way rays of light bounce off the water vapor in the clouds. You're going to look at it and see God. This is what happens when you make this choice. God has always been everywhere. Now you're going to start to see him.

You push on the door with all your strength and energy and still nothing. Still out in the cold. Psst . . . the sign says "pull." Open your eyes that you may see.

11.04

HERE IN THE PRESENT

Come near to God and he will come near to you. Wash your hands, you sinners, and purify your hearts, you double-minded.

[James 4:8]

You can make a sandwich—sit down, eat it, enjoy every bite—there is nothing wrong with that. But if you make a sandwich while volunteering at a soup kitchen, the feeling will be entirely different. There are actions we do for ourselves, and actions we do for God. The actions we do for God are different. We can feel the presence of God in these actions. God breathes into us when we are doing his work. We feel different inside. Is this to say you shouldn't make yourself a sandwich and enjoy it? Of course not. This is to say there's a difference that can be felt. It's a mistake to think a sandwich is just a sandwich—an action is just an action. One is a holy union with God.

—————————— OZ Says ——————————

The feeblest saint who transacts business with Jesus Christ is emancipated the second he acts; all the almighty power of God is on his behalf. We come up to the truth of God, we confess we are wrong, but go back again; then we come up to it again, and go back; until we learn that we have no business to go back. We have to go clean over on some word of our redeeming Lord and transact business with Him. His word "come" means, "transact." "Come unto Me." The last thing we do is to come; but everyone who does come knows that that second the supernatural rush of the life of God invades him instantly.

————— Just Between You and God —————

Do something today that is entirely for God. Volunteer in love somewhere. Sing a song. Put your hand on the shoulder of a friend who needs support. Ask God to breathe his Holy Spirit into your actions and into the one you help.

A sandwich is not just a sandwich. An action for God is holy. You can feel it.

11.05

CLAY

But rejoice inasmuch as you participate in the sufferings of Christ, so that you may be overjoyed when his glory is revealed.

[1 Peter 4:13]

Ever watch potters with a lump of clay? They will bash it, pound it, roll it, and cut it to make sure it's ready to be made into a work of art. Every tough experience you go through as a servant of God is to make you ready for something else down the road. You may think God is testing you, or you may think God has forgotten about you altogether. This is not so. Everything you experience from this point on has a purpose. You may meet people who are going through hard times, and you will be able to tell them, "Yeah, I've been there." Then the reason for your own hard times will be made clear to you. To think you are being shaped by the potter for no reason puts limits on God. There are no limits.

--------------------- OZ Says ---------------------

Are we partakers of Christ's sufferings? Are we prepared for God to stamp our personal ambitions right out? Are we prepared for God to destroy by transfiguration our individual determinations? It will not mean that we know exactly why God is taking us that way, that would make us spiritual prigs. We never realize at the time what God is putting us through; we go through it more or less misunderstandingly; then we come to a luminous place, and say—"Why, God has girded me, though I did not know it!"

--------------------- Just Between You and God ---------------------

This isn't easy, but say thank you to God for whatever hard times you're going through right now. If you believe it's for a reason so that he can use you later on—then the hard times are a gift. Say thank you.

Fire makes the clay hard. The river shapes the rock. Hard times shape the soul. Create something new and wonderful.

11.06

ZOOM IN

. . . whoever lives by believing in me will never die. Do you believe this?

[John 11:26]

How often do we see Jesus get called on the carpet? Think this through. Martha was quite possibly experiencing the worst moment of her life. Her brother was dead, and to her mind, it wasn't necessary. He would still be living if Jesus had just hustled a little. Thoughout the scriptures we see Jesus meet people where they are. He does not expect they will understand what he's talking about. He meets them where they are. He meets Martha in her grief and in her stress and in her pain. He's right there with her in the midst of it. This is where Jesus meets us—in the midst of what we are going through. We know this because we believe. When we believe, we feel his presence during our worst moments. It is when we say "Yes. I believe" in our worst moments that we become true servants of a living God.

OZ Says

To believe is to commit. In the programme of mental belief I commit myself, and abandon all that is not related to that commitment. In personal belief I commit myself morally to this way of confidence and refuse to compromise with any other; and in particular belief I commit myself spiritually to Jesus Christ, and determine in that thing to be dominated by the Lord alone. When I stand face to face with Jesus Christ and He says to me—"Believest thou this?" I find that faith is as natural as breathing, and I am staggered that I was so stupid as not to trust Him before.

Just Between You and God

Think back about your worst moments so far. You're still here, aren't you? You got through them, didn't you? If you look closely, you will see the hand of God on your life, and then wonder how you missed it the first time.

You survived! Good for you! Congratulations! Wait . . . did you think you did that on your own?

11.07

TAKE THIS

And we know that in all things God works for the good of those who love him, who have been called according to his purpose.

[Romans 8:28]

God is in you. God is with you in every situation. He is with you when you meet people and realize they need God just as much as you do. That's when your connection with God lets you talk to God about their needs. God put you where you are, so don't question your circumstances. You were put there to learn something. You were put there to do something. This is all the work of God. Because God is in you, God is present wherever you are. And because God is in you, others can experience his love through you. Don't take the words "all things" lightly. God is in all things. All things. Everything. God is there.

─────────────── OZ Says ───────────────

Your part in intercessory prayer is not to enter into the agony of intercession, but to utilize the common-sense circumstances God puts you in, and the common-sense people He puts you amongst by His providence, to bring them before God's throne and give the Spirit in you a chance to intercede for them. In this way God is going to sweep the whole world with His saints.

─────────── Just Between You and God ───────────

When you see spring show up after a long, cold winter, you appreciate it more. It is this sense of appreciation that is sometimes lacking in our prayers. Ask God for his presence today and then open yourself up to appreciating each new moment.

What part of "all" are you missing? God is in alllll things.

11.08

UNINTENTIONAL PRAYERS

In the same way, the Spirit helps us in our weakness. We do not know what we ought to pray for, but the Spirit himself intercedes for us through wordless groans.

[Romans 8:26]

God is in us. The Holy Spirit moves through us and inhabits us. He's in our thinking. He shoots out the ends of our fingers. We can pray until we're exhausted—and even when we can't pray any more, the Spirit (that connection) takes over and God knows our needs. God knows our problems. The connection created by the Holy Spirit can't be broken. Clouded, clogged, or frayed, maybe—but never broken. We're the landlords of this property the Holy Spirit of God inhabits. We owe it to the tenant to take care of it.

OZ Says

Have we recognized that our body is the temple of the Holy Ghost? If so, we must be careful to keep it undefiled for Him. We have to remember that our conscious life, though it is only a tiny bit of our personality, is to be regarded by us as a shrine of the Holy Ghost. He will look after the unconscious part that we know nothing of; but we must see that we guard the conscious part for which we are responsible.

Just Between You and God

If you were given a few years to build a church and guaranteed God would visit, wouldn't you build something amazing. You've invited God into your "temple." You must take care of it. Stay healthy. Take care of your body. God needs you.

Take care of yourself. You have much to do. God lives there too.

11.09

CREATING SPACE

Now I rejoice in what I am suffering for you, and I fill up in my flesh what is still lacking in regard to Christ's afflictions, for the sake of his body, which is the church.

[Colossians 1:24]

We must allow God to be God in our lives. We must have faith to believe that the words we say will stick in the hearts of those who listen, and allow God to do what he does best—change lives. We actually do more harm than good when we add our own spin to the words. It's when we want to hear someone say, "Oh, she's very good at this" or "He's very special" that we create a roadblock to the presence of God. Jesus gave us the words and the stories. They affected us and moved us to change. They will affect others in completely different ways. Our job is to put them out there and let God be God.

OZ Says

It is not the strength of one man's personality being superimposed on another, but the real presence of Christ coming through the elements of the worker's life. When we preach the historic facts of the life and death of Our Lord as they are conveyed in the New Testament, our words are made sacramental; God uses them on the ground of His Redemption to create in those who listen that which is not created otherwise . . . The danger is to glory in men; Jesus says we are to lift Him up.

Just Between You and God

Ask God to use you today as his messenger. Then ask for strength to not promote yourself as the message.

God's words. Not yours. God's job. Not yours. There's a difference.

11.10

CLEAR DIRECTIONS

We sent Timothy, who is our brother and co-worker in God's service in spreading the gospel of Christ, to strengthen and encourage you in your faith . . .

[1 Thessalonians 3:2]

The person who truly believes in the calling of God can never write an essay entitled, "What I Want to Be When I Grow Up." True servants of God believe God will put them where they need to be. Does this mean you should just give up on all career plans and sit at home until some divine call comes telling you where to go? Get real. Make your interests in line with God's interests, and God will take you places you never thought possible. Should you ignore the career-path classes offered in school? No. But consider God when making your choice. God can use you as a pro-basketball player. God can use you as an art teacher. God's only request is that you have faith and trust him to put you where you can best serve.

──────────── OZ Says ────────────

After sanctification it is difficult to state what your aim in life is, because God has taken you up into His purpose by the Holy Ghost; He is using you now for His purposes throughout the world as He used His Son for the purpose of our salvation. If you seek great things for yourself—God has called me for this and that—you are putting a barrier to God's use of you. As long as you have a personal interest in your own character, or any set ambition, you cannot get through into identification with God's interests. You can only get there by losing forever any idea of yourself and by letting God take you right out into His purpose for the world, and because your goings are of the Lord, you can never understand your ways.

──────────── Just Between You and God ────────────

Seek guidance today. God is the ultimate guidance counselor. There may be paths you haven't thought of. There may be new ways to become what you've always dreamed of being.

God's will. Your will. Two lines drawn on paper. How often do they touch each other? That's kind of up to you.

11.11

KNOWING WHEN

Then God said, "Take your son, your only son, whom you love—Isaac—and go to the region of Moriah. Sacrifice him there as a burnt offering on a mountain I will show you."

[Genesis 22:2]

If God says, "Go," don't get a second opinion. God has thought this out more than you, and you shouldn't ask, "Why? How? Where? Are you sure?" or any other questions. We don't have a better idea. We don't have a more convenient time. We don't have an alternate solution that will accomplish the same thing. God is God. We can't do better than that. If God gives you your very own pint of premium ice cream, eat it with celebration and thanks. If God gives you a plate of dried spinach, eat it and know that there's a purpose, and the ice cream will come later.

OZ Says

The wonderful simplicity of Abraham! When God spoke, He did not confer with flesh and blood. Beware when you want to confer with flesh and blood, i.e., your own sympathies, your own insight, anything that is not based on your personal relationship to God. These are the things that compete with and hinder obedience to God.

Just Between You and God

God has the advantage of seeing the big picture. All of space and time are in front of him. Questioning his decisions will only delay the inevitable. Yes, all things work for the benefit of God. It doesn't mean you have to fight your way there.

You know how the cops on TV say, "Keep your ears open?" Is that really a choice? God won't say listen without following it up.

11.12

CH-CH-CH-CHANGES

Therefore, if anyone is in Christ, the new creation has come: The old has gone, the new is here!

[2 Corinthians 5:17]

Remember a special toy you wanted for Christmas when you were little? Whether or not you got it is irrelevant, but you wanted it so badly you couldn't imagine not getting it. Looking back, it may seem silly now. It's probably gone or stashed in the closet somewhere. It's not nearly as important as it was at the time. God does this with your old life. When you become a servant of God, your wish list changes. The things that used to be so incredibly important aren't so important any more. You become a new creation. You're a new person, and what you can do with the new you will simply blow away the old you.

—————— OZ Says ——————

If you are born again, the Spirit of God makes the alteration manifest in your actual life and reasoning, and when the crisis comes you are the most amazed person on earth at the wonderful difference there is in you. There is no possibility of imagining that you did it. It is this complete and amazing alteration that is the evidence that you are a saved soul.

—————— Just Between You and God ——————

Examine your internal wish list. Are you still wanting things that will be forgotten when they go out of style? See what you can put on your list that comes from God. Pray for those things today.

God's gifts that are used . . . are never "used." Got it?

11.13

ALWAYS EVERYWHERE

I have been crucified with Christ and I no longer live, but Christ lives in me. The life I now live in the body, I live by faith in the Son of God, who loved me and gave himself for me.

[Galatians 2:20]

When do we recognize that we're connecting with Jesus? We can go to Bible study on Wednesday nights and feel like we're connecting. We can sing "What A Friend We Have . . ." in church and feel like we're connecting. We can listen to a song. We can read a book. We can do all these things and feel like we've achieved a true connection with God, and we might be completely correct. But there's more. Jesus wants to be a part of us—the living, breathing, doing part of our makeup. We let others make up the rules and regulations about what we have to do in order to connect. Jesus didn't make these rules. We did. Jesus said he was with us, and he is with us. It's our own insecurities that make us question his presence in us.

--- OZ Says ---

Think Who the New Testament says that Jesus Christ is, and then think of the despicable meanness of the miserable faith we have—I haven't had this and that experience! Think what faith in Jesus Christ claims—that He can present us faultless before the throne of God, unutterably pure, absolutely rectified and profoundly justified. Stand in implicit adoring faith in Him; He is made unto us "wisdom, and righteousness, and sanctification, and redemption." How can we talk of making a sacrifice for the Son of God! Our salvation is from hell and perdition, and then we talk about making sacrifices!

--- Just Between You and God ---

Pray today with confidence. Pray what you will, but pray with the confidence of knowing that the connection between you and the Son of God already exists. Don't pray arrogantly, but in confidence and gratitude for his presence in you.

Jesus is already here. He always was. He always will be. He's been waiting. Connect.

11.14

TRAVELING HERE

Praise be to the Lord, the God of my master Abraham, who has not abandoned his kindness and faithfulness to my master. As for me, the Lord has led me on the journey to the house of my master's relatives.

[Genesis 24:27]

When you are looking for directions to drive from one place to another you might check several sources—maps, the Internet, or a friend who's been there. If you make the trip often enough, you'll no longer have to ask for directions. This doesn't work with God's road trip. God will send you in roundabout ways that you didn't know existed. But even though you might be unfamiliar with the path, you don't need to worry because God is making the journey with you. The danger is thinking the lost feeling you may have isn't God's plan for you. If you're wandering out there, look for God. You're out there to learn something. Learn it and move on. There's no single way to get where you're going. God is in the highways and in the back roads, and you'll spend your share of time on both.

OZ Says

We can all see God in exceptional things, but it requires the culture of spiritual discipline to see God in every detail. Never allow that the haphazard is anything less than God's appointed order, and be ready to discover the Divine designs anywhere.

Just Between You and God

Look for God in the details today. Anybody can spot God in the big and flashy, but it takes some work to see God in the small and dingy. Also, it's usually the small and dingy that has the most to teach you.

Lost? You can't be. You're where God wants you. All the time. Just ask directions.

11.15

UNREQUITED OPINION

When Peter saw him, he asked, "Lord, what about him?"

Jesus answered, "If I want him to remain alive until I return, what is that to you? You must follow me."

[John 21:21–22]

We have an ability . . . in our studied-the-Bible-worked-in-missions-found-the-peace-of-God-in-our-stressed-out kind of lives . . . to royally mess up someone else's. People see your "centered-ness." They sometimes see the God that is in you and ask for your help or advice. We're in no position to do that. We can only point them to God. If we do give advice, we should ask God for the words. We are the GPS. We are the search button. Anytime we give advice there is still that small piece of self-thinking that exists. We like it when people come to us for help. It's rewarding, but when we start working from that place . . . we've left God out of the process.

―――――――――― OZ Says ――――――――――

If there is stagnation spiritually, never allow it to go on, but get into God's presence and find out the reason for it. Possibly you will find it is because you have been interfering in the life of another; proposing things you had no right to propose; advising when you had no right to advise. When you do have to give advice to another, God will advise through you with the direct understanding of His Spirit; your part is to be so rightly related to God that His discernment comes through you all the time for the blessing of another soul.

―――――――――― Just Between You and God ――――――――――

Ask to be God's mouthpiece. Ask to be God's funnel. You can be these things, but you can't be God. There's only one God, and sometimes we just have to get out of his way.

Show someone the truth, then let the truth do its own thing. God's been doing this longer than you have.

11.16

NEVER LEFT

So whether you eat or drink or whatever you do, do it all for the glory of God.

[1 Corinthians 10:31]

Jesus showed up more than once after his death. The Scriptures say he showed up many times, but it was never with a triumphant blast of a heavenly trumpet. Once he just showed up quietly on a beach and had breakfast with his friends. This is how our lives need to show God to the world—quietly. We have this tendency to want the triumphant blast of the horn. At the very least we enjoy having people look at us and think that we're very close to God. That separates us from the people Jesus wants us to help. We're there for the breakfast. The truth of the matter is that the closer we get to Jesus, the more we should disappear. It's our normal, everyday relationships that should be the very manifestation of Jesus.

--------- OZ Says ---------

Oh, I have had a wonderful call from God! It takes Almighty God Incarnate in us to do the meanest duty to the glory of God. It takes God's Spirit in us to make us so absolutely humanly His that we are utterly unnoticeable. The test of the life of a saint is not success, but faithfulness in human life as it actually is. We will set up success in Christian work as the aim; the aim is to manifest the glory of God in human life, to live the life hid with Christ in God in human conditions. Our human relationships are the actual conditions in which the ideal life of God is to be exhibited.

--------- Just Between You and God ---------

At various times during every day we are doing things that are completely unspiritual. The minutia of living day to day goes by without us thinking. Today think about God in those moments. Ask him to give those small moments big meaning.

Not trumpets. Sighs. Not storms. Breezes. Not shouts. Whispers. Not banquets. Brown bags.

11.17

INCLINED TOWARD ACQUIESCENCE

The angel of the LORD called to Abraham from heaven a second time and said, "I swear by myself, declares the LORD, that because you have done this and have not withheld your son, your only son . . . through your offspring all nations on earth will be blessed, because you have obeyed me."

[Genesis 22:15–18]

All of the wonderful things we read about God and the blessings he has waiting for us don't matter one bit until we actually do what we're told. You can read a thousand cookbooks, you can study the greatest recipes of chefs, you can read the instructions on a tube of frozen cookie dough, but none of these will get you a plate of warm chocolate chip cookies until you actually bake them. What Abraham was willing to do must be one of the hardest things any parent has ever been asked to do (with one exception). When he was obedient—willing to do what God told him to do—he became the father of all nations.

─────────────── OZ Says ───────────────

The promises of God are of no value to us until by obedience we understand the nature of God. We read some things in the Bible three hundred and sixty-five times and they mean nothing to us, then all of a sudden we see what God means, because in some particular we have obeyed God, and instantly His nature is opened up. "All the promises of God in Him are yea, and in Him Amen." The "yea" must be born of obedience; when by the obedience of our lives we say "Amen" to a promise, then that promise is ours.

─────────── Just Between You and God ───────────

Today do what you're told. Think of one thing in the Scriptures that God has told you to do, and do it. Start there.

If the recipe calls for baking powder, you can't use baking soda—they aren't the same thing.

11.18

SPONGE

So if the Son sets you free, you will be free indeed.

[John 8:36]

Ever wash a car? There's a difference between putting a sponge into a bucket that's almost empty and putting it into a bucket that's overflowing with water from a hose. When you started on this path you were asked to give up a lot. You were asked to leave things behind. You were asked to give up certain baggage that you didn't need any more. Now you're like a sponge. You can absorb. There are a lot of things out there in the world that can be absorbed. You get to choose. Anything we soak up that is out of our own selfishness will not fill us. We will need to absorb more and more, and we won't feel full. Or we can absorb God. Through prayer, obedience (there's that word again), and Scripture we can bring God into us, and God will fill all those places. God will fill us so full we'll have to squeeze it out and share it with others, and there will still be more.

OZ Says

Personality always wants more and more. It is the way we are built. We are designed with a great capacity for God; and sin and our individuality are the things that keep us from getting at God. God delivers us from sin; we have to deliver our selves from individuality, i.e., to present our natural life to God and sacrifice it until it is transformed into a spiritual life by obedience.

Just Between You and God

Where do you put yourself (the sponge you)? Do you put yourself into situations where you'll be absorbing the wrong things? Look around you today. Are you in an empty bucket or a full one?

Soak up. Squeeze. Soak up. Squeeze.

11.19

NEARER

When he comes, he will prove the world to be in the wrong about sin and righteousness and judgment.

[John 16:8]

Imagine a young boy walking with his mother in a mall, his little hand in her big one. They come to an escalator, and the child decides to see what will happen if he doesn't step on but stays at the bottom. The child watches as his mother gets farther and farther away, until suddenly a fear begins to set in—then tears—then terror. Then a kind stranger comes, calms his fears, and helps him onto the moving steps. A lesson has been learned, and his relationship with his mother is forever different.

Our relationship with God can work like this. We make choices that separate us from God. Unlike the child, we may get angry and blame God when it seems that he has moved away from us—when in fact it's we who have made the decision to let go of his hand and stay behind. But God, like the mother, is waiting at the top of the steps for us—not angry, just waiting with open arms. The lesson has been learned, and our relationship with God is forever different.

OZ Says

The love of God means Calvary, and nothing less; the love of God is spelt on the Cross and nowhere else. The only ground on which God can forgive me is through the Cross of my Lord. There, His conscience is satisfied. Forgiveness means not merely that I am saved from hell and made right for heaven (no man would accept forgiveness on such a level); forgiveness means that I am forgiven into a re-created relationship, into identification with God in Christ. The miracle of Redemption is that God turns me, the unholy one, into the standard of Himself, the Holy One, by putting into me a new disposition, the disposition of Jesus Christ.

Just Between You and God

Any separation we feel from God is our own doing. God doesn't push us away.

Hold tight. Stay close. God will hold your hand the whole time.

11.20

THIS IS REAL

In him we have redemption through his blood, the forgiveness of sins, in accordance with the riches of God's grace.

[Ephesians 1:7]

Yesterday was your sugar. Today is your medicine. All the blessings that God has given you, the forgiveness for every time you mess up, the welcoming back every time you get scared and walk away, the promise of eternal life—all that came with a price. You weren't asked to pay it. God did. Jesus did. Think about the tragedy that is the cross. To allow that to be done to you when you could stop it with a word—to watch that done to your Son when you could easily reach down and save him—that is what Jesus did. That is what God did. You are loved that much.

OZ Says

Compared with the miracle of the forgiveness of sin, the experience of sanctification is slight. Sanctification is simply the marvellous expression of the forgiveness of sins in a human life, but the thing that awakens the deepest well of gratitude in a human being is that God has forgiven sin. Paul never got away from this. When once you realize all that it cost God to forgive you, you will be held as in a vise, constrained by the love of God.

Just Between You and God

It's one thing to say thank you and another thing to show gratitude. Do something today that shows gratitude to God. Help someone. Offer consolation. Forgive another. Do something.

Love. Forgiveness. Eternal life. That's the start! We're talking complete and total emersion into the unconditional depths of a creator and creating God.

11.21

NO MORE AND EVERYTHING ELSE

I have brought you glory on earth by finishing the work you gave me to do.

[John 17:4]

The universe has two beginnings for us. The first is in the opening chapters of Genesis. The great detail and ultimate creativity of God are evident in every verse. There was nothing—then there was everything. It's an impossible idea to grasp. There's a second beginning to our universe—when Jesus hung on the cross and said, "It is finished." Everything else began at that moment. All that we are, all that we'll ever be, began at that moment. That moment changed every person on this planet who had ever lived or would ever live. Jesus' death changed the moment you are in now . . . holding this book . . . reading these words . . . the rest of your day . . . the rest of your life—all of that started the moment Jesus said, "It is finished."

OZ Says

The Death of Jesus Christ is the performance in history of the very Mind of God. There is no room for looking on Jesus Christ as a martyr; His death was not something that happened to Him which might have been prevented: His death was the very reason why He came.

Just Between You and God

Imagine all the possibilities. All of them. What is possible for you? Your family? The world? What's the best case scenario for the planet in a thousand years? Imagine ALL the possibilities. Now realize those possibilities exist because Jesus did what he did.

It all began. Then it ended. And began.

11.22

BABY BABY

So whether you eat or drink or whatever you do, do it all for the glory of God.

[1 Corinthians 10:31]

Imagine all of life as a swimming pool. All of time and space are just one really nice, really big swimming pool. Too often we want to be seen as the person who spends all her/his time in the deep end. Thinking the deep thoughts. Doing deep important deeds. The shallow end does not concern us. We're the deep people. But in the shallow end there are games. Children laughing. Parents teaching. In the shallow end are people who have never experienced water before dipping their toes in and testing the waters. Deep-end living is going to help them at all. The son of God showed up as a baby . . . splashing and playing. Come and play.

———————————— OZ Says ————————————

Our safeguard is in the shallow things. We have to live the surface common-sense life in a common-sense way; when the deeper things come, God gives them to us apart from the shallow concerns. Never show the deeps to anyone but God. We are so abominably serious, so desperately interested in our own characters, that we refuse to behave like Christians in the shallow concerns of life.

————————— Just Between You and God —————————

Think of all the little things you will do today. Find a way to show the God-part of you as you do them.

Deep is good. But it's lonely. God is good. But must be shared.

11.23

SOUL POINTING

Have mercy on us, LORD, have mercy on us, for we have endured no end of contempt.

[Psalm 123:3]

It's not so much the world that separates us from God, but our own state of mind that has done so. If we follow simple common sense it contradicts everything we know about God. To examine the whole concept of God and grace with the rational mind would point us in the exact opposite direction of where we need to go. We must approach God not from a human point of view but from a soul point of view. If we look at the world from a human standpoint, we might wonder how any God could allow such unhappiness, and begin to question his existence. If we look at the world from a soul point of view, we see God in every place and in all things. God gives us a mind so we can see what needs fixing. By doing so we become so filled with God that those looking from the human point of view will see God in us.

––––––––––– OZ Says –––––––––––

The thing of which we have to beware is not so much damage to our belief in God as damage to our Christian temper. "Therefore take heed to thy spirit, that ye deal not treacherously." The temper of mind is tremendous in its effects, it is the enemy that penetrates right into the soul and distracts the mind from God. There are certain tempers of mind in which we never dare indulge; if we do, we find they have distracted us from faith in God, and until we get back to the quiet mood before God, our faith in Him is nil, and our confidence in the flesh and in human ingenuity is the thing that rules.

––––––––– Just Between You and God –––––––––

The universe and all its glory from the microbes to the vast galaxy was created on purpose for purpose. The creator of all that exists in you. How can you look and see nothing but the ugly? Look with your God-eyes.

Half empty? God gave you the water. So it's all good.

11.24

FURTHER

As the eyes of slaves look to the hand of their master, as the eyes of a female slave look to the hand of her mistress, so our eyes look to the LORD our God, till he shows us his mercy.

[Psalm 123:2]

This is all far from over. Yes, you may have come through the dark valley but you are not done. You must keep learning. Keep striving. Keep doing. God is limitless and so, therefore, is your need to know God. You don't get to stop. That's a blessing. Luckily God does not expect us to understand all that he is in order for us to love all that he is. Try and wrap your mind around LIMITLESS. If you can even come close to understanding that concept you'll just be at the beginning of understanding God.

OZ Says

Spiritual leakage begins when we cease to lift up our eyes unto Him. The leakage comes not so much through trouble on the outside as in the imagination; when we begin to say—"I expect I have been stretching myself a bit too much, standing on tiptoe and trying to look like God instead of being an ordinary humble person." We have to realize that no effort can be too high.

Just Between You and God

Pray today with questions. Try these—"What else? What more? What's next?" Be ready. You might get an answer.

There's more. More to do. More to receive. More to learn.

11.25

DUCT TAPE

May I never boast except in the cross of our Lord Jesus Christ.

[Galatians 6:14]

When anyone who is on this journey says, "I will follow the carpenter," there's a certain amount of mental, emotional, physical, and spiritual chaos. It's easy to feel like we don't know whether we're coming or going. Paul took it back to the basics—God and Jesus. Everything else starts there.

We allow things to get out of control. We make lists, rules, laws, decisions, form committees—and God and Jesus get lost in our being religious. When things begin to feel like they're coming apart, we need to get back to the basics—what God did and what Jesus did. (Not what would Jesus do, but what he did). When we embrace these things, it will bring all the chaotic pieces of our lives back together and hold them there so we can keep going.

—————————— OZ Says ——————————

In the apostle Paul there was a strong steady coherence underneath, consequently he could let his external life change as it liked and it did not distress him because he was rooted and grounded in God. Most of us are not spiritually coherent because we are more concerned about being coherent externally. Paul lived in the basement; the coherent critics live in the upper story of the external statement of things, and the two do not begin to touch each other. Paul's consistency was down in the fundamentals.

—————————— Just Between You and God ——————————

Imagine all your stress, schedules, duties, and agendas are all in a basket beneath a hot air balloon. You're clinging to the bottom. What to do is up you to. Today, just for one prayer, pray like you are letting go and falling back into arms of God. Pray like that.

God. Jesus. Holy spirit. Start there. The next time it all comes apart . . . you have the place to start again.

11.26

MORE THAN WORDS

. . . the cross of our Lord Jesus Christ, through which the world has been crucified to me, and I to the world.

[Galatians 6:14]

You can stand on the stage in the school play and read the lines from a script, and they're just words. But any director or actor will tell you there comes a time when the words become your own. They cease being just words on a page.

The same sort of principle applies to our life in Jesus. We know about the cross. We know what happened there and what it means, but has it become our own? There must come a time in this journey when the complete and total idea of what the cross is becomes like our own words. The actor studies his lines, he doesn't just get the gist of it. He knows what the words are and studies them until he can say them with meaning. We must study the cross. We must think about it, ponder on it, dwell on it—eventually the story will become something more than just words on a page. Once that happens, the whole production changes.

OZ Says

Concentrate on God's centre in your preaching, and though your crowd may apparently pay no attention, they can never be the same again. If I talk my own talk, it is of no more importance to you than your talk is to me; but if I talk the truth of God, you will meet it again and so will I. We have to concentrate on the great point of spiritual energy—the Cross, to keep in contact with that centre where all the power lies, and the energy will be let loose.

Just Between You and God

The coloring page and the movies and the hymns will get you only so far. Ask God for the moment when it becomes real. Read the story again. Say it aloud to yourself as you drive. Let yourself become part of it. Ask God to make it part of you.

More than words. More than a story. This is the truth (small T). It must be your Truth (capital T).

11.27

STAGES

The world has been crucified to me, and I to the world.

[Galatians 6:14]

It's interesting that the people who most disliked Jesus when he was here on earth were the ones considered to be the most religious. Think about it. The religious people who were the most respected in his time hated Jesus. They constantly tried to trip him up and point out inconsistencies in his life. Jesus ate with the prostitutes and the tax collectors. The Pharisees called him a drunkard and said, "See, this is why you can't trust him." The reality is that there was never a person more in sync with God than Jesus. He was connected with God in all he did. Whether it was preaching, healing, or eating a meal with the outcasts, he was ultimately connected to God. Just as an actor can be in the play, but not of the play, so we can be in the world but not of the world. We belong to God, but we must exist in a world that doesn't. But being in the world doesn't stop us from being the children of God.

OZ Says

Our Lord was not a recluse nor an ascetic. He did not cut Himself off from society, but He was inwardly disconnected all the time. He was not aloof, but He lived in an other world. He was so much in the ordinary world that the religious people of His day called Him a glutton and a wine-bibber. Our Lord never allowed anything to interfere with His consecration of spiritual energy.

Just Between You and God

Consciously think about God in all you do today. Make the effort to retain the connection in everything. Eventually you'll get to the point where you no longer have to make yourself connect. The connection will already exist.

God in all things. God in all places. God in all actions. God in all hearts. Starting with yours.

11.28

ARRANGEMENTS BEING MADE

. . . and all are justified freely by his grace through the redemption that came by Christ Jesus.

[Romans 3:24]

Fancy robes, nice car, golden candles, rings on every finger, complete and total Scripture recall—wow, that guy must be one of God's favorites. Or, see her—the one who gave up everything to go feed the hungry and shelter the homeless? She must be the one God really likes. You know what? It doesn't work that way. Grace is not earned. Grace is a gift. That's why it's called grace. You don't earn it or deserve it. You have it handed to you. Understand that. When you get spiritually down, that is when God says, "Here you go. No charge." All the things that we think make us good Christians are just frosting. God will give you the gift when you need it most.

OZ Says

We have to realize that we cannot earn or win anything from God; we must either receive it as a gift or do without it. The greatest blessing spiritually is the knowledge that we are destitute; until we get there Our Lord is powerless. He can do nothing for us if we think we are sufficient of ourselves; we have to enter into His Kingdom through the door of destitution. As long as we are rich, possessed of anything in the way of pride or independence, God cannot do anything for us. It is only when we get hungry spiritually that we receive the Holy Spirit.

Just Between You and God

All your preparations are just that—preparations. None of what you've done earns you grace or entitles you to it. It's God's pleasure to hand it to you. You get to say thank you.

Grace is not cheap. Grace is not expensive. Grace has no price. Grace can only be given, not taken. How much do you need?

11.29

SURE

He will glorify me because it is from me that he will receive what he will make known to you.

[John 16:14]

Ever hear the old story about the guy who went to a new church for the first time? He sang loudly and laughed out loud. During the time of greeting he hugged and slapped people on the back, and when the congregation read from the bulletin he read loudly as if he meant every word. Finally, someone went and told him this was inappropriate behavior and asked him to leave. As he sat outside on the steps of the church, Jesus came up to him and said, "It's okay, Buddy. I've been trying to get in for years." Too often we're so busy being religious that we forget to invite Jesus to church. To many people today he has merely become a plastic figurine, a portrait hanging on the wall, or an advertisement. He is far more than this. Jesus is the embodiment of the gospel of God. He's the reason we're here. When we commit ourselves to the idea that Jesus is infinitely more than we understand, we'll receive a gift from God—understanding.

OZ Says

The type of Christian experience in the New Testament is that of personal passionate devotion to the Person of Jesus Christ. Every other type of Christian experience, so called, is detached from the Person of Jesus. There is no regeneration, no being born again into the Kingdom in which Christ lives, but only the idea that He is our Pattern. In the New Testament Jesus Christ is Saviour long before He is Pattern. Today He is being dispatched as the Figurehead of a Religion, a mere Example. He is that, but He is infinitely more; He is salvation itself, He is the Gospel of God.

Just Between You and God

Part of the beauty of knowing Jesus is that we're not expected to understand him. Understanding that we don't understand shows we know more than we think we do.

Believe there is more, and you'll see it. Understand that you can't, and you will.

11.30

THAT I AM

But by the grace of God I am what I am, and his grace to me was not without effect. No, I worked harder than all of them—yet not I, but the grace of God that was with me.

[1 Corinthians 15:10]

Okay, somebody needs to sing along with Kermit, "It's Not Easy Being Green." Why is it we always compare ourselves to others? We look around our school and think, "She's a better athlete, he's a better student, she's prettier, he has more money." Then we go to church and do the same thing. "She's holier than I am, he knows the Scripture better, she goes to Bible study more often than I do, he sings in the choir." But God doesn't make inferior products (i.e., you and me). God makes treasures. Of all that God created, he loves us the most. Every time you think you don't measure up you're telling him, "Sorry, God, you dropped the ball on this one." Is that something you want to say to the One who created the universe?

—————— OZ Says ——————

The way we continually talk about our own inability is an insult to the Creator. The deploring of our own incompetence is a slander against God for having overlooked us. Get into the habit of examining in the sight of God the things that sound humble before men, and you will be amazed at how staggeringly impertinent they are. "Oh, I shouldn't like to say I am sanctified; I'm not a saint." Say that before God; and it means—"No, Lord, it is impossible for You to save and sanctify me; there are chances I have not had; so many imperfections in my brain and body; no, Lord, it isn't possible." That may sound wonderfully humble before men, but before God it is an attitude of defiance.

—————— Just Between You and God ——————

Yes, you are a unique and amazing creation of a creator and creating God and you have the right to ignore anyone who tells you otherwise.

Hold your head up. Higher. God made you. Just as you are. Enjoy! You are glorious.

12.01

UNLIMITED

For whoever keeps the whole law and yet stumbles at just one point is guilty of breaking all of it.

[James 2:10]

You want equality? Here it is. You and me, the guy who said, "No room," the President of the United States, and the homeless woman who yells at people on the street corner are all exactly the same when it comes to the law of God. God laid it down. Here it is: Do it. He doesn't take into account your past behavior (good or bad). God doesn't look at your resume. God doesn't look at the history of your country or family album. God laid down his law and said, "This is it. Absolutely. No negotiating." And there isn't one of us who can measure up to it. However—and this is a big one—if you say to God, "I will obey your law," God will do whatever it takes to help you do just that.

OZ Says

The moral law does not consider us as weak human beings at all, it takes no account of our heredity and infirmities, it demands that we be absolutely moral . . . When we realize this, then the Spirit of God convicts us of sin. Until a man gets there and sees that there is no hope, the Cross of Jesus Christ is a farce to him. Conviction of sin always brings a fearful binding sense of the law; it makes a man hopeless—"sold under sin." I, a guilty sinner, can never get right with God, it is impossible. There is only one way in which I can get right with God, and that is by the Death of Jesus Christ. I must get rid of the lurking idea that I can ever be right with God because of my obedience—which of us could ever obey God to absolute perfection!

Just Between You and God

Messed up on that whole honor mom and dad thing? God loves you. Tried to make it the week without taking his name in vain and failed? God loves you. Didn't quite love your neighbor as you loved yourself? God loves you. It's not cause and effect. It's grace.

Here's the law. No discussion. Impossible? Keep trying.

12.02

GROOVE

Not that I have already obtained all this, or have already arrived at my goal, but I press on to take hold of that for which Christ Jesus took hold of me.

[Philippians 3:12]

L et's make a mental list. Write the word "All" at the top of your mental blank sheet. Now list all the things you'll have when you have it all. Your list is different from mine, and mine is different from the next guy's. What will you have when you have it all? Now let's make a new list for God. Still title it *All*, and list the things you need to have if you have it all as a child of God. This will be a shorter list. It only has one thing on it—God. When you start down the way, that is, with Jesus, the other list becomes scrap paper. We see other people who seem to have it all, and they don't seem to have a need for God. The harder we work toward getting everything on God's *All* list (i.e., God) the more God will give us to get us closer to that goal.

--------------------- OZ Says ---------------------

It is a snare to imagine that God wants to make us perfect specimens of what He can do; God's purpose is to make us one with Himself . . . The thing that tells for God is not your relevant consistency to an idea of what a saint should be, but your real vital relation to Jesus Christ, and your abandonment to Him whether you are well or ill.

--------- Just Between You and God ---------

Ask God to use you today. (You've done it before, but this is different.) Your goal is to obtain what's on your list. Ask God to use you, but ask so that whatever you're given to do will be done for one purpose—to get closer to him.

You can have it all. (No. Not that all.) God is all. All is God. Have a sample.

12.03

TRUTH

My message and my preaching were not with wise and persuasive words, but with a demonstration of the Spirit's power . . .

[1 Corinthians 2:4]

There's an old road trip game . . . name a movie that would be better with Zombies in it. You can have miles of fun with that one. When we are discussing Truth, there is nothing to add. You can't make it better. Truth is truth. If you are trying to share the truth of God's love with people, you can't make it better. You can't add to it. You can only let the Truth do its own work. Give someone the Truth and then step aside. Let the Holy Spirit work inside of them. Pray for them to see the truth as it is. God loves them, as they are, where they are. You don't need to beat people over the head with it. You just give it to them. Allow it to seep inside like milk does with a cookie—it will eventually soften them up. If God wants your help, he'll let you know.

———————————— OZ Says ————————————

If in preaching the Gospel you substitute your clear knowledge of the way of salvation for confidence in the power of the Gospel, you hinder people getting to Reality. You have to see that while you proclaim your knowledge of the way of salvation, you yourself are rooted and grounded in faith in God. Never rely on the clearness of your exposition, but as you give your exposition see that you are relying on the Holy Spirit. Rely on the certainty of God's redemptive power, and He will create His own life in souls.

———————— Just Between You and God ————————

Ask God not just for his message but also for his wisdom. It's selfish and egotistical to think we can do his job better than he can.

How can you follow God's way if you can't get out of your own?

12.04

STRUGGLE

Whoever has ears, let them hear what the Spirit says to the churches. To the one who is victorious, I will give the right to eat from the tree of life, which is in the paradise of God.

[Revelation 2:7]

If you lived on board a space station for a few years and then returned to earth, you'd have a very hard time lifting your hand, standing, or even moving. We need the force of gravity working against our muscles to strengthen them. That continuous force against force is what makes us able to get through life, day after day. Without it, our muscles would weaken and vanish. In the spiritual world we have the same idea. As we move through our day as believers, we'll constantly come up against forces that will try to put us down. Ultimately they can't. But it's that continuous day-in and day-out pushing that makes a life in Christ worthwhile.

—————— OZ Says ——————

Life without war is impossible either in nature or in grace. The basis of physical, mental, moral, and spiritual life is antagonism . . . And spiritually it is the same. Jesus said, "In the world ye shall have tribulation," i.e., everything that is not spiritual makes for my undoing, but—"Be of good cheer, I have overcome the world." I have to learn to score off the things that come against me, and in that way produce the balance of holiness; then it becomes a delight to meet opposition.

—————— Just Between You and God ——————

The ONLY way to lose this game is not to play. Lots of roadblocks will appear. People. Temptations. Pain. Stress. Shame. Guilt. Ego. But there is nothing . . . NO THING . . . that can keep you from getting to God in the end. Every roadblock makes your stronger. Today say thank you to God for the roadblocks. After all, they've done so much for you.

Irritation. Stress. Strength. Voilá . . . a pearl.

12.05

ROOM FOR THE SACRED

You shall be in charge of my palace, and all my people are to submit to your orders. Only with respect to the throne will I be greater than you.

[Genesis 41:40]

Imagine a house. What kind and how big is up to you. Let's imagine God has given you this house and has said he's going to live in it. Where would you start? Clean out the clutter? That's probably first. The easy fixing and cleaning can be done early on. The insulation problems need taking care of. The windows must be clean so the light can come in. Eventually, you'll need to get down to the foundation to make sure it's solid. We must have things that will make God comfortable when he arrives. Getting all this? Sound silly? God has given you a house—you! Paul called it a temple. If you're inviting God to come and live inside your temple, what do you have to do to make it ready?

––––––––––––––––– OZ Says –––––––––––––––––

I have to account to God for the way in which I rule my body under His domination . . . It means that I have to manifest in this body the life of the Lord Jesus, not mystically, but really and emphatically. "I keep under my body, and bring it into subjection." Every saint can have his body under absolute control for God. God has made us to have government over all the temple of the Holy Spirit, over imaginations and affections. We are responsible for these, and we must never give way to inordinate affections. Most of us are much sterner with others than we are in regard to ourselves; we make excuses for things in ourselves whilst we condemn in others things to which we are not naturally inclined.

––––––––––– Just Between You and God –––––––––––

Today invite God to your house. You may still have a lot of work to do, but get the invitation out there. You don't know when God may come knocking.

Life is a sanctuary. A soaring place for the Holy Spirit. The maintenance man? Over there. The guy with the "I am" written on his tool belt.

12.06

COVENANT

I have set my rainbow in the clouds, and it will be the sign of the covenant between me and the earth.

[Genesis 9:13]

This sounds more difficult than it is. Waiting for God to prove himself is a waste of time. God has already provided us with everything we need. God builds a mansion where we can live and grow. Then, we as human beings will stand outside and say, "Gee, I wish God would give me a house."

We demand evidence of the God connection. As long as we demand proof, we will not be able to enter the house. Demanding proof shows a lack of faith. If we show up with suitcases and say "I'm ready to move in," God will hand us the keys.

OZ Says

Waiting for God is incarnate unbelief; it means that I have no faith in Him; I wait for Him to do something in me that I may trust in that. God will not do it, because that is not the basis of the God-and-man relationship. Man has to go out of himself in his covenant with God as God goes out of Himself in His covenant with man. It is a question of faith in God—the rarest thing; we have faith only in our feelings. I do not believe God unless He will give me something in my hand whereby I may know I have it, then I say—"Now I believe." There is no faith there. "Look unto Me, and be ye saved."

Just Between You and God

Don't ask for anything. Don't promise anything. Don't demand anything. Tell God you're willing to take the next step, and the path will be lighted for you.

If you go to church and pray for rain . . . do you take an umbrella?

12.07

TOWARD AND AWAY

Godly sorrow brings repentance that leads to salvation and leaves no regret, but worldly sorrow brings death.

[2 Corinthians 7:10]

Eventually people come to the point where they take a good, long look at themselves and see the things they can no longer hide from God. (Not that they were hidden anyway. We just thought they were.) We don't need to ask the world for forgiveness. We need to ask God. There's pain there. But it's different from the pain we get from the so-called real world. There's a pain that comes from our inability to keep our secret things secret. The Holy Spirit brings us into a wide, open space where we have nowhere to hide and no one to help us. It comes down to just God and us. We must work it out together. We must be sorry for causing a separation between God and ourselves. We created it. God didn't. We must be sorry—not with our words, but with our whole beings. Then we can be forgiven, and then we can continue on.

--------- OZ Says ---------

The marvels of conviction of sin, forgiveness, and holiness are so interwoven that it is only the forgiven man who is the holy man, he proves he is forgiven by being the opposite to what he was, by God's grace. Repentance always brings a man to this point: I have sinned. The surest sign that God is at work is when a man says that and means it. Anything less than this is remorse for having made blunders, the reflex action of disgust at himself.

--------- Just Between You and God ---------

You know what you need to do today. You just don't like to admit you know. Take the time. Get quiet. Tell God everything.

Riding in the back seat you scoot away from Jesus, as close to the door as possible . . . yet somehow you both wind up at the destination. Hmmm.

12.08

LOCKS

For by one sacrifice he has made perfect forever those who are being made holy.

[Hebrews 10:14]

Imagine standing in a room full of doors—all different shapes, sizes, thickness, locks, and knobs. There's one particular door. It's not as strong, ornate, or sturdy, but Jesus is standing there holding it open for us. He must smile and chuckle at our refusal to walk toward him. Over and over again we try to pick the locks on the other doors, shove against them, or count up our good deeds and I'm-sorrys in the belief that we can use them to buy a key. Jesus is standing there with the door open. We might see him, but we pretend we don't. If we go that way, we might have to admit we're not perfect. If we go that way, we might have to actually encounter him. If we go that way, we might have to look at those hands and see the blood. That's too much for some of us. We'd rather go pounding on doors that don't open.

OZ Says

It does not matter who or what we are, there is absolute reinstatement into God by the death of Jesus Christ and by no other way, not because Jesus Christ pleads, but because He died. It is not earned, but accepted. All the pleading which deliberately refuses to recognize the Cross is of no avail; it is battering at another door than the one which Jesus has opened . . . "There is none other Name . . ." The apparent heartlessness of God is the expression of His real heart, there is boundless entrance in His way.

Just Between You and God

If you show up at God's door with all your files in order (baptism certificate, Sunday School papers, confirmation pictures, community service forms . . . ALL your proof), Jesus is going to toss them in the air and shout, "Happy New Year!" You don't need them. You can't earn your way in. Jesus already paid the admission price. You are in! Now go live your life like you appreciate it.

And Jesus said, "Behold I stand at the door and . . . hold it open!!"

12.09

UTMOST?

Those who belong to Christ Jesus have crucified the flesh with its passions and desires.

[Galatians 5:24]

Exactly what did you think the word "utmost" means? Here's how we see ourselves: we aren't intentionally sinful or evil. We don't revel in dishonesty. We're not mean-spirited people. We're the good guys. We're honest, kind, and compassionate, and we consider ourselves to be on the right track with God. Now is when the utmost comes in. Are we really willing to take this one step further? Can we completely turn away from not only the bad things in this world but also the good things, and become one of God's servants? Are you willing to put aside everything—not just what you don't like about yourself but also what you want to hang onto—and say, "I'm one hundred percent God's"? Can you say that? That is what "utmost" means. It's not easy.

─────────── OZ Says ───────────

It is not a question of giving up sin, but of giving up my right to myself, my natural independence and self-assertiveness, and this is where the battle has to be fought. It is the things that are right and noble and good from the natural standpoint that keep us back from God's best. To discern that natural virtues antagonize surrender to God, is to bring our soul into the centre of its greatest battle. Very few of us debate with the sordid and evil and wrong, but we do debate with the good. It is the good that hates the best, and the higher up you get in the scale of the natural virtues, the more intense is the opposition to Jesus Christ.

─────────── Just Between You and God ───────────

You gave God your concerns and your baggage. Can you give up all that you love too? Being a servant may require just that. It's a no-brainer to give up bad stuff. We think it's a big deal to offer good things to God. But today surrender your best to him.

Utmost. Everything. All. Kit and caboodle. Ball of wax. Whole schmear. It's what God gives and what God is.

12.10

LIVING THE GOD-LIFE

For it is written that Abraham had two sons, one by the slave woman and the other by the free woman.

[Galatians 4:22]

We're talking about two different lives, and they both belong to us. There is the everyday, walking-around, breathing, scratching life. And then there is the God-life. In the everyday version of life we give God our baggage and the natural things that make up our lives. We can give a few hours to volunteer in the community. We can give a voice to the choir. We can give some cash to the mission fund. In the God-life, we give God ourselves. "I'm here, God. Use me" is the most dangerous, and at the same time most rewarding, statement you can make—if you truly mean it.

―――――――――― OZ Says ――――――――――

Abraham had to offer up Ishmael before he offered up Isaac. Some of us are trying to offer up spiritual sacrifices to God before we have sacrificed the natural. The only way in which we can offer a spiritual sacrifice to God is by presenting our bodies a living sacrifice. Sanctification means more than deliverance from sin, it means the deliberate commitment of myself whom God has saved to God, and that I do not care what it costs.

――――――― Just Between You and God ―――――――

Are you ready to move on? Are you sure? Ask God to give you the once over. There may be stuff you aren't aware of that will trip you up as you move forward. You've worked this hard. It's better to be sure. God will see what you don't and make you aware of what you need to work on before you enter the next phase.

God doesn't need your stuff. God doesn't need your garbage. God wants you. Just you.

12.11

COMPONENT

Then Jesus said to his disciples, "Whoever wants to be my disciple must deny themselves and take up their cross and follow me."

[Matthew 16:24]

We belong to God. God made us all that we are. He has given us what we need to survive in the world. But we also have a free will. We can stand up and say, "This is who I am—if you don't like it, tough cookies." The problem that arises is that this tough shell can also keep us from God. "I've gotten this far on my own. What do I need God for?" We all need God. There's a need to connect with God. There's a need to connect with Jesus. When we hold our independence up like a hard shell, God can't get in, and soon we'll have a very hard time getting out. That's not free will; that's free won't.

―――――――― OZ Says ――――――――

Watch yourself when the Spirit of God is at work. He pushes you to the margins of your individuality, and you have either to say "I shan't," or to surrender, to break the husk of individuality and let the personal life emerge.

―――――― Just Between You and God ――――――

Still not letting that go? Pride gets in the way sometimes. We think if we don't admit it to ourselves then God won't see it. God has known about it since before you started. Pray from that deep inner place for God to come in and heal what's broken. You won't be judged. He just wants you to be whole.

Remember that stuff you squirt on ice cream and it makes a candy shell? It's not concrete. God can break through whatever walls we build around ourselves.

12.12

THE WE

I have given them the glory that you gave me, that they may be one as we are one.

[John 17:22]

We're not just one person—at least it doesn't always feel that way. There are many different aspects to each of us. There's the student, the son or daughter, the brother or sister, the only child, the athlete, the artist, the singer, the believer—there are dozens of you. All of them make up part of who you are. We think, "There are so many of me that I don't understand myself." This is probably true. The only one who understands all that you are is the one who created you. God's goal is for all these *you*'s to merge with him. God wants you to be one with him. This was Jesus' most important prayer— "that all may be one." God wants that connection. Imagine what you could become if you allowed all the individual pieces of who you are to merge with the Creator of the universe!

OZ Says

An island in the sea may be but the top of a great mountain. Personality is like an island, we know nothing about the great depths underneath, consequently we cannot estimate ourselves. We begin by thinking that we can, but we come to realize that there is only one Being Who understands us, and that is our Creator . . . If you give up your right to yourself to God, the real true nature of your personality answers to God straight away. Jesus Christ emancipates the personality, and the individuality is transfigured; the transfiguring element is love, personal devotion to Jesus.

Just Between You and God

Combine all of yourself. The dancer, poet, player, singer, worker, artist, writer, planner, engineer, mathematician, son, daughter, all of those other people who make up you. Have them all pray together. God will speak to the world through them all.

I am in you and you are in me and you are in them and we are in they, and when they are in we and I am in they—oh then how happy we'll be . . . will be.

12.13

TAKING REQUESTS

Then Jesus told his disciples a parable to show them that they should always pray and not give up.

[Luke 18:1]

We are a caring people. We hate to see our friends hurting, children hungry, seniors lonely, and our world in turmoil and bloodshed. We get on our knees and pray to God for what we think others need. But it's not our job to decide. We pray for a friend going through hard times and want it to be over—but consider whether God might have put that person in those hard times for strengthening. God knows exactly what he's doing. Don't pray for the lost to find a way, pray that they will find God. Don't pray for those in pain to find relief, pray that they will find God. This is called intercession.

——— OZ Says ———

Intercession is the one thing that has no snares, because it keeps our relationship with God completely open. The thing to watch in intercession is that no soul is patched up; a soul must get through into contact with the life of God. Think of the number of souls God has brought about our path and we have dropped them! When we pray on the ground of Redemption, God creates something He can create in no other way than through intercessory prayer.

——— Just Between You and God ———

Think of one or two individuals you know who are having problems. Don't pray for an end to whatever they're going through. Pray for their strength. Pray for their patience. Pray that they'll know God.

The question, "What do you pray for?" has two different meanings. Figure out which one is most important and answer it.

12.14

PEACE

Peace I leave with you; my peace I give you. I do not give to you as the world gives. Do not let your hearts be troubled and do not be afraid.

[John 14:27]

God did not cause you to be in a fender bender. God did not give you the "D" on the test. God did not undercook your meal. God did not give Grandma cancer. God did not ignore you when your parents divorced. God does not cause our problems. We do. Trust God. This is part of something much bigger than you. You can kick and scream all you want, but that's kind of like fighting against a wave. You're pretty much just going to get knocked on your butt. Don't fight. Ride it out. See where God takes the situation. When you are prepared to "Let go and let God," the wave will take you to places you never imagined.

—————— OZ Says ——————

Whenever you obey God, His seal is always that of peace, the witness of an unfathomable peace, which is not natural, but the peace of Jesus. Whenever peace does not come, tarry till it does or find out the reason why it does not. If you are acting on an impulse, or from a sense of the heroic, the peace of Jesus will not witness; there is no simplicity or confidence in God, because the spirit of simplicity is born of the Holy Ghost, not of your decisions. Every decision brings a reaction of simplicity.

—————— Just Between You and God ——————

Say a prayer that acknowledges God is in charge. Make it as simple as "All right, Lord. I'm all yours. I'll go where you say." If you don't get a sense of peace, wait for it. Don't think, "Well, that got me nothing." God will give you his peace.

Life changes like the ebb and flow of the tide. Stand with your feet in the water. That sound? It's God breathing. Breathe with him.

12.15

SPEAK UP

Do your best to present yourself to God as one approved, a worker who does not need to be ashamed and who correctly handles the word of truth.

[2 Timothy 2:15]

Have you ever said this to yourself, "I'm not going to stand up and speak. I'm not a minister. I'm not an expert. No one will listen to me." Ever said that to yourself? Guess what? You're wrong. Say what you want. Look inside yourself and you'll find what you believe. You may have to dig for it, but it's there. You can read great books and then spout off what you read, but those are not your words. It may not be easy, but don't give up. If you keep your mouth shut, you'll miss opportunities to influence others. The teacher you learn the most from is not the one who teaches you something you didn't know. The teacher you learn the most from is the one who can bring out what has been buried deep inside you all the time.

OZ Says

If you cannot express yourself on any subject, struggle until you can. If you do not, someone will be the poorer all the days of his life. Struggle to re-express some truth of God to yourself, and God will use that expression to someone else. Go through the winepress of God where the grapes are crushed. You must struggle to get expression experimentally, then there will come a time when that expression will become the very wine of strengthening to someone else . . .

Just Between You and God

Ask God to look deep inside of you. Deep in the places you don't usually look. Look there. Ask God to help you bring that out into the light. There it can grow and become something amazing. Keep it buried and you'll never find out what it could have become.

Say what you mean. Mean what you say. One thing leads to another.

12.16

RUMBLE

And pray in the Spirit on all occasions with all kinds of prayers and requests. With this in mind, be alert and always keep on praying for all the Lord's people.

[Ephesians 6:18]

Don't be fooled by the phrase "Let go and let God." You are in charge of your choices. You make your own decisions. It's when we confuse our decisions with God's will that we get in trouble. Just because you want it for yourself doesn't mean that God does, *but* God will allow you to venture down the wrong path until you figure it out and then turn back. (Note: the road back may be harder, depending on how many bridges you burned.) It is not God's will that you get tossed around like a dish towel in the dryer. God's plan is purposeful . . . never random. God wants you to make a decision and go with it. Wrong or right. Good or bad. Make a decision. God will stay beside you the whole time.

OZ Says

You have to wrestle against the things that prevent you from getting to God, and you wrestle in prayer for other souls; but never say that you wrestle with God in prayer, it is scripturally untrue. If you do wrestle with God, you will be crippled all the rest of your life. If, when God comes in some way you do not want, you take hold of Him as Jacob did and wrestle with Him, you compel Him to put you out of joint.

Just Between You and God

Thank God for choices. It would be so much easier if he just threw down a giant flashing arrow and pointed the way, but he doesn't. He gives us the choice, and no matter what we choose, God will still be beside us.

There is a difference between what God wants and what God allows.

12.17

CIRCLES

The person without the Spirit does not accept the things that come from the Spirit of God but considers them foolishness, and cannot understand them because they are discerned only through the Spirit.

[1 Corinthians 2:14]

In spite of what you may hear on the nightly news, a lot of teenagers today have good hearts and a strong sense of self. However, it's when things are going well and we have that strong sense of self-image that we don't think about God. There is in every individual a specific need for God. We need God in our lives whether we're aware of it or not. As we recognize that need for God, we become aware of how much more we need him. The more we get to know God, the more we need to live the God-life, and then nothing can satisfy that hunger except God. In effect, God creates the need for himself in those who ask him to.

--- OZ Says ---

It is God Who creates the need of which no human being is conscious until God manifests Himself. Jesus said, "Ask, and it shall be given you," but God cannot give until a man asks. It is not that He withholds, but that that is the way He has constituted things on the basis of Redemption. By means of our asking, God gets processes into work whereby He creates the thing that is not in existence until we do ask.

--- Just Between You and God ---

To ignore God's presence or to say "I've got this one on my own" is just selfish. We know God is there, yet we think we're strong enough without him. Sometimes we just need to get over ourselves and ask God.

God creates a need for God. God fills the need for God. It works out pretty well that way.

12.18

PASSENGER

And we know that in all things God works for the good of those who love him, who have been called according to his purpose.

[Romans 8:28]

We say it but we don't believe it. "God is in charge." It seems when things are going bad it must be God's fault, but when things are going well we're more than willing to take credit for our happiness. God is in charge of everything. Take a look backward at your life so far. Look at the ways certain things have happened to you as a result of other things happening to you. Some of the times when you didn't want to get up off the floor eventually became the starting points for some of the best times of your life. Yet at the same time you made decisions that took you to places, both good and bad. We see the plan from our point of view, which is extremely limited. God sees the whole picture. We must remain loyal to God. It's not about us doing work for God, but about him doing his work through us.

OZ Says

It is only the loyal soul who believes that God engineers circumstances. We take such liberty with our circumstances, we do not believe God engineers them, although we say we do; we treat the things that happen as if they were engineered by men. To be faithful in every circumstance means that we have only one loyalty, and that is to our Lord. Suddenly God breaks up a particular set of circumstances, and the realization comes that we have been disloyal to Him by not recognizing that He had ordered them; we never saw what He was after, and that particular thing will never be repeated all the days of our life.

Just Between You and God

Look for God's presence in your past triumphs and tragedies. Can you see it? Do you really think you were on your own? From here forward ask for God's continued presence. Watch for it. Seek it. You will find it.

Everyone in the Bible who shakes their fist at the sky and demands answers gets the same one. "Because I'm God."

12.19

DISTANCE

Do not suppose that I have come to bring peace to the earth. I did not come to bring peace, but a sword.

[Matthew 10:34]

Picture it this way—we're rock climbing, hanging on to the face of a mountain by the tips of our fingers and our toes. We climb up the sheer face and arrive at a rock outcropping. On the other side Jesus says, "I'm here. Reach out." But in order to do that we have to let go of the little bit of ledge we have. Too many of us will stay right where we are until our fingers bleed rather than reach around to something that we can't see.

If people are having trouble communicating with God, the problem is on their end, not the Creator's. Some people don't want to hear about faith because it means giving up control. They don't want to hear about a new life because they are scared to give up the life they know—no matter how bad it is. The life Jesus offers is so far beyond what they have that they can't conceive it. Often Jesus must take his sword and use it to separate us from what we cling to. It can hurt. But often that's what it takes for us to finally let go and cling to him.

───────────── OZ Says ─────────────

If God has had His way with you, your message as His servant is merciless insistence on the one line, cut down to the very root; otherwise there will be no healing. Drive home the message until there is no possible refuge from its application. Begin to get at people where they are until you get them to realize what they lack, and then erect the standard of Jesus Christ for their lives—"We never can be that." Then drive it home—"Jesus Christ says you must." "But how can we be?" "You cannot, unless you have a new Spirit."

───────── Just Between You and God ─────────

Pray to hear and trust God's voice. Have the faith Peter did when he stepped out of the boat. Let go of all you know and believe that something better is waiting.

Listen for Jesus. Have faith in his hands. Let go. Grab hold.

12.20

MUD

And I, when I am lifted up from the earth, will draw all people to myself.

[John 12:32]

Getting to know God is not a how-to list. There's no prescription. There's no do this and don't do that. The only way to God is through God. He sent his Word, his prophets, his preachers, and finally his own Son to tell us about love. We must show Jesus to the world, not in pretty songs or flowery words, but in the bottom-line way that we live. God is in you. When people look at you, they should see God. Sometimes it's necessary to get in their faces. It's not always easy. Poems, prayers, and songs don't always do the trick. Sometimes you have to get your hands dirty.

OZ Says

The one thing we have to do is to exhibit Jesus Christ crucified, to lift Him up all the time. Every doctrine that is not imbedded in the Cross of Jesus will lead astray . . . The calling of a New Testament worker is to uncover sin and to reveal Jesus Christ as Saviour, consequently he cannot be poetical, and he must be sternly surgical. We are sent by God to lift up Jesus Christ, not to give wonderfully beautiful discourses. We have to probe straight down as deeply as God has probed us, to be keen in sensing the Scriptures which bring the truth straight home and to apply them fearlessly.

Just Between You and God

God is love. Love is God. If you love, you know God. If you know God, you love. If you don't love, you don't know God. Why? Because God is love. One is the other. You must know both. If you only think you know one, you really know both.

Every action speaks. Are you shouting or whispering? You are the God teacher. Lesson number one . . . ?

12.21

MIRACULOUS

What we have received is not the spirit of the world, but the Spirit who is from God, so that we may understand what God has freely given us.

[1 Corinthians 2:12]

God doesn't give himself out with an eyedropper. You don't have to stand in line for a share of him. We think that maybe we can get a teaspoon, when all the time God is waiting with an ocean. God is waiting to send the Holy Spirit to envelop, surround, and permeate you. We just have to believe that Jesus is at the center. Through him we know God, and through the Holy Spirit we are blessed. We say thank you by using the gifts he gives us, and when we say thank you, the whole thing starts all over again.

—————————— OZ Says ——————————

. . . I am led out of myself all the time; I no longer pay any attention to my experiences as the ground of Reality, but only to the Reality which produced the experiences. My experiences are not worth anything unless they keep me at the Source, Jesus Christ.

————— Just Between You and God —————

You don't have to ask for air or gravity, do you? You accept them. They surround you. Think of God this way. Stop asking for his presence and breathe deep.

Imagine the best roller coaster ever. Now imagine that until this moment you never even knew what a roller coaster was. God says, "Hang on. This is going to be great."

12.22

GREEN LIGHT

No one can come to me unless the Father who sent me draws them, and I will raise them up at the last day.

[John 6:44]

We choose to believe. That's the beauty of belief. From this point on, for the rest of your life, you'll meet people who'll want to know why you believe. They'll want to know why you believe in a God no one has seen. How can you believe in a virgin birth? How can you believe in a God of love when there is so much suffering in the world? The answer is simple. Say to them, "I decided to." We choose to believe in God, and we can spend the rest of our lives supporting that belief. Others can choose not to believe and spend the rest of their lives supporting their decision. The more we believe—the more we spend our time praying, loving, praising, and getting closer to God—the more reason we'll be given to continue believing. Those who choose the opposite will have to fight harder and harder as they fall farther and farther away.

OZ Says

Belief must be the will to believe . . . Every man is made to reach out beyond his grasp. It is God who draws me, and my relationship to Him in the first place is a personal one, not an intellectual one. I am introduced into the relationship by the miracle of God and my own will to believe, then I begin to get an intelligent appreciation and understanding of the wonder of the transaction.

Just Between You and God

We are surrounded by doubts. "But what if . . . ," "How come . . . ," "Why does God allow . . . ," "If there is a God then . . ." You have so many questions. That's okay. Choose one. Make that the focus of all your prayers today. See what happens.

Decide to believe. Then believe. That's it.

12.23

COME TOGETHER

May I never boast except in the cross of our Lord Jesus Christ, through which the world has been crucified to me, and I to the world.

[Galatians 6:14]

There's magic in all this. Not the kind where the wires hold up the woman floating in the air, and not the kind of magic you get at a carnival. There's something that happens, something beyond our understanding that occurs when we truly identify with Jesus.

When we understand that the mission trip is not about the work . . .
When we understand that communion is more than bread and wine . . .
When we understand that prayer is a two-way communication . . .
When we understand that worship is not just singing . . .

Something happens. Jesus makes his presence known.

———— OZ Says ————

Every now and again, Our Lord lets us see what we would be like if it were not for Himself; it is a justification of what He said—"Without Me ye can do nothing." That is why the bedrock of Christianity is personal, passionate devotion to the Lord Jesus. We mistake the ecstasy of our first introduction into the Kingdom for the purpose of God in getting us there; His purpose in getting us there is that we may realize all that identification with Jesus Christ means.

———— Just Between You and God ————

Jesus is here now. Jesus is beside you. Jesus has his hand on your shoulder as you read these lines. Close this book and pray—doesn't matter what. Just pray.

Some things are so far beyond our comprehension we can't even conceive what they are. Are you open to seeing it all?

12.24

HIGH WIRE

For you died, and your life is now hidden with Christ in God.

[Colossians 3:3]

Some people want you to believe that a life as a follower of Jesus is like walking the high wire in the circus. Nothing could be more wrong. Walking the tightrope is a better analogy to a life *without* God. Believers start the long climb up the stairs, and from our perspective the steps at the top look narrow and difficult to keep our footing on. As we get higher, we realize the steps are wider and easier to stand on than they were when we started. To those back on the ground, it looks as though we're in danger of falling backward, but where we are we feel more secure than we ever did before. Jesus said, "Do not let your heart be troubled." Once you get into an experience you know is from God, there's no way your heart can be troubled. It isn't possible. You'll feel the peace Jesus promised to leave with you.

─────────── OZ Says ───────────

The Spirit of God witnesses to the simple almighty security of the life hid with Christ in God and this is continually brought out in the Epistles. We talk as if it were the most precarious thing to live the sanctified life; it is the most secure thing, because it has Almighty God in and behind it. The most precarious thing is to try and live without God. If we are born again it is the easiest thing to live in right relationship to God and the most difficult thing to go wrong . . .

─────────── Just Between You and God ───────────

You are in the presence of God and there is nothing that can separate you. Nothing. Not your past. Not your bad decisions. Not your doubts. Not your mistakes. Nothing. Accept that. From here it's all going to be different.

Stand firm. Plant your feet. Jesus is here. And he's not going anywhere.

12.25

BABY PICTURES

Therefore the Lord himself will give you a sign: The virgin will conceive and give birth to a son, and will call him Immanuel.

[Isaiah 7:14]

Jesus existed in this world and he EXISTS in this world. On the timeline from the creation of the universe to the present moment, Jesus showed up. God became man. The word became flesh and blood. Jesus was born. In that small place and for the next 33 or so years . . . Jesus existed. Flesh and blood.

Jesus exists now in this moment. When we say, "I want to follow Jesus." When we give a blanket to those who are cold. When we give food to those who are hungry. When we listen to a person who just wants someone to talk to. Jesus exists in those moments just as real as when he walked on this earth. We are the hands and feet and eyes and ears and heart of Jesus. Jesus exists because we do.

OZ Says

He is not man becoming God, but God Incarnate, God coming into human flesh, coming into it from outside. His life is the Highest and the Holiest entering in at the Lowliest door. Our Lord's birth was an advent. The characteristic of the new birth is that I yield myself so completely to God that Christ is formed in me. Immediately Christ is formed in me, His nature begins to work through me.

Just Between You and God

Show off your Christmas gift—Jesus—inside you. Allow him to continue his work with your ears, your eyes, your hands, your feet, your mouth, and your heart.

Unto us a child is born. Into us a child is born. Believe.

12.26

TO DO LIST

**But if we walk in the light, as he is in the light, we
have fellowship with one another, and the blood of
Jesus, his Son, purifies us from all sin.**

[1 John 1:7]

We're aware of some of the things that separate us from God. There are others that we're not aware of. We have the tendency to make a list of "Things That Separate Me from God," fold it six ways, and shove it down deep into our beings. We think it's buried and will no longer be a problem. Then we stand in the light of God—a light so bright nothing can hide. We are lit up. God sees that list and sends his Holy Spirit to grab it, unfold it, and read it back to us. When that happens, we often find we no longer need those things, and we allow the Holy Spirit to take them away from us. At the same time, the light illumines other things we didn't know were there. We don't need these either, but if we didn't stand in God's light, we would never know they existed until they came out and started to do damage.

OZ Says

If I walk in the light as God is in the light, not in the light of my conscience, but in the light of God—if I walk there, with nothing folded up, then there comes the amazing revelation, the blood of Jesus Christ cleanses me from all sin so that God Almighty can see nothing to censure in me. In my consciousness it works with a keen poignant knowledge of what sin is. The love of God at work in me makes me hate with the hatred of the Holy Ghost all that is not in keeping with God's holiness. To walk in the light means that everything that is of the darkness drives me closer into the centre of the light.

Just Between You and God

You don't need to hide. You think the creator of the universe doesn't see you there? God is not waiting to punish you. Step out into the light and let God remove all the things that separate you from him.

Hold the beach ball underwater. Easy, right? Now hold six. Seven. Is there a problem?

12.27

THE DRENCHING

"If you, Israel, will return, then return to me,"
declares the LORD. "If you put your detestable idols
out of my sight and no longer go astray . . ."

[Jeremiah 4:1]

This truly is just between you and God. You stand looking up at a beautiful waterfall of love pouring down and know in your heart that you can't step from the bank into the lovely waters—not just yet. This is not a battle that can be fought in the real world; this must be done alone, just between you and God. You can say, I-am-your-servant-God-I-am-your-servant-God-I-am-your-servant-God-I-am-your-servant-God, but until you believe this with all your heart, you'll stand at the base of the waterfall and try to be satisfied with the drops that splash up at you. You can even drench yourself in the spray, but it's entirely different to step under the waterfall itself or the exciting, swirling waters in front of you.

OZ Says

The battle is lost or won in the secret places of the will before God, never first in the external world. The Spirit of God apprehends me and I am obliged to get alone with God and fight the battle out before Him. Until this is done, I lose every time. The battle may take one minute or a year, that will depend on me, not on God; but it must be wrestled out alone before God, and I must resolutely go through the hell of a renunciation before God. Nothing has any power over the man who has fought out the battle before God and won there.

Just Between You and God

This is the ultimate form of multi-tasking. Live your life—your extra-ordinary amazing life AND your ordinary everyday life—while simultaneously thinking "God loves me." Never let that thought slip away. Eventually it's going to open a door and an ocean of love is going to deluge in.

Downpour. Drenching deluge. Waiting. Waiting.

12.28

PETER PAN

And he said: "Truly I tell you, unless you change and become like little children, you will never enter the kingdom of heaven."

[Matthew 18:3]

Jesus said we need to be like children to understand the kingdom of God. We can handle that most of the time. But children grow up. Some overly religious people think we have to become like adults as soon as possible. What Jesus is talking about is a simple child-like faith. The problem is that our bodies grow. Obviously we can't be physical children forever, but when we allow our outside-grown-up-self to dictate the actions of the inside child-of-God-self we find ourselves growing away from God instead of toward him.

OZ Says

The hindrance in our spiritual life is that we will not be continually converted, there are wadges of obstinacy where our pride spits at the throne of God and says—I won't. We deify independence and wilfulness and call them by the wrong name. What God looks on as obstinate weakness, we call strength. There are whole tracts of our lives which have not yet been brought into subjection, and it can only be done by this continuous conversion. Slowly but surely we can claim the whole territory for the Spirit of God.

Just Between You and God

Begin today with a prayer you remember from your childhood. "God is great. God is good." or "Now I lay me down to sleep . . ." Then continue your prayers with that same faith you had as a child, the one that says, "Jesus loves me this I know."

Get older. Don't grow up. Children know. Child-like is not childish.

12.29

WHERE'S MINE?

From this time many of his disciples turned back and no longer followed him.

[John 6:66]

Questions come up. It's inevitable. We ask: "I'm a good person; why can't I have what he has?" "I've done everything I've been asked to do; where's my reward?" "He does all the things Jesus said not to do, and he still gets ahead in this world. It's not fair!" "Where's mine?"

Here's the thing—you don't get to ask these questions of God. You don't get to judge what other people have or how other people live. It isn't your place to decide who gets what, and when they get it, and how much they get. That's not your job. Part of saying that you believe God is in charge is actually *believing* that God is in charge. God knows what you need. Trust him. God has a plan for everyone, including you. If you stop and look at what's going on in other people's lives, you can't keep going. You're stopped. Don't worry about what he has or what she did. Keep your eyes on God. Follow the way and focus on Jesus.

OZ Says

You have to walk in the light of the vision that has been given to you and not compare yourself with others or judge them; that is between them and God. When you find that a point of view in which you have been delighting clashes with the heavenly vision and you debate, certain things will begin to develop in you—a sense of property and a sense of personal right, things of which Jesus Christ made nothing. He was always against these things as being the root of everything alien to Himself. "A man's life consisteth not in the abundance of the things that he possesseth."

Just Between You and God

All those questions . . . the ones that annoy and anger and puzzle. Those questions. Mentally put them in a box. Tape it shut. Write "Not my job" on the lid. Now pray and give God the box. He already knew, but it's good to get it off your plate.

Mine. Yours. God's. Hmmm.

12.30

OURS

As they make music they will sing, "All my fountains are in you."

[Psalm 87:7]

You've been driving the same highway for a long time. Along the way you always stop at Benny's Rest Stop. Then one day, after traveling quite far, you pull off the road and see that Benny's is closed. Your source of re-fueling will have to change. The same is true as you grow in your spiritual life. As you journey, your source of refueling—for things like comfort and self-worth—will change. You will need to find new sources by going to the Scriptures, to church, or to God in prayer. This is that new you that needs feeding. The old you is going away and doesn't need to stop any more. The new you finds inspiration in the resurrection life of Jesus. The new you is God's you. God can reach in any time, any place, in any way, and refresh your soul.

--------------- OZ Says ---------------

Watch how God will wither up your confidence in natural virtues after sanctification, and in any power you have, until you learn to draw your life from the reservoir of the resurrection life of Jesus . . . The sign that God is at work in us is that He corrupts confidence in the natural virtues, because they are not promises of what we are going to be, but remnants of what God created man to be. We will cling to the natural virtues, while all the time God is trying to get us into contact with the life of Jesus Christ which can never be described in terms of the natural virtues. It is the saddest thing to see people in the service of God depending on that which the grace of God never gave them . . .

--------- Just Between You and God ---------

Ask God now. Don't think about the old places you went for comfort and affirmation. Ask God now. Regardless of where and what you're doing. Ask God now.

What was broken is fixed. Run your fingers along the seam where the crack was. Soon that will be gone too. Scars fade.

12.31

NOW WHAT?

But you will not leave in haste or go in flight; for the LORD will go before you, the God of Israel will be your rear guard.

[Isaiah 52:12]

YESTERDAY: Take a look back at your year. Thumb through this book if you want to. Remember that one? See, didn't that work out? Told ya so! What amazes us most when we look back is how much God was part of all we did, and we never noticed. God is the God of our yesterdays. He allows our pasts to be used for his purposes. The past never goes away, but it can always be a part of who we are . . .

TODAY: Let today be a clearing out. All that you have been through is gone, and you can't change it. All that you're going to be going through is ahead, and there's nothing you can do to know what it will be. Take today to pray, praise, and thank God for what has happened, and what will happen . . .

TOMORROW: Do you remember where we began? We said at the first that this book would begin and end with God. You've been through a journey. You are not the same person you were when we started. It may or may not have been the book, but you are changed. God has been with you through the changes. God will continue to be with as you go from here. Look forward. God is waiting. Ready to keep moving?

————————— OZ Says —————————

Leave the Irreparable Past in His hands, and step out into the Irresistible Future with Him.

————— Just Between You and God —————

TOMORROW: Step into it. Don't throw yourself head first into the future—you'll just hurt yourself. Step into it, and know that God is beside you. He always has been, but now you're aware of it. Let every step you take reflect that to yourself, the world, and back to God.

Past. Present. Future. God. You. Amen. And amen.

Not a Fan
Student Edition

What does it mean to really follow Jesus?

Kyle Idleman

If someone asked, "Are you a fan of Jesus?", how would you answer? You attend every movie featuring a certain actor, you know the stats of your sports hero, and you can recite lyrics from your favorite songs. In short, you're a huge fan. But are you treating Jesus the same as the other people you admire? The truth is Jesus wants more than the church attendance, occasional prayer, and the ability to recite Scripture—the fan response. He's looking for people who are actually willing to sacrifice in order to follow him. In this student edition of Not a Fan, Kyle Idleman uses humor, personal stories, and biblical truth as he challenges you to look at what it means to call yourself a Christian and follow the radical call Jesus presents. So, will you be a fan, or a follower?

Circle Maker Student Edition

Dream Big. Pray Hard. Think Long.

Mark Batterson with Parker Batterson

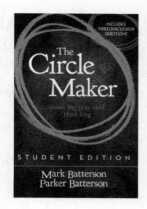

Pray Circles around Your Greatest Dreams and Biggest Fears

Prayer can sometimes be a frightening thing—how do you approach the maker of the world, and what exactly can you pray for? In this student adaptation of *The Circle Maker*, Pastor Mark Batterson uses the true legend of Honi the circle maker, a first-century Jewish sage whose bold prayer saved a generation, to uncover the boldness God asks of us at times, and what powerful prayer can mean in your life. Drawing inspiration from his own experiences as a circle maker, as well as sharing stories of young people who have experienced God's blessings, Batterson explores how you can approach God in a new way by drawing prayer circles around your dreams, your problems, and, most importantly, God's promises. In the process, you'll discover this simple yet life-changing truth: God honors bold prayers; bold prayers honor God. And you're never too young for God to use you for amazing things.

Available in stores and online!

All In Student Edition

*Mark Batterson with
Parker Batterson*

Halfway is no way to live.
    Quit holding back. Quit holding out.
    It's time to go all in and all out for God.
    The good news is this: If you don't hold out on God, God won't hold out on you. If you give everything you have to follow Jesus, you'll receive amazing spiritual rewards. But this reality also comes with a deeper truth: Nothing belongs to you. Not even you.

    In *All In: Student Edition*, Mark and Parker Batterson explore what going all in can mean for your life, sharing unique illustrations and unforgettable stories, as well as compelling accounts of biblical characters. Throughout, they demonstrate the amazing things that can happen when you surrender to the Lordship of Jesus Christ.

    Mark Batterson writes: "When did we start believing that God wants to send us to safe places to do easy things? Jesus didn't die to keep us safe. He died to make us dangerous."

Available in stores and online!

ZONDERVAN®
.com

Me I Want to Be Student Edition

Becoming God's Best Version of You

Bestselling author John Ortberg with Scott Rubin

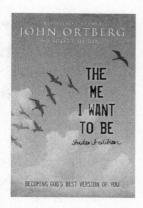

Maybe you've gone to church and just not felt like you were connecting to the service like everyone else. Perhaps you have been trying to get closer to God but simply hit block after block and feel more frustrated than faith-filled each time you sit down to pray or worship. Or maybe you feel like you are doing okay spiritually, but feel you're missing something you can't quite define. And on top of everything else, you're simply trying to figure out who you really are inside and what you're supposed to be doing with your life.

The good news is you're not alone, and you don't have to feel discouraged. Though in the pages of *The Me I Want to Be Teen Edition*, bestselling author John Ortberg focuses on what makes you who you are, looking at how you spend your time, your unique experiences, your relationships, and your overall world to help you see where you are now, as well as providing exercises and quizzes that help uncover God's plan for you and the positive directions you can now go. Find out what it can look like when you discover what the best version of you looks like, as well as the life God has always desired you to have.

Available in stores and online!

Case for Christ Student Edition

A Journalist's Personal Investigation of the Evidence for Jesus

New York Times Bestselling Author
Lee Strobel with Jane Vogel

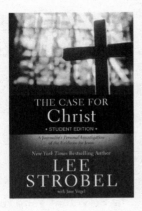

There's little question that he actually lived. But miracles? Rising from the dead? Some of the stories you hear about him sound like just that—stories. A reasonable person would never believe them, let alone the claim that he's the only way to God! But a reasonable person would also make sure that he or she understood the facts before jumping to conclusions. That's why Lee Strobel—an award-winning legal journalist with a knack for asking tough questions—decided to investigate Jesus for himself. An atheist, Strobel felt certain his findings would bring Christianity's claims about Jesus tumbling down like a house of cards. He was in for the surprise of his life. Join him as he retraces his journey from skepticism to faith. You'll consult expert testimony as you sift through the truths that history, science, psychiatry, literature, and religion reveal. Like Strobel, you'll be amazed at the evidence—how much there is, how strong it is, and what it says. The facts are in. What will your verdict be in The Case for Christ?

Available in stores and online!

ZONDERVAN®
.com

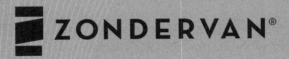

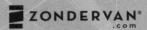